THE CANDYMAKERS

THE CANDYMAKERS

WENDY MASS

Little, Brown and Company
New York Boston

Copyright © 2010 by Wendy Mass
Illustrations by Steve Scott
Excerpt from *The Candymakers and the Great Chocolate Chase* copyright © 2015 by Wendy Mass

Little, Brown and Company

Hachette Book Group
1290 Avenue of the Americas, New York, NY 10104
Visit us at lb-kids.com

Little, Brown and Company is a division of Hachette Book Group, Inc.
The Little, Brown name and logo are trademarks of Hachette Book Group, Inc.

The publisher is not responsible for websites (or their content)
that are not owned by the publisher.

First Paper-Over-Board Edition: May 2015
First published in hardcover in October 2010 by Little, Brown and Company

Library of Congress Cataloging-in-Publication Data

Mass, Wendy.
The candymakers / by Wendy Mass. — 1st ed.
p. cm.
Summary: When four twelve-year-olds, including Logan, who has grown up never leaving his parents' Life Is Sweet candy factory, compete in the Confectionary Association's annual contest, they unexpectedly become friends and uncover secrets about themselves during the process.
ISBN 978-0-316-00258-5 (hc) — ISBN 978-0-316-26499-0 (pob)
[1. Candy — Fiction. 2. Secrets — Fiction. 3. Contests — Fiction. 4. Friendship — Fiction.] I. Title.
PZ7.M42355Can 2010
[Fic] — dc22   2010008621

"Be not forgetful..." quote on page 10 from the King James Bible, Hebrews chapter 13, verse 2;
"Be kind..." quote on page 76 commonly attributed to Plato; "List your blessings..." quote on page 384 by Garrison Keillor.

10 9 8 7 6 5 4 3 2 1

RRD-C

Book design by Alison Impey

Printed in the United States of America

For my mom,
who never kept candy in the house,
thus ensuring
I ate it every chance I got

"It's not what you look at that matters,
it's what you see."

—Henry David Thoreau

"There are no rules of architecture
for a castle in the clouds."

—G. K. Chesterton

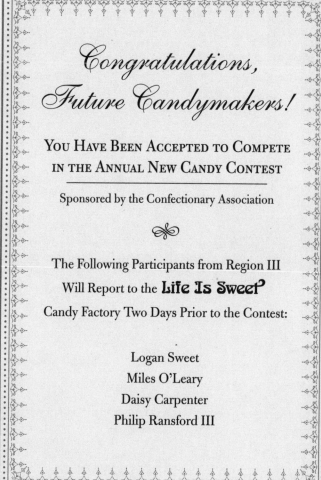

Congratulations, Future Candymakers!

YOU HAVE BEEN ACCEPTED TO COMPETE IN THE ANNUAL NEW CANDY CONTEST

Sponsored by the Confectionary Association

The Following Participants from Region III

Will Report to the **Life Is Sweet**

Candy Factory Two Days Prior to the Contest:

Logan Sweet

Miles O'Leary

Daisy Carpenter

Philip Ransford III

BREAKING NEWS

The results are finally in from the Confectionary Association's annual new candy contest. Thirty-two 12-year-olds from around the country were invited to create a brand-new candy to enter in this highly respected hundred-year-old competition. According to insiders, the competition was particularly fierce this year. The contest day was marked by surprises that rocked the very foundation of the candy industry, including the shocking news that one of the country's most celebrated candy factories will close its doors. The winning candy will soon be available nationwide. However, the factory that will manufacture the winning candy has not yet been decided.

THINGS YOU NEED TO KNOW

O nce there were four children whose names were Logan, Miles, Philip, and Daisy. Each of them had recently turned twelve, and although none of them knew it yet, their lives would never be the same.

You might ask, what makes them so special that their essays were selected over hundreds of others? Why do they each want to win the contest so badly they are willing to risk everything?

Perhaps it would be best to show you.

Let's start with Logan, since he *is* the Candymaker's son, after all. But don't think he has an edge in the contest just because he was born smelling like chocolate.

Logan has the hardest task, for he must be your eyes and ears. Pay close attention to what he tells you about the others — and himself — and what he doesn't.

The others will get their chance, too, but it's only fair to start with Logan because if it weren't for his father's generous invitation to help prepare the others for the contest, Miles, Daisy, and Philip wouldn't be standing outside the **Life Is Sweet** candy factory right now, wondering if they should knock on the huge wooden door or just let themselves in.

PART ONE

LOGAN

CHAPTER ONE

L ogan didn't have to open his eyes to know that morning had arrived. The sweet smell of cotton candy wafting into his room worked better than any alarm clock. He rolled over so his nose nearly touched the air vent.

You might think that if your bedroom were inside a candy factory, your bed would be shaped like a lollypop. But Logan had gotten rid of the lollypop-shaped bed last month when he turned twelve — it had become uncomfortable not being able to bend his knees while he slept.

Logan loved the start of a new day, when the air was thick with possibilities (and, in his case, with the smell of chocolate, caramel, nougat, and spun sugar). The breeze through his open window brought the room to life. The pages of his comic books rose and fell as if they were taking deep breaths. Paper drawings on the walls fluttered. The fur of his stuffed dragon rippled, making it appear to be moving very quickly without actually moving at all.

Logan focused his attention on his breath, as he did first thing every morning. He breathed in and breathed out.

With each breath he recounted the things he was grateful for. The new day. Being here to enjoy it. His parents. The factory. All the people who worked there.

In...out...in...out. He matched his rhythm with the familiar hums and whirs of the candy machines powering up for the day. The sizzle of licorice root on the stove made him pause, mid-inhale. Soon his mother would start scraping cinnamon bark onto the oatmeal she made each morning, and he always liked to be in the kitchen for that part.

"So what are we gonna do today?" his dad sang outside Logan's door.

"Make some candy!" Logan replied automatically, his voice still scratchy.

"And why are we gonna do it?" Without waiting for Logan to answer, his father continued the chant as he did every morning. "To make the whole world smile!"

To make the whole world smile, Logan hummed to himself as he hopped out of bed to dress. All the factory workers wore white collared shirts and tan pants (those who worked outdoors wore shorts). Logan didn't officially work for the factory yet, but he wouldn't think of wearing anything but the official uniform during the day.

Plus all his play clothes were in piles on the floor. Truth be told, most things in Logan's room were in piles on the floor. His parents had long since given up asking him to clean it. Who could spend time cleaning when there were so many exciting things to do right outside the door?

To his surprise, he heard his mother beginning to scrape

the cinnamon bark already. He turned to look at the clock on his desk. They usually didn't eat breakfast for another half hour. Then his breath caught in his throat. The other contestants in the Confectionary Association's annual New Candy Contest would be arriving any minute! How could he have forgotten? But even as he asked himself that question, he knew the answer: having three other kids spend two whole days at the **Life Is Sweet** candy factory was so out of the ordinary, so different from his usual routine, that he hadn't really believed it would ever happen. Their factory had never hosted any contestants before, and this year he was finally competing himself!

The only problem was that Logan didn't have much experience with other kids. Sure, he played Name That Cloud on the lawn with the workers' kids sometimes. But most of them were much younger. The factory's annual picnic used to bring people from all over Spring Haven to the grounds, but it had been so long since the factory held a picnic that he barely remembered them. Every time he asked his parents why they'd stopped holding picnics, their answers were always vague. Too busy, too hard to control the crowd, that sort of thing. Eventually he just stopped asking.

Up till now his life's steady routine hadn't wavered much. His only outings were short trips into town to visit the local candy shops, an occasional checkup at the doctor or dentist, and the family's annual trip to the Confectionary Association's convention. Not that daily life at the factory didn't bring surprises—it did, every day. But he usually knew what to expect—a candy machine that had ground to a halt, a clogged irrigation tunnel on the farm, the labels for the pink Sour Fingers getting stuck on the blue Sour Fingers container, or some other issue that could usually be fixed with a squirt or two of oil. If only making friends were as easy.

He raced into the bathroom to perform the quickest face-washing–toothbrushing in recorded history. He reached for his rarely used comb, only to watch it slip right through his fingers. He was used to dropping things. A career as a ball-player was not in his future.

Holding the comb firmly this time, he ran it through his shaggy hair, wincing as he encountered a knot. With his father's olive skin and his mother's wheat-colored hair, Logan resembled no one else he'd ever seen. He didn't look in the mirror very often, but when he did, he was always surprised to see he'd gotten older.

He arrived in the kitchen (sliding the last ten feet in his socks) just as his mom pulled a jug of fresh milk from the dumbwaiter built into the wall. She swung the metal door shut and the old gears creaked into action, pulling the tray back down to the Dairy Processing Room. The Candy-maker took the pitcher and poured out three creamy white glasses. He took a big gulp from the largest one, nodded in satisfaction, and flicked a switch labeled MILK on the wall. This signaled the farmers to send the milk to the Cocoa Room and other areas of the factory that needed fresh milk every day. As a main ingredient in so many products, one could never be too careful. One day it would be up to Logan to determine if the milk was good enough.

His dad handed him a glass. Logan grasped it with both hands, took a small sip, and swished the milk around in his mouth for a few seconds before swallowing. "Bessie?" he asked.

The Candymaker shook his head. "Cora."

Logan frowned and plopped down into his chair. He had been so certain. Bessie's milk had a slightly nutty taste. Cora's was thicker and mint-flavored, which he chalked up to the fact that the field where the cows grazed bordered the peppermint plants. Was he losing his touch? Being able to distinguish between the milk of two different cows was a basic skill for a candymaker.

The Candymaker reached past his generous belly and ruffled his son's hair. "Just kidding. It was Bessie's."

Logan sighed in relief. His mother shook her head disapprovingly, but her husband just grinned. "Gotta keep the boy on his toes." He tossed a few slivers of dark chocolate into his milk and stirred briskly.

"Now, Logan," he said between sips, "be sure not to make the other kids feel insecure today. After all, you grew up here, and this is their first time visiting a candy factory."

"I'll be sure not to shout out the temperature at which sugar boils," Logan promised.

The Candymaker laughed. "I'm sure you won't."

"Here you go," Logan's mom said, handing him a folded piece of notebook paper. He tucked the paper into his back pocket without reading it. This tradition had started when he turned eight and his mother was trying to find some way to make him enjoy reading more. She had found a poem called "Keep a Poem in Your Pocket." Now each morning he got to carry a poem or a quote in his pocket. He *almost* always remembered to read it.

She also handed him a homemade breakfast bar — which was just her usual oatmeal compressed into bar form. "Eat this on your way downstairs," she instructed, pointing to a small video monitor on the counter. "Your fellow contestants are here."

Logan eagerly leaned forward for a better look. The screen showed the view outside the factory's front door. A blond girl in a yellow sundress caught his eye first. Her dress was so bright it rivaled a Neon Yellow Lightning Chew, one of the factory's biggest sellers.

Two boys stood beside her. He couldn't see their faces or hear their words, but from the looks of it, they were having a very heated debate. The girl planted her hands squarely on her hips and shook her head, her ponytail whipping around. The taller boy (in a blue suit! and a tie!) stamped his foot. Logan turned to peer at the smaller boy, more casually dressed in shorts and a T-shirt. He kept shifting his large backpack from shoulder to shoulder. It must be very heavy.

"You might not want to leave them out there much longer," Logan's mom said. "Looks like things are heating —"

Logan was halfway out the door before she finished her

sentence. He practically inhaled the breakfast bar as he ran along the steel walkway that led from the apartment into the main section of the factory. Years of eating while on the move had trained him in the art of making sure he didn't choke.

He could run and chew and still determine every ingredient of what he was eating. In the case of the breakfast bar: beets, barley, oats, molasses, licorice root, pine nuts, cinnamon, and a dash of salt. His mom may have been a whiz at making meals out of random ingredients, but Logan was a whiz at taking them apart.

He could also tell, merely by sniffing from across the room, if a vat of chocolate needed one more teaspoon of cocoa butter. When he was younger, he could identify the color and variety of any kind of chocolate by feel alone. He had discovered this talent by blindfolding himself and sticking one clean finger into the warm mixture. After that the Candymaker had special plastic gloves made for Logan's four-year-old hands.

Even though he could no longer perform this trick, he still found ways to make himself valuable around the factory. He spent all his early years watching his grandfather's handmade machines turn out candy of all sizes, shapes, colors, and smells. Just by looking, he could tell if a batch of marshmallow needed one more egg white. If an Oozing Crunchorama came down the conveyor belt with one too few hazelnuts, he would toss in a nut before the chocolate shell hardened around it.

But every night, after he listed all the things he was grateful for (which took a solid twenty minutes) and when the comforting shapes around him became too dark to see, the fear crept in and whispered in his ear, *You don't have what it takes to be a candymaker*. To be a candymaker, you actually had to know how to *make candy*. He couldn't follow a recipe, couldn't do even the simplest multiplication in his head. He knew that if he went to a real school, he'd probably be left behind.

Fortunately, his parents didn't believe in traditional schooling and had always educated him themselves. His father taught him to be kind, generous, and hardworking; his mother, to read and write and tell right from wrong.

Biology and baking he learned at the elbow of the Candymaker's right-hand man, confectionary scientist Max Pinkus (the genius responsible for creating the famous Icy Mint Blob, among other best sellers). From Mrs. Gepheart, the factory's librarian, he learned storytelling and philosophy. Everything else he learned by playing on the great lawn behind the factory and helping with the animals and crops. Logan used to think all that knowledge was enough.

But now, only six years away from stepping into his role as official assistant candymaker, he feared otherwise. Sure, he was great at working with the candies they'd already created, but ask him to create his own nougat, for instance, and it would be a scorched mess in no time. He couldn't translate ounces into cups or keep sugar at a steady boil, although he'd tried for years. Heating sugar to exactly the right temperature was the very foundation of candymaking. A few degrees too high, and your gummy dinosaur would turn into a lollypop!

But if he were to somehow win this contest, as his father and grandfather had when they were his age, he would not only prove to the candymaking community that he had what it took to make great candy, he would prove it to his parents and to himself.

"Hey, are you winning the race?" Henry, the head of the Marshmallow Room and one of Logan's favorite people, called out as he ran by.

"I've got a good head start," Logan replied, inhaling the smell of fresh marshmallows roasting. For as long as he could remember, they had had the same exchange every time Logan ran past Henry's room — sometimes ten times a day. (He ran a lot.)

Greetings flew at him from all sides as he raced past the Taffy Room and the Nougat Room, his sneakers squeaking on the shiny linoleum floors. He waved in response, in too much of a hurry to chat.

His feet slowed as a thought struck him. The other kids would know a lot more about the world than he did. What if they didn't like him? What if he didn't fit in? He came to a full stop.

Luckily, he had stopped right outside the Candy Laboratory, where no one could focus on anything but candy. Logan loved to watch Max and the assistant candy scientists in action.

Today Max's team was testing how long it took for their tongues to return to normal temperature after sucking on Fireball Supernovas, their newest invention. Each one held a stopwatch and a clipboard. A few were red-faced. One was panting.

Logan glanced around the room. Max's bald head made the group easy to find. He stood beside one of the large steel kettles in the back, stirring the spicy cinnamon brew for the Supernovas with a long wooden spoon. Every few seconds he added a drop of red pepper oil. In the opposite corner of the lab, the recently harvested carrageen crop lay soaking in large metal pans.

Logan wrinkled his nose at the marshy smell of the reddish purple seaweed, which wafted all the way out to the hall. After being processed, carrageen produced the gel for all the Candymaker's gummy products, including Gummzilla and Gummysaurus Rex, which, at thirteen inches tall, were the world's largest commercially sold gummy dinosaurs. The gel was also used on products that required a sugar coating (like the High-Jumping Jelly Beans) or a chocolate coating (like the Oozing Crunchorama). Logan had spent many a messy afternoon coating caramel balls with carrageen before rolling them in chocolate.

He could watch the scientists all day, but he knew it would be rude to keep the other kids waiting any longer. So he turned away, breathing deeply. His lungs expanded with the fresh air that was constantly pumped into this section of the factory to keep the temperature in the ideal 70- to

72-degree candymaking range. Refreshed, he ran without stopping to the large front entryway.

He heard the bell ring a few times as he approached the thick wooden door. But when he reached it, his hand lingered on the brass doorknob. What would he say to the newcomers? Why hadn't he prepared a welcome speech like those he'd heard his dad give to new employees on their first day?

Well, he might not have a speech, but at least he had a poem. He reached into his pocket, took a deep breath, and swung open the door in time to hear the boy in the suit say, "And that's just the way it is." Then three faces turned expectantly toward his.

In that moment, all their fates were sealed. They just didn't know it yet.

I t's about time," said the boy in the suit. The other boy pushed up his glasses, reddened, and smiled shyly. The girl grinned brightly and pulled her ponytail tighter.

Logan cleared his throat, held up the notepaper, and read, "*'Be not forgetful to entertain strangers, for thereby some have entertained angels unawares.'*" Then he refolded the note (not as gracefully as he would have liked) and stuck it in his pocket. He knew he could rely on Mom to pick out the perfect quote for any occasion.

The girl clasped her hands together. "Lovely!" she exclaimed.

The shorter boy beamed.

The boy in the suit rolled his eyes, looked at his watch, and said, "We're losing daylight here. Let's get this show on the road." He picked up a large brown leather briefcase and strode past Logan into the factory.

"Hi, I'm Daisy Carpenter," the girl said, sticking out her hand.

Logan stared at it for a second before reaching out to

shake it. He'd never shaken hands with someone his own age before. It made him feel very mature. He again found himself distracted by her yellow dress, which glowed even brighter up close. He couldn't help noticing that one of her socks was pink and the other blue with white spots. Maybe she was color-blind. He'd never met someone who was color-blind before. What if you thought you were choosing blue cotton candy but it turned out to be pink?

"I'm Logan," he replied, forcing his gaze away from her feet. "I'm, uh, the Candymaker's son."

"Nice to meet you," she said, then tilted her head toward the boy in the suit, who was already a few feet inside. "That charmer is Philip."

The short boy with the big backpack stepped up next to Daisy. "I'm Miles." He didn't extend his hand, though, so Logan gave a little wave and said hello.

Miles flashed a smile and seemed about to say more. Instead, he just shuffled his feet. Logan was glad to see that someone else felt as shy as he did. He stepped aside to let them enter. The square white pocketbook slung over Daisy's right shoulder hit him on the arm as she passed. He rubbed his arm quickly so she wouldn't notice. What could be in there, bricks? He was about to ask, when he remembered that his mother had taught him never to ask what was inside a lady's purse.

"Wow!" Miles exclaimed as he crossed the threshold. "This place is amazing!"

"Utterly!" Daisy added in an awed tone.

Logan closed the door and smiled. He always liked watching people's faces when they first entered the factory. Philip had turned toward the window of the Cocoa Room, so Logan couldn't see his face. But Miles and Daisy were wearing similar expressions: eyes wide and shining, jaws slightly open, heads bobbing around to soak it all in. The glass ceiling overhead threw sunlight onto the white floors and bounced it off the silver fixtures, making everything shimmer and glow as though lit from within. The bronze statue of his grandfather loomed over the entryway, his kind and welcoming smile the first thing guests saw when they entered.

Logan watched Miles and Daisy slowly turn in a circle, taking in the chocolate fountain, with its continuous stream of smooth chocolate, the barrels of taffy in every color of the rainbow, the gleaming machines behind the long windows of the Cocoa Room.

"Look!" Miles said, pointing to a large display case. "It's a giant Gummysaurus Rex! That's my favorite candy!"

"That one was the prototype," Logan explained. "The first of its kind, I mean. If you look closely, you can see where the tail broke off in the mold. We had to keep adding more acacia-tree gum until we got it right."

"So cool," Miles said, leaning forward eagerly to get a better look at the broken tail.

"And look at this!" Daisy exclaimed, running up to a gold plaque on the wall. She read off the words that Logan could recite in his sleep: "The Confectionary Association is proud to bestow the honor of Best New Candy to Samuel Sweet, for his invention of the Pepsicle." Then she hurried over to the next one.

Logan felt his stomach twist but managed to keep a pleasant smile on his face as she read the plaque. "The Confectionary Association is proud to bestow the honor of Best New Candy to Richard Sweet, for his invention of the Neon Yellow Lightning Chew." She turned to Logan, a look of admiration on her face. "That's your grandpa and your dad, right?"

Logan nodded, his stomach twisting again.

"Must be a lot of pressure on you, huh?" Philip asked, joining them. He tapped the empty space next to the Candymaker's plaque. "I bet your parents expect to see your name right here. Too bad you have to be up against me. I don't lose."

Logan took a step backward. He wasn't used to having anyone talk to him this way. The need for him to win was his own, not his parents'. "No, it's...it's not like that," he insisted. "They only wanted me to enter if it's what *I* wanted. They don't care if I win."

But Philip wasn't listening. He was reading the first plaque again. "The *Pepsicle?* Your grandfather won the candy world's biggest honor for a *peppermint ice pop?*"

"Things were, um, different back then," Logan stammered, still feeling off balance from the boy's mocking tone. "I mean, people were just starting to have freezers in their houses. Creating the first frozen candy was a big deal."

"Boy," Philip muttered. "Competition must have been slim pickings that year."

"I happen to love Pepsicles," Daisy said, turning her back on Philip. "So does my best friend, Magpie, and she's very particular."

Logan threw her a grateful smile.

"What kind of girl is named Magpie?" asked Philip.

"What kind of boy is named Philip?" replied Daisy.

"Sooo...," Miles said, turning toward Logan. "Is Sweet really your last name?"

Logan nodded, hoping he wasn't going to get teased about that, too.

Miles grinned, and his glasses rode up a bit on his nose. "I guess with a name like that it's no wonder your grandfather opened a candy factory!"

"Yeah," Daisy added. "If your last name was Carpenter, like mine, you might be the Cabinetmaker's son instead of the Candymaker's son!"

The three of them laughed. Philip rolled his eyes yet again. Logan wondered if all that eye-rolling would give Philip a headache one day. He turned to Daisy. "Is that what your dad does? Makes cabinets?"

She shook her head, her long ponytail actually skimming Philip's nose. "Oops," Daisy said when Philip backed up in annoyance, rubbing his nose. Logan and Miles stifled a laugh, and Logan suspected that Daisy had known exactly where her ponytail would wind up. "My dad's not a carpenter," she said. "He's a musician. He plays the violin."

"He plays what?" Philip asked, keeping a good distance from Daisy.

"The violin," she repeated.

"Not much money in that," Philip mumbled.

"Money doesn't buy happiness."

Philip shrugged. "Only people who don't have any believe that."

"What does *your* dad do, then?" asked Daisy. "Rule the world?"

"Maybe someday."

"What does *that* mean?" she asked.

But Philip had turned and walked over to the chocolate fountain. He stuck his fingertips into the flow, the chocolate spilling over his hand and back into the fountain. Digging a handkerchief out of his pocket to wipe off his hand, Philip said, "Doesn't seem very sanitary. I wouldn't be surprised if leaving food out like this is a serious health-code violation." He whipped a black spiral notebook out of his briefcase, scribbled a few words, and slipped it back inside.

Logan gritted his teeth. "It's for display purposes only, not for eating. Still, you're not supposed to stick your hand in it."

"That's true," a deep voice said from behind them. "But we can let it go this time. You haven't learned the rules yet."

The familiar voice made Logan relax instantly. He turned around to see Max wearing a broad grin, his ever-present clipboard tucked under one arm. "Hi, Max," Logan said.

"These are the other contestants—Miles, Daisy, and Philip."

Daisy bent at the waist in an awkward curtsy. "Max?" she asked in an awed voice. "Max Pinkus? *The* Max Pinkus? The man who invented the Icy Mint Blob, the High-Jumping Jelly Bean, the Oozing Crunchorama, the Ten-Minute Taffy?" Her voice rose as she rattled off the name of each candy.

For a brief second Logan allowed himself to think that if he won the contest, a girl like Daisy might feel that way about *his* candy. As far as he knew, his contest idea had never even been *conceived* of before. The Bubbletastic Choco-Rocket would be the first candy in history to turn from chocolate to gum...and back again. Of course, it would take a miracle to pull it off. But that didn't mean it was impossible. Or at least that's what Logan had told himself every day for the last year.

Max laughed at Daisy's starstruck reaction. "Guilty as charged," he said. "But I had some help with the Ten-Minute Taffy." He put his arm around Logan's shoulders and winked. Logan knew that all he'd done was suggest they use more cornstarch and less butter, but still, he stood a little straighter. He realized with a start that he had grown nearly as tall as Max now. Although, in all fairness, Max was pretty short for an adult.

While Daisy stared in open admiration, Miles said a shy hello. Logan worried that Philip would say something rude, but instead the boy offered Max his hand and in a very formal voice said, "This is truly an honor, sir. I've admired your work for years."

Max shook his hand, a bemused smile on his face. "Have you, now? That's most flattering indeed. It's my pleasure to meet you all. I trust you're getting acquainted?"

No one answered right away, so Logan shrugged and said, "Sort of."

"Well, there'll be plenty of time for socializing at lunch. I've been entrusted with the job of overseeing your visit to the factory, and I'd like to start by going over the rules."

Max's eyebrows rose when Philip took out his notebook again, holding his pencil at the ready. "After the rules, we'll go on a tour of the factory. The sooner you learn your way around, the more comfortable you'll feel here."

Daisy's eyes gleamed, and Miles bounced a little in anticipation. Logan couldn't help smiling. He liked both of them already. Philip had started scribbling away, even though Max hadn't gone over the rules yet. He couldn't imagine why someone like Philip would want to make candy in the first place. No one had ever insulted the chocolate fountain before. Not to mention the Pepsicle, without which his grandfather might never have had the confidence to believe he could be a great candymaker. Without the Pepsicle, this whole factory wouldn't exist.

Philip moved his notebook closer to his chest so no one could see what he was writing. Each scratch of his pencil made the hair on Logan's neck stand up a little. He forced himself to look away. Daisy caught his gaze and pretended to scribble madly on her arm. Logan stifled a laugh.

"You don't need to take notes, Philip," Max said calmly. "There won't be a test on this."

Philip snapped the notebook closed but didn't put it away.

"All right, then," Max said, holding out the clipboard and flipping a few pages. "Here are the official rules of the Confectionary Association's annual New Candy Contest. First, all contestants must be twelve years old as of the day of the contest. Each contestant may enter only one confectionary item in the contest, which must fall into the gum, chocolate, or sugar-based candy categories. Cookies, cakes, pies, and pastries are not admissible. You will be competing against twenty-eight other young people across the eight regions of the country, all using the same tools and list of approved candymaking ingredients. The winning entry will receive a one-thousand-dollar cash prize. But of course that's not the best part." He leaned toward them as if he were about to share a big secret, instead of telling them something they all knew well. "The best part...is that the winning candy will be produced and distributed for the whole world to enjoy!"

Daisy and Miles began to whisper excitedly. Logan felt a shiver that was half anticipation and half fear. Even with his limited math skills, he knew that twenty-eight plus the four of them equaled a lot of contestants. Max continued over the whispers, "The Candymaker and I are honored to welcome you all to **Life Is Sweet**. We will do our best to help each of you succeed."

The murmurs instantly quieted. The three visitors looked at Logan, although Miles quickly glanced away. Logan jutted out his chin and didn't flinch under their scrutiny.

Max cleared his throat. "Let me assure you, no preferential treatment will be given to anyone. You will all have access to the same supplies, ingredients, and assistance."

Philip muttered something under his breath that sounded like "Doubt it."

Max continued as though he hadn't heard. "After the tour, we'll have lunch in the cafeteria. Then it's off to the lab for the rest of the day. Today I'll be going over the basic tools, equipment, and raw ingredients you'll be using. Tomorrow morning I'll teach you the basics of candymaking—boiling sugar to make different types of hard and soft candies and tempering, panning, and enrobing chocolate. Tomorrow afternoon you'll use what you've learned to create your submission for the contest. Along with your entry, you'll need to present the judges with a copy of your recipe, including all the ingredients and the instructions on how to make it. Are there any questions so far?"

Daisy raised her hand. "Um, may I go to the bathroom?"

Max sighed. "Are there any questions actually related to the contest rules?"

Miles began firing off question after question about what

kinds of ingredients there would be, how they'd know if they picked the right ones, and how many pieces of their candy they would need to make. All the while Daisy shifted her weight from one leg to the other and made little whimpering sounds. Finally Max turned away from Miles and pointed Daisy down the hall. "First left, second right, around the bend, and it'll be on your left by the Neon Yellow Lightning Chews Room."

"Left, right, left," Daisy repeated. "Got it." She ran off down the hall, her pocketbook bouncing against her hip. Logan figured she must have a big bruise from whatever it was in there that weighed a ton.

Once she had gone, Max said, "Any other questions?"

Miles opened his mouth. But one warning look from Philip, and he shut it again.

"All right, then. We'll go over the rules specific to the factory itself as we go on the tour." Max looked pointedly at Philip and added, "Things like wearing gloves before we put our hands in the raw ingredients."

Philip seemed not to hear as he turned to face the Cocoa Room window.

They all watched as a load of football-sized yellow pods tumbled out of a chute along the back wall and landed in a heap on a clear plastic tarp.

"What are those?" Miles asked.

Logan opened his mouth to reply, but Max said, "Let's wait until Daisy returns. This will be our first stop on the tour."

30

Long minutes went by. Had Daisy gotten lost? To someone who wasn't familiar with it, the factory could seem like a maze of hallways. Logan was about to suggest looking for her, when Miles turned away from the window and said, "In the afterlife, no one has to use the bathroom."

He said this as if it were a totally normal thing to say. Logan's mouth dropped open a bit. Philip rolled his eyes (for a change) and leaned his forehead against the window, his breath fogging it up.

"Is that so?" Max asked, sounding genuinely interested.

"Oh yes," Miles assured him. "People in the afterlife don't eat real food or drink or even need to sleep."

"What else happens there?" Max asked kindly.

"Don't encourage him," Philip warned, not turning away from the window. "He'll just keep talking."

Miles frowned and shifted his weight.

"I'd like to know, too," Logan said.

Miles brightened. "All sorts of things happen. Parties and movies and rubber-duck races—"

"Like the rubber-duck races we used to have here at the annual factory picnic!" Logan exclaimed.

"Yes!" Miles replied excitedly. "That was my favorite part of the picnic!"

"Me, too!" Logan said. The boys grinned at each other.

"I liked the egg toss best," Daisy said a bit breathlessly as she rejoined the group. She must have been running— an activity highly frowned upon in the factory because of the likelihood of bumping into someone carrying trays filled with freshly made candy. Not that that ever stopped Logan.

"Finally," Philip grumbled, glancing at his watch. "Can we get on with the tour now?"

"Sorry," Daisy said, addressing her apology to Max, not Philip. "I got lost, and when I stopped at the Some More S'mores Room to ask how to get back here, well, it was hard to leave that place. All that silky, warm chocolate and those buckets of gooey marshmallows and those freshly baked graham crackers…" Her voice trailed off, the longing evident.

"You should try one straight out of the oven," Logan said earnestly.

"You'll soon get your chance," Max said. "We'll be sampling everything today as part of your training."

Daisy and Miles cheered. Philip twisted his watch back and forth anxiously. Logan wondered if that boy ever relaxed for even a minute.

Max clapped his hands and said, "Now let's get to work, people!"

They all lined up along the window and watched the chocolate-making process unfold. Logan had seen it every day of his life (except Sundays, when the machines were cleaned out) but never tired of it. The Cocoa Room was the domain of Lenny and Steve, brothers who had been at the factory for ten years. They had grown up on a real cocoa plantation and loved chocolate so much they were always the first people in the doors in the morning and the last to leave.

Lenny tied on his apron (which would stay white for about three seconds) and waved at them. They all waved back except for Philip, who apparently couldn't be bothered. Lenny then grabbed a hatchet from a hook on the wall and began to break open the large yellow pods, spilling gooey white beans on the counter. Steve gathered the beans in his gloved hands, rinsed them off in a big metal sink, and tossed them into a giant revolving cylinder. The waves of heat rising from the beans as they roasted mesmerized all of them. Max had to snap his fingers in front of their faces to regain their attention. He led them to the other end of the window to watch the hulling machine crack the beans in half.

"Cool!" Miles said as tiny bean nibs popped out of the shells.

Logan wondered what it must feel like to be seeing this for the first time. He tried to pretend he'd never seen the machine that was now compressing the nibs (along with milk from Bessie and sugar from the factory's sugarcane crop) into a gooey cocoa butter. Or the one that ground up the rest of the bean into a fine brown powder. Alas, he couldn't do it.

"This is my favorite part," he whispered to Miles.

They watched as the cocoa butter was blended with the cocoa powder to make a thick paste. Then, for the final touch, Steve pulled out a square tin from the cabinet above him, peered inside, then sprinkled a pinch into the mixture. The result? Nothing less than the best-tasting chocolate in the world. At least Logan thought it was the best, and he'd tasted a LOT of chocolate in his lifetime.

"What's in that tin?" Daisy asked, pointing to the last ingredient the brothers had used.

Max smiled. "Ah, my dear. You have stumbled upon one of the Candymaker's few trade secrets."

She tilted her head. "What's a trade secret?"

Philip rolled his eyes again. Logan wondered if the boy needed to see a doctor about that. Maybe his eyeballs were loose or something.

"A trade secret," Philip explained, tucking his pen behind his ear, "is something that a businessman does not reveal. If everyone knew about it, they'd be able to duplicate his product."

"That's it in a nutshell," Max said. "That's how we protect our recipe."

Daisy glanced back at the cabinet where the tin was now tucked away again. She turned to Logan. "You must know all these secrets, living here and all."

"You'd think so," he replied, pretending to glare at Max. He'd been asking about that secret ingredient since he learned how to talk, but Max steadfastly refused to answer. It was the one ingredient in all of their products that Logan couldn't identify by taste. He turned back to Daisy. "Believe it or not, I don't know either."

"Dad's afraid you'll sell it to a competitor, eh?" She gave him a playful nudge.

Logan grinned. "That must be it." Truthfully, though, the unwritten code of honor among candymakers would never allow that to happen.

Max patted his shoulder. "All will be revealed the day you officially come on board, my boy. That's the tradition."

Logan swallowed hard. Everyone took for granted that he could follow in his father's sizable footsteps. He forced a smile and took some deep breaths. He wished he could get outside for a few minutes. His mind always felt clearer under the sky. He took one last peek through the glass ceiling before Max led them deeper into the factory. He only had time to look for one cloud, one shape.

A monkey riding a bike, he thought. *While eating a grape Blast-o-Bit.* He instantly felt better.

But not for long.

H i, everyone! Come in, come in!" Fran, the superenergetic head taffy maker, welcomed them to their next stop on the tour. Her muscles rippled as she motioned them inside the Taffy Room. Fran could probably have won an arm-wrestling contest with any of the men in the factory, except maybe Avery in the Tropical Room. Climbing trees all day made you even stronger than stretching taffy.

Daisy's and Miles's eyes widened as they took it all in. Even Philip couldn't stop looking around. The Taffy Room held the unofficial title of Most Colorful Place in the Factory; only the Cotton Candy Room came close. Rows of liquid-filled jugs lined the walls, representing every color of the rainbow and every color that *should* be in the rainbow but isn't. Each flavor had been lovingly created from fruits and vegetables grown right on the factory grounds.

"Look around, children," Fran said, spreading her arms wide. "You can see taffy in every stage of creation. Those kettles over there? Cane sugar and butterfat, boiling at exactly 238 degrees. That table to your right is called a cooling table. That's where the taffy hardens. Water circulates underneath to keep the surface at the correct temperature. How cool is that? Pun intended!"

They all agreed it was very cool.

They watched assistant taffy makers roll a huge blob of yellow taffy back and forth between them until it took on a thick snakelike shape. It even curled and twisted like a real snake. Next to them a machine sliced purple taffy into perfect squares, and another wrapped the squares in small pieces of wax paper faster than you could blink. Bags of sugar and large containers of corn syrup, cornstarch, and butter passed from worker to worker.

"My best friend, Magpie, would love this place," Daisy said, whistling appreciatively.

"Who would like to pull some taffy?" Fran asked, slinging the roll of yellow taffy — now as thick as Logan's leg and twice as long — onto a metal hook on the wall. She made it look easy, but the last time Logan tried to lift a roll onto the hook by himself, he'd sunk down to his knees under the weight. Pretty embarrassing.

"I'll help!" Daisy offered. She laid her pocketbook on the floor and hurried forward. Fran handed her a pair of rubber gloves and then instructed her to hold on to each end of the taffy roll, sling the middle over the hook, then mush the two ends together. Daisy did it with ease. Fran showed her how to pull the taffy until it was taut, then to sling it back over the hook until it softened up.

"This will put air into the taffy to give it a lighter texture,"

Max explained as they watched Daisy, who didn't seem to be struggling under the weight of the taffy at all. "And the friction helps deepen the flavor."

Daisy kept pulling and slinging as if she could do it all day. Logan put his hand on his upper arm and squeezed. Not mushy exactly, but not rock-hard either. He made a mental note to start doing push-ups.

Max must have been thinking the same thing (about Daisy, not the push-ups) because he said, "You're stronger than you look, young lady. That's backbreaking work!"

Daisy rested her arms for a second, the taffy dangling precariously close to the floor, and said, "It *is* pretty heavy. Maybe someone else should take over?"

Fran quickly stepped up. "Great start, young lady. You may have a career in taffy pulling in your future."

For a second Daisy beamed, then with a little shrug said, "Thanks. It was fun." As she returned to the group, she picked off tiny scraps of taffy that had stuck to her dress. Logan didn't know why she bothered. It was the exact same yellow.

Max handed them each a freshly wrapped piece of still-warm purple taffy. Miles and Daisy unwrapped theirs eagerly and tossed the mushy squares into their mouths. Logan was about to instruct them on how you can get more taste out of something if you place it on just the right part of your tongue, but he never got the chance. The unthinkable was unfolding right in front of his eyes. He saw, as if in slow motion, Philip tossing his unopened piece of taffy back to Max.

"No thanks," he told the world-famous confectionary scientist. "I don't like candy. It rots your teeth."

All voices and chewing and rolling and pulling came to a halt. Only the whirring and slicing and wrapping of the automatic machines still echoed through the room. Every face turned to gape at the boy in the suit, who busily clicked the latches open and shut on his man-sized briefcase.

Logan's mind simply could not process what had just happened. Never, not even once, had he seen someone turn down candy fresh off the line. And to be so rude about it, too. Rudeness did not have a place at **Life Is Sweet**. Who could be rude when the very air molecules pulsed with sugar?

No one spoke. Taffy hung loosely on the hooks, slowly congealing.

"In the afterlife," Miles said, breaking the silence, "no one gets cavities."

His comment hung in the air. The boy certainly knew a lot about the afterlife.

Daisy stepped forward until she was only a few inches from Philip's face. He took a step backward, sending a rack of wooden mixing spoons toppling to the floor. "Why would you want to create the world's best new candy," she demanded, "if you don't even eat candy?"

Philip shrugged, grabbed his briefcase, and headed toward the door. "A contest is a contest. You never want to get too close to your subject, anyway. You'd all be wise to follow that advice. It might even give you a chance at winning something one day."

The door swung closed behind him. A few seconds later, activity resumed, as if a switch had been turned on again.

"Wow," Fran said, staring after him. "Where'd ya dig up *that* kid?"

Max shook his head. "I'm not sure that *is* a kid!"

"More for the rest of us," Daisy said with a shrug, grabbing two more pieces of taffy from the wrapping machine.

"That's the spirit," Max replied. Resting his hand on Logan's shoulder, he asked, "You all right, son?"

Philip's words were still swimming around Logan's head, but another thought began to push through. Did *he* want to win just to win? His top priority, of course, was to create something that would bring people joy. But his motives weren't entirely unselfish either. Maybe that made him no better than Philip. A depressing thought.

When Logan didn't answer right away, Miles grabbed him by the arm and tugged. "Logan!" he cried. "Are you all right?"

"Um, Miles?" Daisy said. "I think you're going to pull his arm out of the socket."

Miles's anxious expression (and vigorous shaking) snapped Logan out of his trance. "I'm fine, sorry. Let's just keep going on the tour, okay?"

"Absolutely," Max declared enthusiastically. "Onward and upward, young candymakers-in-training! We're off to the Cotton Candy Room!" With a quick goodbye and muttered apologies to Fran and the other taffy makers, they hurried from the room. Philip was waiting for them in the hall, seemingly oblivious to the drama he had just caused.

As they headed toward the next wing, Miles kept up a stream of steady questions. How did the fruits and vegetables turn into food coloring? Did Fran make taffy all night, too? Why didn't everyone at the factory weigh five hundred pounds? Max answered cheerfully *(compressed and mixed with water; all the machines are turned off at five; exercise and restraint)*, but the others remained quiet with their thoughts.

As soon as they turned the corner, the unmistakable smell of spun sugar filled the air. Logan inhaled deeply. He saw the others do the same, even Philip. Filing inside, they watched the granules of colored sugar dance in the air inside huge wind-tunnel machines. Slowly the streams of sugar transformed themselves into massive cottony balls of fluff.

"It's like magic," Miles breathed.

Logan nodded in agreement. He'd always thought so, too.

After they had sampled each of the five flavors being created that morning — chocolate, pineapple, blueberry, lemon-lime, and carrot (which tasted better than it sounded) — the tour continued. They visited the Icy Mint Blob Room, the Oozing Crunchorama Room, and the Leapin' Lollies Room (which shared space with the Blast-o-Bits and the High-Jumping Jelly Beans). Max nearly had to drag Miles out of the Gummy Dinosaurs Room, and Daisy from Some More S'mores.

In each room Philip would ignore the offer of candy and jot something down in his book before shutting it tight.

After a quick stop at the Neon Yellow Lightning Chews

Room (currently not operating because of an overproduction the day before), Miles asked Max why the factory didn't offer regular tours to the public. "I bet it would be a good way to make money," he said. "Not, I mean, that you need more money or anything. I mean, I'm sure you guys do great." Miles reddened. "Er...you know what I mean."

Max laughed. "I do know what you mean. For years we did offer tours during the annual picnic. One day a plastic toy truck wound up in a vat of chocolate, and we had to dismantle the whole piping system to retrieve it." He pointed up at the ceiling, where thick white pipes sent the molten chocolate, caramel, and cream to different parts of the factory throughout the day. "After that, we had to stop giving tours. Things have been so busy around here that we never started them back up again."

"That's too bad," Daisy said. "I bet a lot of people would want to visit."

Logan thought so, too, but whenever he brought it up to his parents, they changed the subject. Just like with the annual picnic.

"In the afterlife," Miles said, "all the candy factories are open to the public and you can eat as much as—"

Philip (who clearly *hated* it when the conversation turned to the afterlife) interrupted Miles with a sharp cough. The cough turned into a wheeze, which became a really bad case of the hiccups. His whole face turned as red as if he'd just sampled a Fireball Supernova. It would be funny if he didn't look so uncomfortable.

Max ducked back into the Lightning Chews Room and came out with a cup of water. "Drink," he commanded.

Philip didn't hesitate. He gulped down the whole thing and handed it back.

"Better?" Max asked.

Philip gave a single nod. The hiccups seemed to have stopped. His face soon faded to the less extreme color of a cherry-flavored High-Jumping Jelly Bean.

"Serves you right," Daisy whispered under her breath.

Philip ignored her.

"Let's keep going," Max said, ushering them all down the hall.

Logan turned his attention away from Philip, anxious to move along to the next stop. He couldn't wait for the others to see this one. They passed the cafeteria (where delicious smells were already starting to fill the hall) and the offices where the "suits" worked. The suits were the people in the marketing, advertising, and sales departments. They didn't really wear suits, but they didn't wear the white shirt/tan pants combination either. "Business casual," they called it, which meant nice clothes, basically. Adults had strange names for things.

The factory's library was right across the hall from the offices. Seeing it reminded Logan that he had a report due on Plato, the ancient philosopher, for Mrs. Gepheart. He gave the room a wide berth as they passed. Miles, however, stopped so abruptly that the others walked right into him.

Philip scowled.

Miles stood, transfixed, in front of the library's glass walls. "You have a *library* here?" he asked, his voice high, his eyes so round they looked like an owl's.

Before anyone could confirm that, yes, the rows and rows of books, the oak-paneled walls, desks, and comfortable chairs did indicate the presence of a library, Miles began to drift toward the door as though pulled by some invisible force. His feet barely touched the ground. Max laughed and reached out his arm to halt him. "You'll have plenty of time to explore the library after lunch. We have a lot of ground still to cover."

But Miles didn't tear his eyes away. "Can't I just go in for a few minutes? I'll meet you at the next place, I promise."

Max hesitated, then said, "Well, I guess that's all right. Far be it from me to keep anyone from a library." He scribbled down the directions, and Miles shoved the paper into his pocket without a glance.

Logan felt a pang of sadness that he wouldn't get to show Miles the Tropical Room. He certainly couldn't imagine feeling drawn to a library the way Miles seemed to be. The Cotton Candy Room, yes, but a library? No.

As the group got farther away from the central part of the factory, the temperature became progressively warmer. As used to it as he was, Logan found himself flapping the bottom of his shirt in a futile attempt to generate a breeze. Daisy tugged at the collar of her sundress. Philip, who was wearing the most clothes by far, pretended not to be bothered by it. But the beads of sweat on his forehead gave him away.

Though tempted to explain the rise in temperature, Logan didn't want to give away the surprise. And it was an *excellent* surprise. Max didn't explain either. A shared glance between them confirmed that he had no plans to.

By the time they reached the enormous glass door at the very end of the longest hallway, they were all full-on sweating. Even Philip openly mopped his brow. The humidity inside the room fogged up the door, fully hiding the treasures within.

"Here we are," Max announced, turning his back to the doors. "The jewel in the crown of the **Life Is Sweet?** candy factory. Our pride and joy, the reason our candy tastes like no other—the Tropical Room!" He whirled around and tugged at the door handle, then sighed in defeat. Logan giggled. No one but Avery (and maybe Fran) was strong enough to open the heavy, pressure-sealed door without assistance. Still, he had to hand it to Max for trying.

Max pretended to glare at Logan, then pushed the red button on the side of the door, which then slid open easily. The humid air rushed out to greet them, a sensation Logan once compared to being hit in the face with a hot, wet washcloth—but in a good way.

They filed in, moving a bit more slowly as a result of the thick air. "Ahoy there!" Avery called down from the top of the sapodilla tree, where he was extracting chicle to make gum. "Can someone pass up the funnel? I left it down by the bucket."

"Sure, Avery," Logan said, scrambling over the tree's

roots to find the metal funnel. For a second he was tempted to shinny up the tree and hand it to him, but climbing the trees was against the rules. This was one of the hardest rules in the whole factory for Logan to obey. Every day he watched the workers slice the bark in crisscrosses until the yellowy goo (which later would be boiled and purified and transformed into gum) slid down into the cloth bags waiting at the bottom. Once the cuts stopped dripping, they hardened, leaving inch-wide diagonal tunnels on the trunk that were perfect for a boy's toes to grip on to.

Logan had to admit, though, that after all the effort the factory had made — going to a real jungle at the equator to get the trees, transporting them here, replanting them, and imitating their natural surroundings well enough to ensure their continued survival — climbing them for sport probably wasn't the best idea. Under the sapodilla tree was his favorite place to be in the whole factory. When he hugged the tree's narrow trunk (which, admittedly, he did a lot), he swore he could feel its heart beating.

Plus it smelled like caramel.

Without his realizing it, his arms had begun to embrace the tree. Common sense quickly warned him that hugging the tree with the other three watching wouldn't be a good idea. He quickly disentangled himself and attached the funnel to the pulley system. He then tugged on the rope until the funnel started moving up among the branches.

"Thanks, mate!" Avery called down as he plucked the funnel from the pulley.

From his position below, all Logan could see of Avery's head was the blue bandana he wore to keep the sweat out of his eyes. The glass roof curved so high above their heads that on sunny days like this, the trees looked as if they could disappear into the blue sky of a real jungle.

A few seconds later, Avery swung his strong legs around a branch and popped his head through the leaves. "Who are your new friends?"

Logan stepped aside as the others tentatively approached the tree. Neither Daisy nor Philip volunteered their names — they were too busy staring, open-jawed. Avery laughed. "First time in the Tropical Room, eh?"

Logan nodded, proud that the room would elicit such a response. "These are two of the other kids in the candy competition with me," he explained. "Daisy and Philip. Miles will be along soon. Max is giving them a tour of the factory."

With the help of the harness around his waist, Avery twisted around until he was hanging completely upside down. He extended his hand, speckled with yellow goo, and the two visitors took turns shaking it. Daisy blushed. Philip, however, took out another handkerchief (Logan couldn't help wondering how many he had in there) and wiped both hands, front and back.

"Have fun, kids," Avery said, adjusting his bandana. "Make some good candy. We could use it around here." He punched Logan good-naturedly on the arm and pulled himself back up the tree.

After a few minutes of letting them watch the gooey liquid darken as it made its way down the trunk, Max continued the tour of the Tropical Room. Daisy lingered so long at the cinnamon tree, stroking its soft bark and smelling it, that Max had to threaten to continue on to the cocoa trees without her. She tore herself away with a final deep inhale.

Stepping carefully over the vanilla vines and around the tall stalks of sugarcane, they approached the section of the room where the cocoa trees grew, under an elaborate sprinkler system that rained water on the trees every few hours. It must have just stopped, because the leaves and the reddish purple pods were still dripping. The cocoa trees, shrouded in shade, grew so much shorter than the other trees in the room that the kids could easily reach the pods on the lower branches.

Logan was about to demonstrate this when he caught sight of Miles trying to untangle a vine from around his ankle. He ran over to help him.

Once Miles's ankle was freed, Logan asked, "So what do you think?" He hoped that Miles loved the room as much as he did.

"S'ti elbidercni!" Miles replied.

"What did you say?" Logan asked, wondering if Miles had spoken in another language. He hoped not. No one at the factory had taught him foreign languages yet.

"I meant to say, it's incredible!" Miles exclaimed, beaming.

"Glad you could join us, Miles," Max said, patting the

nearest trunk. "This is where it all begins, my friends. A chocolate bar is only as good as the bean it comes from. These trees are cultivated in the finest soil and given the perfect amounts of shade, sun, heat, and rain." He glanced at his watch and then up at the roof. "In fact, it's just about time to let in the sun."

A minute later they heard a grinding sound high above, as the long metal slats that covered the roof began to slide into grooves on the wall. Sunlight slowly filtered in, streaming through the leaves and sending a shiver of pleasure down Logan's spine. He saw Miles shiver, too, and it made him wish again that the factory hadn't stopped giving tours. Everyone should get to experience stuff like this. He'd even offer to lead the tours so no one would have to leave their posts.

"C'mon," he said to the others. "I want to show you something really neat."

He was about to lead them over to the long rows of drying cocoa beans when Max's walkie-talkie crackled to life. Max slipped it off his belt, held up one finger for them to wait, and stepped a few feet away.

"Do you come down here a lot?" Miles asked Logan as they waited.

Logan nodded. "I like to check on the trees first thing in the morning. The sapodilla's my favorite."

"Are you allowed to climb them?" Daisy asked, glancing back at her beloved cinnamon tree.

Logan shook his head.

"Don't you want to?" she asked.

"All the time. But only Avery and his crew are allowed. Someday I hope to work on the sapodilla."

Philip made a noise that sounded halfway between a guffaw and a sneeze.

"Are you okay?" Logan asked warily. He hoped another hiccupping fit wasn't on the way.

"You're the heir to an entire candy factory, and all you want to do is drain sap from a tree?"

Before Logan could think of a response, Max returned with a worried expression on his face. "That was Randall in Quality Control," he explained. "He's concerned about the nougat. He said it tastes 'off.'"

"Off?" Miles repeated.

Randall had been the factory's quality-control guy for twenty years, and Logan admired him greatly. Randall's taste buds were even more finely tuned than his own. If Randall said something tasted off, then it was off.

Logan silently checked the list of ingredients in nougat — sugar, corn syrup, vanilla, butter, salt, egg whites, and honey. Could there be an egg-quality issue? Their chickens were fed the highest-quality food, and the farmworkers monitored the health of all the animals very closely. Any problems would have been discovered before now. Then Logan remembered something that Paulo in Beekeeping had said a few days ago.

"I bet it was the honey!" he exclaimed. "Paulo told me the queen of the hive didn't have long to live. If she died, the worker bees would be really depressed. Maybe that's what happened."

Max nodded thoughtfully. "Yes, that would do it! This calls for a bit of a detour on the tour. *Detour on the tour . . .* that's funny." He shook his head at his own joke. This time it was Logan's turn to roll his eyes.

"That was pretty bad, boss," Daisy said, grinning.

"Let me get this straight," Philip said, pushing low branches and leaves out of his way as they headed back toward the entrance. "Bees get depressed over another bee dying, and the honey somehow tastes different? Is that what you're saying?"

"The queen's not just any bee," Logan said. "She's the glue that holds the whole hive together."

"Bees don't make glue," Philip pointed out. "They make honey."

"You know what I mean," Logan said calmly, refusing to rise to Philip's bait. "Without the queen, the worker bees don't know what to do. It's like they forget how to make the honey. And we need a lot of honey here. We use it in about half our recipes."

"So what are *you* supposed to do about it?" Philip asked Max. "Isn't your job in the lab?"

"Well, Philip," Max said as he pushed the button to open the door, "at **Life Is Sweet**, we all like to help out when we can. Logan here has a way with bees, don't you, son?"

"A way with bees?" Miles repeated as they walked down the hallway. The moisture rising from his face made him look oddly pale.

Logan tried hard not to blush. "I don't know. They seem to listen to me or something."

"Now don't be modest," Max chastised as they hurried down the long corridor that led to the Bee Room. "Logan has a way of charming bees. And girls." Max winked.

Logan's cheeks burned. He kept his gaze forward, hoping Daisy hadn't heard Max's comment. As if he'd ever charmed a girl in his life!

They didn't say much as they traveled through more long corridors, up one staircase and down another. By the time they reached the Bee Room, Logan's embarrassment had faded enough that he was able to hand Daisy the required protective gear—helmet, goggles, and long gloves—without avoiding her eyes.

"Thanks," she said, plopping the helmet on her head and adjusting the goggles. "Do I look like an alien?"

"Sort of," Logan admitted.

"I'll just wait here," Miles said when Logan tried to hand him his gear.

"No need for concern," Max assured him. "The bees aren't dangerous at all. The gear is really only for insurance purposes."

Miles still hesitated.

"Unless you're allergic?" Max asked.

Miles glumly shook his head and held out his arms for the gear.

"We're *eventually* going to learn how to make candy, right?" Philip asked. "The contest is in two days!"

"Yes, of course," Max promised. "But this is part of your training, too. To understand how candy works, you have to know how the ingredients come together. Without honey, for instance, you'd be very limited in what you could make for the contest."

Philip muttered something about not needing honey for his recipe.

With a nod from Max, Logan pushed the door open slowly, making sure none of the bees flew close enough to escape. As usual, the buzzing reached his ears before he actually saw any bees. The large room — the second largest in the whole factory — had two solid walls and two made of giant screens. Sunlight streamed through the screens and threw thousands of tiny crisscross shadows onto the opposite walls. Daisy gasped when they reached the huge garden that filled the center of the room.

Usually the bees hungrily sucked the nectar from the hundreds of colorful flowers to take back to the hive. Today only a few stragglers buzzed around the plants, flying lazily, as if their hearts just weren't in it. Miles stopped near the first bed of flowers and seemed intent on going no farther.

As Logan wound his way through the flowers and shrubs, the buzzing became progressively louder. He found Paulo kneeling on the floor, peering into the largest of the hives, where the queen resided. Totally engrossed, Paulo didn't even look up. He just kept making little clucking sounds as the bees flew in and out erratically, not in their usual smooth rotations.

Logan liked Paulo a lot. He was completely dedicated to the well-being of the bees, and, at twenty-five, he was one of the younger workers. He always called Logan "dude." After a minute passed, Logan cleared his throat. Paulo jumped up, clearly surprised to find he was no longer alone in the big room.

"Oh, hey, dude," he said, sounding more subdued than Logan had ever heard him. Noticing Daisy and Philip, he added, "And, um, other dude and dudette, who I don't know." To Logan he said, "The queen has passed. The worker bees are in mourning. Will you join me in a moment of silence?"

Logan nodded and knelt beside his friend. Out of the corner of his eye, he saw Daisy yanking Philip down. Logan knew his world differed from that of most other people. Most kids did not mourn the death of a honeybee, queen or no. But for two years that queen bee had been the reason the other bees had made the honey that flavored the candy at **Life Is Sweet**, indirectly bringing pleasure to thousands of kids.

Max joined them, and they all bowed their heads as Paulo gave a short prayer of thanks for the queen's years of service. The other bees seemed to silence their buzzing, too. No one spoke (or buzzed) for a full minute.

Then Miles screamed.

CHAPTER FOUR

I'm okay," Miles insisted as the others rushed around him. He lay sprawled on the ground, halfway between a marigold bush and a batch of white clover. "I bent down to look at this butterfly, and then it landed on... I mean, then I sort of tripped."

Daisy leaned down to tap Miles's helmet. "Good thing you had this on."

Miles smiled weakly.

"I don't see any butterfly," Philip said, looking from side to side.

Miles pushed himself up on his elbows. "He must have gotten away."

Logan reached past the marigold bush to help him up.

"You're sure you're all right?" Max asked, peering closely at Miles's face. "When people scream in a factory, it's often bad news."

Miles nodded, straightening his helmet and goggles.

"In that case," Max continued, "let's agree to save the screaming for when an appendage gets caught where it shouldn't. And since no one is going to stick a hand inside a moving blender, that means no screaming, period."

Miles nodded. "Got it."

Paulo joined them. "Everything okay here?"

"Nothing to worry about," Max assured him. "Now, what can we do to help get your bees back on track?"

Paulo led them to the hives and pointed to the largest one. "The new queen is in there, but the colony hasn't taken to her yet. They need to get their usual routine back in gear."

"Isn't Logan supposed to be some kind of bee charmer?" Philip asked. "Can't he just tell them what to do?"

"Logan is indeed a friend to the bees," Paulo said, waving him forward. "It's worth a shot, dude."

Logan had no choice but to kneel down in front of the hives. He cleared his throat. "Um, hi, bees," he whispered, trying to ignore his audience. "I know this is a hard time for you, but cheer up. You'll like the new queen. She's, er, *peppier* than the old one. I mean, she's alive and all. I'm sure she'll take great care of you. All you have to do is keep bringing that nectar and, you know, mixing it with bee spit to make that tasty honey of yours."

A few bees circled Logan's head and then took off again.

Logan sighed. "Did you try the smoke machine yet?"

Paulo shook his head. "I was hoping I wouldn't have to. It relaxes them, but it makes them eat their own honey. I didn't want to use up our reserves."

"It's okay if we're a little low on honey for a few days,"

Max said. "Henry in Marshmallows has at least a few days' worth stored up. And the nougat can wait, too."

Paulo nodded thoughtfully. "All right. Let's do it."

Max ducked out to tell Randall of their plans. The others helped haul the smoke machine out of the closet (except for Philip, who claimed that the cost of dry cleaning his suit would be prohibitive).

"He better put on an apron when he starts cooking," Paulo muttered to the other kids as they bent over the equipment. "Wouldn't want powdered sugar to get on that fine material."

"Or bee spit!" Daisy said, and they all cracked up.

Paulo plugged in the machine, which looked like the mutant offspring of a vacuum cleaner and a toaster oven, and showed them how to place wood chips in the bottom. Then he lit the wood chips with a long match and aimed the metal contraption at the opening of the hive. Puffs of smoke wafted around the hive and then blew straight in.

Almost immediately the bees, which had been flying haphazardly around the room, raced back to the hive, and the buzzing inside grew louder and louder. In response, Philip, Daisy, and Miles retreated to the other side of the bushes, but Logan stayed to watch.

After a minute Paulo turned off the smoker. The bees soon began leaving the hive in a steady stream. Logan stepped back quickly to let them pass. It was never a good idea to get in their way when they were hungry. Soon the bees had returned to their usual routine — sucking nectar from flowers and carrying it to the hive, then going back to do it all over again. Paulo scraped some fresh honey off the comb with a wooden spatula and held it out for the kids to taste.

Philip declined, and Miles had disappeared to the marigold bushes again.

Daisy tried it. "Um, good, I guess?"

"Perfect," Logan declared, licking his lips.

Max, who had just returned, gave his thumbs-up, too.

Paulo let out a long breath. "That's a relief," he said, stowing away the smoke machine. "You can tell Randall everything's going to be fine. And I'll bring some of the bees out to pollinate the vanilla vines this afternoon."

Logan took one more lick of the honey, then took a small jar off a nearby table and let the rest drip into it. Randall would want to sample it for himself. "Later, Paulo!"

"Later, dude. And other dudes. And dudette."

"*Now* can we make some candy?" Philip asked as they stripped off their gear in the hall.

"Soon enough," Max promised. "Right now it's lunchtime. Chocolate pizza's on the menu today!"

Miles's stomach growled so loudly in response that everyone laughed.

"I'll drop off the honey jar at the Quality Control Office and meet you there," Logan said with a backward wave. He hurried up and down the staircases and along the corridors now bustling with workers on lunch break. He weaved in and out, holding the honey jar close. He loved the way the unprocessed honey glowed a deep orange. It took a lot of restraint not to stick his finger in.

Randall stood outside the door of his office, beaming, as Logan approached. The tall, thin man took the jar of honey, stuck a finger in, and swirled it through the thick orange goop, then licked his finger.

"Good job, my boy!" Randall said. "I knew if anyone could get to the bottom of the problem, it would be you."

Logan smiled up at him. Randall never missed an opportunity to build up his confidence. Now that Logan was twelve, he knew what Randall was doing, but he didn't mind. "See ya, Randall!" he said, taking off again. "It's chocolate pizza day!"

"Don't run in the halls," Randall teased.

"I won't!" Logan called back, laughing.

The cafeteria was only around the corner, and he knew the others wouldn't have gotten there yet. He was lost in thought, thinking of all the different ways he would eat his chocolate pizza slices, when they arrived. And someone else was with them. Logan could spot that mop of bright white hair from miles away. Henry from Marshmallows had been at the factory ever since Logan's grandfather founded it fifty years before. When his grandfather left a few years ago for that special part of heaven reserved for people who have made other people's lives sweeter, Logan began spending more time with Henry. He always had good stories to share of the olden days at the factory, and Logan never tired of listening to them.

"Hi, Henry!" Logan said. "I'm sorry I didn't get to stop by this morning."

Henry put his hand on Logan's shoulder. "That's okay, my boy. I just had the pleasure of meeting your new friends. They came by to tell me to expect a new batch of honey in a few hours. What an exciting journey you're all embarking upon! And what nobler calling is there than inventing a new way to make people happy?"

"I told you so," Daisy said to Philip. "You should be making candy to make people happy, not just to win."

Logan expected Philip to have a quick comeback, but he merely nodded absently, looking at Henry out of the corner of his eye almost suspiciously.

"C'mon, kids," Max said, handing them each a green plastic tray and ushering them into the line. "I thought we'd get our pizza and take it out to the lawn for a picnic."

Logan beamed at this welcome news. He disliked being inside for more than a few hours at a time. Plus the caterpillar he had been watching for the past few weeks would be shedding its chrysalis any day now. He wanted to chart its progress.

While they waited on line, Max told the others that if they were interested, he would take them out on the pond after lunch. "We have a few rowboats and a canoe, so there would be plenty of room for everyone."

Both Philip and Miles shook their heads and answered at the same time, which made it hard to hear either one.

Max bent down a bit toward them. "Sorry, what was that?"

"I just want to get to work," Philip repeated.

"I'm allergic to rowboats," said Miles.

Daisy asked it first. "How can someone be allergic to rowboats?"

Miles shrugged. "I just am."

By this point they had reached the front of the line, so getting chocolate pizza onto their trays took priority over boat allergies. Daisy asked for four slices. She got a raised eyebrow from Mary, the chocolate pizza maker. But she got her request.

"Two for you?" Mary asked Logan, holding out his slices.

Logan nodded. "Thanks, Mary."

To look at Mary, with her chocolate-stained apron and her ability to slice pizza into perfect triangles without losing a single tiny marshmallow in the process, you'd think she'd worked there for years instead of only months. But that's how it went at the factory. When a new employee arrived, it seemed as though the right job had been there all along, waiting for just that person to fill it.

Unable to resist, Logan leaned down and bit the point off one of his slices. The dough was sweet, the chocolate sauce and marshmallow topping warm and gooey.

Philip watched him with a look that bordered on disgust. "Do you have anything else?" he asked Mary.

She stopped cutting midslice. "Anything else? Like what?"

"I don't know," Philip said. "Like regular pizza? You know, with cheese? And tomato sauce?"

Mary wiped off the chocolate pizza slicer on her apron. "We do indeed have regular pizza," she said. "If you don't mind waiting a few minutes, I can whip one up for you."

Philip gave his usual single nod.

"I'd like to be at the Marshmallow Room when the new batch of honey arrives," Henry said, leaning over the counter and carefully lifting off two slices. "So I can wait in here with the young man — Philip, is it?"

"That work for you, Philip?" Max asked, handing everyone an apple and a small carton of milk.

Philip hesitated as if he were about to argue, then nodded grimly.

The back door of the cafeteria let them out in the middle of the lawn. To their right lay the pastures where the cows and chickens roamed inside their tall white picket fences. To their left, acres of red and yellow and orange fruits and green vegetables provided a colorful contrast to the wheat and barley and cornfields.

And the smells! The smells in the factory, as wonderful as they were, had a slightly *processed* odor, even though they all came from pure ingredients. The air outside smelled like earth and newly growing things. Logan looked over at the pond glittering in the distance. The empty boats bobbed welcomingly in the slight current. "Definitely allergic to rowboats, eh?" he asked Miles as they followed Max and Daisy through the groups of factory workers enjoying their lunches.

"Yup, sorry."

"It's okay," Logan said, wondering what form an allergy

to rowboats would take. Hives? Throat closing up? Something totally weird like an inability to see the color red anymore? He thought it would probably be rude to ask.

"I can't believe you actually live here," Miles said.

"I know," Logan agreed. "I'm very lucky." As soon as he said the words, he wished he could take them back. After all, he didn't really know anything about Miles's life. He wouldn't want to make anyone feel bad just because they didn't live in a candy factory.

Max led them to an empty red-and-white-checked blanket near a thicket of elm trees. They quickly settled around it, placing their trays gently on the ground in front of them. Within seconds, everyone had a slice of chocolate pizza in hand.

"This is the best thing I've ever eaten," Daisy said, chewing slowly and deliberately.

Miles nodded enthusiastically. "I may never eat anything else."

"You know what would be perfect?" Daisy said. "A tall stack of buttermilk pancakes for breakfast, chocolate pizza for lunch, a Pepsicle for snack, and then this again for dinner!"

Logan had to agree, although he'd throw in a lot more candy throughout the day.

Miles said, "I agree with everything except the breakfast part."

"Why?" Daisy laughed. "Are you allergic to pancakes, too?"

Miles nodded. Daisy stopped laughing. "Seriously?"

Miles nodded again.

"Anything else?" Daisy asked.

"The color pink," he replied, glancing warily at Daisy's one pink sock. "Hot pretzels with mustard, merry-go-rounds, and jazz music."

No one spoke.

"You are very strange," Daisy finally said, shaking her head.

Miles shrugged. "In the afterlife, everybody's strange because nobody's trying to impress anyone."

"Like I said, *strange*."

"I think everyone is strange in some way," Logan said. "I mean, I am, at least."

Miles glanced at Daisy, who put her hand on Logan's arm. "Do you want to talk about it?"

Their serious expressions made him hesitate. Even Max had stopped chewing. What did they think he was talking about? He shook it off. They were probably just playing around. He laughed. "It's nothing *serious*. My pinky toe sticks out sideways." He reached down to his sneaker. "Do you guys want to see?"

"No!" they all said at the same time.

"Don't you have anything weird about you?" Logan asked Daisy, glad that the serious mood seemed to have quickly passed. He must have imagined it.

She looked down at her own feet. "Well, I can never find matching socks!"

"That's it?" Miles asked.

She shrugged. "I'm allergic to bees. Don't know if that's exactly weird, though."

Max, Logan, and Miles all stared at her with concern. "You're allergic to bees?" Max repeated. "And yet you came into the Bee Room with us?"

Daisy frowned. "I guess I didn't really think about it."

Miles and Logan shared a look. "What happens if you're stung?" Logan asked.

"I don't remember. I was only stung once, when I was really little. I was out with my grandmother. She must have gotten me to a hospital or something."

Max just shook his head. "Anything else you'd like to tell us before we put your life at risk again?"

"If I think of anything," Daisy said with a laugh, "I'll let you know." She stood up and pointed a few feet away. "Is it okay if I go read under that tree over there?"

"Of course," Max said. "Do you have a book with you?"

Daisy patted her pocketbook. "Always."

"Me, too," Miles said, then frowned. "Well, except today."

She headed off to the tree, and Logan turned to Miles. "So how do you know so much about the afterlife?"

"I'm just interested in it," Miles said, biting into his apple. After chewing for a long time, he added, "I do a lot of research."

"Like in the library?" Logan asked. Mrs. Gepheart had shown him books on different religions and philosophies, but he didn't recall anything about the afterlife.

Miles nodded. "Sometimes, but people tell me things,

too." He took another bite and chewed it so slowly it was clear he didn't plan on elaborating.

Logan glanced over at Daisy. He couldn't be sure, but it looked like she was reading her book upside-down! She must have realized it, because she soon flipped it the right way again.

Philip showed up with his *(ugh)* regular cheese pizza.

"Did you have any trouble finding us?" Max asked, sliding over.

Philip placed his tray and briefcase on the ground before straightening out his suit and sitting. "No. The sun glinted off your head and made you easy to spot."

Max laughed and rubbed his shiny head. "I knew this thing would come in handy one day." Looking at Philip's tray, he said, "You only got one piece? Is there something else you'd prefer?"

"This is fine. I don't believe in eating too much at meals. Digestion slows down the brain."

"Actually, son, food provides energy for the brain."

"Can you please just keep talking about whatever you were talking about before I got here?" Philip asked.

"That would be the afterlife," Max said, the corners of his mouth twitching.

Philip groaned. "Anything but that." He squinted in the sun.

"Do you want to switch places?" Logan offered.

"It's okay," Philip mumbled, shading his eyes as he ate. Logan got the distinct feeling that Philip didn't spend much time outdoors. This suspicion was confirmed when Max suggested they all go for a run around the pond to get some oxygen into their systems, and Philip asked, "Why would anyone run unless he was being chased?"

"Well, we can stay right here, then," Logan said, lying down on his back. "And play Name That Cloud."

Miles flopped onto his back, too. "I love that game!" Looking up and shading his eyes, he pointed to a big fluffy cloud. "How about that one?"

"Hmm," Logan murmered, deep in thought. "A frog sitting on a phone book eating an Icy Mint Blob!"

"That's exactly what I was going to say!" Philip said. Logan and Miles lifted their heads in surprise. "Really?" they asked at the same time.

Philip, who wasn't even looking at the sky, shook his head. "No, not really."

They lay back down with a groan. "Some people have no imagination," Miles said, loud enough for Philip to hear.

"I don't know," Logan said, staring back up at the clouds. "Maybe some people just haven't tried."

Logan turned his head slightly to glance at Philip. He was too busy scribbling in his notebook to pay any attention to their conversation. What could he be taking notes on out here? He considered walking behind him and stealing a quick look but thought better of it. He wouldn't like it if someone peeked at his sketchpads without asking, and this was pretty much the same thing. He turned back to Miles. "Wanna see if my caterpillar turned into a butterfly yet?"

"Sure," Miles replied, pushing himself up. "I'll go see if Daisy wants to come, too."

"Be back in five minutes," Max said.

As Logan made his way around the blanket, he mistakenly kicked Miles's backpack, which was lying in his path. It slid onto the grass, so he reached down to move it back to the blanket. From the size of it, he expected it to be heavy; instead, it felt as light as air. But it was full — thick and bulky, as if there was a balloon inside, which couldn't possibly be the case.

He quickly caught up to Miles, and they approached Daisy together. She was leaning back against the tree, holding the book right up to her face and reading out loud.

"*Love's Last Dance*?" Miles asked, looking at the cover.

Daisy quickly closed the book and laid it down in her lap.

"I wouldn't have pegged you as a romance reader," Miles said.

"Why not?" Daisy replied, crossing her arms.

"You just seem more, I don't know, practical."

"Can't a girl be both?"

"I have no idea," Miles replied.

"I used to read out loud to myself, too," Logan said.

"It's a bad habit," Daisy admitted. "And a little embarrassing when the book is called *Love's Last Dance*!"

"A little," Logan agreed. "Do you want to come check on my caterpillar with us?"

Daisy shook her head and gestured to the book. "I'm at a

good part. The son of the ranch owner is about to propose to the cowboy's daughter!"

"Wow," Miles said in mock sincerity. "That really *does* sound like a good part!"

Daisy kicked him playfully in the shin.

"C'mon," Logan said, taking Miles by the arm. "Let's let her read in peace. We only have a few minutes."

Miles made a big show of rubbing his shin as they left. Logan led the way to the far corner of the field, where the milkweed, clover, and marigolds grew. He tiptoed to the white clover bush and knelt in front of it.

"He's still there," Logan whispered, pointing to the underside of a leaf.

The caterpillar's chrysalis hung by the thinnest of threads, like a silver strand of spun sugar. Logan had rigged up a temporary shelter for it out of some twigs and gauze. That way, if it rained or a big wind kicked up, it should be protected.

He tested the twigs to make sure they were still sturdy, then took out his pencil and notebook, flipping quickly to the chart on the last page. He wanted to make sure Miles didn't see his drawings. Not because they were bad—he freely admitted they were—but because most of them were of dinosaurs, some with two heads. He had a sneaking suspicion that at his age drawing dinosaurs was no longer acceptable unless you were planning on being a paleontologist. Which, of course, he wasn't.

Logan entered the date on his chart and quickly sketched

what he saw. The pod looked bigger than yesterday and thinner, too. He swore he could see butterfly wings stuffed in up there, just bursting to get out. It was three weeks exactly since the black-yellow-and-red-striped caterpillar had spun the tight casing around itself, and Logan knew that any day it would emerge as a butterfly. Every spring he tried to catch one doing its final molting. And every spring he had failed.

"It's really cool," Miles said, his eyes wide.

"I know," Logan agreed. "If you look closely, you can see the colors that the butterfly's wings will be when it's born."

Miles bent down for a closer look. "Red, right?"

Logan nodded and flipped his sketchpad closed. "Come on, we should get back."

They stood up just as Max came around the bend with Daisy and Philip following.

"What *is* that thing?" Philip said, peering at the thin thread that held the fledgling butterfly.

"It's a butterfly chrysalis," Logan said. "Haven't you seen one before?"

"You should take it down," Philip scoffed. "It's diseased. It's going to kill that whole bush."

Logan moved in front of it protectively. "There's nothing wrong with it. That's how they're supposed to look."

Philip shuddered.

"Okay, enough nature for one day," Max said, putting his arm around Philip's shoulder and leading them all away. "The rest of the afternoon you'll get to be in a nice environmentally controlled room with no windows. Does that make you happy?"

"Ecstatic," Philip said dryly.

"Good!" Max thumped him on the back.

Over the last few hours, the lab had been divided into four sections, each with its own lab table, burners, and equipment. The center of each table held a place card with the name of one of the four contestants. Logan saw only one sign of the earlier Fireball Supernova testing; Alvin, one of Max's assistant confectionary scientists, held a bag of ice to his tongue and whimpered as he rinsed out a beaker in the sink.

"Guess you need to turn the Supernovas down a notch?" Logan whispered to Max as they passed the unfortunate man.

"What makes you say that?" Max asked innocently.

The others couldn't wipe the smiles off their faces as they found their stations. Logan wondered if Philip knew he looked like a totally different person when he smiled. Probably not. Unless he was in the habit of smiling at himself in the mirror, which Logan doubted.

"Now," Max began, walking among the stations. "What you see before you are the tools of a master confectionary scientist. You are welcome to add any other ingredients you like, as long as they're on the approved list. Everything you need to take the contest judges by storm is this equipment, the raw ingredients in the right combination, and a huge helping of imagination."

"Oh, is that all," Daisy said dryly.

"Let's take a few minutes to get familiar with our workstations. I'll walk around and answer any questions you may have."

"I have a question," Miles said, raising his hand. "What does this do?" He turned the knob on the Bunsen burner, and a thin purple flame shot a foot in the air. He leapt out of the way as Max ran over and switched it off. "Never mind!" Miles said, bowing his head.

"Let's all agree to ask questions first and act later, all right?" Max asked.

Logan sent Miles a sympathetic glance. It was hard not to play with the burners. He and Henry often toasted marshmallows over them, mostly as an excuse to stare into the purple flame. Logan looked over his supplies: pans, candy and chocolate thermometers, a small scale, a blender, bowls, steel and wooden spoons, a marble slab, wax paper, a mixer, spatulas, and measuring cups and spoons.

Max led them through some supposedly basic experiments, like heating sugar to different temperatures and making buttermilk and cream, which seemed easy for the others. It was fun watching the concoctions boil and bubble and sizzle. And colorful, too, when they started adding all-natural fruit flavors.

Logan knew a lot would have to change in the next two

days for his dream of winning to become a reality. He'd really need to work hard at it, perhaps harder than he'd worked on anything before. He'd have to quiet that voice in his head that told him he wasn't smart enough. Could he really do that? Could he focus well enough? He doubted it.

But if he *could* pull it off, if he could make the Bubble-tastic ChocoRocket turn from chocolate to gum and back again, it would do more than take the contest judges by storm. It would make **Life Is Sweet?** famous the world over.

He wished he were back outside, staring up at the clouds and naming their shapes. *That* he was good at. Why couldn't there be a contest for that?

CHAPTER FIVE

When Logan arrived at the Marshmallow Room the next morning, ten large pans of marshmallows were cooling on the counter. Henry had wasted no time whipping up a fresh batch. The others would be arriving at the factory in a few minutes, but Logan didn't want another day to go by without his morning visit to Henry. He had so much to share.

Henry whistled as he flipped over pans and peeled off wax paper with an ease and swiftness that came from decades of practice. Logan unwrapped the two sticks they had carefully handpicked in the woods near the factory a year ago. Henry divided up the marshmallows, and they took up their spots on either side of the largest burner, holding their sticks exactly two inches above the flame.

Logan watched the flames arc gracefully toward the marshmallows, enjoying the ever-shifting shapes they made as they leapt. The marshy smell drifting from a fresh bundle of mallow plants in a box on the counter drew his attention.

"I would have helped you harvest those," he said. He enjoyed accompanying Henry into the swamp beside the pond.

Henry kept his eyes on his marshmallow, always more careful not to let his burn. "We'll go together next week," he said, rotating his stick slightly. "Right now you have more important things to do."

Logan couldn't help grinning. "Seriously, Henry, you should have seen it yesterday. After Max went over how to use the equipment, he gave us samples of the raw ingredients. Little containers of cane sugar and beet sugar and powdered sugar and flour and milk and all the nuts and different flavors of chocolate and egg whites—" Logan stopped to take a breath. "And food coloring and spices and cut-up fruit and all the sticky things like acacia gum and lecithin and carrageen, chicle and molasses and corn syrup and honey. And then Max got all serious and said something like 'From these building blocks you can create something no one has seen before. I have faith in all of you.'"

Henry lifted his marshmallow away from the flame and blew on it. "That sounds very profound indeed."

Logan nodded and pulled his marshmallow from the flame, too. "But what if he's wrong? To have faith in me, I mean. After all, I've been trying—and failing—to make this work for years. Why would that change with only one day left before the contest?"

Henry shrugged. "Things change when they're ready to change. People change when they're ready, too. You can never predict these things. You still haven't told Max your idea, I gather?" Henry popped his perfectly toasted marshmallow into his mouth.

Logan shook his head. "No one except you."

"Don't worry," Henry said, switching off the flame. "No one's going to laugh at you."

Henry had an uncanny ability to read Logan's mind. "You're sure?" he asked.

"And if they do, well, they'll just be jealous they didn't think of it first."

Logan grinned. "That's right!" He bit into the marshmallow and slid it off the stick. Then he placed the stick back in the cabinet for next time.

"Good luck," Henry said, placing his stick next to Logan's. "By the way, how are you all getting along?"

"Great," Logan replied, surprised by the question. "Well, I guess Philip pretty much does his own thing. He's not, um, very pleasant."

"Don't be too hard on him," Henry said, opening the door for Logan. "Perhaps he's insecure in this new environment."

Logan nodded, although it seemed as if Philip had made himself right at home, bossing everyone around like he owned the place. He remembered the paper in his pocket and pulled it out: *"'Be kind, for everyone you meet is fighting a battle you know nothing about.'"*

"See?" Henry said. "What did I tell you?"

Logan grimaced. "I'll try to be kind." With a final wave,

he ran the whole way to the front door, managing to get there before the others arrived. He walked outside and took a deep breath of the crisp morning air. Along with the air came sweet scents from the field — peppermint and clover, apples and peaches, and a decidedly earthy smell from the barn.

He sat on top of the old-fashioned milk jug to wait. Before his grandfather started keeping cows, milk for the chocolate had been delivered from the local dairy. For the last forty years, the large tin jug had stood empty by the side of the door. It always reminded Logan of his grandfather, and he suspected that's why his dad had never gotten rid of it.

For a brief second he worried that the others had changed their minds and dropped out of the competition. For an even briefer second he realized that in that case, he'd have a better chance of winning. He banished both of those thoughts from his head, and a minute later a small blue car pulled up. Miles hopped out, his big backpack over his shoulder again. Logan jumped up from the milk jug to greet him.

"This is my dad," Miles said, pointing to the man behind the wheel.

Logan ducked his head inside the window to introduce himself. Miles's dad had black hair streaked with gray and looked about ten years older than the Candymaker. Although his smile was nothing but friendly, Logan could see a weariness in his face, as if he hadn't gotten enough sleep in a long time.

"Thank you for being such a wonderful host," Miles's dad said. "Miles couldn't stop talking about the place yesterday."

"Dad!" Miles protested, the tips of his ears turning red.

Logan laughed. "It's been fun for me, too."

"Well, you two stay out of trouble, and, Miles, try to eat something other than chocolate for lunch today."

"Dad! I told you we ate apples, too!"

They sat down on the stoop to wait for the others. They laughed for a solid minute about Philip getting powdered sugar all over himself in the lab the day before, then debated whether Gummysaurus Rex would win in a battle against Gummzilla. Both presented valid arguments, and then the sound of hooves clomping on the driveway drew their attention away.

Their mouths fell open as Daisy approached, not in a car, but on a large black horse. Instead of the yellow sundress, she was wearing jeans and a purple T-shirt with orange flowers on it. When she saw the two of them watching, she pulled on the reins and the horse slowed down.

"Um, is this how she arrived yesterday, too?" Logan asked in a low voice.

"She was here before me," Miles whispered. The horse let out a snort and shook its mane as Daisy made clucking sounds at it.

Daisy came to a halt right in front of them. The horse swished his tail a few times and grunted. Logan crinkled his nose. Miles pinched his closed.

"Oops," Daisy said, looking behind the horse at the steaming pile on the driveway. "I'll clean that right up." She swung down in one fluid movement and pulled a brown paper bag from the bundle tied to the saddle. With a pat on the horse's flank, she bent down to sweep the droppings into the bag. Logan noticed that her socks didn't match again, but at least neither of them was pink.

"Sorry about the unusual transportation," she said, straightening. "My parents couldn't drive me this morning, so I had to take the horse. She's old but reliable. She used to work on my aunt and uncle's farm. You know, pulling carts of hay and stuff."

Miles jumped back a bit as the large beast swung its head in his direction.

"You don't have to be afraid of her," Daisy said. "She's harmless." She rubbed her flank again and turned back to Logan. "My dad will come later to pick her up. Where should I leave her?"

"You could put her in the barn by the cow pasture," Logan offered. "There's plenty of hay and water and people to watch her."

"Sounds perfect," she said, picking up the reins. "I'll meet you guys inside."

"Don't you want me to show you where it is?"

Daisy shook her head. "I saw it yesterday at lunch."

"Wait," Logan said as she turned to go. "You should bring your dad in when he comes. I'm sure my parents would love to meet him."

She quickly shook her head. "He isn't really the social type. You know how musicians are."

Logan didn't, having never met a real musician. "Oh, okay. Well, see you inside." They watched her lead the horse around the side of the factory. "I've never seen a real horse before," Logan admitted to Miles as they sat down again to wait for Philip.

"Me neither. Bigger than I thought they'd be."

Logan nodded in agreement. "I wonder where her aunt and uncle's farm is."

Miles shook his head. "I didn't think there were any farms around here. I mean, except for yours."

"I didn't think so either. But then again, I don't get out too much."

Miles looked as if he were about to say something, but he changed his mind and picked quietly at a loose thread on his shorts. Logan wondered if he had said something wrong.

"Do you think we should go in?" Miles finally asked. "Maybe Philip's not coming today."

Logan checked his watch and nodded. He had planned on taking Henry's advice and being extra friendly to Philip. He couldn't do that if Philip didn't show up, though. "I guess he knows the way."

To their surprise, Philip was already in the lab when they arrived. He wore the same suit, but no tie this time. Logan opened his mouth to say hi, but Philip had already turned away. Oh well, he'd tried.

They took an inventory of their supplies, as Max had instructed the day before. Daisy arrived a few minutes later. A strong odor of peppermint wafted from her. She must have walked through the peppermint plants on her way from the barn. Logan was about to ask her more about the horse when Max clapped his hands. "All right, future candymakers. Let's begin!"

He passed around the box of rubber gloves, and they each pulled out two and fitted them on. Then they followed him up to the long lab table at the front of the room, where he'd set up a small enrobing machine, a rotating drum for panning, and a tempering machine.

Next to the equipment sat a metal tray of Oozing Crunchoramas (lined up in perfect rows of ten) and a bowl of High-Jumping Jelly Beans. But not the finished products — only the centers, which Miles, Daisy, and Philip examined with interest. No one outside the factory had ever seen these.

"We're going to start with panning," Max said. "This machine is used to give a candy its hard shell. You can pan with a sugar mixture or chocolate. For demonstration purposes today, we're going to coat jelly beans. Everyone stand back."

Dutifully, they did as they were told. Max tossed a bowl of the jelly beans inside the metal drum and flicked the switch. The urn started rotating slowly at first, then picking up speed. The jelly beans tumbled around like clothes in a dryer, flinging themselves against the sides, top, and bottom. Max handed Philip a cupful of bright red liquid and, talking loudly over the sound of the beans bouncing hard off the metal, instructed him to fling it into the urn.

Without hesitating, Philip flung. Unfortunately, he forgot to hold on to the measuring cup. It flew out of his hand, banged against the side of the urn, and clattered to the floor. They all instinctively stepped back as the red liquid shot through the air.

"And that's why we use plastic measuring equipment," Max said, reaching for the cup, which had rolled to a stop against his foot. He switched off the panning machine, and the beans fell into a pile on the bottom.

"Sorry," Philip mumbled, slipping the paper-towel roll off the dispenser on the wall. He seemed not to know what to do with it, though, so it hung limply from his hand.

Miles leaned over and ripped a piece from the roll. He took off his glasses and wiped the red splatters off the lenses. Then he handed Philip back the soiled towel.

Philip just stood there, holding it and waiting for instructions.

"Here, let me take that," Max said, lifting the paper towels from his hands. "Don't worry, that's why they call them accidents."

"Accidents?" Philip repeated, sounding unfamiliar with the word. As if he'd never made a mistake before. Logan wondered if maybe he hadn't.

Max poured more of the red liquid into a new measuring cup. "We need to remember to focus on what we're doing at all times. These machines can be pretty powerful. And these are only the traveling versions of the full-sized ones in the other rooms. Try again." He handed the cup to Philip and switched the machine back on.

This time Philip hesitated for a few seconds before tossing the liquid (and only the liquid) into the urn. It sloshed all over the beans and coated them as the urn rotated.

Max gave them each a cupful to throw in, and within a few minutes, a thick coating had built up on the beans. To finish it off, Max tossed in a quarter cup of melted beeswax, which gave the beans their shine. As they glinted under the bright laboratory lights, Max switched off the machine and grabbed a handful. He held out his palm, and they each took one.

Philip deposited his directly in his lab-coat pocket. Miles and Daisy threw theirs on the floor, obviously familiar with why they were called High-Jumping Jelly Beans. Both beans bounced up high over their heads. They reached out expertly to catch them before popping them into their mouths.

Philip looked pained. "You both ate food off the floor, are you aware of that?"

They laughed. "That's how you're supposed to eat these," Daisy explained. "Haven't you ever had one before? Wait, of course you haven't."

Philip smoothed out his lab coat. "I'm not in the habit of eating where people walk. Who knows where your shoes have been?"

Daisy fumed.

"Moving right along," Max said, stepping down the line to the enrobing machine. "This little beauty is one of my favorites." He placed the tray of bare Oozing Crunchoramas on the conveyor belt of the enrober, then flipped open the lid on top of the machine. He handed Daisy a funnel and a jug full of the chocolate that had been simmering in a copper pot on the back of the stove. She still looked as if smoke could come out of her ears.

Max turned the switch to the ON position. The conveyor belt began to move.

"Now?" Daisy asked.

"Good a time as any."

She tilted the funnel over the opening on the top of the enrober. A thin curtain of chocolate flowed down as the belt began moving the Crunchoramas along. The result? Each row of Crunchoramas emerged from the chocolate waterfall draped with a shiny coating of deep brown chocolate. A quick burst of air whooshed out from a small tube to create perfect ripples on top of each piece.

Logan loved those ripples. He could watch the silky stream of chocolate cascade down all day, and sometimes he did. But no time for daydreaming today. Max was already herding them toward the tempering machine. Daisy, transfixed, had to be dragged away from the enrober by Max.

"In the old days," he began, "we would temper the chocolate by hand, carefully heating and cooling it until the crystals inside the chocolate molecules reached the perfect level of stability. Now, in the interest of saving time, we use this handy tempering machine." He patted the contraption lovingly.

Logan could hear Max talk about crystals and molecules and stability all day, and it *still* wouldn't make sense. All he knew was that if you wanted to cook with chocolate, it needed to be in a certain state. Basically, a blob of mushy chocolate fresh from the Cocoa Room went into the machine, got sloshed around, then was heated, cooled, heated, and cooled again. About an hour later, the chocolate came out shiny and more solidified. He'd need to learn how to do it by hand one day—all good candymakers knew how—but Logan feared he wouldn't be able to follow the instructions.

"I'd like you to spend the next few hours practicing with these machines and your raw ingredients," said Max. "Also feel free to go back to some of the rooms we visited yesterday, where anyone will be happy to answer your questions. After lunch I'll meet with each of you in private to discuss your chosen project. Do any of you know what you want to make yet?"

Philip's hand shot up.

Daisy muttered, "Why am I not surprised?"

"Preparation is the key to success," Philip declared. "I've been working on my contest entry for weeks." He waved his hand dismissively at the long lab table. "And I won't need any fancy machines to make it."

Logan glanced worriedly at Max. These machines were like his children. Max's eyebrows rose in response to Philip's comment, but all he said was, "Wonderful, Philip. I look forward to seeing what you've come up with. Anyone else?"

Logan glanced at Daisy and Miles, but they both shook their heads. With a deep breath, Logan slowly raised his hand. He'd dreamt about the Bubbletastic ChocoRocket for so long, it had begun to feel like just a dream. But now the time had come to make it real. He had opened his mouth to speak when Philip stepped forward and pulled on Max's sleeve.

"Yes, Philip?" Max asked, turning toward him. "Are you so eager to share your plans that you can't wait your turn?"

Philip shook his head. "I just wanted you to know I'm not going to show my candy to anyone before the contest. Like you said yesterday, you can't copyright a recipe. There's nothing to keep anyone at the factory — or any of you guys, *no offense* — from stealing my idea, mass-producing it, and making a fortune. Then I'd have to sue, and it would get messy."

Miles gasped. Daisy shook her head disapprovingly. Logan stared, aghast. "But that would never happen!" he insisted. "Not here at the factory. Not from one of us!"

Philip shrugged. "I prefer to win the contest first, and then I can control what happens next." He crossed the room to his station and pulled out his notebook. Apparently, the conversation didn't interest him anymore.

Silence descended on the room and hung there. Even Max couldn't seem to find the right words. The only time

Logan had ever seen that happen was when Miss Paulina called from **Miss Paulina's Candy Palace** with the news that twenty boxes of Oozing Crunchoramas had oozed all over the store when the electricity went out, and she was standing in a river of chocolate.

No one moved until the door swung open with a bang. Then they all jumped.

CHAPTER SIX

How's everybody doing?" the Candymaker boomed as he and Logan's mom entered the room. "It's so quiet in here I figured I'd find you all huddled over your lab tables creating something delicious and award-winning!" He grinned, making sure to meet everyone's eyes.

The Candymaker's high spirits were enough to lift the dark mood that had fallen on the room. Philip kept his head down, but Miles and Daisy eagerly approached Logan's parents with shy smiles. Introductions were made and hands shaken.

"We had hoped to get here yesterday," Logan's mom said. "But things always get a bit crazy before the big show."

"That's what people in the candy business call the annual convention," Logan explained to the others.

"That's right," Mrs. Sweet said. "And we always get a few visitors passing through on their way to the show, so you may notice a few more men around here today who look like my husband." She reached over and affectionately patted the Candymaker's belly. "We're always happy to show other candymakers how we do things. And we learn from them as well. I'm sure you're all helping one another, too."

Logan squirmed a bit but didn't look over at Philip. He didn't want to put him on the spot.

His mom then put her arm around Daisy's shoulders. "It's nice to have another girl around here. If there's anything you need, just ask me."

Daisy beamed.

"Nice to see you again, Philip," the Candymaker's wife said.

They all turned to look at Philip in surprise. When had she met him?

"Ah, so this is Philip!" the Candymaker exclaimed, crossing the room.

Philip quickly stashed away his notebook (no doubt full of his top-secret recipe) and stood up. "Yes, sir."

"Sir?" Miles mouthed at Logan.

"Well, Philip, I heard you're quite the go-getter."

"You...you did?" Philip said, stuttering a bit. For the first time, he seemed a bit nervous. Logan supposed the Candymaker's, er, *girth,* could be a little intimidating if you didn't know him.

The Candymaker nodded. "Henry in Marshmallows told me he had a nice chat with you at lunch yesterday. You impressed him with your ambition."

Philip gave a quick nod but didn't say anything.

Logan listened to this exchange with interest. Henry was impressed with someone's ambition? Henry, the man blissfully content to make marshmallows day after day for forty years? Leave it to Henry to find something nice to say about everyone.

"Well, children," the Candymaker said, turning back to the others. "Enjoy your stay here with us, and I'll look forward to seeing what you each come up with. Including you, son." He ruffled Logan's hair playfully. Logan's mom gave Daisy a final squeeze and off they went.

Logan busied himself by picking up the measuring cup at his station, examining it in the light, and putting it down again. Maybe no one had heard his father's parting words. No luck. All three contestants swarmed him.

Daisy said, "Your own parents don't know what you're making?"

Logan shook his head.

"Why?" asked Miles.

Logan hesitated, not sure how to answer. Before he could figure it out, Philip took his turn. "I'm sure his parents know. How could they not? He's pulling your leg."

"I assure you he is not," said Max, coming to Logan's rescue. "He has kept me in the dark as well, although the rules don't stipulate that the contestant can't use other resources."

"But why, Logan?" Miles asked. "Don't you want your dad's help? And Max's?"

Logan took a deep breath. "It's sort of complicated. I always thought if I made it into the contest, that this was the candy I wanted to make. So if I had everyone's help, then it wouldn't be mine anymore. I need to do this myself. The way you guys are. It wouldn't be fair otherwise."

"Aw, shucks," Daisy said, punching him playfully on the arm. "That's very big of you. Don't you think so, guys?"

Miles nodded enthusiastically. Philip shook his head. "No. I think it was stupid. You had an advantage and you tossed it aside. That's not how you win, that's how you lose."

Daisy's fists clenched again, but Max stepped in before she could respond. "Come now, children," he said, ushering everyone back toward their stations. "This is a friendly competition. We're making *candy*, after all, not running for political office."

"That may be," Philip said, crossing his arms, "but I'd like to request some sort of structure around my station."

"A structure?" Max repeated.

Philip nodded. "Like a curtain."

Max's forehead furrowed. "What would I hang a curtain from?"

They all looked up at the gleaming rows of pipes that ran along the ceiling, then back down at Philip.

"Well, some sort of temporary wall, then," he demanded. "I believe the contest rule book will back me up."

Max opened and closed his mouth like a fish. Logan looked back and forth from Max to Philip, who stood with his arms crossed.

Finally Max sighed. "I'll look into it during lunch."

Philip appeared satisfied and sat down on the stool behind his station.

Max addressed all of them. "Now everyone scram. Go visit some of the rooms, talk to the assistant candymakers, see what excites you. We don't have much time left to prepare. The four of you will meet for lunch in the cafeteria in an hour."

The contest had begun! They were about to take the first step toward winning. The moment should have been electrifying. No one, however, moved a muscle. Max clapped his hands. "Go, go, go!"

Still no one moved.

Max sighed again. "Okay, what's the problem?"

Miles raised his hand. "I don't know where to go."

"Did any of the stops on the tour yesterday interest you more than the others?"

"I guess so ..."

"Good!" Max said. "Start there. Now, how about you, Daisy?"

Daisy tugged at her ponytail. Logan noticed she did that whenever she felt unsure of something. "I really don't know. Maybe I should make something with taffy?"

Max nodded. "You certainly have the strength to work with taffy. I'm sure you can come up with something the taffy world hasn't seen before."

"If you say so," Daisy said, sounding unconvinced.

Max turned to Philip. "I won't even ask."

Philip gave his standard curt nod, picked up his briefcase, and strode from the room.

All eyes turned to Logan. He gave a weak smile. "Tropical Room. I need to, um, learn about the properties of gum. You know, from the source."

Max smiled. "So your new candy is gum-based? It seems you were about to tell us before but got cut short."

Logan shifted his weight, then nodded. "It's sort of gum-based. Sort of chocolate."

"C'mon, Logan," Daisy said. "You can tell us. We're all friends here."

Logan looked around at the three faces smiling at him and knew she was right. "Okay, but I don't even know if it's possible." He took a deep breath. "I want to invent the Bubbletastic ChocoRocket, which turns from chocolate to gum . . . and back again!"

He waited for them to laugh, but instead they all started talking at once.

"Sounds great! Wow! You should totally do that!"

"You really think so?"

Max hesitated for only a second. "I'm not saying it will be easy, but yes, I think you can do it."

Logan felt a weight lift just by telling them his plans. Keeping a secret always made him uneasy.

"No time to waste," Daisy declared, linking her arm through his. "Gotta get you off and running!"

Miles joined them, and the three left the room, talking excitedly about their plans.

"See you guys at lunch," Daisy said, turning down the corridor toward the Taffy Room.

"Good luck." Logan waved, then turned to Miles. "Do you want me to take you somewhere?"

Miles shook his head. "I'll be okay."

As Miles strode away, he looked smaller, somehow, than he had yesterday. It took only a second to realize why. No backpack on his shoulder! Logan considered getting it for him but realized he didn't know where Miles was headed. How strange to have the others wandering around the factory on their own. Unheard-of, really. But his dad had said he wanted them to feel at home.

Logan hurried to the Tropical Room and searched the trees for Avery. He couldn't find him anywhere. He circled around again, then stopped to break off a stalk from an aloe plant, which he stuck in his pocket for later.

"Ahoy there, matey!" Avery's voice came from one of the many loudspeakers dotted throughout the room.

Logan ran from tree to tree. He started laughing. "Where are you?"

"In the office. A guy's gotta do paperwork sometimes. It's not all fun and games, ya know."

Logan wound his way back to the office, which he had passed right by. "It's not? All fun and games, I mean."

Avery grinned as he shut a file drawer with his hip. "Mostly it is. So what brings you here in the middle of the day? Aren't you supposed to be inventing the world's next great candy?"

Logan nodded. "That's why I'm here. I need to learn all there is to know about gum."

Avery narrowed his eyes in suspicion. "You know as much about gum as I do, mister. What's really up?"

Logan sighed. Avery was probably right — he *did* know a lot about gum. "Well," Logan said sheepishly. "There's one thing I really need to know — how do I get gum to turn into chocolate, and, er, back again?"

Avery laughed. Logan's shoulders sagged.

Avery stopped laughing. "Oh, you're serious?"

Logan nodded.

"Sorry! Okay, gum to chocolate and back again. Like, over and over or just the one time?"

"Um, over and over. You know, if possible."

Avery reached into the corner of the office and grabbed two canvas bags from a big pile. He tossed one to Logan. "Well, sounds like you've got a challenge in front of you. Help me collect some fresh chicle, and we'll talk."

So Logan helped, and Avery talked. By the time they'd finished harvesting, Logan had a pretty good idea of how to proceed. All he'd need is the fresh chicle, the exactly right cooling and heating temperatures, powdered sugar, acacia gum, some tempered chocolate, nougat, edible wax, and a handmade mold.

Oh, and that whole miracle thing.

Logan found Miles waiting outside the cafeteria at lunchtime. He was leaning against the wall, backpack at his feet, reading a note. He held it out to Logan.

> Hi guys, have lunch without me,
> went to go check on ~~the horse~~ the horse.
> Hugs, Daisy.

"What do you think she crossed out?" Logan asked, handing the note back to Miles.

Miles peered down at it and shook his head. "Can't tell." He tucked it into his pocket. "So, do you think we should wait for Philip?"

Logan nodded. "At least a few minutes."

"Okay."

Neither of them spoke as they watched the workers stream into the cafeteria. Everyone greeted Logan with a high five or a hearty hello. They all had a smile for Miles, too.

"Everyone here is really nice," Miles commented.

"Yes," agreed Logan. Now that the two of them were alone, he wanted to ask Miles about himself, his family, school, and so on, but he didn't know how to begin. He didn't even know if Miles had any brothers or sisters. He opened his mouth to ask where Miles had spent the last hour just as Miles blurted out, "Do you think Daisy's pretty?"

Logan thought about it. Her hair was definitely shiny and a nice shade of yellow. And she smelled kind of good. When she smiled, her whole face lit up. "Yes," he said, fairly confidently. "I'm pretty sure she is. Pretty, I mean. Do you think so?"

Miles nodded, less certainly. "I think so. I'm not really

sure." He looked down. "To be honest, I'm not really used to thinking about girls. Well, one girl I liked, but she, um, moved away."

Logan was relieved. "Me neither. Thinking about girls, I mean. I don't see many of them."

Miles nodded, then said, "I don't think Philip's coming."

Logan looked at his watch, then turned to scan inside the cafeteria. No sign of him. "I think you're right. Let's get something to eat."

"Chocolate pizza?" Miles asked hopefully.

Logan laughed. "That's only on Thursdays. But I know where we can get some. C'mon."

He took off running, with Miles close on his heels. When they arrived at Logan's apartment, they were out of breath. Logan's mom opened the door right as he reached for the knob.

"Logan Sweet," she said, hands on her hips. "Were you running again?"

"Um, no?" Logan replied, panting. Miles giggled.

His mother shook her head disapprovingly and ushered them inside. "So how's the Bubbletastic ChocoRocket coming?"

Logan sighed. "Max told you already?"

His mother nodded. "Of course. There are no secrets in this place."

"It's true," Logan told Miles. "If you sneeze in the Sour Fingers Room, someone in Icy Mint Blobs will say *God bless you*. It's weird."

"Well?" his mother prompted.

"I have some ideas," he replied honestly.

"How about you, Miles? How's your project coming?"

"I'm not sure," Miles replied, the tips of his ears turning a bit red. "I . . . I think it's going to work. It's nowhere near as cool as Logan's, though."

Logan opened the refrigerator and pulled out the box of chocolate pizza. "Mine's only cool if I can make it work," he reminded Miles.

"Here, let me warm these up for you." Logan's mom took the box from his hands.

"She's afraid I'll drop them," Logan explained good-naturedly.

"Hush," his mom said, pretending to swat him with her free hand. "Why don't you go show Miles your room? These will be ready in five minutes."

So Logan gave Miles a tour of the apartment. When they reached the bathroom, he dug the thick aloe leaf out of his back pocket and rested it on top of the pile on the counter.

"Good for the skin," Logan explained.

Miles nodded knowingly.

Logan wondered if Miles used aloe, too. "You can have some if you like," he offered. "I can always get more. You know, because I live in a candy factory." He grinned.

Miles grinned back. "Right. That's what I figured. But no thanks, I'm good."

Logan tried to think of ways to keep stalling so he didn't have to show Miles his bedroom. What if Miles thought it looked like a little kid's room, with all the stuffed dinosaurs and drawings tacked up and the curtains with moons and stars on them? To say nothing of the mess. Fortunately he was saved by his mom yelling for them to come for lunch.

Miles gobbled down two slices of pizza before coming up for air. "Honestly, Mrs. Sweet, I could eat this at every single meal. My dad would love it, too. He says he's a chocoholic."

"Why don't you invite your parents for dinner tonight at six?" she suggested. "We'd love to have them."

Miles glanced at Logan, who nodded eagerly. "Okay, sounds great." He went into the next room to call his parents.

"That's okay with you, right, honey?" Logan's mom asked.

He nodded, reaching for another slice. He ate it quickly, too excited to hear Miles's mom's answer to even taste it. The only guests they ever had for dinner were people from the candy business who had known the family forever. He vaguely remembered a time when his parents entertained a lot more, but that was years and years ago. He wondered why his mother suddenly wanted to invite new people. But he didn't ask. He didn't want her to change her mind.

"All set!" Miles said, returning to the kitchen. "My mom said she'd bring dessert, but I told her I thought you had that covered."

They all laughed. For the first time in a long, long time, maybe ever, Logan felt like a normal kid, hanging out with a friend, eating chocolate pizza, and looking forward to later. After slurping down one of his mom's famous all-natural milkshakes, it was time to get back to work. Miles went to use the bathroom as Logan helped his mom clean up.

"How are you doing with everything?" she asked him. "You've had a lot of new things to deal with all at once."

"I'm good," Logan said. "It's been fun." He thought of Philip. "Well, mostly fun."

She gave his shoulders a squeeze. "You know it doesn't matter if you win, don't you? Your father and I couldn't be more proud of you."

"Sure." Logan nodded. He hoped he sounded convincing.

Miles returned. "Hey, is it okay if I leave my backpack up here, since I'll be back for dinner?"

"Of course," Logan's mom said. "Why don't you go drop it on Logan's bed? If you can find it, that is."

"Ha ha," Logan said, his cheeks growing hot.

It felt as if Miles was gone a long time, but it couldn't have been more than a minute. All he said was "Cool room."

"Um, thanks," Logan said, relieved. He glanced over at his mother. She just smiled and pushed them toward the door. On the way down to the lab, they resumed their debate on who would emerge the victor in a fight between Gummzilla and Gummysaurus Rex. Since they couldn't come to a conclusion, Miles suggested the two gummy dinos team up to end the reign of the giant monster Philipsaurus the Third, who threatened to rule the planet with the evil plans hidden inside his impenetrable Briefcase of Darkness.

They were still laughing over that idea when Logan pushed open the door to the lab. Daisy met them at the door, her face grim.

They stopped laughing. "What's wrong?" Logan asked.

She gestured behind her with her thumb. "Welcome to Corporate America."

She stepped aside, and Logan gasped.

The laboratory looked like an office in downtown Spring Haven! Temporary walls five feet high hid each of the stations, turning them into cubicles. Logan looked over at Philip's area but couldn't even tell if he was in there or not. Max approached from the back of the room, carrying a bucket of caramel in one hand and marshmallows in the other.

"I know, I know, it's awful," Max said wearily. "But Philip was correct. The rule book does say that each contestant's privacy should be respected and all that."

"You didn't have to put them around my station," Logan insisted. "I don't need any privacy from you guys."

"Me neither," Daisy and Miles said in unison.

"Technically, I had to put them around everyone's," Max replied. Lowering his voice, he added, "If we want the factory to host another group in the future, I wouldn't want anyone reporting that we didn't follow the rules to the letter."

None of them needed to ask which "anyone" he was referring to.

So off they went to their individual cubes. Logan instantly felt lonely. He peeked around the side of his cube, then giggled when he saw Daisy and Miles peeking around theirs. Nothing to do but get to work.

As promised, Max took his turn with each of them (even Philip, which was shocking after his insistence on being left alone). The thick walls muffled the conversations, so Logan could only catch bits and pieces. When it was his turn, he told Max what he'd tried already, and Max steered him in a few other directions.

The hours sped by as he mixed, mashed, rolled, and tasted, then started all over again. There was no denying that when he wasn't worried about following directions, he loved the different shapes the candy took as he worked with it, the tastes that emerged when he added a pinch of one ingredient or another. But after a while, every bit of him itched to be outside under the wide sky, with the sun warming his skin. Every once in a while Max would stop by to see how things were going. Logan stuck on a smile and said, "Couldn't be better!" He knew Max wasn't fooled.

Once he heard Max threaten loudly to take away a certain romance novel if Daisy kept pulling it out of her bag. "It's for your own good," he insisted.

Daisy muttered something Logan couldn't hear but went back to work. Every hour on the hour Philip left the room for ten minutes. (Logan knew the exact time because checking the clock gave him an excuse to poke his head out.)

At one point Paulo (whom Logan rarely saw outside of the

Bee Room) delivered a jar of fresh honey to Miles, who gave a shy little wave, clutched the jar to his chest, and ducked back into his cube. Before leaving, Paulo made a second stop—at Philip's station. Logan couldn't tell what he dropped off, only that it was shaped like a square and wrapped in foil. You can't wrap fresh honey in foil. Beeswax, maybe?

The last hour of the day was a frenzy of activity. All four took turns using the machines Max had set up in the center of the room—Philip had clearly decided he needed them after all. They crisscrossed the room, boiling candy in various-sized pots and kettles, putting trays in the fridge, grabbing more supplies.

They scribbled down recipes, then scratched them out. They baked candy in the ovens, they enrobed, they panned. They made a huge mess. With all the comings and goings, Logan couldn't help catching glimpses now and then of the others' work.

Philip's idea involved chocolate in some capacity and whatever Paulo had brought him, but more than that Logan couldn't guess.

All he knew about Miles's idea was that it included honey, and Logan thought he smelled black licorice wafting from his cube now and again. Daisy's... well, it looked like a glob of goop. A green glob of goop, to be precise.

As for his own, he'd managed to get the chocolate to turn to chocolate-flavored gum after inserting tiny pieces of chicle into blocks of cocoa and heating it at a very high temperature. But getting it to turn back again? Not so much.

At five o'clock the factory bell rang, and Logan jumped. He had just added carrageen and salt and was about to stir the final mixture.

"All right, everyone," Max called out from the center of the room. "Let's gather and discuss plans for tomorrow."

Logan looked down at the tray in front of him, which was covered with pieces of this, clumps of that, nothing even remotely recognizable as a Bubbletastic ChocoRocket. His only hope (besides that whole miracle thing) was that some inspiration would hit him overnight. At least a little hope was better than no hope at all.

Never one to dwell on problems, Logan put the direness of the situation out of his mind. If he hurried, he'd have time to go outside before dinner. He had something to show Miles. So when the bell rang, Logan sprang up from his station, the first one to emerge.

Miles came next. His eyes were a little bloodshot — no doubt from the strain of the last few hours — but he gave Logan a thumbs-up. Daisy skipped over to them, her ponytail bopping with each step. Logan guessed that meant her green glob of goop had actually transformed itself into some brand-new kind of candy. He was happy for her. For her and Miles both.

Philip emerged last, and Logan realized he hadn't seen more than the back of his head since before lunch. His expression was a mixture of determination, weariness, and something that Logan couldn't quite identify. He gave no indication that his candymaking efforts had been successful, and no one asked.

"Great job, everyone!" Max said. "You should all be proud of yourselves. You've had a crash course in being a candy scientist, and you all proved you have what it takes."

Logan wasn't so sure about that, but he didn't interrupt.

"We'll meet here in the lab at eight o'clock, and you'll each make a fresh batch of candy to submit to the judges. We'll leave promptly at ten for the drive up to the city. I'll be taking us in one of the factory's vans. Now, everyone get to bed early and eat a big breakfast. Tomorrow's going to be a long day. Any questions?"

They all looked at Miles, who said, "Why is everyone looking at me?"

"Okay, then," Max said, securing his clipboard. "If Miles doesn't have any questions, I'll see you all in fifteen hours."

Philip wasted no time in bolting from the room.

"Let's walk out together," Daisy said. "I just need to grab my bag."

As Daisy disappeared into her cube, Miles whispered, "Maybe we should invite Daisy to dinner tonight? I mean, I wouldn't want her to feel left out."

Logan nodded. "Good idea." Just as he reached her cube, he heard her whisper, "All I'll need is twenty minutes." She reached over and gave a loving little pat to the green glob of goop, which honestly didn't look any different from when Logan had seen it last.

"Twenty minutes for what?" he asked.

Daisy jumped a bit when she heard him, then glanced at the glob. She smiled. "Believe it or not, all this little guy needs is twenty minutes in the fridge, and it'll turn the candy world on its head."

"Really?" Logan asked, excited.

"Yup! I wanted to show you guys, but the whole privacy thing, I just don't think we're supposed to."

Logan backed away, covering his eyes. "I didn't see a thing. I didn't hear a thing. I know nothing."

Daisy swung her bag over her shoulder. "That's not very convincing."

"I'll work on it."

As the three of them left the room together, Miles turned to Daisy and asked, "So, are you coming?"

"Coming where?"

"I didn't get a chance to ask her," Logan explained.

"Ask me what?"

"If you wanted to come to dinner. You know, at our apartment. With my family. To um, eat. And Miles's family. Did I say it's at six?"

"Smooooth," said Miles.

"I don't have much practice inviting people to dinner," Logan admitted. "You were my first."

"You did just fine," Daisy assured him. "And thank you, but I can't come. My dad conducts an orchestra at the elementary school, and I promised I'd go to their recital tonight. You haven't lived until you've heard third-graders perform Beethoven's *Ode to Joy*."

Logan and Miles laughed. "A bunch of the factory guys put a band together once," Logan said. "They weren't very

107

good either, but they had a great time playing. All their instruments are still around somewhere, though, in one of the storerooms."

"Did you ever try playing one of them?" Miles asked. "Like the guitar or keyboard or something?"

Logan shook his head. "I have a tendency to drop things. I think my instrument would wind up being played more by the floor than by me."

"I haven't seen you drop anything," Daisy said kindly.

Logan smiled. "I hold on very tight."

A car honked outside. "Well," Daisy said, "that's my ride. See you guys tomorrow, bright and early."

They accompanied Daisy to the front step. "You arrive on horseback and leave in an old brown pickup?" Miles asked. "I was expecting something a lot more exciting than that. Hot-air balloon maybe."

"Or a unicycle!" offered Logan. "That would have been cool."

"Sorry to disappoint you," she said.

"Is that your dad?" Logan asked, peering at the driver's seat. But instead of a dad, a boy around seventeen or eighteen was sitting behind the wheel, tapping on the dashboard as if he were playing a keyboard or trying to fix something that was stuck. Hard to tell.

Daisy opened the passenger-side door. "This is my cousin, Bo. He bought this lovely truck with his winnings from the motorcycle-pulling contest at the state fair last year."

Miles's eyes grew big. "Is that where they pull motorcycles with their *teeth?*"

"Well, with what was left of them after so many attempts," she said, shaking her head sadly. "Now all he can do is grunt until he gets his new teeth."

Logan and Miles nearly fell off the stoop trying to see the boy better. Daisy got into the car and said, "Say hi, Bo."

"Grunt," said Bo.

"See?" Daisy said. "Sad." She reached over to pinch his cheek. "Let this be a lesson to you boys."

"What, not to pull a motorcycle with our teeth?" asked Miles.

"Exactly," said Daisy.

"Grunt," added Bo as Daisy shut the door with a final wave.

Logan and Miles stared after the truck as it rattled its way down the long driveway. "Do you think the motorcycle was running when he pulled it?" Logan asked.

"I sure hope not," Miles said. "Hey, I bet tomorrow Daisy rides in on that unicycle."

"Or flies in on a flying carpet!"

"Or glides down on a parachute!"

Logan nodded. "I bet that'll be the one." Instead of going back inside, Logan led Miles around the side of the factory. The scent of cow from the barn quickly faded as they approached the Peppermint Field.

"Where are we going?" Miles asked, glancing anxiously at the pond off to their left.

"There's something I want you to see. It's right over here, between the Strawberry Patch and the Orange Grove."

"We don't have to take a boat to get there, do we?"

Logan shook his head and led Miles away from the pond to the cornfields, where the stalks were taller than both of them. "You up for going straight through? We could go around, but it would take a lot longer."

Miles glanced warily at the corn stalks but nodded. Logan turned and plowed through them, stopping every few feet to make sure Miles was behind him. Logan loved walking through the corn. Something about not being able to see where he was going or where he had come from gave him a little thrill. He also liked to imagine the view from above as he ran. What new shapes were formed by his path? And then the end, when he burst out of the corn into the openness of the Strawberry Patch, that was a good part, too. He did that now and waited for Miles.

For a few seconds, he worried that he'd lost Miles. Then out he burst, twenty feet down the field.

Logan ran to meet him. "Pretty cool, right?"

"Uh, sure," Miles said with a wobbly smile.

"C'mon, we're almost there." Logan pointed toward the large clump of trees in front of them.

"Maybe on the way back we'll walk *around* the corn?" Miles suggested.

"We better hurry, then," Logan said, picking up speed. "We don't have much time." They ran through the perfect rows of strawberry plants, stopping only once to pick two berries. Before handing one to Miles, Logan asked, "You're not allergic, are you?"

Miles shook his head and accepted the bright red strawberry.

Logan popped his into his mouth and took off again. "We're almost there," he called back to Miles, who was still standing in the same spot, munching his strawberry. "Hey, you've gotta learn to eat on the move!"

Miles caught up and said, "Didn't your mother ever teach you not to run with food in your mouth? You can choke and die that way!"

Logan almost laughed, but something in Miles's expression warned him not to. "Of course she has. But I'm not afraid of choking. Or dying."

Miles stopped walking. "You're not afraid of dying?"

Logan shook his head and shrugged. "I figure when my number's up, my number's up."

Miles squinted up at him. "What do you mean?"

Logan thought for a minute. "Well, if you enjoy life while you have it, then it doesn't matter how long you have it for. No one knows how long they get to live. It's like a deal you make when you're born, you know, to accept what happens to you."

"Is that what you do, just accept what happens?"

Logan shrugged. "I guess so. What else can you do?"

"Well, you can dwell on it and play it over in your head a hundred different ways."

Logan tilted his head. "Does that help?"

Miles sighed. "No."

"Well, c'mon." Logan tugged on Miles's arm. "We'll both have to accept the wrath of my mom if we don't hurry. She has a pet peeve about people being late for her cooking."

After running along the short path beside the Orange Grove, they came to a small clearing. "Here we are," said Logan. He watched Miles's expression turn from anticipation to surprise to something like dread as the old merry-go-round came into view. Though the painted horses and elephants and giraffes were half buried in the tall grass, it was evident what they were.

"What's wrong?" Logan asked as he watched Miles's fear turn to shock. "I thought you'd think it was neat, since, you know, you used to love the annual picnic..."

Miles didn't reply; he just stared at the broken merry-go-round. Then slowly his face began to change, and he started to smile.

Relieved, Logan said, "My parents must have wanted to keep it for some reason. Not too many people know it's out here."

Miles reached out to touch a horse, which still had flecks of gold and red on its mane. "I don't remember it from the picnic," Miles said. "But it's...it's really cool."

Suddenly Logan realized why Miles had reacted so strangely. He slapped his forehead. "Duh! You're allergic to merry-go-rounds! You told us at lunch yesterday, and I totally forgot. Sorry!"

"It's okay. I think I'm getting over my allergy." Turning

away from the merry-go-round, Miles said, "We'd better get back."

This time they ran around the cornfields, not through them. Logan let Miles set the pace, let him lead them all the way to the back entrance of the factory. Before they went in, though, Miles surprised him by ducking over to the bush where the butterfly chrysalis hung. They bent down to look.

At first Logan didn't see it. He moved some leaves aside and then realized he couldn't see the glossy white clump hanging among the branches because it was lying on the ground, broken open.

He'd missed it. *Again*. Logan scanned the nearby bushes for signs of black, yellow, and red wings but could find none.

"I'm sorry," Miles said softly.

"It's okay," Logan said, trying to hide his disappointment. "There's always next year, right?"

"Right. And I'm sure you'll see him around here soon. Sometimes things can be right in front of you and you don't see them. Then suddenly you do."

"You think so?"

Miles nodded.

Logan wasn't so sure, but he hoped Miles was right.

By the time they got up to the apartment, both sets of parents were there to greet them.

"Sorry we're late," Logan told his mom as he tried to ignore the cramp in his side from running.

"Actually, you're right on time," Miles's dad replied. "We got here early."

Miles's mom looked just as Logan would have guessed. She was short, with dark, straight hair and glasses, which made her look smart, just like Miles. She had the same tired circles under her eyes as her husband.

His mom outdid herself with the meal. She had prepared six different dishes, all from ingredients produced at the factory. And for Miles's dad, his own personal chocolate pizza. The man seemed so happy, Logan thought he might ask to move in! Then a thought occurred to him. "Mom? Can Miles sleep over tonight? Since we have to leave so early tomorrow and everything?" He turned to Miles and said, "I mean, if you want to."

Miles nodded eagerly. They waited for both sets of parents to answer.

"We'd love to have Miles stay," Logan's mom replied. "I'll make sure to give him a big pancake breakfast before the contest."

"Miles is allergic to pancakes, Mom."

Miles's parents lifted their eyebrows, and Miles gave a weak smile.

"Oh. Well, I'm sure I can find something else," Logan's mom said.

"So can I stay, Mom?" Miles asked.

His parents exchanged a glance. "It's okay with us," his mom answered. "But what about pajamas? And clothes for the contest?"

"He can borrow mine," Logan said. "I have some stuff that'll fit."

The Candymaker raised his glass of cocoa. "To new friendships," he boomed.

"To new friendships," the others repeated, clinking glasses.

Then the Candymaker asked, "Do you want to take your sleeping bags to the Tropical Room and sleep down there?'"

Logan's mouth fell open. "Seriously? But it's not my birthday!"

Everyone laughed. "The night before the big contest is a special occasion," his father said. "Just make sure you two get some sleep. You'll want to be sharp tomorrow."

Logan could barely sit still for the rest of the dinner, which seemed to drag on and on. Seriously, grown-ups found the most boring things to talk about, although judging from the laughter and refills of cocoa, *they* must not have thought so. He and Miles kept sharing frustrated glances.

Finally Miles's dad said, "Thank you for this lovely meal. I'm afraid if we stay any longer I may need another chocolate pizza!" He pushed back his chair, and the others followed.

"It was our pleasure," Logan's mom assured him. "We don't have visitors very often."

An awkward silence fell, making Logan even more anxious to get moving. Finally Miles's mom stepped over to Miles and gave him an extra-long hug. Miles eventually pulled away, clearly embarrassed.

After another ten minutes of small talk at the door, during which Logan thought he might scream, the O'Learys finally left. Logan's mom went with them so they wouldn't get lost.

As soon as the door clicked closed, his dad said, "Well, what are you boys waiting for? Get going!"

Logan didn't have to be told twice. In five minutes flat, he yanked down two sleeping bags from the hall closet and filled a duffel bag with pajamas, toiletries, towels, snacks, a battery-operated alarm clock, and two flashlights. "I'm ready!" he announced, slinging the bag over his shoulder.

Miles slipped his backpack over his shoulder and tucked a rolled-up sleeping bag under each arm.

"Do you want to take a walkie-talkie with you?" the Candymaker asked, holding one out.

Logan shook his head. "We'll be fine. If I need to reach you, I'll use the intercom."

"What if *we* need to reach *you?*" the Candymaker asked. Then, seeing Logan's pained expression, he laughed and said, "Okay, we'll leave you alone. Be good. And no climbing the trees, or I'll never hear the end of it from your mother!"

"Don't worry," Logan assured him. "We'll see you in the morning." Before the Candymaker could issue any more orders, Logan and Miles hurried out the door.

"Have you ever slept in the Tropical Room before?" Miles asked as they made their way through the darkened factory. Small lights set into the ceiling shed enough light to see by, but only barely. They had to watch their steps carefully.

Logan nodded. "Each year on my birthday, but never without one of my parents."

As they turned the corner by the lab, they nearly bumped into Logan's mother on her way back from showing Miles's parents out. "Don't forget to turn off the rain," she reminded them. "Or you'll get a wet surprise in the middle of the night."

"I won't," Logan promised, although he totally would have forgotten if she hadn't said something.

"You sure you have everything you need? Toothbrush? Your aloe?"

He'd forgotten the aloe but could get more from the aloe plant. "Mom, I'll be fine."

"All right," she said, reluctantly. "And no —"

"I know, no climbing," he said.

"That's right. And if you're not back up by seven in the morning, I'll come get you."

"Thanks," Logan said, pushing Miles forward. "Gotta go!" he called over his shoulder. He could tell without turning around that his mom was watching. This would be his first night apart from them.

A little while later they passed the library, and this time Miles pressed his face right up to the glass. "You're so lucky," he said earnestly. "A whole library inside your house."

Of all the things Logan felt lucky about having in his

house, the library fell very low on the list. "Why do you like books so much?" he asked.

Miles answered without taking his face away from the window. "You never know what you'll learn when you open one. And if it's a story, you sort of fall into it. Then you live there for a while, instead of, you know, living here."

Logan couldn't understand why anyone who lived where he did would feel the need to live anywhere else. But he supposed if you *didn't* live in a candy factory, you might feel differently.

Miles finally peeled himself away from the window, and they continued down the long corridors. As they got farther away from the main section of the factory, the lights grew dimmer. But even in total darkness, the rising heat would have told them they were nearing the Tropical Room. Logan stopped to fish the flashlights out of his bag. He handed one to Miles.

"Hey, can I ask you something really weird?" Miles said as they continued, the flashlights illuminating their way.

"Sure."

"If you could climb the tree without getting caught, would you?"

"I don't know," Logan admitted. "If I did, I'd probably wind up slipping and falling and get caught anyway as they carted me off to the hospital. Why?"

"Well, I know this is terrible . . . but I really want to stick my hand in the chocolate fountain. I've wanted to ever since I saw Philip do it."

Logan laughed. "Why didn't you just say so? Let's leave this stuff here and go over there now."

Miles hesitated. "I kind of need to do it alone."

"Oh," Logan said, surprised. "Are you sure?"

Miles nodded. "It'll only take two minutes."

"Okay. I'll get our stuff set up inside."

They knocked flashlights, and Miles headed back the way they'd come, shining the beam on the floor ahead of him. Logan waited until he'd turned the corner, then pushed the button to open the Tropical Room door. He made sure the setting for the automatic rain was securely in the OFF position and turned on the row of lights.

One by one, the trees lit up until the room was so bright, it might as well have been broad daylight outside. He fumbled with the switches a little and managed to dim the room until it looked like dusk settling over the treetops. Before they went to sleep later, he'd lower the lights even more, along with the temperature.

He was able to get all their stuff underneath his favorite sapodilla tree in one trip by rolling the sleeping bags with his feet. He laid down the duffel and slid Miles's backpack off his other shoulder. It dropped to the ground, nearly weightless. Logan stepped toward the tree, the urge to put his arms around it as strong as ever.

But as he stepped, his foot snagged on something, and he looked down to investigate. A zipper on Miles's backpack had gotten caught on his sneaker. He yanked at it and succeeded in not only freeing the zipper but opening the backpack a few inches in the process. Something soft and bright orange peeked out. A big stuffed animal, maybe? Is that what Miles had been carting around with him everywhere?

He quickly zipped the bag closed without exploring any further. He'd never want Miles to think he had been snooping.

He started unrolling the sleeping bags when it dawned on him that a lot more than two minutes had passed. What if Miles had gotten lost? Or his flashlight battery had burned out?

Grabbing his own flashlight, Logan set out. He'd assumed he would meet Miles along the way, but he reached the fountain without running into him. Strange. He turned to look around, and his right foot slid out from under him. He caught his balance before he fell. Turning his flashlight beam at the floor, he saw the smear of chocolate his foot had made.

"Aha!" he said out loud. He felt like a detective searching for evidence. Wherever Miles had gone, he had definitely been here.

Logan was about to retrace his steps to look for more clues when he saw movement and a flash of light out of the corner of his eye. He turned toward its source and found himself facing the long windows of the Cocoa Room. His first thought was that he'd found Miles. His second thought was that no way would Miles be inside the Cocoa Room without him. At least he didn't *think* he would be.

He clicked off his flashlight and ducked down just in

time, as the other beam of light scanned the area outside the window. When whoever was in there turned away, Logan lifted his head slowly until he could see inside again. The flashlight beam was now focused on the cabinets against the wall by the bean grinder.

Another sudden movement caught his eye. Someone was crouching, low to the ground, a few feet behind the person near the cabinet. The only people besides his father and Max who had after-hours access to this room were Steve and Lenny. As dedicated as they were to their jobs, they rarely showed up at night. Why would they be using flashlights? Or crouching?

And why would the person with the flashlight be standing in front of the cabinet?

The cabinet! That could only mean one thing. Someone was stealing the Candymaker's secret ingredient! But who? Why?

It was up to him to find out.

PART TWO

MILES

CHAPTER ONE

Miles's dad stuck his head out the window. "Mom wants to leave for the factory in ten minutes."

Miles nodded. "Ll'i eb thgir ni."

As always, his father waited for a translation. If he'd just spend a minute going over the words, he could figure it out. After all, it was his dad who had bought him his first book on the subject — *How to Write in Code and Make Up Your Own Language*. In the last year he'd made up three fairly serviceable alphabets (the foundation of every language) and taught himself to say words backward.

"I'll be right in," Miles translated with a sigh.

He waited for his father to disappear back through the bedroom window, but instead he climbed out, all sharp elbows and knees, and made his way across to Miles with careful steps.

Most parents might have had something to say about their son sitting out on the roof for hours each day, but this section over the garage inclined only slightly, and a fall wouldn't be very far — seven feet eight inches, to be precise.

Miles had measured it once by hanging a tape measure off the edge. He figured that if he did topple off somehow, he might break his arm, but he'd escape serious harm.

"You're not going to talk backward around the other kids, are you?" his father asked warily, sitting down next to him.

Miles tried to look serious. "You don't think it would be a good way to make friends?"

His dad shook his head. "First charm them with your theories about the afterlife, *then* unleash the backward talk on 'em."

"Got it. Afterlife first, neht drawkcab klat."

After a moment's silence, his dad said, "You don't have to do this, you know."

Miles nodded again, hugging his knees tight. "I know. But I don't want to let Mrs. Chen down." Mrs. Chen knew him perhaps better than anyone else. She was the children's librarian in town, and he'd spent half his life inside the library or on the benches outside.

"She'd understand," his father said. "She only told you about the contest because she thought...well, she thought...."

"Don't worry, Dad. I know why she did it. She thinks it will bring me back to the land of the living. She thinks I'm still dwelling on it too much."

Dwelling. Miles repeated the word to himself. It was a strange word. But he loved words, and he loved strange words best of all. *D*'s and *w*'s rarely hung out next to each other. And any word with a double *l* in the middle — like *yellow* and *ballad* and *idyllic* and, well, *dwelling,* had a special appeal. So even though the word meant "spending too much time thinking about something negative," he still liked it.

"I have to agree with her," his father said. "It's been over a year since the day at the lake. You need to get out there and do things again, the way you used to. But I only want you to do this if *you* want to."

Before Miles could answer, a yellow, black, and red butterfly landed silently on the edge of the roof. Neither he nor his dad moved as the butterfly lazily flapped its wings. A minute later, just as silently as it had arrived, it lifted off again. Miles had seen butterflies up close before. But never one with red in it. And never on the roof.

He watched the now butterflyless spot for a moment. He knew that after something stressful or traumatic happened, you were supposed to stay away from things that reminded you of the event so that the emotions you had worked so hard to overcome wouldn't overwhelm you. The black and yellow of the butterfly's wings reminded him of bees, and bees were one of the things he wasn't supposed to dwell on.

He knew his dad was waiting for an answer. He *did* want to participate in the contest. He loved candy of all kinds (even more than words and languages, and he loved those a lot). The thought of getting to see how some of his favor-ites—like the Gummysaurus Rex and the High-Jumping Jelly Beans—were made was undeniably exciting. He'd been to the factory a few times before, back when they held an annual picnic, but he'd never been inside.

And he had to admit, he was curious to meet the Candymaker's son, who everyone knew rarely left the factory grounds anymore. Yes, he wanted to go. But he didn't want to forget about the girl either. Of course, forgetting wasn't *really* an option. She went everywhere with him. He had created his whole afterlife so she'd have a safe place to live, and his head was always churning out new additions to it. Just that morning he'd enrolled her in a dance class. Girls liked dance classes. Or at least he hoped they did.

Would the girl *want* to go to the candy factory?

His dad put his hand on Miles's shoulder, as though reading his mind. "Not letting yourself live your life isn't going to change anything. You know that by now."

"I know," he replied. "It's just..." Miles bit his lip. He had promised himself (and his parents and Mrs. Chen, the librarian) that he wouldn't ask that question again — *why couldn't I have done something?*

The answer never changed anyway. It was always something like *you were too far away* and *it happened too fast* and *we can't always control everything* and, the one he hated the most, *maybe it was a trick of the eye.*

"Well, then," Miles said, getting to his feet. "Looks like I'm off to **Life Is Sweet?**."

His father nodded approvingly. "I think I'll enjoy the view from here for another minute. I'll look forward to a full report later." Then he added, "And some chocolate."

Miles laughed. His father liked candy almost as much as he did. "I'll try my best. They might frown on thievery on my first day."

"I have faith in you," his dad called out as Miles propelled himself through the window, landing on his bed with a bounce.

His mother waited for him by his bedroom door. "Ready?"

Miles nodded and grabbed his green backpack from the end of his bed.

"Why don't you leave that home today?" she asked gently.

He shook his head. "Can't do that." He slung the backpack over his shoulder and reached for the five books on the desk.

His mom stepped directly in front of them. "Those I think you *can* leave here. I'm quite sure you won't have time for reading today."

He wanted to tell her that he didn't actually *read* the books, not entirely anyway. But he liked keeping some things secret. "Okay, Mom," he said. She was right anyway. He doubted he'd have time for reading at the factory.

"Good. Now let's go. I don't want you to be late."

Miles dutifully followed his mom out to the car, knowing they had plenty of time. His mother had never been even a moment late in her life. She set her watch (and alarm clock and car clock) a full half hour earlier than the real time. Miles was usually the only kid waiting outside the still-dark school each morning during the school year. He had to wait until a janitor came to unlock the door so he could slip into the library for a while before the halls filled with kids. Fortunately for him, he loved libraries more than anyplace in the world. He would live in one if he could. All that knowledge. All those worlds hidden inside the covers.

They got into the car, and his mother pulled on her yellow driving gloves. Yes, she wore driving gloves like a professional race-car driver. She said it helped her feel more connected to the car. Miles once argued, wouldn't her bare hands on the wheel actually connect her more to the car? She said he'd understand when he was old enough to drive. Miles doubted that he would.

"The invitation to the factory said three of the other contestants would be there, too, right?" she asked, peeling out of the driveway. Oh yeah, his mom *drove* like a professional race-car driver, too.

"Yes, three, including the Candymaker's son."

"And you're going to talk to them, right?"

"Yes, Mom. Dad already warned me. No talking backward."

"I'm fine with that as long as you're actually talking."

"Why wouldn't I talk to them?"

"Well, Miles, you can get awfully shy in new environments, and you've been keeping to yourself a lot."

Miles didn't answer. What could he say? She was right.

"And one's a girl," she added.

"I've spoken to girls before, Mom. Every day at school, in fact."

"I know, it's just that you're at that age..."

He might be "at that age," but the only girl ever on his mind was the one he couldn't save.

"Oh, never mind, just be nice."

"I'm always nice," he argued.

"But don't be too nice," she said. "You don't want anyone to push you around."

"Mom, you're driving me crazy."

"Sorry, hon. This is a big deal, that's all."

"I know." He'd heard rumors of a hundred applicants for every contestant who was selected. He was sure his essay on why he wanted to make candy was only chosen because Mrs. Chen had helped him write it. He tried to enjoy the colorful buildings of downtown Spring Haven, but their car zoomed by so fast, the background blended all together. *Zoomed.* He liked the way that one made his tongue vibrate when he said it silently. *Zoooomed.*

"So have you decided what new candy to make yet?"

Miles shook his head. He'd lain awake for hours the night before, hoping for a burst of inspiration that never came. No doubt the others had theirs all figured out. As they zipped through the quiet streets of east Spring Haven, he tried again to think of the perfect candy. Something no one had ever tasted before or even dreamt of.

Chocolate-covered jelly beans? Caramel-covered marshmallows on a stick? Both sounded yummy, and he did enjoy things covered in other things, but neither was creative enough to win the contest.

Because his mom took the posted speed limits as suggestions rather than laws, they arrived at the candy factory very soon — before he'd thought of anything worthy of entering. The only new idea that had occurred to him was whether, in the afterlife, people gained weight if they ate a lot of candy. He decided that they didn't.

His mom drove up the long circular driveway and stopped in front of a huge wooden door, easily three times bigger than any door Miles had ever seen before. The factory itself was partly glass and partly deep red bricks. He'd never seen it up close like this; at the annual picnics, the townspeople hung out on the vast lawn in the back. And the picnics had stopped when he was only four or five, so his memory of the place was fuzzy at best. He felt his excitement stirring and knew it would be hopeless to try to suppress it.

"Well, will you look at that," his mom said, pointing to the front stoop or, more precisely, to the girl sitting on it reading a book. "You're not the first one here."

"There's a first time for everything, I guess," Miles replied. He leaned over and kissed his mom on the cheek before climbing out.

The girl on the stoop wore a bright yellow dress and held her book so close to her face that all he could see was her eyes. She looked up when the car door closed, as though surprised to find she wasn't alone anymore. Any book captivating enough to keep someone from hearing the rumbling engine of his mother's old car was one Miles wanted to know about. But before he could ask for the title, she had jumped to her feet and stashed the book away.

"I'm Daisy," she said, pumping his arm up and down and grinning.

Daisy, he repeated inside his head. He enjoyed the roundness of the word. A perfect name for this sunny girl in yellow, a double-*l* word! Hopefully these were signs that he and Daisy would get along just fine.

He heard his mom chuckle approvingly as she pulled away. He did his best to pretend he hadn't. "I'm Miles."

"Hi, Miles! I guess you're here for the contest, too?"

He nodded and pushed up his glasses, a habit he had when he felt nervous. Okay, so maybe he didn't have much experience talking to girls, especially not pretty girls with blond ponytails who were a good head taller than him. He straightened up to his full height, readjusting his backpack as he did so. He was still a head shorter than Daisy.

"Aren't you totally excited?" she asked, her eyes gleaming. "I can't believe this day is finally here." She lifted her arms and spun around in a perfect circle, as if her excitement wouldn't let her stand in one place.

Twirling. One of his very favorite words — that rare pairing of *t* and *w*. Plus it sounded just like what it meant.

He nodded in response to her question. He *was* excited, but he wished that was all he felt. He had to smile, though, as Daisy twirled around again and came to a stop. It would be impossible to think of sad things around this very full-of-life girl.

He knew it was his turn to say something. "Do you know how many contestants there are from our area?"

She lifted an eyebrow. "Don't *you* know?"

He shook his head. "I, um, don't know too much about the contest."

She stared at him. He pushed up his glasses. Clearly he had said the wrong thing. She'd probably counted down the days until she turned twelve and could enter this contest, and he was acting like he'd just entered last week. Which, of course, he had.

"There are four of us," she eventually said. "You, me, one other kid, and Logan, the Candymaker's son. He's the one to beat." She reached up to adjust her ponytail, which had started to slip from all the spinning.

Miles wanted to ask Daisy if she knew anything more about what had happened to Logan, but he couldn't think how to ask without sounding nosy or rude. Before he could find some tactful way to bring up the subject, a car pulled up next to them. This was no ordinary car — long and black, with tinted windows. A limo, if ever he'd seen one. Which, outside of the movies, was never.

Daisy let out a long whistle. They watched as the driver stepped out, walked the length of the car, and opened the back door. A boy in a blue suit, brown shoes, and a striped tie climbed out, a briefcase clutched under one arm. The driver tilted his hat at the boy and, without receiving so much as a *thank-you*, got in and drove away.

Miles had never seen a boy dressed like a man before.

This boy wore it well, though. It helped that he was tall and broad in the shoulders. Miles suddenly felt very underdressed (and even smaller than he'd felt two minutes ago) in his white shorts, tan shirt, and sneakers.

The three of them stood there, eyeing one another, until Daisy stuck out her hand and introduced herself and then introduced Miles.

"Philip Ransford," the boy replied. "The Third."

Daisy laughed. When the boy's expression didn't change, she said, "Oh, you're serious! I'm sorry."

Philip rolled his eyes, and Miles had to stifle a laugh.

"Don't let me interrupt whatever you were talking about," Philip said. "I'm sure it was fascinating."

"Actually," Daisy said, "we were talking about how Logan's the one to beat."

"Hardly," Philip said, resting his briefcase against the front stoop.

"Oh, really? How do you know?"

Miles watched the exchange with interest. He'd never seen two people take such an obvious dislike to each other so quickly.

"Because *I'm* going to win," Philip replied. "I always do."

"Oh, yeah?" Daisy stuck her hands on her hips. "How do you know I won't win? Or Miles here?" She gestured toward Miles with her thumb.

"Me?" Miles said, reddening under their gaze. "I probably won't win, so, um, don't worry."

Philip sniffed. "I never worry."

Daisy just glared.

"Hey," Miles said, anxious to break the tension. "Um, what do you guys know about Logan anyway? I mean, about what happened to him?"

Instead of breaking the tension, though, his comment only seemed to heighten it. Neither one answered him, and now Daisy's glare had shifted from Philip's face to his. He backed up a step. He already missed the cheerful twirling Daisy.

"Neither of you better say anything to him," she warned. "I'm sure he's very self-conscious, and we're guests here. I don't want to get thrown out because one of you says something mean."

"I would never...I just meant..." Miles trailed off. He *knew* he shouldn't have said anything.

"Don't look at me," Philip said. "I don't know what happened, and I don't care. I'm not here to make friends."

"Obviously," Daisy muttered, but her expression relaxed a bit.

No one spoke for a minute, then Miles blurted out, "In the afterlife everyone is friends with everyone else."

"Excuse me?" asked Philip.

"In the afterlife, you know, after you die. Everyone is like, really good friends because no one *wants* anything. When you don't want anything, there's no competition."

"I like that idea," Daisy said, her old cheerfulness mostly back. "I hope you're right."

Philip rolled his eyes. "There's no such thing as the afterlife. This is your only life. The sooner you realize that, the more successful you'll be."

Miles opened his mouth to argue, but Philip had already turned away and was climbing the steps. "How many times have you rung the bell?" he asked. "It's quite rude of them to leave their guests out here so long."

"We haven't," Daisy replied with a shrug. "I figure they'll come get us when they're ready."

"Maybe we should see if it's open?" Miles suggested.

Philip shook his head, as if he couldn't believe how clueless they were, and pressed the doorbell, then pressed it again. Then a third time. He tried the doorknob, but it didn't budge.

"Rude," he muttered, glaring at the door as though the door itself were to blame for being locked.

"Not as rude as ringing the bell three times," Daisy whispered to Miles.

Philip began to pace back and forth, clutching his briefcase.

"In the afterlife," Miles whispered back, "all the doors are always open."

"The afterlife is an old fairy tale," Philip said angrily, coming to a stop. "And that's just the way it is."

As he spoke the last few words, the door swung open, surprising them all. And there he stood. Logan. The Candymaker's son.

It was so much worse than Miles had imagined.

Attacked by a bear? Licked by flame while fleeing a smoke-filled room? Chased into a volcano by a pirate? Miles couldn't imagine what had happened to cause those scars.

Then the Candymaker's son said something about strangers and angels, and Miles listened, spellbound. Logan's voice sounded like the kind of voice you hear in your head when you're reading a really good book. Familiar and hopeful and exciting all at once.

In an instant, Miles knew he wanted more than anything to be this boy's friend. It wasn't because he felt sorry for him or anything like that. Logan radiated something that felt like goodness. In a weird way, he made Miles feel peaceful, which he usually felt only when he was on his roof or working on one of his alphabets. He wished, as he often did when something important happened, that the Girl He Couldn't Save could be here. He bet she really would have liked Logan, too.

Daisy was kind enough to make the introductions, and it took all of Miles's willpower not to blurt out, *What happened to you?* He knew that if he did he'd never forgive himself. Plus he'd have the wrath of Daisy to deal with, and he wanted to avoid that at all costs. He wished he hadn't let his mother talk him out of bringing his books. He'd just checked them out of the library the day before and hadn't even opened them yet. He knew they'd tell him what he needed to know. They always did.

All rational thought flew from his mind as soon as he stepped inside the factory. The shafts of light from the glass ceiling threw gold in every direction. The walls, the floors, the ceilings — everything glittered and glowed. Miles didn't know what to look at first.

Logan explained about the gummy dinos in the case, and the more he spoke, the more excited Miles felt to be there. Mrs. Chen had been right. This is exactly where he needed to be. He wanted to eat everything, touch everything, to be a part of this place the way Logan clearly was.

When Philip inexplicably stuck his hand into the chocolate cascading from the fountain, Miles wished he could feel the silky warmth on his own hand. But he'd never have done that. He watched Philip take out a notebook and scribble something in it. He held his pencil in a really weird way, with his thumb at the top instead of the bottom.

Miles knew that when he was working on one of his alphabets or adding to his picture of the afterlife, he could get so absorbed that everything around him disappeared. But that was nothing compared with the intensity on Philip's face as he wrote in his notebook. Miles had the sickly feeling that Philip would do anything he had to in order to win. He definitely must have meant it when he said he didn't care about making friends. He must have insulted Logan and the factory ten times in the first ten minutes. How could anyone be mean to Logan?

Daisy was quick to rise to Logan's defense each time and didn't let Philip get away with anything. Miles was very grateful she was here. He didn't think he'd be able to stand up to Philip on his own, and Logan was way too nice to insult him back.

Daisy left for the bathroom before the tour began, and Miles made a silent plea for Philip not to start anything without her there as a buffer. His mom needn't have worried that he wouldn't talk, because when he got anxious, he got talkative. And when he got talkative, it usually led to talking about the afterlife and the cool things they had there.

Logan and Max seemed interested in hearing him talk about it, though, which was a nice change from his parents. And teachers. And classmates.

As pleased as it made him to think of the girl living in the nice place he'd created for her, there was a downside. Having his head half in this world and half in the next meant that he saw potential death everywhere he looked. First Logan had gone into shock or something in the Taffy Room, and now Philip was having a hiccupping fit in the hall outside the Neon Yellow Lightning Chews Room just because Miles had mentioned that in the afterlife all the candy factories were open to the public.

All he wanted to do was focus on the amazing things around him, but it was hard when he had to worry every few minutes about one of his fellow contestants dropping dead.

Logan was obviously excited about the next stop on the tour. The second Philip stopped hiccupping and gasping, Logan started off down the hall. He was walking really fast and kept glancing back at the others, his eyes gleaming even more than usual. Miles found it hard to keep up.

"You okay?" Daisy asked, stepping back to walk with Miles. "You look a little green. Don't let Philip and his dramatics bother you. Serves him right for interrupting you again. I don't know why he minds hearing about the afterlife so much. I think it's really interesting."

He smiled weakly. It was nice of her to say that, but if Philip didn't want to hear about the afterlife, he'd try not to mention it. He didn't want any more fits. Plus he thought he'd seen something in Philip's face during his attack of hiccups, something like fear. He didn't want to see it again.

They rounded the corner past the cafeteria and suddenly there it was, in all its oak-paneled glory. A library! He wouldn't need his books from home to make him feel better. He skidded to a halt. Max tried to rush him along to the next stop, but Miles was too busy thinking about the treasures those shelves must hold to wonder where Logan was leading them. "Can't I just go in for a few minutes? I'll meet you at the next place, I promise."

Max finally agreed and gave him the directions. Logan

looked a little disappointed, but Miles knew he'd catch up in a few minutes. This never took long.

The others went on their way, and Miles approached the wooden door. It was one of the few he'd seen in the factory that didn't swing open and shut. It felt a little like intruding, but he turned the knob and ducked his head in.

"Hello?"

"Back here," a woman's voice called out. "Behind the armchair."

Miles left his backpack by the door and made his way toward the voice. He wound through the stacks of books till he found a brown leather armchair and a white-haired woman sitting on the floor behind it. She had books spread around her like a fan and was stamping **PROPERTY OF Life Is Sweet** inside their front covers.

She looked up, rubber stamp in hand. "Hello there, can I help you?"

"Hi. I'm Miles, one of the, um, contestants for the candy contest this weekend? I was wondering if I could just look at some books. I wouldn't need to take them out or anything."

"Certainly, Miles," she said with a smile. "Can I help you find anything?"

Miles shook his head. "I already know what I'm looking for."

"Okay. I'm Mrs. Gepheart if you need anything."

She resumed her stamping. It was really very rhythmic. Open, stamp, close, slide. Open, stamp, close, slide.

Miles thanked her and headed back to the shelves. As soon as he was far enough away, he closed his eyes, reached out, and grabbed a book. Then he went a few feet farther, turned to the opposite shelf, and grabbed another. He went to the next aisle and did the same thing. He did this until he had a total of five books in his arms.

He spread the books out on a small wooden desk to see what he'd come up with. This was his favorite part.

THE HISTORY OF THE CONFECTIONARY ARTS, VOLUME 2: FROM BEETS TO CANDY CORN

THE HOLOGRAPHIC UNIVERSE

MY LIFE AS A PROFESSIONAL POOPER SCOOPER

CHARLOTTE'S WEB

I'M A MONKEY'S UNCLE…AND SO ARE YOU!

Miles rubbed his hands together with excitement and dug into his shorts pocket for a pencil and notepad. One by one, he opened each book to a random place, closed his eyes, and let his finger drop onto the page. Then he wrote down whatever sentence his finger landed on. When he'd done this with all five books, he returned them to their rightful places on the shelves.

Only then did he read what he'd written.

Butterscotch was first created in England two hundred years ago. The universe, and everything in it, might not actually exist. Over time, I've learned to tell the breed of the dog by the appearance of its bowel movements. "You have been my friend; that in itself is a tremendous thing." Humans and chimpanzees share over 98 percent of their DNA; humans and butterflies share at least 25 percent.

Miles flipped the notepad closed and held it tight to his chest. He felt much better now. He knew that sometime soon at least one of those sentences would help him in some mysterious way. He called out a goodbye to Mrs. Gepheart, who was still busy opening, stamping, closing, and sliding.

The directions Max had written were to someplace called the Tropical Room. As he walked, the halls got emptier and emptier and hotter and hotter. Was he going toward the boiler room? He was about to double-check the instructions when he turned one more corner and found himself in front of a huge, steamed-up glass door. To the side of the door a red button marked OPEN flashed at him. He pressed it and admired the slow but smooth path of the door as it slid into the wall.

He stood with wide eyes as the heat wrapped around him like a blanket. He could easily imagine that he'd left Spring Haven and stepped right into a real jungle. At the top of a tall tree with very wide branches, a guy with a bandana around his forehead swooped from branch to branch. Miles wondered if perhaps some humans shared *more* than 98 percent of their DNA with monkeys!

He was so busy looking up as he walked that he didn't see the vines at his feet until he got stuck. Logan came to his rescue and expertly untangled him.

"So what do you think?" Logan asked eagerly.

"S'ti elbidercni!"

Logan tilted his head. "What did you say?"

Oops! Miles recovered quickly. "I meant to say, it's incredible!"

Logan shivered with obvious glee, even though it must have been 90 degrees in the room.

Max gave a little lecture about the cocoa beans, then went over to the far wall and pulled a big lever. The huge metal slats on the roof began to open. Sunlight flooded in through the glass ceiling, but instead of feeling even warmer, Miles felt a cold chill run down his spine as another scene of shadow and sun, from a little over a year ago, filled his mind. His mother had just passed the oars of the rowboat over to his father when the sun appeared from behind thick clouds. They'd all tilted their faces up toward it. He'd never forget the peacefulness of that moment — the sun warming their cheeks, the light breeze swaying their boat — because it was in such stark contrast to what came next.

The buzz of Max's walkie-talkie cleared Miles's head. He

needed to shake off the memory, to focus on the here and now. Think about all the candy he sampled that morning! Think about what his books told him. Think about holograms! Think about dog droppings. (No, don't think about dog droppings!)

He breathed in the warm, humid air and reached out to touch the rough bark of the nearest tree. Just the solidity of the tree made him feel better. That is, until Max announced that a problem had arisen with the nougat, and Logan, who seemed to know everything about the factory, said, "I bet it was the honey!"

So now they were all supposed to go see the bees. Bees! Of all things!

The memories flooded back again. How the bees had swarmed over their boat and then over the shore. How the girl sitting on the shore had run into the lake to escape them. She didn't flail around, she didn't duck or scream, she just ran straight into the water until it covered her head. And then she didn't come back up.

It all happened so fast, and so quietly, that his parents didn't even see it happen. By the time they reached the shore, there wasn't even a bubble on the water. Only a pink ribbon that the police kept as evidence. Other people had been on the shore of the lake earlier—a couple holding hands and an older woman—but they had left by the time he and his parents rowed frantically ashore.

The merry-go-round in the center of the park was still full of kids, and the pretzel vendors had long lines, but no one had seen the girl run into the water. Why had she been all alone on the shore? Why had no one come to look for her?

He'd asked himself those questions over and over and had come up with all sorts of answers. At one time or another, the girl was an orphan or had run away from a hard life in the circus. And once, after a particularly tough day at school, Miles convinced himself that she was from another planet and that the portal back to her own world had been under the lake.

His parents had ever so gently suggested that perhaps the shadows had played tricks on him, that what he'd seen was nothing more than a pile of leaves blowing into the water. But he knew the difference between a girl with long brown hair and a pile of leaves. He knew what he had seen.

A room full of bees was just about the *last* place Miles wanted to go. He tried to get out of it, and when he couldn't, he lingered as long as he dared with the protective gear. He trailed behind once they got inside the Bee Room, not eager to surround himself with them, no matter how well protected he might be.

The plants and flowers provided a good excuse to stop, so he pretended to be fascinated by them. His gaze lit upon a particularly full plant covered with heads of tiny white flowers. But it wasn't the plant itself that caught his attention. It was the yellow, black, and red butterfly flapping its wings above it.

Miles glanced around. The others were all occupied with the beekeeper. He crept closer. He knew it couldn't be the same butterfly he'd seen on the garage roof earlier, since that would be impossible. Still, the resemblance couldn't be denied.

He crept closer. And then—he could swear it—the butterfly landed right on his nose!

He shouted in surprise, backed up, and fell right into another row of plants. Flat on his back, he stared up at the leaves and tiny flowers and considered his situation. A butterfly, one that looked exactly like the one from his roof, had just landed on his nose.

In the last year, Miles had become a master at finding hidden meanings, in his books and in the world around him. A few minutes ago he'd learned that people and butterflies really weren't that different. Then he was visited by a butterfly for the second time in one day? And it happened here in this room full of bees. Definitely a sign.

This butterfly had *clearly* been sent from the afterlife to give him a message from the girl. And the fact that it had landed on his nose here in the Bee Room of the candy factory could mean only one thing: the girl wanted him to win the competition. In honor of the girl who never came out of the lake, he would make the best candy the world had ever seen. It would be black and yellow, like a bee. Then the girl would be at rest because, as *Charlotte's Web* had told him, he was her friend, and that was a big deal.

"Are you all right?" Logan asked, appearing at his side and startling him.

Miles figured he must look pretty weird, splayed out on

the floor half under a bush. "I'm okay," he said, blushing, as the others joined Logan in a circle around him. "I bent down to look at this butterfly, and then it landed on...I mean, then I sort of tripped."

Daisy rapped her knuckles on Miles's helmet. "Good thing you had this on."

He gave her a small smile.

"I don't see any butterfly," Philip said, clearly doubting his story.

Miles didn't see it anymore either. But that's how it always was with signs. Very fleeting.

After promising Max he wouldn't shout at random anymore, he went to watch Logan charm some bees. As interesting as that was, Miles's head was elsewhere.

He was armed with a new purpose and something he hadn't truly possessed until that moment, the desire to win the contest. And he knew that if he really put his mind to it, he could do it.

CHAPTER THREE

Miles learned three things at lunchtime:

1. HE COULD EAT NOTHING BUT CHOCOLATE PIZZA FOR THE REST OF HIS LIFE AND BE TOTALLY HAPPY.

2. DAISY READ ROMANCE NOVELS — OUT LOUD!

3. ANOTHER BUTTERFLY WITH RED WINGS WOULD SOON BE BORN.

And he learned one thing after lunch:

4. UNLESS HE STOPPED THINKING ABOUT THESE THINGS AND FOCUSED ON PAYING ATTENTION IN THE LAB, HE MIGHT BURN HIS EYEBROWS OFF WITH THE BUNSEN BURNER.

So he focused his attention on examining the equipment at his station, marveling at how each object served a unique function. They practiced weighing and measuring various ingredients while Max rotated around the room, observing each of them individually.

"You have a very light touch," Max said as he watched Miles sift powdered sugar into a small bowl. "Have you ever baked before?"

Miles shook his head, a little embarrassed at being praised in front of everyone. "I had a chemistry set when I was younger that I used to play with a lot. You know, mixing things and watching them turn into other things."

"Is that what got you interested in creating a new candy?"

Miles knew the others could hear everything. How could he explain the real reason he had entered the contest? But he couldn't lie either. He still felt bad about saying he was allergic to rowboats at lunch. And all those other things, too. How could someone be allergic to rowboats? And the color pink?

But again, how could he explain how each one reminded him of that day at the lake? The pancakes he'd had for breakfast before the boat trip that later sat in his stomach like a rock. The merry-go-round at the park, whose music kept going even after the police had cleared the area. If Max hadn't asked if he was allergic to bees earlier, he never would have thought of claiming allergies to any of those things.

Max was waiting patiently for a response, so Miles just said, "The librarian at my school knew I liked chemistry and told me about the contest." There. That may not have been the whole truth, but all of it was true.

"Excellent!" Max said. "Now, are you all ready to boil some sugar?" Everyone nodded except Logan, who, Miles figured, had been boiling sugar for years.

"Good," Max said, stepping over to the burners in the front of the room to demonstrate. "Now, this is the first step in candymaking. It may look easy, but I assure you, it requires careful attention. If you get the sugar too hot, it will melt; too low, and it will harden. The difference between a jaw-breaker and a piece of caramel is all about the temperature of the sugar."

Each of them followed along, trying to keep the temperature steady. Logan kept taking his thermometer out and shaking it, and once his sugar mixture boiled over the side of his pot. Maybe, Miles thought, Logan was just pretending to struggle to make the rest of them feel better. He probably wasn't pretending, though, when a measuring spoon or a piece of cinnamon bark slipped through his fingers and fell to the floor. Every time something fell, Miles quickly pretended to be absorbed in his own work so Logan wouldn't know he'd noticed.

He heated his second batch of sugar until he could make flat, bendable sheets out of it. He had just stood up to admire his handiwork when a cloud of powdered sugar flew up into the air at Philip's station. This was followed by a few choice words from Philip as the white dust fluttered down like snow onto his head and shoulders. Unable to help himself, Miles started giggling.

Logan and Daisy laughed, too. For a split second it seemed Philip would join in, but then he scowled and began wiping at the mess with his handkerchief. Daisy launched into a sneezing fit as the sugar wafted over to her station, and she had to leave the room.

Max hurried over to the sink and wet a few pieces of paper towel. He handed them to Philip.

"No thanks," Philip said, grabbing his briefcase from the tabletop and wiping a layer of powdered sugar off it. "I'll go to the bathroom and do it properly. If this stains, you'll be getting my dry-cleaning bill." With that, he stormed out.

Max told them to keep working, but Logan kept blowing powdered sugar into the air and cracking Miles up. When Daisy returned, her nose was so red from sneezing it looked swollen. She kept touching it and wincing.

When it was time to leave for the day, Daisy stopped by Miles's station to say goodbye. "Thanks for driving Philip crazy with all that afterlife stuff."

He laughed. "No problem. I've got a lot more where that came from."

"Good!" Daisy said. "See you tomorrow."

Miles wondered if he should mention that his shin still ached where she had kicked him at lunch when he made fun of her book, but he didn't want to make her feel bad. She just didn't know her own strength. Daisy said goodbye to

Logan, then gave Max a hug and skipped out of the room. Although the lab's white walls and overhead fluorescent lights made the room extremely bright, it seemed to grow dimmer after Daisy left.

"I have to do some homework," Logan told Miles. "But if there's anything else you want to see again, like the Gummy Dinosaurs Room, I can take you there."

Miles shook his head reluctantly. "My parents are probably waiting for me."

"Okay, see you tomorrow, then," Logan said, waving goodbye.

Miles recognized the look on Max's face when Logan left the room. It was a combination of fierce loyalty, genuine affection, sympathy, and concern. He had seen it on many of the faces of the people they'd met that day. Miles felt that same way about Logan, and he'd only met him that day! No wonder he didn't leave the factory very often. Living here was like living inside a well-protected cocoon.

The whole ride home Miles couldn't stop talking about the factory and how the air itself tasted like candy and how the next day they'd be making their own. His father kept interrupting and making him start over.

"What do you mean Logan *charmed bees?*"

"He just talked to them in this, like, soothing kind of voice, and they listened to him. Even though Paulo still had to use this smoke machine thing, I think Logan really did it."

"What again did he do exactly?"

"He made the bees accept the new queen."

"Uh-huh," his dad said, clearly a little skeptical.

Undeterred, Miles continued. "The thing that's most amazing? Logan doesn't even seem to notice his scars. Like they don't even matter."

"Maybe they don't," his father said, pulling into their driveway. He turned off the car, but neither of them got out.

"But, Dad, they're really bad. There's one down the side of his face, like by his ear. And his arms and his hands... sometimes he can't hold on to things."

"It must be very difficult for him."

Miles nodded. They sat in silence for a few minutes, the breeze coming through the open car windows. Then Miles climbed out and said, "I'll be on the roof if you need me."

"Be careful," his dad replied automatically.

"I lliw."

His father groaned.

Miles raced upstairs and climbed out onto the roof. He needed some good-quality thinking time. Using his back-pack as a pillow, he stared up at the trees that overhung a portion of the roof. The sky, now a pale blue, shimmered between the leaves. He thought about how his dad had said to be careful. How could a kid who carried a life jacket with him all the time be any more careful?

Leaning up on his elbows, he searched the edge of the

roof for the butterfly. He didn't see it. He hadn't really expected to. So he stared up at the sky and began to talk to the girl, as he often did. He did it out loud only if no one else was around.

"I got your message from the butterfly," he whispered. "I'm going to come up with a really good candy for you." Then he added, "Of course, if you'd like to help me, you know, to think of one, that would be cool. I'll watch for another sign."

But when it came, he almost missed it.

Gummzilla is by far superior," Miles insisted, shading his eyes from the bright morning sun. "His tail alone could toss Gummysaurus Rex to the next city block!"

Logan shook his head. "So wrong. Gummysaurus Rex could trample Gummzilla with one foreleg!"

Miles had been very happy to see Logan waiting for him when he arrived for Day Two. Still, he had to insist that Gummzilla would tower over Gummysaurus Rex. He started to tell Logan this, but an odd clip-clopping sound made him stop. It almost sounded like a horse.

A giant black horse, in fact. A giant black horse with Daisy on its back. His thoughts raced back to the day at the lake. After he and his parents reported the incident, the whole area had been roped off and everyone asked to leave. The merry-go-round had gone around and around with its empty horses. Merry-go-rounds and their ghost riders gave him the chills.

Any dark thoughts vanished, though, as soon as they were inside and Miles saw the candymaking machines set up in the center of the lab. He rushed over to peer at the insides of the High-Jumping Jelly Beans. The *insides!* He never could have dreamt of seeing such a thing. Sure, he was used to seeing inside when he bit into one, but this was entirely different. Now he could see the *outsides* of the insides. And who ever got to see that?

When he got his turn to fling the glaze into the urn of rotating beans, he held on really tight, not wanting to make the same mistake Philip had. The liquid streamed out in a long arc, spraying and coating the jelly bean insides as they banged around in the rotating urn. He felt like a real scientist.

When the chocolate in the enrober began cascading onto the Oozing Crunchoramas, Miles literally had to lock his hands behind his back. The urge to feel the chocolate running over his open palm was nearly overwhelming.

"Do any of you know what you want to make yet?" Max asked.

Philip was the only one to respond. He sounded so confident and so protective of his recipe that Miles began to doubt anyone would be able to beat him. Not that he'd ever tell him that.

When Max shooed them out of the room to go do research, Miles had only one place to go. He wanted to tell Logan about his project, especially after Logan shared his amazing idea for the Bubbletastic ChocoRocket, but he felt weird about it. He didn't really know enough yet.

"Hey, you're the little dude who fainted," Paulo said

when Miles walked into the Bee Room ten minutes later, fully decked out in his protective gear.

"I didn't faint," Miles said, eyeing a bee buzzing dangerously close to his nose. "I *fell*. It's different."

Paulo wiped his hands with a wet rag, wrung it out, and laid it over a nearby post. "If you say so. So what brings you back? There isn't a problem with the honey again, is there?"

Miles shook his head. "Actually I just came to ask you a few questions. About honey."

"Then I'm the guy you want." He gestured Miles over to a bench away from most of the activity. They sat, the bees buzzing in the background adding a sort of musical undertone.

"Basically," Miles explained, "I want to make some sort of honey-based candy. But with a soft consistency, not like a hard candy that could hurt your teeth. Oh, and I'd like it to look like a bee."

"A bee?" Paulo repeated.

Miles nodded.

Paulo rested his chin on his hands and said, "Interesting, very interesting. Well, I can help you with the honey part. Making it look like a bee is up to you."

For the next twenty minutes, Paulo explained how bees made both honey and wax, how you could distinguish between different types of honey, which were best for baking, and how long and laborious a task it was for the bees to make it in the first place. By the end of the lesson,

Miles had begun to second-guess his plans. He worried that it wouldn't be fair to make a honey-based candy when it would take so many bees to do it.

"Let me guess," Paulo said, leaning back on the bench. "You're feeling guilty."

Miles looked up, surprised. "How'd you know?"

"I saw that same expression on Logan's face when he was four years old. He saw how the process worked and asked if taking the bees' honey was like stealing. I explained that making honey is what bees do. It's their *purpose*. They make it to eat themselves, but they make much, much more than they need. Since then Logan's made it his duty to make sure the bees know they're appreciated for their hard work." Paulo shook his head. "Great kid, great kid."

"Wait," Miles said, "you were here that long ago?"

Paulo nodded. "I've been here since I was fifteen. The Candymaker hires teenagers during the summer and sort of grooms us to work here when we get out of school."

Miles saw his opportunity and took it. "So you were here when Logan, um, when whatever happened to Logan... happened?"

Paulo let out a long breath. "Indeed I was, little dude, indeed I was."

"Can you, um, tell me about it?" Miles held his breath.

"Logan didn't tell you?" Paulo said, not really sounding surprised.

Miles shook his head.

Paulo put his chin in his hands again. "Well, I figure it's Logan's tale to tell, if he wants to. I will tell you it was pretty bad. A lot changed around here after that. If Logan hadn't been such a good kid, had such a big heart, it wouldn't have happened, you know?"

Miles shook his head.

Paulo smiled sadly and stood up. "That's the best I can do. I'm sure if you ask him, he'll tell you."

But Miles didn't think he could. He thanked Paulo for his help and promised to bring him a sample of the bee candy if he figured out how to make it.

His next stop was the Taffy Room, where he expected to run into Daisy. Most of the taffy makers must have gone to lunch, because Fran was the only one there. Miles watched from the door as she lifted a soft roll of orange-and-white-striped taffy onto the hook and started working at it so intently that he felt bad barging in. He purposely made a lot of noise by bumping and kicking the door so she wouldn't be startled. She looked up and seemed genuinely glad to see him.

"Miles!" she exclaimed. "Back for some more grape taffy?" Without waiting for an answer, she reached over to a heaping barrel and tossed him handfuls of the individually wrapped pieces. He laughed as he tried to catch them all.

Stuffing them into his pockets, he said, "Actually, I'd really like some of the yellow ones for my project. I mean, if that's okay."

She beamed. "Wonderful! I hoped someone would use

taffy in their entry. C'mon!" She led him across the room to where a foot-long glob of yellow taffy sat cooling on a marble slab. "Would this be enough?"

"Even half of that would be great."

She took a very sharp knife, cut it neatly in half, wrapped the chunk in wax paper, and presented it to him like a gift. Miles clutched the warm package to his chest.

As they walked back to the door, something Fran had said came back to him. "Fran, you said you hoped one of us would use taffy in our project. Didn't Daisy come to see you?"

Fran shook her head. "Nope. And that girl has potential. Good arm strength, very important."

Miles crinkled his brows. "You're sure?"

"I'm sure. But if you see her, tell her to stop by."

"Okay," Miles promised. "Thanks for everything." He headed back to the lab, wondering why Daisy had changed her mind about the taffy. He had to go right past the Some More S'mores Room, so he poked his head in to see if Daisy had gone there. The intoxicating aromas of chocolate and graham crackers and marshmallows overwhelmed him (but in a good way), and he had to hold on to the door.

"Has anyone seen Daisy?" he asked, trying not to salivate as the S'mores came down the conveyor belt not two feet away from him.

One of the S'more makers, a roly-poly guy who looked enough like a younger version of the Candymaker to be his brother, looked up from pouring a tray of marshmallows onto a slab of chocolate. "The girl in the bright yellow dress who you kids had to drag out yesterday?"

Miles nodded. "That's her."

The Candymaker's look-alike shook his head. "Haven't seen her since yesterday."

"Okay, thanks anyway." He took one last inhale and forced himself to move on. He passed a closed unmarked door to a room where someone — one of the workers on a break, probably — was listening to classical music. His own parents were more light-rock types, so he never heard classical music except in elevators or at the eye doctor's office. He didn't realize he had slowed down until he noticed that his feet were no longer moving forward.

That music! So powerful! So full of both sorrow and beauty! He was rooted to the spot. Tears sprang to his eyes, and he wiped them with the back of his hand, horrified at himself. He couldn't let anyone see him crying at classical music of all things! Finally the music stopped, and he was able to move again. He hurried to the lab, trying not to think about what had just happened.

The first thing he saw when he ducked into his station was the backpack on the floor next to his stool. He stared at it for a full minute. He hadn't left it behind in all this time, and now he'd abandoned it without a second thought. He sighed and placed the taffy carefully in the center of the lab table. It looked as if it belonged, which he took as another good sign that he was on the right track.

Before he forgot everything he had learned on his journey,

he quickly wrote down what ingredients he'd need and how to prepare the honey to get the consistency he had in mind. He closed his notebook with a satisfied smile. He liked his plan. He was sure the girl would, too. It was time to meet the others for lunch. He grabbed his backpack and was halfway to the door when Philip strode in.

Miles noticed that Philip looked flushed, and his eyes were shiny. Either he had been crying (which he highly doubted Philip was even capable of), or he was excited because his project was going so well.

Miles cleared his throat and, as cheerfully as he could, asked, "Hey, how's it going?"

Philip stared at him like he'd just said bunnies could talk.

Miles edged closer to the door. "Well, see ya. I was just dropping something off. You know, for my project." Then, unable to resist, he added, "It's pretty good, I think."

"Is that so?" Philip asked, crossing his arms. "You think you'll win?"

"Um, I don't know. Probably not. I mean, Logan's idea is so great. Not that yours isn't, I'm sure. Or Daisy's."

Philip laughed. "I'm not planning on losing to Daisy. Just because she's pretty doesn't mean she's going to win. And I bet Logan doesn't even have a clue of what to enter. He's not the brightest, you know. Or are you too busy buttering him up to notice?"

Miles wanted to lunge at him. Or at the very least, to throw a bowl of jelly beans at his head. Instead, he gritted his teeth and said, "Oh, yeah? Logan's idea is great! No one has ever been able to make chocolate turn into gum and back again. If anyone can do it, *he* can."

"Chocolate into gum?"

Miles nodded fervently. "And back again!"

"Interesting," Philip mused, moving over to his station. "Very interesting."

Miles suddenly wished he'd kept his mouth shut. What had bragging about Logan's idea done except tip off Philip to his plans? Ugh! Miles shifted his backpack and stormed out. Every once in a while he thought he saw a flash of something behind Philip's eyes, some sort of pain hidden really, really deep. Now he wondered if he'd just wanted to believe it was there, wanted to believe that everyone had some good inside them. Maybe it just didn't work like that.

He hurried to the cafeteria, trying to convince himself that after all, Logan hadn't specifically *hidden* his idea from Philip; it just happened that Philip hadn't been in the room when Logan told everyone. At least he hoped Logan would see it that way when he found out.

He scanned the cafeteria but didn't see Logan anywhere. Mary, the woman who had given them their chocolate pizza yesterday, spotted him and waved him over. "Miles, right?"

He nodded, surprised.

She reached into her apron pocket, leaned over the counter, and handed him a note.

"Um, thanks," he said, going back to wait for the others.

*Hi guys, have lunch without me,
went to go check on ~~Daisy~~ the horse.
Hugs, Daisy.*

He showed the note to Logan when he got to the cafeteria a minute later. Miles was glad to have a distraction so he wouldn't focus on the fact that he'd revealed Logan's project.

To keep himself from blurting out his blunder, he said the first thing that popped into his mind. "Do you think Daisy's pretty?"

Great, Miles thought as soon as he'd said it. *Now he thinks I have a crush on Daisy.* So he pretended he used to like a girl who'd moved away, which wasn't even a complete lie. The girl at the park had in fact "moved away," just to a very different place, not the next town over.

Fortunately Logan didn't ask any questions. After agreeing that they'd waited long enough for Philip, they went to Logan's apartment for chocolate pizza. It was just as Miles had imagined Logan's home would be — cozy and colorful, with thick rugs and red brick and lots of windows, and it smelled REALLY GOOD.

The living room walls were lined with photographs — the older ones in faded black and white — of men and women standing next to various candy machines. He recognized the Candymaker as a young man and a white-haired man who could only be the original Candymaker, Logan's grandfather.

Lots of pictures showed Logan as a little boy — on his father's shoulders or kneeling down at the great rubber-duck race or blowing a huge pink bubble. After age five, the pictures of Logan became more sporadic, maybe two a year. His smile was still just as wide.

A lump formed in Miles's throat, and he had to blink back tears.

Thankfully, before Logan could notice that anything was wrong, Logan's mom suggested they take a tour of the place.

Logan showed him the framed candy-bar wrappers that lined the walls of the hallway. "Every candy **Life Is Sweet** has ever made is up here," he said proudly.

"Wow," Miles said, glad to be talking of candy and not scars. He recognized most of the candies, even some that hadn't been made for years.

He thought he was doing okay until they got to the bathroom. Seeing the huge pile of aloe leaves made him choke up again. He knew aloe was used for healing wounds — they had learned that in fifth-grade science class.

They didn't get to Logan's room because the Candymaker's wife called them in for lunch. Miles felt slightly relieved. What if there was more skin stuff in there and he had to pretend he didn't see it?

The chocolate pizza tasted just as good the second day. Maybe better, if such a thing were possible. And now he had the promise of dinner at the apartment to look forward to.

"Is it okay if I move in?" he asked the Candymaker's wife. She laughed. "I think your parents might miss you."

He shrugged. "As long as I send home chocolate, my dad will be okay."

After lunch he washed his hands in the bathroom and accidentally knocked over a few aloe leaves when he reached for the towel. He scrambled to pick them up, hoping he hadn't harmed them in any way. Suddenly, carrying around a life jacket all day seemed so pointless. He'd carried it faithfully every day. Only his parents and Mrs. Chen at the library had known what was in his backpack. But he could no sooner turn back the clock and give it to the girl to wear as she ran into the water than Logan could undo what had happened to him.

As he let the backpack fall onto Logan's bed, he felt much lighter. He almost laughed out loud to think that a life jacket had actually weighed him down, which is the opposite of its purpose.

It felt so natural to fall right back into joking around with Logan that he was almost sorry when they reached the lab for the afternoon session. He was even sorrier when he saw the walls that had been erected around their stations.

The only thing to do was dive right in, so that's what Miles did. He gathered all the ingredients he thought he'd need and put some butter in a pan. When it started to sizzle, he added sugar, milk, and corn syrup.

Max dragged a stool over to Miles's station. "So, young man, what have you got for me?" Max peered into the pan.

"Caramel!" Then he picked up a small vial of black liquid, pulled out the cork, and sniffed. "Anise!"

Miles nodded, pleased.

"You're making black licorice–flavored caramel!"

Miles nodded again. Then he leaned in and whispered, "It'll go around a ball of honey. Then tiny strands of yellow taffy will circle around it."

Max clapped his hands. "You're making a bee!" He lowered his voice. "Out of candy!"

"That's the plan, at least!"

Max squeezed his shoulder. "Wonderful!" He did a quick inventory of Miles's station and said, "You're going to need more honey. I'll send for Paulo to drop some off."

The rest of the afternoon went by much too fast. Miles baked, boiled, cooled, rolled honey, flattened caramel, got taffy under his fingernails, and loved every minute of it. The only thing that lowered his spirits was seeing Logan struggle. Every once in a while something would crash to the floor, and then Logan would go out to the cabinets or the refrigerator to replace what he'd dropped.

When the five o'clock bell rang, Miles felt ready to go. He'd done all he could. Daisy seemed pleased with her progress, too. He hadn't been able to figure out what kind of candy she was making—he had caught a glimpse of what looked like a green glob of goop, but surely that couldn't be it. He was sorry she wouldn't be joining them for dinner. He would have bombarded her with questions until she gave in and told them what her candy was.

It seemed so natural walking out of the factory with Logan and Daisy. As if they'd been doing it their whole lives instead of only two days. He tried not to think about the fact that they'd only be together for one more day.

Outside, the exhaust from an old brown pickup truck greeted them. Miles wouldn't have admitted it to the others, but he was glad that the horse hadn't returned.

Daisy opened the door of the passenger seat. "This is my cousin, Bo. He bought this lovely truck with his winnings from the motorcycle-pulling contest at the state fair last year."

Miles couldn't wait to see what someone would look like who could pull a motorcycle with his teeth. He probably had bulging muscles and teeth the size of fingers!

He and Logan practically fell over each other to get a peek. Miles was disappointed to see that Bo looked like a regular guy. Too bad about the teeth, because otherwise he was good-looking enough to be on television.

After Daisy and Bo pulled away, Logan got that now-familiar gleam in his eye that meant he was excited to show Miles something. He led the way around to the back of the factory, and at first Miles thought he was going to suggest again that they go boating.

But he stopped in front of a huge cornfield instead. "You up for going straight through?" Logan asked. "We could go around, but it would take a lot longer."

The pale yellow stalks swayed and rustled in the breeze, reaching a good foot above their heads. Miles didn't want to disappoint Logan by chickening out, so he followed behind, trying not to bend the stalks as he squeezed between them.

At first it was fun making his way through the stalks, but then he fell too far behind and couldn't see anything except the sky above his head. "Logan?" he called out.

He waited a few seconds for an answer, but none came. Nothing to do but keep going, so he pushed through the stalks, turning this way and that, and suddenly it felt like drowning. In all the times he'd thought of that day at the lake, he'd never allowed himself to imagine what the drowning part must have been like. It would have been too awful.

Gasping for breath, Miles swung his arms, and a long minute later he found himself flying out of the stalks and into rows of evenly spaced strawberry bushes.

"Pretty cool, right?" Logan asked, running up to him.

He didn't know whether to laugh or cry, so he ate his strawberry, not tasting it.

He wished he could be more like Logan, accepting what came his way as just another part of life. He knew his parents wished that, too.

Was it really possible to simply accept that at any minute something terrible could happen to you or to someone you care about or to someone you saw across an empty lake? And what about the fact that once that person is gone, everyone after them goes, too, like bubbles popping?

What if the girl at the lake had grown up, gotten married, had kids and even grandkids? And what if one of those grandkids discovered a way to end world hunger? Now that kid would never get the chance — they'd all died before ever being born.

He wanted to explain this to Logan, to explain why a person shouldn't run and chew at the same time. How he needed to take more care, how everything could change in an instant. But he couldn't tell him that. Partly because he suspected that after his accident Logan must already know it and partly because he recognized the truth of Logan's words. We *don't* know how long we'll get to live, so we might as well make the best of it while we're here. Could it be that simple?

His head still full of these thoughts, Miles couldn't understand at first what Logan was trying to show him in the clearing beyond the Orange Grove. When he saw the broken merry-go-round half buried in the tall grass, he instinctively shrank back as the image of the merry-go-round moving with no riders flashed in his mind.

"What's wrong?" Logan asked, clearly concerned. "I thought you'd think it was neat, since, you know, you used to love the annual picnic…"

But Miles could only stare at the rusty poles, the flakes of yellow paint on the giraffe's neck, the green peeling off the frog's back. Then the late-day sun sent a beam of light directly onto the spire in the middle of the merry-go-round, and it came to him in a flash. The merry-go-round was a sign! If he was successful in creating the winning candy, he could make the girl live forever. The afterlife had a lot of merry-go-rounds, and he bet she was riding one right now, probably one of the horses or the zebras, her long, dark hair streaming out behind her.

With some kind of mutual understanding, he and Logan broke into a run. Running around the cornfield was exhilarating. All the fruits and vegetables smelled so fresh and ripe that his stomach growled. At the last minute, he turned toward the white clover bushes, thinking Logan might like to check on the butterfly.

But all that remained of the chrysalis lay broken on the ground. The butterfly had molted already.

"I'm sorry," he said. Logan had followed the caterpillar and watched over it for so long. He handled it pretty well, but Miles could tell he was disappointed to have missed seeing the butterfly do its final molting.

When they got back up to the apartment, Miles wasn't at all surprised to see that his parents had arrived early for dinner. He had a sneaking suspicion the adults had been talking about them, because they all had that slightly guilty look when he and Logan walked in.

Mrs. Sweet made her famous Sweet Family Sweet Stew for dinner. As far as Miles could tell, she gathered ingredients from every part of the factory, mixed them all together, and baked it.

As he ate the delicious meal, he was tempted to ask again if he could move in. It might insult his parents, though, to ask right in front of them. Logan must have read his mind when he invited him to sleep over. Of course it would have been preferable if he hadn't mentioned Miles's so-called pancake allergy. He tried not to meet his mom's eyes for the rest of the meal.

When his mom hugged him goodbye, she whispered in his ear, "So now you're allergic to pancakes?" He tried to end the hug, but she held tight. "I'm sure there's a good reason you told him that, and I'll look forward to hearing it." All the while, she kept a smile on her face, finally letting go of the hug after what seemed like a really long time.

If there was anything cooler in the world than walking with flashlights through a darkened candy factory with all the smells of the day still hanging in the air, Miles couldn't think what it might be. He felt so lucky. But that's not all he felt. As he walked the halls, he sensed that the girl was with him.

He realized he'd felt her presence ever since arriving at the factory yesterday, but never as strongly as he did now. It gave him a strength he hadn't had in a long time. In fact, it gave him the courage to admit to Logan that he couldn't walk by the chocolate fountain without wanting to stick his hand in it. Fortunately, Logan didn't laugh at him. Well, he laughed, but not in a mean way, and he didn't insist on coming with him.

Walking the halls of a darkened candy factory all alone felt a little less cool. With Logan at his side, he hadn't paid any attention to the creaks and groans of the factory settling down for the night, but now every sound seemed magnified. He didn't dawdle and he was relieved when he reached the fountain. The moon shining through the glass ceiling provided only a tiny bit of light.

He put the flashlight down on the floor and flexed the fingers of both hands in preparation. Even though he was alone, and the fountain deep in shadow, he felt kind of silly for what he was about to do. Not silly enough to keep him from doing it, though.

One finger slid under the chocolate waterfall, then another and another, until the chocolate was cascading over his entire hand. Then his other hand. He splayed his fingers and watched the chocolate slide between them in perfect arcs. It felt just the way he'd imagined it would, warm and soft. And it shimmered like liquid gold.

It also felt sticky. Really, really sticky.

"Uh-oh…" He pulled his hands out from under the stream and shook them. Drops of chocolate splashed back into the fountain, but most of it remained stubbornly coating his hands. He briefly considered licking it off, but remembered Logan had said it was for display only, not eating.

The nearest bathroom was outside the Lightning Chews Room, which meant he'd have to head in the opposite direction from the only person who knew where he was. Well, couldn't be helped. He'd just have to be brave. He bent down and grabbed his flashlight. Or rather, *tried* to grab it. It flew right out of his chocolate-covered hands and into the fountain, where it managed to splash his face, neck, and one side of his glasses before sinking to the bottom.

Without thinking, Miles thrust his hand in after it, too intent on retrieving it to fully enjoy having his hand and forearm immersed in warm chocolate. His hand wrapped around something, but it didn't feel like a flashlight.

He pulled his hand out and opened it. At first he couldn't tell what the object was. He used the bottom of his shirt to rub some chocolate off until the thing revealed itself in the faint moonlight. A small rubber duck with a sailor's hat! Just like the kind they'd used for the rubber-duck race. How had *that* gotten into the fountain? Maybe it had been hidden in there for years.

He shoved the duck into his pocket and reached in again for his flashlight. After feeling around in the fountain for a few seconds, his fingers tightened around it. He wiped it off as well as he could, held his breath, and turned it on. It still shone, although in a lightbulb-smeared-with-chocolate kind of way. It was, however, still bright enough to show Miles the mess he'd made on the floor. Not to mention the one on his arm, hands, and clothes.

"Great," he muttered, stepping carefully to avoid making chocolate footprints. Perhaps this hadn't been the brightest idea after all.

The bathroom door creaked when Miles pushed it open. It was the kind of creak you wouldn't notice in the day, but in the dark it sounded REALLY LOUD. The moonlight filtering in from the windows sent an eerie kind of half-light bouncing off the white-tiled walls. Miles almost expected a ghost to charge out of one of the stalls, wailing. He'd read a lot of books. He knew it was possible.

Rather than waiting around to find out, he quickly scrubbed his arms, hands, face, neck, and eyeglasses and grabbed a roll of paper towels from the wall to take back.

His flashlight had now faded to the point of being barely usable. He could hardly see a foot in front of him the whole way back to the fountain. But as he got closer, it suddenly became easier to see. Had his eyes adjusted to the dark? He glanced up at the ceiling above the fountain. The lights were still off. Then he saw where the light was coming from. The Cocoa Room!

Miles froze. No one had been there just two minutes earlier, he was sure of it. But now someone was definitely shining a flashlight around the room. That could mean only one thing — an intruder had broken in!

His mind raced back to the sentences he'd copied from the books in the factory's library. He hoped one of them would tell him what to do right now. One by one, he discarded them. No dogs doing their business here, thankfully. No monkeys swinging, and no butterscotch boiling. What about that universe one — something about things not really existing? He was pretty sure that whoever was wielding that flashlight existed. That line about friendship was the only one that fit. Again.

His hand tightened around the roll of paper towels. A

flimsy weapon if ever there was one, but he had no choice. He had to protect the factory!

Holding tight to the paper-towel roll, he crept over to the door of the Cocoa Room. He planned to stay as low to the ground as possible until he saw what the intruder was doing. Then he'd make his move. He didn't know what that move would be, but he knew he had to make one.

Bracing himself for whatever he'd find, Miles inched the door open until he could fit through. On his hands and knees, he crept a few feet into the room. Fortunately, the same tables and machines that blocked his view of the intruder also blocked the intruder's view of *him*.

He hadn't gone three feet when his elbow brushed against a huge mound of cocoa-bean pods piled on the floor. He reached out to steady them, not breathing. He didn't breathe again until he was sure that not a single pod would slip from the pile and give him away.

Sweat had begun to roll down his forehead, sending his glasses on a one-way trip down his nose. He used the bottom of his shirt to wipe the sweat off them. This turned out to be a bad idea, since he'd forgotten that the bottom of his shirt was covered in chocolate.

He reluctantly abandoned his now useless glasses and continued crawling past the long metal table where earlier they'd watched the beans get stripped of their shells.

He'd crept about a foot past the table when a hand reached out, grabbed hold of his ankle, and yanked him underneath.

PART THREE

DAISY

CHAPTER ONE

Daisy snuggled deeper under her blanket and sank back into her favorite dream, the one where, as the best twelve-year-old spy in the biz, she lived in a mansion with ten of her best friends (all pretty and smart, although none as accomplished a spy as she). She dreamt that her closets were bursting with clothes of every color and design and that every day brought new and exciting adventures.

Her dream bedroom overflowed with all the newest high-tech gadgets. The tiny transceiver that fit into her ear and picked up the smallest whisper. The video communicator hidden inside what appeared to be a romance novel. The pen that not only wrote in invisible ink and shone a light so bright it could be seen from outer space but also could effortlessly slice through glass and metal. The block of wax that could reshape itself to match any object it came in contact with — especially useful for opening locked doors.

In her dream, her top rank among the girls guaranteed that the hardest jobs, the most grueling tasks, were given to her. She got the most important assignments because she never complained, always got the job done, and didn't get emotionally involved.

The sound of her grandmother's voice calling her name forced the dream to dissolve until only a feathery wisp remained. Clinging to it like a life preserver, Daisy opened her eyes and blinked. Grinning, she let go of the last wisp and laughed.

"What's the joke?" her grandmother asked, her voice reaching Daisy through the tiny transceiver hidden deep in her left ear. She really had to remember to take that thing out when she slept—it both sent and received sounds. She wouldn't want someone to hear her snoring! (Not that she snored...much.)

Daisy stretched and rubbed her eyes. "I was laughing because in my dream I didn't complain about anything. Oh, and all the other girls in the mansion were my best friends."

Her grandmother laughed. "That really *is* funny!"

When her grandmother laughed, it sounded like tinkling glass, like wind chimes. No wonder she was widely considered one of the best spies of her generation. Everyone who met her fell instantly in love. Daisy had been a spy since she could walk, and most of what she knew she'd learned by watching her grandmother work.

If she were being totally honest, she would have told her grandmother another difference from her real life. In the dream, she was always happy and couldn't ask for anything more out of life. In reality, though, things weren't so black and white.

Even though she couldn't see her grandma at the moment, Daisy knew she was probably sitting cross-legged in the

Zen garden behind the mansion, sipping tea. "Hold on, Grammy, let me turn on my book so I can see you."

Daisy reached over to the night table and picked up her copy of *Love's Last Dance*. She propped herself up on the pillows, switched on the screen, and typed in the coordinates for the Zen garden. No Grammy, only Mo, the gardener. Daisy pressed more buttons.

The screen zoomed in on the kitchen, where one of the older girls, Courtney, stood by the counter, holding her nose and guzzling down Grammy's foul-tasting green instant-energy breakfast drink.

Courtney looked every inch the ballerina in her black leotard and pink tights, her hair pulled so tight into a bun that she wore an unintentional look of surprise. Daisy had been very relieved not to be given the assignment to infiltrate the Spring Haven Ballet Company. Although she was fully trained in almost every sport (including cricket and synchronized swimming), she usually managed to have a stomach bug on the days she was scheduled to practice dancing.

Courtney gave a little shudder as she finished the drink and placed the glass on the counter. Her eyes rose to the wall screen. Daisy waved, and in response Courtney did some kind of ballet move, rising up on her tiptoes with her hands arched gracefully over her head. Daisy laughed.

Even though Courtney was a few years older, she never treated Daisy like a little kid, unlike most of the other older girls. Not that they were outright mean or anything. They couldn't be, since Daisy's grandmother ran the whole show. But still, she would hear them laughing in their rooms at night, and they never invited her to join them.

Daisy waved a quick goodbye to Courtney and typed in the coordinates for her grandmother's car. Empty. She tried the office next. Nope. Just a stack of folders piled high on the desk. Odd. Those were Grammy's regular early-morning haunts. "Okay, Grammy, I give up. Where are you?"

She could hear others in the background as her grandmother replied, but she couldn't make out what they were saying. "Put in coordinates Alpha Delta seven-five-one," her grandmother instructed, "then hit the GPS button."

A few seconds later, Grammy's face flickered onto the screen. Behind her was a grassy field and a tall metal structure. Daisy squinted. "You're in *Paris?*"

"Yes! I mean, *oui!*" she replied, tapping her purple beret.

"You always did look excellent in hats," Daisy admitted, "but something tells me you're not in Paris to go hat shopping!"

"Darling, Paris is one of the world's top travel destinations." For effect, she zoomed in on the Eiffel Tower, fifty yards behind her. "How do you know I'm not here on vacation? You and your parents are always after me to take one."

Daisy yawned. It might be midday in Paris, but it was still near dawn on the outskirts of Spring Haven. "Maybe normal people go to Paris on vacation, but not you. You're on a mission, aren't you? Remember the whole delegating thing? You can't take all the missions for yourself. You're no spring chicken anymore."

Her grandmother laughed. "Where did you hear *that* expression?"

"I'm like a sponge," Daisy said proudly. "I absorb everything around me."

"That's what makes you such a good spy, my darling granddaughter."

"Don't change the subject."

"Okay, okay, I'll hand off the next case that requires a sixty-year-old silver-haired lady, I promise. You're as relentless as your parents."

"Thank you!" Daisy glowed. When your parents were two of the most sought-after spies in the world, any comparison to them was a good one. She couldn't be prouder of their success, even if it meant that except for the rare times the three of them were on a case as a family, she saw her parents only a few times a month. Sometimes for only a few hours at a time. She would never ask them to change what they did on her account, though, and only partly because she knew they wouldn't. But, hey, they never missed her birthday, and that said a lot.

Her grandmother glanced to the left at something Daisy couldn't see. "I only have a minute or two," she explained, "but I want to wish you luck on your mission today."

"No worries, Grammy. Should be an easy job. Get in, get the secret ingredient, get out."

"That's why I wanted to wish you luck. It's always —" Her grandmother paused to step aside for a group of camera-wielding tourists. Lowering her voice, she said, "It's always the easy ones that turn out to be the hardest. Have you read the file carefully?"

"Er, sure," Daisy fibbed, glancing guiltily at the file waiting, unopened, on her desk. She had meant to go through it before bed but was too tired after spending the day riding Magpie. Daisy didn't ride as gracefully as some of the other girls, or as sure-footedly, but she loved being on that horse's back more than anything else in the world. Except for successfully completing her missions, of course. "Hey, if you're away on another mission, who's going to be my handler?"

Her grandmother adjusted her beret and winked. "You must know that, since you read the file so carefully."

She should have known she couldn't put anything over on that woman. "Oh, right!" Daisy said brightly. "I remember now!"

They both laughed.

"Love you, Grammy, be careful."

"You, too, dear. Don't give Mrs. Peterson a hard time. The last time I left her in charge, you convinced her that Magpie should eat supper in the dining room with all the girls."

Daisy recalled the look of horror on the caretaker's face when Magpie put her big head into the spaghetti bowl.

"And remember our motto," her grandmother continued. "When in Rome, act like the Romans. When you're a kid in a candy factory, act like a kid in a candy factory."

Daisy smiled. "Does that mean I get to eat all the candy I want?"

"Of course! And give AJ my love." The screen went blank.

AJ? *AJ?* Daisy jumped out of bed, tossing the book onto the pillows behind her. No, it couldn't be. She ran over to the desk and picked up the orange folder with the day's assignment in it. She skimmed through the paperwork outlining the mission until she came to the section marked HANDLER. And there it was, in bright red ink: *AJ.*

Every spy worth her salt had an arch-nemesis. AJ was hers. Five years older, ten times better-looking (or at least *he* thought so), and a constant thorn in her side. All the other girls lost a hundred IQ points when he walked by, but they hadn't been at the mansion as long as she had. They didn't remember when he was six years old, the youngest spy in the biz, and the only boy in the mansion. He bragged about both nonstop.

Well, to be honest, she didn't quite remember that time either, since she was only a baby then, but she *did* remember when he was ten and she was five. They had to pretend to be brother and sister to infiltrate a traveling circus, and he told the ringmaster she was mute so she couldn't say a single word for two weeks. He'd probably done it just so she couldn't remind him that *she* was now the youngest working spy, beating his claim to fame by a full year.

She went into her bathroom to wash up. No use whining over it. She was a professional. She could work with anyone.

Plus this assignment was short — only three days — and she figured she'd need only one day to get the secret ingredient. Once she had it, she'd make up some excuse to get out of the candy competition and leave. She could put up with AJ for one day, she decided, and pressed the intercom on the wall.

"Ready for prep," she announced, wondering who would show up. Whoever wasn't on active duty got assigned to help prep the others. Last week she had prepped ten-year-old Janel, whose mission was to infiltrate the Buttons and Bows Junior Miss Pageant. Daisy had dressed her in lots of poofy skirts and curled her hair until she looked like a poodle. A very puffy poodle. It took almost a whole can of hair spray to keep her hair that way. Very messy business, the whole prepping thing. Daisy much preferred being on a case than prepping someone else.

She picked up the folder and leafed through the thin stack of pages again. The research department had found grainy surveillance pictures of both the inside and the outside of the **Life Is Sweet** candy factory.

A small photo clipped to the top page had the words "Logan, the Candymaker's son" scribbled across the bottom. The picture showed a boy of about four or five with olive skin and blond hair. A butterfly sat on the tip of his nose, making his eyes look slightly crossed. His expression was one of pure astonishment and glee. Daisy had to admire the skill of the photographer in capturing both the boy *and* the butterfly without being seen by either.

A note from the background checker explained that the factory interior shots were from a very old data-gathering trip, as was the photo of the boy. There had been no time to update the records. The upcoming contest provided the best opportunity for someone to be in the factory unescorted, and the research team had worked day and night to get Daisy enrolled as a contestant.

She had just begun to read the notes about the factory's founder when Clarissa and her twin, Marissa, barged in, way too bright-eyed for so early in the morning. Once again, Daisy had to remind herself that she was a professional and could work with anyone.

Being an identical twin was a great asset when it came to spying. Clarissa and Marissa could essentially be in two places at once, a very handy trick when you're trying not to be seen in the wrong place. Relentlessly perky and armed with a fashion sense much keener than the typical fifteen-year-old's, they were never suspected of having a devious thought in their heads. That's what made them such good spies.

"I thought you guys were on a case," Daisy said, holding out the folder. Clarissa grabbed it and flipped it open, scattering the pictures on the rug. Marissa bent down to pick them up.

"Sorry!" Clarissa squealed.

"We finished the town-hall job yesterday," Marissa said, tossing the photos on the bed. "Got the plans for the new water tunnels with no problem. So we're all yours!"

"Swell," Daisy muttered.

The twins huddled together and skimmed the file. Then, with a nod, Clarissa swung open the door to the walk-in closet and stepped in. Marissa clapped her hands with excitement. "This is going to be a fun one!"

The two of them pulled out dress after dress until Clarissa said, "Got it!" and held up a short yellow dress so bright Daisy had to shield her eyes.

"You're kidding me," she said, pretty sure they weren't. "Why that one? Can't I wear something more, I don't know, sophisticated?"

"We think your personality for this mission should be fun and cheery. What says fun and cheery better than this?" She held the dress up high.

"And these?" Marissa asked with a giggle, holding up two socks — one pink and one blue with polka dots.

Daisy sighed. She knew they were right. The twins were the best preppers in the mansion. "All right, let's do this."

They marched her into the bathroom, where they poured a whole bottle of Sunshine Blond on her naturally light brown hair. It stung her scalp, but she didn't complain. Daisy actually preferred looking like a different person on the job. It helped her get inside the character. Twenty minutes later, the dye had done its job, and Clarissa blew her hair dry.

On to the outfit. The twins twirled and giggled as they dressed her. Marissa whipped out her needle and thread to make some tiny adjustments to a seam, which somehow made the dress fit perfectly. Clarissa got to work on her hair, pulling it into a ponytail so tight Daisy cried out. "I'm not a ballerina, ya know!"

"Sorry!" Clarissa loosened it a bit and then twirled the end around her finger to form a curl. On went the mismatched socks and white sneakers and a dab of pink blush, which they swore would "wake up her face." When they were done, they turned her toward the mirror. Well, she definitely looked the part of "fun and cheery contestant," and that's all that mattered.

Her wall screen blinked on, and AJ's face appeared, one hand covering his eyes. "Everyone decent?"

The twins beamed and Daisy glared. "Just barely! Don't you ever knock?"

AJ lowered his hand and made a big show of pretending to knock on the screen. The twins shrieked with laughter.

"Nice outfit, Oopsa," he said with a grin. "Did a piece of you break off from the sun?"

"Ha ha," she said, wishing she could have thought of something more clever. She hated it when he called her Oopsa, short for Oopsa Daisy. Refusing to let him get to her so soon, she straightened up, smoothed down her dress, and said, "Let's get this show on the road. I've got a lotta candy to eat."

Ten minutes later, she sat behind AJ, clutching the edges of his black-and-silver moped for dear life. Her pocketbook, complete with a handful of gadgets and her fake romance novel, banged hard against her hip as AJ managed to hit each pothole on the dirt road that led from their estate out to the main road.

"Can't you go any less than a hundred miles per hour?" she yelled into the wind.

In response AJ leaned into a corner, sending the ground swimming up toward Daisy's face. She closed her eyes. The next time her parents showed up, they'd get an earful from her about this.

After a fifteen-minute ride that felt eternal, AJ screeched to a halt at the edge of the factory's long driveway. Daisy hopped off and waited for her pulse to return to normal. She knew that if she complained again it would make him drive twice as fast when he picked her up. Instead she ripped off her helmet and stuck it on the end of the handlebar.

"Okay," AJ said, unsnapping his helmet strap but leaving it on his head. "Let's go over last-minute stuff. You are Daisy Carpenter. You're fun—"

"Carpenter?" she interrupted. "Why'd you choose that name?"

"Why not?"

She shrugged. She didn't want him to know that the one time she'd actually made a friend during a mission—a real friend—the girl's name had been Rebecca Carpenter. But it didn't really matter. Names were things spies took on and off like clothes. She'd had more last names than she could remember. Truth be told, she didn't even know her real one. None of the kids living at the mansion did. It was for their own protection in case they slipped up and blew their cover. She'd learn it when she turned eighteen.

"May I continue?" he asked. Not waiting, he said, "You are fun, cheery, excited to be here, and ready to win. You get along with everyone. They need to like you and trust you if you're going to get the job done."

"Got it," she said. "This isn't my first time, you know."

He crossed his arms over his leather driving jacket. "Then of course you've read the file."

She smiled innocently. "Isn't that what handlers are for?"

He narrowed his eyes at her and sighed. "I've set your earpiece frequency to my own. I'll alert you if you need to know something."

"Just keep your yakking to a minimum," she instructed, fixing her ponytail, which had come loose during the ride. "I won't be able to concentrate on my job with you going on about sports or video games or whatever it is guys talk about."

He pretended to look insulted. "Is that what you think of me? I actually have some very highbrow interests, you know."

"Like what?" Daisy asked, glancing up the driveway. The smell of chocolate had just made its way out to the street. She felt her pulse quicken. She loved chocolate.

"That's for you to find out," AJ said. He hopped back onto the bike, saluted once, and took off with a screech.

"Yeah, I'll get right on that," she muttered under her breath.

"I heard that!" AJ's voice came through her earpiece, clearer than if he were still beside her.

Daisy kicked at the ground. What she wouldn't give for privacy every once in a while. At least no one could read her thoughts. Not yet anyway! No doubt the tech department was working on it. She began the long walk up the driveway. When she reached the front entrance, she quickly surmised that not much, if anything, had changed since the photos she had seen were taken. The smell of chocolate was even stronger, and her stomach growled. If her grandmother had been home, she never would have let Daisy leave without drinking her breakfast goop. She debated whether to knock on the door, but it was so heavy she knew no one would hear her. Ringing the doorbell seemed rude, somehow, so she sat on the stoop to wait.

A minute later, her pocketbook beeped, and she scrambled to pull out her book. Flipping it open, she immediately switched it to vibrate so it wouldn't give her away later. At first all she could see on the screen was a lot of white fuzz. It slowly cleared to reveal her mom's face, nearly completely covered with a ski hat, scarf, and goggles. Where could her mom be skiing in late June? She must be literally on the other side of the world.

"Hi, honey!" her mom said through blueish lips. "Hope you're warmer than I am right now!"

Daisy held the screen away and pointed the camera at her outfit.

Her mom laughed. "Is that your dress or the sun?"

In her ear she heard a muffled chuckle from AJ.

Ignoring both, she asked, "Where are you, Mom? Is Dad with you?"

"Can't tell you, honey, you know that. But we're fine. We miss you."

"How come you always know my missions, but I don't know yours?"

"When you turn eighteen we won't know yours either. Assuming, of course, that you want to continue this life."

"Of course I do!" Daisy said, shocked. What other life was there?

Her mom smiled. "I'm glad to hear that. Have fun today."

She frowned. "I'm here to do a job, not to have fun."

Snow began gently falling around her mother's face. "Lighten up, honey. You're twelve. You're allowed to have fun at a candy factory. In fact, I order you to."

"Me, too," AJ's voice said.

"This is a private conversation!" Daisy snapped, her hand reaching up to her ear.

"Daisy!" her mom admonished. "That's no way to talk to your grandmother, even through an earpiece."

"It's not Grammy, Mom. It's *AJ*. Grammy abandoned me to go on a mission to Paris!"

The snow was falling more heavily now. "She did, eh? I'll have another talk with her. At her age, she should be —"

"Don't mean to interrupt," AJ's voice cut in, *"but is that a car I hear?"*

Daisy looked up in time to see a short boy climbing out of a rather beat-up blue sedan, not ten feet away from her. She usually didn't allow herself to get so distracted. She'd have to be more careful. Daisy quickly shut the book without saying goodbye. Her mom would understand.

"Okay," AJ's voice said. *"It's show time."*

Daisy planted a smile on her face and jumped up. *Fun and cheery,* she told herself, channeling her inner Clarissa and Marissa as she introduced herself. She could tell it was working, because Miles — who had looked a little shell-shocked when he got out of the car — was now relaxed and smiling.

"Are you twirling?" AJ's voice teased a minute later. *"I hear your hair whipping around. That might be overkill."*

She stopped twirling.

Then Miles asked her a question about how many kids were in the contest and she said something snarky like "Don't you know?" and instantly felt bad. But she didn't want to admit she didn't know, either. All she could do was wait for AJ to come to the rescue. She heard pages being turned frantically. Seconds passed, and she began to squirm. Miles looked uncomfortable, too.

"There are four of you," AJ's voice finally said. He listed the names, telling her his bet was on Logan.

She repeated the information to Miles, hoping he hadn't wondered about her hesitation. Grammy always warned the girls that it was usually some very small thing that broke a spy's cover. She couldn't risk blowing this assignment. Not with her parents and Grammy away and with AJ living inside her head.

A sleek, shiny black limo pulled up in front of them, reminding Daisy of Magpie. If Magpie had wheels instead of legs. She figured the Candymaker himself would get out of the limo, but instead, a tall boy in a suit and tie stepped out and walked toward them, head held high with self-importance. Daisy's eyes widened. She didn't know his name, but she'd know him anywhere. The only time she'd had to be replaced on a job, it was because of him.

She'd been hired a few years back to investigate a claim of cheating at the regional spelling bee, held at a local elementary school. She had pretended to be a student at the school, sneaking around the building during classes and blending in when kids filled the hallways. After only a few hours, she located the supply room where the judges kept the index cards with the words for the final round of the bee. She suspected they had two stacks, one with difficult words and one with easier ones and were putting certain kids through to higher rounds by giving them the easy words.

The supply room was right next door to the music room, where a recording of some famous violinist was being played, drowning out the sound of her pushing open the squeaky supply room door. She thought she'd locked the door behind her — she'd been so sure of it — and had been about to pick the lock on the metal box that held the cards, when in walked *this* boy.

He was shorter back then and wore regular school clothes rather than an ill-fitting suit, but he already had the superior attitude he displayed now. He started yelling that he was going to report her for trying to look at the words. She kept telling him that she wasn't even *in* the spelling bee, but he wouldn't listen. He kept going on and on about how he'd studied for months for the bee. She realized that the music next door had stopped, and any minute the music teacher would come in. Daisy had no choice but to run out, humiliated, before her cover was fully blown.

"Introduce yourself," AJ's voice prompted in her ear, making her jump.

She forced herself to do as instructed. She was trained to notice even the subtlest shift in a person's body language, and as she and Philip shook hands she thought he flinched ever so slightly. She knew he couldn't recognize her, though. She'd been a redhead then, with large tortoiseshell glasses that covered half her face. Fun and cheery went out the window when she laughed as Philip said his ridiculously stuffy name.

"Daisy . . . ," AJ warned. He began growling at her when she started arguing with Philip over who would win the contest.

It didn't take lessons in reading body language to know that their bickering was making Miles uncomfortable, but Philip was so obnoxious, she just couldn't back down. She suddenly wanted to win the contest simply so Philip would lose. Not that she'd given the contest any thought whatsoever, since she'd been so certain she wouldn't need to stick around long enough to actually participate.

She suddenly became aware that AJ had gone from growling to screaming. He was telling her something like the whole plan could be jeopardized if one of the boys insulted Logan and everyone got kicked out. So she warned them that no one should say anything mean to Logan, while having absolutely no idea what that was all about. Poor Miles looked terrified, and she instantly felt bad for letting herself get worked up over Philip. She really needed to calm down and focus on the present mission, not one that was closed three years ago.

"Daisy!" AJ barked in her ear. *"What's gotten into you?"*

She couldn't answer him, of course, not until she was alone. And she didn't relish the idea of dredging up her one failure. AJ would just love that. In the meantime, she'd have to pretend that Philip was no more than an annoying boy, not the face she saw in her head each time she thought of that day. Then Miles started talking about life after death, and things lightened up a bit.

Then the door opened, and she realized why AJ was so adamant that no one upset Logan. That poor kid! She'd seen a lot in her long career, and she knew that life didn't treat everyone fairly. Logan's hands trembled a bit, and she could tell he was nervous. He greeted them by quoting scripture about how everyone has a bit of an angel inside them—or at least she *thought* that's what it meant. She swallowed hard and clapped. "Lovely!"

The scars down the left side of his face couldn't hide that same sweetness, that same happy, hopeful grin he'd worn as a child in the old photograph when he hadn't known he was being watched. All thoughts of Philip went straight out of her head. This time she didn't need AJ's prompting to be polite. She stuck out her hand. "Hi, I'm Daisy Carpenter."

Logan didn't respond right away, and Daisy panicked for a second, afraid she'd done the wrong thing. Maybe he didn't like people touching him or maybe it hurt to shake hands. But then he took her hand, and as he did, she felt it.

Beneath the raised, uneven skin, this boy was electric.

CHAPTER TWO

From the second she stepped inside, Daisy knew she wouldn't have to pretend to be a kid in a candy factory. Her senses burst to life: the gentle hums and whirring of the machinery, the sweet smells that filled the air, the bright colors, the beams of light from the ceiling. All of it captivated her completely. It took AJ clearing his throat to remind her that she was actually on a job. Miles had clearly fallen under Logan's spell, too. She could tell by the way he kept stealing worshipful glances at him.

Her hand still tingled from touching Logan's. Philip didn't seem the least bit fazed by either Logan's appearance or the place itself. He'd barely glanced at Logan since their arrival, and he kept his back to all of them now, which suited her just fine.

She excitedly read the plaques on the wall, anxious to learn about the factory's history, since she hadn't gotten to that part of the file.

"Good job!" AJ said encouragingly. *"You sound really interested, you're really getting into the role."*

She wanted to laugh, since of course she wasn't acting at

all. But then Philip started being mean to Logan and her mood changed. She switched into protective mode.

"I happen to love Pepsicles," she said, totally truthfully. And then, before she could stop herself she added, "So does my best friend, Magpie, and she's very particular." This, too, was true. Sometimes, on really hot days, Magpie would eat a whole box of Pepsicles.

AJ burst out laughing. *"Your horse is your best friend?"*

Daisy wanted to pull the transceiver out of her ear but knew she couldn't. All she could do was try to ignore him. She was succeeding pretty well until Philip asked what Daisy's dad did for a living, and she couldn't remember her cover story. *Why* hadn't she read that file? Of course, now that she needed him, AJ was silent. So she said the first thing that popped into her mind. That sent AJ into another fit of laughter. *"Your dad is a violinist now? Classic! Good luck keeping that cover story going."*

While the others were occupied by the chocolate fountain, Daisy stepped away and whispered furiously, "Why are you here if you're not going to help me out?"

"Sorry," AJ said, still giggling. *"Just trying to picture your dad with a violin in his hand. He'd crush it!"*

That was probably true. Her dad had the big, broad build of a football player. A violin would look tiny in his large hands. Not that it mattered. No one here would ever meet her parents. She pretended to examine a barrel of taffy. "Just do your job!" she whispered.

"I said I was sorry," AJ said, his voice muffled as he

chewed. *"I went to grab a sandwich. All this talk of candy is making me hungry. That Philip kid? You're lucky he's there."*

"How's that?"

"He's a good diversion. He'll be the bad kid, so you can get away with more."

Daisy grunted, but what he said made sense. A short, bald man with a warm, open face entered the hall, and she dropped the pieces of taffy she'd been sifting through and stepped back toward the rest of the group. Logan introduced the man as Max Pinkus.

"That guy's the big cheese," AJ said with a sense of urgency. *"You need to turn on the charm."*

AJ rattled off all the candies Max had been credited with making, and Daisy repeated them, doing her best to seem awed by his accomplishments.

Philip actually greeted Max in a civilized manner, which meant he was brownnosing him, too. He probably had all his plans for world domination written down in that notebook of his.

When Max finished going over the contest rules, she wanted to tell the others they didn't need to worry about her entry, since she wouldn't be here that long. But of course she couldn't say anything. She heard the tapping of keys in her ear.

"I just pulled up some old blueprints of the factory," AJ said. *"Try to get away for a few minutes to a secure location so we can go over them."*

The only thing she could think to do was ask to use the bathroom. She felt ridiculous as she squirmed around until Max sent her away. As soon as she was out of earshot, Daisy said, "Okay, where should I go?"

"What are you passing now?"

She told him, all the while nodding happily at the workers ducking in and out of rooms with trays of marshmallows, buckets of melted chocolate, and, in one case, ears of corn. He directed her down a few more hallways to a door marked STOREROOM.

She tried the door. "It's locked."

"So?"

She sighed and reached into her bag. So quickly that anyone passing by would never even notice, she pinched off a bit of the high-tech wax and stuffed it into the lock. A few seconds later, she pulled out a perfect replica of the key, which she then reinserted. The lock clicked open. She smushed the key back into the ball of wax.

"I'm in," she said, pulling a cord that dangled from the ceiling. A faint light flickered from the single bulb hanging there. Judging from the dust on the cardboard boxes surrounding her, the storeroom hadn't been used in years. She sat down on the nearest box, only to fall right in.

"Whoa!" She scrambled to stand up and then laughed.

"What's so funny?"

"I just fell into a box of rubber ducks!"

"Of what?"

"Rubber ducks," Daisy repeated. "Yellow ones. Some

are wearing sailor hats, if you must know." She inventoried the small room. A large first-aid kit. Two more boxes of rubber ducks, one box, labeled EGG TOSS, full of multicolored blindfolds, two large piles of burlap sacks, a bunch of musical instruments with a layer of dust covering the keys and strings, a stack of cracked hula hoops, a large wicker basket filled with balls of different sizes, a sink, a few rolls of paper towels, and a dusty satchel with what looked like old gardening clothes inside.

"I think this stuff is from the annual picnics they used to have here." She bent down to fix the box the best she could.

"C'mon, Daisy, you need to focus. Have you seen the secret ingredient yet?"

"I'll keep my eyes open during the tour," she said, reaching for a duck that had slid across the room. "Do you have my exit strategy yet?"

"There are some back-door exits that don't seem to have surveillance and some old tunnels running through the basement. I'll have the route mapped out by tonight."

Daisy tossed the last yellow duck into the box and closed it back up. "I need it today. I plan to be done before tomorrow and on to the next job. No offense, of course."

"Fine by me," AJ said. *"Babysitting you isn't exactly my dream job either."*

"Babysitting?" she repeated, bristling. "I'm hard at work here. I'm wearing a yellow dress for goodness' sake! I match these ducks!"

"You're doing pretty well so far," he admitted. "Logan and Miles seem to like you a lot. Two out of three ain't bad, as they say."

She thought once again of explaining how she'd met Philip before but didn't see that any good could come of it. The organization's rule book clearly stated that if the operative thought that someone recognized them from another job, she was supposed to alert her handler and pull out before getting nabbed. No way was she going to allow Philip to have her taken off *another* case. She was still confident that even though he gave her strange looks, he didn't recognize her.

Putting the issue of Philip temporarily out of her head, she sat down on a creaky metal step stool. "Hey, why didn't you tell me about Logan? Wait, don't answer that. It was in the file, wasn't it?"

"*Actually, no,*" AJ said. "*And I don't know too much. Some kind of accident when he was a little kid. We got some info on a bunch of trips to the burn clinic at Spring Haven Hospital, but no details.*" AJ cleared his throat. "*Is it bad?*"

"Yes," she said without hesitation. "But it's weird. After a few minutes, you don't really notice the scars."

"*Well, just keep being nice to him. His trust is a key component to your success in this mission.*"

"I know," she said, feeling the twinge of an unfamiliar emotion. She pushed it away and stood up. Emotions got in the way of a clear head. She'd never had much time for them, especially on a mission.

"I've already been gone too long," she told AJ as she pulled the string. The lightbulb flickered off as she reached for the door, making sure not to knock over any more ducks. It wasn't until she had left the Some More S'mores Room five minutes later, armed with the alibi for her delay, that she realized what the unfamiliar emotion had been.

Guilt.

It didn't take long — another fifteen minutes, to be exact — for the secret ingredient to make its appearance. Daisy had watched every step of the chocolate-making process with a close eye and knew that the ingredient her client was looking for must be in one of the metal tins in the Cocoa Room. She innocently asked what the square tin contained, and her hunch was confirmed.

It drove her crazy to have to pretend to Philip that she didn't know what a trade secret was, but she wanted to keep Logan and Max talking about it. She watched one of the workers put the tin back in the cabinet and close it. She couldn't see the front of the cabinet from this side of the window, but there didn't appear to be any locking mechanisms.

"If you just found the secret ingredient," AJ said eagerly, *"bark like a dog."*

Ignoring him, she tried to pry all she could out of Logan without raising any suspicions. No matter how easy it would be to nab the small tin, she had learned that the direct route was usually the best. If Logan felt like revealing the secret, that sure would make things simpler. But he claimed not to know, and she was inclined to believe him.

"Very funny," she whispered to AJ as the group headed to the Taffy Room. "The day I bark like a dog will be the day I hand in my badge."

"You don't have a badge."

"You know what I mean."

Philip glanced back at her, and she waited until he was a few feet ahead before daring to whisper again. "I did find it, though. Doesn't appear to be locked or guarded at all. Should be easy peasy."

"Roger that," AJ said, crunching hard on what could only be potato chips.

"Do you *ever* stop eating?"

Another crunch. *"I'm a growing boy."*

"Can you at least lower your microphone while you eat? I'm getting a bit nauseous listening to all the chewing and swallowing."

"Yes, boss," he joked. But he lowered the volume.

It was perhaps the first time Daisy could remember AJ taking a request of hers seriously. So it was with an extra bounce in her step that she volunteered to pull the taffy when the taffy maker asked. She was really getting into it when she realized everyone was looking at her. Apparently most twelve-year-old girls couldn't lift and twist the taffy like that.

She'd been strength-training her entire life, doing drills

and exercises every morning when she wasn't on a case. She could run without being heard, enter a room without breathing, carry fifty pounds on her back for a whole mile without breaking a sweat. Lifting the taffy required no effort at all. Still, she couldn't let them know she wasn't an ordinary twelve-year-old, so she had to pretend she'd exhausted all her energy.

When Fran complimented her, she allowed herself for one split second to imagine how easy and uncomplicated life would be if she could make taffy all day. No prepping in the mornings, no handler in her ear, no files to read. But there would be no Mom and Dad either, or Grammy. No gadgets, no Magpie. It would be someone else's life, and she liked her own.

She almost changed her mind, though, when she tasted the fresh taffy. She was about to ask for a second piece when Philip announced that candy was bad for you. She saw Logan go rigid, as if someone had slapped him. She couldn't contain herself.

"Easy, girl," AJ warned when Daisy started yelling at Philip.

Even though he'd raised the volume on his microphone again, she could barely hear him over the buzzing in her head. Why did this boy keep baiting Logan? Didn't he have any feelings at all? One well-placed karate chop, and Philip would go down. He wouldn't even see it coming.

"Remember," AJ said, *"the worse he behaves, the less people will focus on you."*

Even so, that karate chop started to sound good a bit later, when Philip pretended to choke just because Miles talked about candy factories in the afterlife. Seriously, Philip should just let it go and leave the kid alone. Sure, it's a strange interest, but to each his own. She'd met a lot of odd people over the years, with all sorts of quirks (including one lady who wore only orange and another who saved the last bite of food from every meal). She'd long ago learned not to judge.

This ability came in handy a few minutes later when Logan started hugging a tree. She didn't think he even realized what he was doing. Logan obviously loved this place, and Avery — the guy in the tree — obviously did, too. Now that she thought about it, everyone they'd come in contact with clearly loved what they did. What a rare place this was.

"Big fan of cinnamon?" Max asked a moment later.

Daisy opened her eyes to see the others gathered around her. Logan and Max looked amused. Philip just looked bored. It took a few seconds before she realized her arms were around the cinnamon tree, her cheek pressed against its smooth bark. She quickly backed away, forcing herself not to blush.

This place — the warm air, the lush foliage — reminded her of the last time she and her parents had been on a family assignment. Of course, that one had been in a *real* jungle. And instead of making candy, they'd been sent undercover to expose a black market for monkeys.

Or was it to *protect* a black market for monkeys? She had been taught not to question the motives of the client. After all, every story had two sides. Who was she to decide right from wrong?

"You're making me hungry again," AJ complained when lunch began. *"Do you think you could stop with all the oohhs and ahhhs?"*

"This is the best thing I've ever eaten," Daisy declared, making sure to chew her chocolate pizza extra loudly. Then, just to further annoy AJ, she started talking about what would be her perfect meals. She hadn't expected it to lead to a discussion on all the strange things Miles was allergic to. How could someone be allergic to a color? She'd have to remember not to let the twins dress her in anything pink the next day. Wait, what was she saying? She wouldn't even be here after today.

For a minute, she felt sure Logan was about to tell them what had happened to him, but as always, he acted as if his arms and hands and the side of his face didn't have pale pink scars running up and down them. That fact certainly overshadowed a weird pinky toe.

AJ started laughing hysterically when Logan asked Daisy to reveal something strange about herself. *"Why don't you tell them how you can speak five languages and cross a busy street blindfolded?"*

"I'm allergic to bees," she admitted.

AJ stopped laughing. *"Hey, that's right!"* he said. *"Why did you go into the Bee Room?"*

Why did he insist on asking her questions when he knew she couldn't answer them? They'd need to have a talk about proper handler etiquette. She couldn't very well tell him *or* the others that when she was on a job she didn't think about the real Daisy, only the Daisy she was pretending to be.

"All right, enough chitchatting with your new friends. We have work to do. Face-to-face. Can you get away again?"

Unwilling to arouse suspicion by wandering off, she went over to a tree far enough away that they wouldn't be able to hear her but close enough that they could plainly see her. As soon as she opened the book, AJ's face popped up. He grinned his self-assured grin at her.

"You have spinach in your teeth," she said.

"You wish," he replied.

She sighed. It was true. Sometimes she did wish AJ didn't look so perfect all the time. Didn't he ever get a pimple?

He pointed above her left ear. "You have purple cotton candy in your hair."

"Very funny."

"No, really, you do."

She reached up, and, sure enough, a strand of purple came off. "Well, you should have seen how that stuff was flying around the room."

She flipped the view on the screen until she could see herself and picked out the rest of the cotton candy. It figured that the boys hadn't told her. A girl would have! When she switched the screen back to AJ, he was holding up a blueprint of the factory.

"Okay," he said, straightening out the page. "Here's the Cocoa Room, where you saw the secret ingredient, right near the front door." He drew a red *X* over it. "The good news is that there aren't any security cameras in the individual candymaking rooms. The bad news is that there's a security camera above the front door, which means you can't use that entrance."

"Wait, there is? The case file didn't mention a camera." She definitely would have remembered that.

"Nevertheless," he said, "it's there. There's another one by the back door."

She thought back to that morning. "I hope they didn't see me talking to my mother."

"Me, too," he replied.

To his credit, he didn't say anything about how she should have been more careful, which he had every right to. Instead, he circled three doors on the blueprint. "These all lead to the basement, where a tunnel runs out to the side of the driveway. They use it to transport grain and other crops from the farm. That's your best bet for an exit route."

She nodded. "Okay. I'll find out when the shifts start and end. Maybe the Cocoa Room is empty for a period of time during the day." She figured daytime was her best chance. Then she could just blend back in with the rest of the people milling around.

"You have the bag?" he asked.

She reached into her pocketbook and pulled out a ziplock bag.

"That's it?" he asked. "That's the high-tech way to store the secret ingredient?"

"Hey," she said, raising her voice. "Don't knock the ziplock. This thing can withstand —"

"*Love's Last Dance?*" Miles said, interrupting her.

She looked up to see Miles's and Logan's smiling faces. She couldn't believe she'd let AJ distract her again. Now she had to pretend she would actually read a book with a title like that. It was so embarrassing. She *may* have kicked Miles a bit too hard in her quest to be playful.

"*Nice,*" AJ said in her ear. "*Love on a cattle ranch.*"

Once Miles and Logan had disappeared into the bushes, she replied, "How about you stop talking to me unless you've got something really important to say?"

No answer. Perfect. Daisy closed her eyes and leaned back against the tree trunk. With the birds chirping and a light breeze grazing her cheeks, it was easy to forget she was on a job. She let her mind wander from the plan to steal a sample of the secret ingredient to riding Magpie when she got home, to Grammy in Paris, to wondering where her parents were, and then back to the plan again. All was peaceful until a boy's voice spoke into her ear. She'd have preferred AJ's voice, which wasn't saying much.

"Thinking about how you're going to lose on Saturday?" he taunted.

She slowly opened her eyes and fixed them on Philip. With the sun behind him, she was surprised to see that he wasn't entirely un-good-looking. This made her even more annoyed at him.

"I'm not going to lose," she replied firmly. In her head she added, *Since I'm not going to be there.*

"Come," Max said, joining them. "Let's go find the others."

Daisy grabbed her pocketbook and walked with Max into the bushes. Philip trailed behind, grumbling. They found Logan and Miles kneeling beside a row of bushes, drawing a cocoon or something. Logan turned to smile at them as they approached, and Daisy felt a shiver. Logan had been in this exact spot in that photograph from so many years ago. She glanced behind her, but all she could see were low bushes and the field with the pond behind it. Nowhere for a photographer to hide. Whoever snapped the picture must have had a really good telephoto lens.

On the way to the lab, Max explained the plan for the afternoon.

AJ made his reappearance in her ear. *"Stay in the game. Remember to act really interested in everything."*

He didn't have to tell her that. When they got to the lab and saw all the fun equipment they'd get to experiment with, absolutely no acting was required. She loved the white lab coats they were given. Wearing one made her feel like a real scientist. She loved cracking eggs into a glass bowl, heating sugar until it hardened, measuring soybean oil to the exact eighth of an ounce.

Every now and then AJ popped in to remind her she was supposed to be doing surveillance on the Cocoa Room. When some pans clattered onto the floor, she took the opportunity to whisper, "I'm waiting for the right moment. I don't want to ask to use the bathroom again. They'll think I have a problem!"

A minute later, though, Philip supplied the perfect diversion. As soon as he sent a plume of powdered sugar into the air, she seized the moment and began to sneeze. Voilà! Banished from the room!

As soon as the lab door closed behind her she said, "Okay, I'm clear. Heading over to the Cocoa Room."

"Roger that."

She hurried down the long hallway that led to the main entrance. She had expected to see Philip ahead of her, but he must know of a bathroom elsewhere. When she reached the long windows that looked into the Cocoa Room, one of the work-ers — Steve, she recalled Max telling them — was intently pour-ing a bucket of bean nibs into the giant roaster. Gooey chocolate oozed its way through one tube and into another. She glanced around but didn't see the other guy. Steve put down his bucket and caught sight of her watching. She waved, and he waved back. Instead of talking loudly to be heard over the roaster, she mouthed the words, "Hi, can I ask you a question?"

He put his hand to his ear, as she'd hoped. She asked again. He held up a finger and disappeared from view. A few seconds later the door to the room opened, and Steve stepped outside.

"That's better," he said, closing the door behind him. "Sometimes I forget how loud it is in there when the roaster's on. Enjoying yourself here at the factory?"

"Oh yes, it's great! You're so lucky you get to work here."

He smiled and wiped his hands on his lab coat. Daisy recalled that at the start of the day it had been white. Now it was various shades of brown.

"Um, did your brother go home for the day?"

Steve shook his head. "He just ran to get more sugarcane. We don't leave until the last bean is processed."

"Wow, when is that?"

Steve looked at his watch. He had to scrape off the chocolate splattered across the face of it before he could read it. "In about two hours, usually." He paused for a second, then said, "Hey, I didn't get a chance to grab lunch today, and its being chocolate-pizza day, I'd like to see if I can rustle up some. Would you mind keeping an eye on things while I'm gone for a minute? If anything goes wrong, just press the big red button on the wall and the whole line will shut down."

"Sure!" Daisy said, barely believing her luck. In her ear AJ whooped. Steve opened the door and let her in. By the time she turned around, he had gone. She immediately headed over to the cabinet where she had seen them place the small tin. Just as she'd suspected, the door had no locking mechanism, just a simple wooden knob.

"Well?" AJ asked impatiently.

"Hold on. I'm about to open the cabinet." She reached

up, took hold of the knob, and yanked. The door swung open much more easily than she'd anticipated, smacking her on the nose. She yelped.

"What was that?"

"Um, nothing," she replied, rubbing her nose with one hand. "Just one of the machines." She stepped back a few feet to make sure Steve or Lenny hadn't returned. She wouldn't be able to hear the door open from here.

"So what do you see? Is it in there?"

She turned back to the cabinet and scanned the shelves. "Yes! It's on the top shelf. I'll need to climb up to reach it. Wait, I don't have a bag with me!"

"Pour some into your pocket, then."

She looked down at her dress in a panic. "I don't have a pocket! Stupid yellow dress!"

"You'll just have to hold it in your hand till you reach the lab. But hurry. You've been in there for almost two minutes already."

She closed the cabinet door and hunted around the room for something to stand on. Her eyes lit on the bucket Steve had just emptied into the roaster. She strode across the room to get it, keeping an eye on the door. She loved the feel of her heart pumping, the adrenaline rushing through her veins, when she was close to completing a mission. As she grabbed the handle of the bucket, a thought suddenly occurred to her. "AJ, do you know why the client wants the secret ingredient?"

"What?" AJ asked. *"Why would you even ask that?"*

She headed back to the cabinet, but more slowly this time. "I know it's not supposed to matter, I ... I'm just curious."

"I don't know any more than you do, Daisy. And you're right, it doesn't matter. Now hurry!"

But time had run out. Lenny walked into the room carrying thick stalks of sugarcane under each arm. She quickly flipped the bucket over and sat on it. He stopped short when he saw her. Before he could say anything, Daisy jumped up and said, "Hi! Steve asked me to watch the place while he went off in search of chocolate pizza."

Lenny nodded knowingly. "My bro does love his chocolate pizza."

"Who doesn't?" Daisy asked. When Lenny turned away to put down the sugarcane, she sneaked a peek at the cabinet to make sure she'd closed it. Luckily, she had. Even if she'd left it open, she'd have found some way to explain it. She'd escaped much closer calls than this. One time she had to persuade a throng of screaming teenagers that she was a pop star, even though she couldn't sing a note. If she could pull that off, she could do this.

"Well, I better get back to the lab or they'll think I fell in," she said, gesturing to the big vat of chocolate simmering next to them. It actually did look kind of inviting. Warm and gooey.

He gave her an odd look but said, "Okay, thanks for holding down the fort."

She hurried back to the lab but stopped a few yards short. No one was around, so she whispered, "Sorry about that."

"Not your fault," AJ said. *"And now you know you can get*

into the cabinet. You'll just need a way to get both guys out of the room again. Shouldn't be too hard."

She sighed. "Looks like I'm coming back tomorrow after all."

"Hope you have some great new candy idea lined up."

She groaned and put her hands over her eyes. "That's right! I'm really gonna have to do that now."

"Why don't you ask Magpie to help you? That's what best friends are for, right?" He started laughing.

"You're just jealous."

"Of a horse?"

"You know," said a voice behind her. "Talking to yourself can be a sign of a serious problem. This isn't the first time I've seen you do it."

Daisy whirled around in time to see Philip push open the door to the lab. Where had he come from? The only possible place was the storeroom she'd hidden in that morning. Someone must have told him about the sink in there. Why would he want to be in that cramped room when he could have simply walked around the corner and used the bathroom? Was he so concerned someone might see him in there not looking perfect?

She took a small bit of pleasure in noting that he still had some powdered sugar on his back, along with some water stains.

If someone had told her at that moment that one day soon she'd be lifting him off the ground so he wouldn't get his feet wet, she'd have said they were a whole hat full of crazy.

CHAPTER THREE

You're awfully quiet," AJ said as Daisy hopped off the back of his moped.

The ride home had been a lot less harrowing than the ride earlier. More traffic meant AJ had to go more slowly and actually stop at stop signs and red lights. She handed him her helmet. "I'm fine. I'll see you tomorrow morning." She strode off toward the stable before he could reply. She was halfway there when she heard the voice in her ear.

"I'm still here, ya know."

She groaned. "Not for long." The small office at the back of the stable had a mirror, so she headed there first. With the help of the long tweezers she always kept in her bag, it took only a second to pull the transceiver from her ear and slip it into the small soundproof case. "There!" she said out loud, relishing the fact that no one could hear her.

Leaving her pocketbook behind, she made her way around to Magpie's stall. It was empty. Daisy's spirits sank. She had really been looking forward to riding her. She did her best thinking on that horse's back.

"Over here," Courtney's voice called out.

Daisy turned around to see Courtney and Magpie emerge from the edge of the woods. Courtney must have gotten home a while ago, since she'd already changed out of her ballet outfit and gone for a ride. Daisy ran to meet them.

Courtney handed over the reins. "So, did you eat a lot of candy?"

Daisy smiled, patting Magpie on her warm flank. "Too much. You haven't tasted candy till you've tasted it straight off the assembly line. How did your gig go today?"

"Good," she replied, stretching her arms overhead and twisting her back. "I'm sore from all the twirling and leaping. I should be done by next week, though. How about you?"

Daisy frowned. "I thought it would just take a day, but it turned out to be a little complicated."

Courtney nodded. "Been there. Hey, at least you get to spend more time in a candy factory, that can't be too bad."

Daisy had to admit that as assignments went, this was a pretty amazing one.

"Well, have a good ride." Courtney gave Magpie a final pat and turned toward the stable.

"Wait," Daisy called out. Courtney stopped. Daisy cleared her throat. "Do you ever wonder about the reasons behind an assignment? Like if the information we're getting for the client is going to hurt the person or group we're getting it from?"

Courtney considered the question. "Well, there're two sides to everything, so it's not up to us to try to figure it out."

"I know that part," Daisy said impatiently. "That's what they drill into us. But what if they say that to keep us from asking too many questions?"

"I'm sure they do." Courtney reached up to pull out a bobby pin that had come loose from the tight bun she still wore. "But it's a good thing. Our mission is to get the job done. If we start questioning whether it's right or wrong, or who's the good guy and who's the bad guy, we'll lose our focus. We'll get sloppy. Your grandmother told me once she never asks why the client wants the job done. If that's good enough for her, it should be good enough for us."

Daisy nodded. "Yes, you're right." But suddenly she knew it wasn't good enough. Not for her. She could ask Grammy what she knew about the case, but it would be midnight in Paris now. She'd just have to find out for herself.

That night, after the other girls and Mrs. Peterson had all gone to bed, Daisy snuck down to her grandmother's office in her slippers and pajamas. The first thing she did was switch off the feed from the wall camera, so that anyone looking for her grandmother wouldn't be able to see into the room. Then she locked the door, turned on the desk lamp, and slid into her grandmother's comfy leather chair. It didn't take long to find the correct folder. Out of the fifteen spies living in the mansion, only half were on active cases. She flipped open the one labeled **Life Is Sweet?** and began to read.

GOAL OF THE ASSIGNMENT:
Obtain a sample of the Candymaker's secret ingredient.

NAME OF SPY ASSIGNED TO THE CASE:
Daisy.

TIME ALLOTTED:
Three days (annual contest).

CLIENT:
Second Enterprises

Daisy held up the paper. *Second Enterprises?* What did that mean?

She flipped through the rest of the file. Mostly it was a duplicate of the one she'd been given, complete with the photos and layout of the factory, along with a brief history. No more info on the client. Not even a phone number. Her grandmother must keep that on her computer. As curious as she was, she'd never go so far as to hack into it. She started to flip the folder closed, when a small square of paper fluttered out. It had been stuck to the back of another page. She bent to pick it up and saw that it was a copy of a hospital admittance form.

PATIENT: Logan Sweet

AGE: 5

REASON FOR ADMITTANCE: workplace accident. Burns on arms, hands, torso, left cheek.

RECOMMENDATION: medication for pain, compress wraps, balms, skin grafts at age 14.

DOCTOR: Vincent Orlando

Why hadn't this been included in her own file? Maybe her grandmother had thought it would upset her or make the assignment harder. She put everything back where she found it and leaned back in the chair. She might not know what Second Enterprises was or what exactly the client was after, but she did know one thing: anyone trying to steal a secret ingredient couldn't be up to any good. She'd have to make some alterations to her plan.

Fortunately, the library on the third floor of the mansion was always open. The shelves overflowed with books on every topic. If there had been more time, she would have been sent here to learn all she could about the art of candy-making in order to be more convincing in her role. She went straight to the section on foodstuffs, although it wasn't candy she was looking for now.

Eight hours later AJ's voice woke her up. "Want to explain this?"

She *really* had to remember to take the transceiver out of her ear before bed. Wait, she *had* taken it out! She rolled over and bonked her head on something hard. "Ow!" She reached up to rub her head, banging her elbow in the process. What was going on? She opened her eyes. The first thing she saw was that she was lying half underneath one of the library tables. The second was that AJ was standing above her, arms crossed.

"Uh, hi?" she said, sliding forward to avoid hitting herself again on the leg of the table.

"Don't *hi* me. You're up to something." He gestured to the books splayed open on the floor. The closest one had the title *Noxious, Foul-Tasting Foods and How to Cook with Them.* "And by the looks of it, I'd say sabotage! Poisoning another contestant's candy? That's low, even for you."

Daisy rubbed her eyes, forcing herself to focus. Her entire body hurt from sleeping on the hard floor. "Wait, what? I'm not trying to poison anyone. Why would I do that?"

"To win, I guess."

"You're way off," she said, getting to her feet.

"So tell me, then."

She shook her head. "I can't."

"Daisy, I'm your handler."

She straightened her pajamas. "That's why I can't tell you. You shouldn't have to take the fall with me."

He narrowed his eyes at her but didn't speak.

"How'd you find me here, anyway?"

"The twins went to your room to prep you, but you weren't there. They're very concerned."

Daisy looked up at the clock over the library door. "Ten minutes," she said, rushing past him. "I'll meet you out front."

"Make it five," he called after her.

With barely enough time to brush her teeth and wash her

face, Daisy couldn't worry about what to wear. She grabbed a pair of jeans, and since she knew the twins would complain that the pants weren't bright or girly enough, she added a purple shirt and mismatched socks. No pink, though, out of respect for Miles and his strange allergies. It took only a minute to gather the material she'd need to put her new plan into action. She pushed it down deep into her pocketbook, then stuck the tiny transceiver back in her ear. AJ must not have turned his on yet, because she couldn't hear him breathing.

AJ was waiting on the front step when she arrived. She looked up and down the driveway. "Where's your moped?"

"I'm not taking you today," he said, his mouth a thin, straight line.

"What? Why?"

"I'm pretty sure I know what you're doing, and you're right, I can't be a part of it. In fact, I should call your grandmother."

Daisy knew she couldn't blame him. She'd probably have felt the same way, even a week before. "How am I supposed to get there, then?"

He shrugged. "Ask one of the girls to drive you."

"But all the ones old enough have jobs today."

"Mrs. Peterson, then."

Daisy shook her head. "She'll know something's up."

"You're resourceful," he said, walking back into the house. "You'll figure it out."

Daisy tightened her ponytail and sat down on the steps to think. A low whinny came from the stables, and Daisy had her answer. She'd never ridden Magpie across town before, but she figured she knew the side streets and back roads well enough to make it without too much trouble.

She scribbled a note for anyone who might come looking for the horse and tacked it up in Magpie's stall. The other horses looked on as Daisy led Magpie to the water trough and then outside. She secured her bag to the saddle, adjusted the stirrups, and climbed on.

The ride took a lot longer on horseback than on AJ's moped, but she made it to the factory without incident. She had hoped to slip in unnoticed, but Miles and Logan were right outside the front door. Nothing to do but keep going. As she pulled up she heard a click in her ear followed by *"Okay, okay, I can't very well abandon you. I still don't approve of your taking matters into your own hands, but I won't let you go alone."*

"Thanks," she whispered without moving her lips.

"Leave Magpie in the barn, and I'll come get her later. Enter the factory through the tunnel—it will give you a chance to get familiar with the layout."

"Roger that," she whispered, then greeted the boys. Five minutes later, she left Magpie happily chomping hay in the barn and ducked into the tunnel. The temperature was at least ten degrees cooler in here. She could see why they'd use it to store the freshly harvested ingredients.

She'd only gone a few feet when she heard AJ again.

"Hide!" he yelled.

Without turning to look back at the entrance, she dove behind a large pile of recently harvested peppermint leaves. She knew they were peppermint because she immediately felt like brushing her teeth. "How come you can see me?" she whispered.

"I'm up a tree in the front yard."

"Why exactly are you in a tree?"

She could hear the rustling of leaves as he shifted on a branch. *"I wanted to make sure you got here okay. Sure took you long enough, by the way. What did you do, walk Magpie here?"*

This wasn't the time to explain about horse hooves and paved streets and traffic, so she didn't reply. Through gaps in the peppermint leaves she could see workers bringing in barrels of milk and buckets of grain and cartons of eggs. This went on for a few more minutes before the coast appeared to be clear. *"Two men in suits are coming into the tunnel. They're wearing visitor's badges. Stay put."*

She ducked lower. She couldn't see them, but she could hear them clearly. "Great place he's got here," one man said to the other. "Wonder how much it's worth."

The other whistled. "Who could put a price tag on it?"

"Big Billy could!" They both laughed at that, shuffled around a bit, and headed back outside. Their words faded, and Daisy had to strain to hear.

"I have to meet with Mrs. Sweet now to go over some arrangements for the convention," one of the men said. "I'll see you later in the Cocoa Room."

"Okay," replied the other. "Should be interesting."

"I'll say!"

Then the voices died out. She rose from her hiding place and pulled a few sprigs of peppermint from her hair. Who was Big Billy? Could he be the man behind Second Enterprises? If those men had gotten visitor's badges, that meant they had access to the factory. It sounded like they knew the Candymaker and his wife. Could they be planning to steal the secret ingredient from right under the Candymaker's nose?

Didn't the client trust her to do her job?

Every spy comes up against this situation now and again — clients who pay good money, then think they can do the job better on their own. It was very frustrating, and it totally messed up her plan. Not only did she still have to obtain a sample of the secret ingredient, she had to do it before they did or lose her credibility.

"Are you thinking what I'm thinking?" she asked AJ as she made her way around all the barrels and cartons to get to the door that led to the factory.

"Are you thinking about a ham and cheese on rye? With a pickle?"

"No."

"Then no, not the same."

She sighed. "I'm thinking this Big Billy character is the client who hired us. Maybe he's a rival candymaker and he's trying to get the secret ingredient for his own factory."

"Anything's possible, I guess. I'll do some research and get back to you."

"Okay." Daisy knocked one more leaf off her shoulder before pushing open the door at the end of the tunnel. She found herself in a corridor she hadn't seen before and stood for a moment trying to decide which way to go. AJ's blueprint would have been helpful, had she remembered to get it from him instead of falling asleep on the library floor.

The nearest door suddenly swung open, missing her nose by mere inches. An elderly man backed out, wheeling a Pepsicle cart behind him. Frost covered the sides of the cart.

"Oh, I'm sorry, young lady," he said, catching sight of her. "Didn't see you there. Are you lost?"

She put on her friendliest smile and said, "Yup! Can you tell me which way to the lab?"

He gave her the directions and asked, "Would you like a Pepsicle?"

"My friend Magpie loves these," she gushed, accepting the one he held out to her. AJ laughed. *"Leave it by the door and I'll bring it to her. But I'm doing this for her, not you."*

The Pepsicle man strode away, pushing the cart and whistling. Daisy left the frozen treat by the door and hurried off to the lab. As she reached the door, AJ said, *"It's more important than ever to keep up the act."*

Daisy found it funny that with all he knew, AJ would think she was just acting as if she cared about being there. Fortunately, the others were too mesmerized by all the cool things Max had set up in the center of the room to notice her delay. Who wouldn't be captivated by the spongy appearance of the insides of the jelly beans and the Oozing Crunchoramas?

She stifled a laugh when Max gave Philip the cup of sugary red liquid and he tossed the whole cup at the machine. He seemed truly shaken up by the incident. It was the first time he'd shown any emotion other than annoyance. It didn't last long, of course, but it showed he was human.

"Ready to dress those Crunchoramas, Daisy?" Max asked, handing her a container of chocolate with a funnel at the end.

"Now?"

"Good a time as any," he replied.

She nodded, took a deep breath, and began to pour the chocolate into the top of the machine. A simple thing, but something happened when she did it. She suddenly became a real part of the candymaking process. She watched as the chocolate looped through the tubes, then flowed along a flat surface until it cascaded over the edge, creating a chocolate waterfall so smooth and shiny she could see her reflection in it.

The candy moved along underneath, each piece emerging cloaked in chocolate. She watched in awe as a blast of cold air made a perfect S pattern on top of each piece.

During the course of an ordinary day, she never got to actually *create* anything. But doing this, making candy, it felt as if a little bit of herself—her *real* self—had become a part of that chocolate. She'd had the same feeling stretching taffy the day before, only she hadn't been able to put it in words.

She understood now why everyone at the factory seemed so happy. They weren't just making candy. They were *making candy*. How could Big Billy or anyone else want to take that away from them? This place was worth protecting at any cost.

Nowhere was this more apparent than when the Candymaker himself walked in. He and his wife had a kind of *glow* to them. They radiated the same kind of energy that Logan did. When Mrs. Sweet told them other candymakers would be visiting the factory that day, Daisy knew her suspicions had been correct. These men were definitely rival candymakers, and they were up to no good.

"Don't even think *about telling her,"* AJ warned.

She had to remind herself that even though AJ couldn't read her mind, he could still tell what she was thinking. She'd never tell Mrs. Sweet the truth and risk destroying her grandmother's entire organization. She'd just have to hope her plan worked. And for her plan to work, she needed to get to that tin before they did.

She was trying to figure out if she should use the bathroom excuse again when Max dismissed them all to go do research. She pretended to walk toward the Taffy Room, then doubled back to the Cocoa Room once Miles and Logan were out of sight. Ugh. The two men in suits were already in there, joking with the Candymaker. The poor man didn't suspect a thing. Daisy took a deep breath, put on a smile, and entered the room.

"Hi!" she said, as cheerily as she could muster. "Mind if I watch a little bit?"

"Not at all," the Candymaker boomed. "Fellas, this is one of the lucky contestants in the contest tomorrow."

"Wonderful, congratulations!" they replied in unison, then laughed.

"We've been working together too long," the older of the two explained. That elicited a round of laughter from all three men.

"He's my dad," the younger one explained.

"Ah, I see the resemblance," Daisy said, not seeing it at all. The father was round, like the Candymaker, while the son was tall and thin and shaped kind of like a bowling pin.

"So, young lady, what's it like going up against the Candymaker's son?" the older man asked. "After all, he's got some mighty big footsteps to follow in."

"Hey, my feet aren't *that* big!" the Candymaker said, raising his leg to show them a surprisingly ordinary-sized foot.

This got them all laughing again. Daisy looked from one man to the other. They must be very good actors, because they didn't seem like the kind of men to double-cross a friend. And it was clear they were friends with the Candymaker. Maybe Big Billy had given them no choice. "You guys are visiting from another candy factory?"

"That's right," the older man said. "Although ours isn't anywhere near as grand as this."

"Ah," said the Candymaker, "but you make the best nougat I've ever tasted."

"Must be that secret ingredient we sprinkle on at the end," the bowling-pin son said, nudging his dad. This started them all laughing again.

"Certainly a jolly bunch," AJ muttered.

Daisy agreed. Joking about the secret ingredient? These guys had nerve!

"Doesn't look like they're going anywhere soon," AJ said. *"Come meet me outside. I did a little research."*

"Well, see you all later," Daisy said.

"That's it?" the Candymaker asked. "Don't you want to watch us whip up a new batch?"

"Aw, let her go," the son said. "Who'd want to hang around us boring old guys when she could play with the other kids?"

Daisy gave a weak smile. Of course he'd be trying to kick her out. Fewer witnesses. She lingered by the door to make sure the Candymaker didn't leave them alone in there.

When it was clear that all three men were staying put, she hurried down to the cafeteria, where she left a note for Miles and Logan telling them not to wait for her. A good spy always has good manners.

She met AJ outside on a bench by the pond. If anyone asked, she'd say he was her cousin, and he'd come to pick up the horse. He handed her a ham and cheese on rye.

"I should have guessed," she said, taking a big bite. She hadn't eaten since dinner the night before and probably could have eaten the bark off the trees in the Tropical Room at that point.

"I did a little research on the visiting candymakers," AJ said. "They seem legit. Worst thing either of them has ever done is ignore a parking ticket."

"Phreeally?" Daisy asked, her mouth full of sandwich. She swallowed. "Even the one who looks like a bowling pin?"

"How can someone look like a bowling pin?"

"You know, long neck, thick legs. A bowling pin!" Daisy dug into her sandwich again.

"Yes," AJ said with a sigh that meant he was only barely tolerating her. "Even that one. I did find the name Billy Foster though, who could be the Big Billy they were talking about. He's the owner of the candy company **Mmm Mmm Good**."

"Your sandwich is that good?" Daisy asked, looking down at her own. "I mean, mine's okay, but nothing to go on about."

He sighed. "Very funny. **Mmm Mmm Good** is the name of Billy's company."

"I know. Just trying to lighten the mood. So these two guys work for him?"

AJ shook his head. "I can't find a connection. I'll keep looking. But I think at this point you need to tell me exactly what you're planning."

Daisy swallowed and nodded. "I'm going to mix something that tastes really bad into the secret ingredient. Then, whatever the client is planning to do with it, it'll backfire on him."

AJ didn't say anything for a full minute, and Daisy began to squirm. Now that she had said her plan out loud, it sounded like what it was — sabotage. Of their own client! "Am I crazy to do this?" she whispered.

"Yes."

Daisy's face fell. "Don't you even want to think about your answer first?"

He chuckled. "You really care about this place, don't you?"

She nodded and returned a wave from Fran the taffy maker, who had settled on a nearby blanket. Softly, so that Fran couldn't hear, she said, "Everyone here is so happy. They love their jobs. And being here, I don't know, I feel like a part of something. Don't get me wrong. I love what we do. It's just that I don't ever feel that way normally, you know, going from one job to the next, always pretending to be someone else."

AJ nodded. "I know what you mean about this place. I was watching the Candymaker's son and that kid with the backpack before you arrived this morning. They seemed so normal. I kind of envied them. And you know, with Logan's, um, condition, you wouldn't think he'd be someone to envy."

"Exactly!" Daisy said. "That's what I mean about him. There's something inside him that just erases everything on the outside."

They sat there for a minute, watching the boats bob on the water. Out of the corner of her eye Daisy saw a flash of black, yellow, and red fly past the bench and out toward the water. She didn't know butterflies could fly so quickly. It made her want to be up and running through the fields or riding Magpie. She watched the butterfly skim over the water until Fran approached and blocked her view.

"Hi, Daisy! And who's this handsome young man?"

Snapping back to attention, she joked, "Well, I don't know about *handsome,* since he's my cousin. His name is Bo."

Fran extended her hand, and instead of shaking it, AJ kissed the back of it.

"Oh!" Fran giggled. "Nice to meet you, Bo. Your family must be very proud of Daisy. She's the best taffy stretcher I've seen in years."

"Oh, we are! We're very proud of our little Oopsa." AJ put his arm around Daisy's shoulder and squeezed.

"And she lights up a room, doesn't she?" Fran asked.

"That she does, that she does."

"Well," Daisy said, standing. She was eager to end this exchange. "I better get back. I don't have much more time to create my contest-winning candy."

"I hope you'll consider putting taffy in it," Fran said.

"Absolutely!" Daisy promised.

AJ rose, too, and they started back toward the factory. "So I'm Cousin Bo now? That's the best you could come up with?"

"I think the name suits you," Daisy replied, tossing her sandwich wrapper into a nearby garbage can.

"Yeah, if I pulled motorcycles with my teeth, maybe."

Daisy laughed, then grew serious. "AJ, are we, you know, trapped in our jobs? I mean, this is all we've ever done. Do you sometimes want to just be a normal guy, go to a real school, that sort of thing?"

He shook his head. "I love traveling all over and meeting all kinds of people. Next year I'll go off to college, and after that, right back to Spring Haven. This is what I'm good at. And as much as it pains me to admit it, you're very good at it, too. You just have to find a way to make it work for you, where you're comfortable. You can't take a job and then sabotage it."

Daisy nodded. "I know. It's just that this time is different. I feel the closest to the real Daisy here." She lowered her head. "Not that I even know who that is."

"What do you mean?" he asked.

"I don't even know my last name," she whispered.

"It's Dinkleman."

Daisy stopped short. *"What?"*

"Your last name. It's Dinkleman."

Her jaw fell open. "I'm *Daisy Dinkleman?*"

"No, I was just kidding. I have no idea."

She punched him in the arm.

"Ow!" he said, rubbing it. "You don't know your own strength."

"Yes," she assured him, "I do."

"Okay, to make up for kidding you about your name, I'll tell you a real secret that you should probably know."

They were at the back door now and stepped to the side so others could get past.

She narrowed her eyes. "For real?"

"For real." He took a deep breath. "When you were three years old, your parents were stuck in Italy on a job during your birthday, so everyone agreed not to tell you it was your birthday. You were too young to notice anyway. The following year, when you turned four, you thought you were turning three. No one had the heart to correct you and tell you about the missing birthday."

Daisy stared in disbelief. "I missed a birthday? That means I'm ... *thirteen?*"

He nodded. "Yup. A full-fledged teenager."

"You are KIDDING me!"

"I kid you not."

She fumed. "But why didn't they tell me after all this time?"

He shrugged. "Spies aren't known for being honest. Maybe they weren't ready for *Daisy Dinkleman, Teenage Girl.*"

She kicked him.

"Hey! What's with the violence?"

She crossed her arms. "I'm a teenager, right? We're famous for being moody and lashing out at those closest to us."

He followed her inside the factory, limping. "I'm sorry I even told you."

"Why did you?"

"I don't know," he admitted. "This place has me all mixed up."

"You probably shouldn't come in," she said, reaching out to keep the door from closing. "I want to see if the Cocoa Room is empty, and I don't want to have to introduce everyone to Cousin Bo."

He nodded and slipped back outside. Before the door closed, he pulled a small white flower from the closest bush and tossed it to her. "Happy third birthday."

She shoved it into her pocket and turned away. *Thirteen!* Her parents would have a *lot* of explaining to do when they returned from wherever they were.

The candymaking machines were all running at full force, and Daisy couldn't help stopping to sniff the air outside each room she passed. The smell of chocolate from the Cocoa Room was, not surprisingly, the strongest of all. She was dismayed to find not only Steve and Lenny in the room but the bowling-pin candymaker as well. Squaring her shoulders, she ducked her head in and said, "Hey, guys! Want me to watch the place again while you go eat?"

"No, thanks," Lenny said, holding up a hot dog. "We're all set."

"Oh, okay. I'll see you later, then." She stepped back out to the hall, letting the door swing shut in front of her. At least she could assume that if the visitors were indeed trying to get the secret ingredient, they hadn't done so yet. Otherwise they wouldn't still be hanging out in the room.

A few minutes later, she entered the lab, only to duck back out again. She checked the sign next to the door. CANDY LABORATORY. Yup, this was the right place. But somehow, during the time she'd been out, walls had grown up around each person's station.

Tentatively, she pushed the door open. The whole room

looked different, like an office in some busy company. She'd miss seeing everyone's faces. Well, almost everyone's.

Voices drifted from Philip's station. "But how will I keep it in the right shape?"

"You're going to have to form them by hand for now," Max said. "It would take too long to make a mold."

She couldn't believe it! Philip had actually asked for help! She stood there in amazement until Logan and Miles arrived. As annoying as it was to be closed off from the others, Daisy had to admit she could use the privacy.

Her pocketbook vibrated a little while later, and she was grateful for the thick walls. She pulled out her comm device and opened it. Grammy's face popped up from her home office.

"Oh, hi, Grammy," Daisy said in a tentative whisper. She wasn't prepared for the wave of guilt that ran through her when she saw that cheery smile. Daisy quickly scanned what she could see of her grandmother's desk to make sure she had left everything exactly as she'd found it. Looked good.

"Hi, honey. Is this a safe time?"

Daisy nodded, holding the book up in front of her face in case anyone peeked in. "We just have to be really quiet. When did you get back?"

"Just a few minutes ago," Grammy whispered. "I ran into the twins, and they said you weren't in your room this morning. Is everything okay?"

Daisy nodded again. "I was in the library doing research. You know, on candy stuff." At least that wasn't exactly a lie.

Her grandmother laughed softly. "You sound like you're actually planning on participating in the contest."

Daisy blushed but didn't know how to answer. *Was* she really planning on entering?

"Surely you'll have completed your mission before then. You know our motto: get in, get it done, get out."

"I know, Grammy."

"Daisy!" Max said, peering over the side of her cube. "Do I need to take that book away? It's for your own good."

"No, sir," she said. She mouthed a goodbye to her grandmother and slipped the book back into her bag.

Max smiled his approval and moved on. Whether or not she went through with the contest, she needed to make it look like she was working on something. She spread out all the ingredients and equipment and started playing. Add a dab of cream, a spritz of lime, a tablespoon of maple-flavored nougat, a dribble of caramel, two marshmallows, and voilà! A green glob of goop!

She tore off a small chunk and tasted it. Not bad. It had a nice feel to it, smooth, but thick. Still, something was clearly missing. She stuck her hands in her pockets to think. Her fingers touched something soft, and she pulled out the flower AJ had tossed her earlier.

"Hey, Max!" she called out. "C'mere."

"You bellowed?" Max asked, appearing at her side.

Daisy held up the flower. "Is this edible? I wouldn't want to poison the judges."

"That would not go over well," Max agreed. "Your flower

is fine. Most flowers are actually edible. A little goes a long way, so you wouldn't want to overpower your —" He glanced down at her tabletop. "Your uh ... whatever that is. I have a book in the back that will teach you how to prepare it."

For the next two hours Daisy worked on perfecting her candy and checking on the status of the Cocoa Room. Every time she went there, people were going in and out. A few times she passed Philip in the hall, either coming from somewhere or heading somewhere, she couldn't tell. Once he almost looked as if he were going to say something to her, but then he turned away and pretended to be fascinated with the statue of the first Candymaker.

AJ had kept quiet most of the afternoon, but after Daisy's third failed trip to the Cocoa Room, he said, *"I think you're just going to have to get it after the factory closes."*

"I think you're right," she said, ducking into a bathroom to talk. "I don't really want to go home, though. I'm afraid my grandmother's going to figure it out somehow."

"You've got to tell her eventually."

"I know. Just not yet."

"Well, where are you going to go, then?"

"I could hide in that storeroom I found yesterday. With the rubber ducks. "

"Too risky. You need to make sure people see you leave. I'll pick you up in one of the cars. We'll walk around town or something."

"Roger that," she said. The door of the bathroom swung

open, and one of the candymakers from the S'mores Room came in.

"Daisy!" she said. "How's it going? Are you excited about tomorrow? The convention is always a great time."

"I'm totally excited!" Daisy replied.

"I'll be there, too. All of us in the S'mores Room are rooting for you."

"Thanks! I'll see you then."

AJ laughed. When she was safely out in the hall she said, "What's so funny?"

"Daisy, you're not going to that contest. Once you have the secret ingredient and you've done your diabolical deed, your job is over."

"I'll see you out front at five" was all she said.

At 8:00 P.M. sharp, Daisy slipped through the door that connected the tunnel to the factory. She withdrew the wax key she'd made and pushed it into her front pocket. "I'm in," she whispered to AJ, who was hiding back up in his tree. "Like I said before, all I'll need is twenty minutes to get in, do what I need to do, and get out." She patted her back pocket, where she'd stored the foul-tasting ingredient in a small plastic bag.

"That's all well and good, but I'm still mad at you for telling those kids I pull motorcycles with my teeth."

She laughed. "I thought we settled that over hot dogs in the park! I explained I was getting you back for making me pretend to be mute for two weeks."

"But that was seven years ago!"

"I have a long memory. Now can we move on, please? Did the car leave yet?"

"Yes. Miles's parents are out of the driveway. Give Mrs. Sweet ten minutes to get back to the apartment before moving."

She pressed herself against the cool limestone wall, waiting for her eyes to adjust to the near darkness. She had her pen with her, which would illuminate the entire place if she switched it on. But that was only for emergencies, since it was bright enough to be seen from miles away. She rarely needed to use it, since all the spies in the mansion had been trained from early on to have excellent night vision. It only took her a minute to expand her pupils well enough to see.

"Okay," AJ said. *"Get moving, but stay close to the walls."*

She crept down the hall, her sneakers making no sound. The factory felt so different at night. She hadn't realized how noisy it was until the machines weren't running. Occasionally she'd pass a room where a fan rotated overhead or a heating unit clicked on or off, but that was pretty much it. The air still smelled sweet, though.

She reached the Cocoa Room and smiled. Finally! No one moved inside the room. Not Steve. Not Lenny. Not the Candymaker or his visitors or any of the zillion people who seemed to spend their day going in and out of that room.

She slipped inside, nearly knocking over a pile of bean pods. Why would someone leave those right by the door? She steadied them and was about to move away when she heard noises out by the fountain. She quickly crouched behind a table. "Someone's out there," she whispered. "What if it's one of the visiting candymakers?"

"Stay down," he instructed. *"It's probably a janitor or a night watchman."* A minute later he asked, *"Do you still hear anyone?"*

"No."

"Okay, keep moving, then."

Staying low, Daisy began to creep down the long room. She'd gotten about halfway to the cabinet when the door swung open and a figure rushed in with a very weak flashlight. Not two steps later she heard a crash. Whoever it was must have tripped right over the cocoa pods. She wanted to laugh but didn't dare. Too many machines separated the two of them, so she couldn't see who it was. After a minute, she heard the person repile the pods.

She just had time to slide under a table as the person ran by her. All she could see was a pair of dirty sneakers. Man-sized sneakers. Okay, so she knew it was a man. She didn't dare peek out to see his face, but judging by how quickly he moved, it probably wasn't the older of the two visiting candymakers. Whichever one it was, he knew what he was looking for.

"Everything okay?" AJ asked. *"I can't hear you breathing."*

Daisy let out the breath she'd been holding, knowing

he'd be able to pick up the sound. She couldn't risk answering.

"Okay, at least I know you're alive. I'll assume you're no longer alone. Don't do anything rash. Stay hidden."

But she couldn't. She had to see this to its end. Ever so quietly, she began to crawl forward again, so low she was practically swimming across the floor. Squeaky-clean floors or not, she was going to need a long bath after this. She had to take the long way around the room in order to stay as close as possible to the tables without bumping them. The guy couldn't know she was there until she wanted him to. Just as she thought it, her knee landed on something squishy that let out the tiniest of squeaks. She held her breath, but miraculously, the flashlight didn't turn in her direction.

She pushed aside the squeaky thing and was only a few feet away from the figure when he suddenly turned toward the long window and shone the flashlight out into the entryway.

Amateur, Daisy thought. All he'd be able to see was his own reflection.

Time slowed as the faint flashlight beam turned back toward the cabinet.

Why wasn't he opening the cabinet? Watching him stand there for what felt like minutes was almost unbearable. Finally, he yanked at the cabinet door, only to find it locked. Judging by the loud groan he emitted, this was as surprising to him as it was to her. He pulled at the door again, but it remained firmly closed.

Daisy allowed herself to hope that perhaps he'd give up and leave. No such luck. She saw him dig into his pocket and pull out some sort of pouch. He used a short, skinny tool to open the cabinet door. Laying the pouch down on the counter, he reached up and pulled out the tin from the top shelf. The time had come.

She sprang to her feet just as the flashlight beam shone directly in her eyes.

"Looking for this?" He held up the tin.

At first she was unable to see anything, since the light, which no longer seemed so weak, had momentarily blinded her. Perhaps this guy wasn't such an amateur after all. But it took only a few seconds for her eyes to adjust.

Standing before her, his hand shaking ever so slightly, was the last person she expected to see. For what felt like an eternity, they stared at each other. AJ kept talking in her ear, asking what was going on, but she couldn't focus on him.

In her head, she counted down: *five . . . four . . . three . . . two . . . one.*

Then she leapt.

PART FOUR

PHILIP

CHAPTER ONE

Philip had been awake for hours by the time his two alarm clocks rang. In fact, he had hardly slept all night. He'd been waiting for this day for years. Literally *years*. Ever since the day they kicked him out of the factory, he'd been looking for a way back in. Turned out all he had to do was turn twelve. Well, turn twelve *and* gain entry to the contest. He knew his essay would get him accepted. His English teacher once told him he could persuade an Eskimo to eat ice cream in the middle of winter.

Then there was the small matter of making sure **Life Is Sweet?** was chosen to host some of the contestants before the contest. But that truly *was* a small matter. Philip only had to throw his dad's name around and pull a few strings. And now, in a few hours he'd be strolling through that huge wooden door like he owned the place.

As he slipped on his freshly pressed suit, he couldn't help thinking that after the contest he would go to his father's tailor and have a whole closetful of suits made just for him. This one had belonged to his brother, Andrew, who had outgrown it long ago and had left it behind when he went off to college. It didn't fit quite right in the shoulders, but he doubted any of the other contestants would know how a suit was supposed to fit.

Dad always said that success was the best revenge. But Philip believed that revenge itself was the best revenge. And winning this contest would be *excellent* revenge. Plus, as a bonus, he'd get to prove he could win a contest that his brother hadn't won. Andrew hadn't even *entered* when he was twelve. Andrew never missed the chance to win anything, so he must have been unaware of its existence.

Philip gave his tie a final tug and turned toward his shelves. Even though he kept his windows firmly closed, dust and pollen and dander and who-knows-what other tiny particles were constantly landing on his trophies. He gave them a quick polishing with the cloth he kept on his desk.

To Philip, the outdoors existed only as a means of getting from one indoor place to another. Outside was either too bright, too hot, or too cold. He knew there had been a time when he hadn't felt that way, when he and Mom and Andrew would play in the grass for hours. But Philip preferred to look at the past only as a way to motivate himself in the present, not as a source of nostalgia. Looking back only kept a person trapped.

Once he won the contest, he'd finally be able to put that humiliating day at the factory behind him. To achieve true greatness, he'd have to plant his feet firmly in the here and now and focus his head on the future.

Or at least that's what Andrew had told him when he left for college last year. His brother had left him with those words of wisdom, the suit, his old briefcase, and a secret.

Actually, it wasn't much of a secret. Philip had known it for years. In fact, it was thanks to Andrew keeping such accurate records of his secret that Philip had won many of his awards and trophies. His brother believed that it was better to hide something in plain sight than to lock it inside a hidden box.

Philip disagreed. To him, hiding something in plain sight simply meant it wasn't hidden at all and therefore was fair game. That's how he'd first stumbled across his brother's notebook. When he flipped it open, he figured he'd see notes from class or perhaps an article Andrew was writing for his school paper. Instead, he found detailed instructions on Andrew's methods for cheating and lying his way through every contest he'd ever participated in. The classic bait and switch. Subtle distractions at precisely timed moments. Breaking and entering, lock picking, bribery. Sabotage.

When Andrew officially handed off the notebook, Philip had to pretend he'd never seen it before. Years of putting his brother's techniques to use had prepared him well for this lie. Andrew assured Philip that the end justified the means. His goal had been to get into one of the world's most prestigious universities, and he'd done it. He no longer needed the book.

Philip had graciously accepted the gift and hidden it in a locked box in his lower dresser drawer. He still consulted it every once in a while, but he had his own notebook now. Although what he wrote in it was quite different, his notebook contained even greater secrets than his brother's.

"We leave in five," Reggie called from the hallway.

"My father's taking me," Philip replied, checking his reflection one more time. He adjusted his collar, then opened the door.

Reggie, his father's longtime driver/bodyguard/assistant, finished tying one black patent leather shoe and rose slowly. Reggie always dressed impeccably. Philip's father insisted on it. As one of the most successful businessmen in the state, his father believed that everyone around him should reflect his success.

Philip glanced down at his own shoes, an old brown pair that didn't really match his suit. He hoped the other contestants were as ignorant about shoes as he believed they'd be about suits.

Reggie shook his head. "Your dad's in a meeting. You're stuck with me again." He held up the limo keys and jiggled them.

With his graying hair and bad back, Reggie was now less of a bodyguard and more of a babysitter. Although neither of them would ever dare use the word.

"What a surprise," Philip grumbled, picking up his briefcase.

"Nice suit," Reggie said, the corners of his mouth twitching. "Didn't your brother wear that to his middle-school graduation? I bet your dad would have spotted you a new one."

Philip didn't reply. He'd actually asked for a new suit, but his father said he was growing so fast it didn't make sense. Philip had been annoyed but figured at least it meant his dad had noticed he was growing.

"Seriously," Reggie said, "why are you wearing that?"

Philip still didn't answer.

Reggie began to whistle, then moved on to inspecting his fingernails.

"Oh, all right," Philip snapped. "Look at me like you don't know me."

Reggie stepped back, sizing him up.

"I look sophisticated, wouldn't you say?"

Reggie tilted his head. "I suppose one might say that."

"I look important. Like someone not to be messed with."

"Sure, okay."

"Well, that's why I'm wearing it."

Reggie turned toward the stairs. "So much for you making any new friends today."

Philip started to follow, but then the battle that raged inside his head every time he ventured into the outside world began. *Just leave it at home! But I need it. No, you don't! Yes, I do!* The struggle kept his feet glued to the hardwood floor.

"Oh, just get it," Reggie said, turning around. "You know you're going to in the end."

Philip threw him a withering look, then darted back inside his room, tugged the notebook out from under the mattress, and slipped it into his briefcase. He didn't meet Reggie's eyes on the way down to the kitchen, where the maid handed him his breakfast wrapped in a paper towel. He kept his eyes straight ahead as they climbed into the car.

He hated that Reggie knew his secret. He supposed it was inevitable, though. Reggie had been a constant shadow since the day his mother died, when he was three.

Philip had just turned eight when Reggie caught him. He thought he was alone in the spare room behind his father's study. He had discovered the room a year before and had gone there often. The small room was filled with his mother's old stuff — art supplies and gardening books and an old violin. He hadn't known any of it even existed. He didn't remember her ever making art or growing flowers or playing a violin. He didn't remember much about her at all, which suited him just fine. You can't miss what you don't remember having in the first place.

That day he'd just finished playing Air on the G String by Bach (which he had taught himself on his mother's violin) when a sniffling sound led him to the back hallway. He found Reggie leaning against a bookshelf, tears running down his face.

Before he could ask if something terrible had happened, Reggie took Philip's hands and told him he had a gift, a real gift. Something that came from deep inside the soul.

Philip, of course, didn't believe in souls or any other spiritual junk. Why should he? He'd certainly never seen any signs of it in his life. Truth be told, his "gift" embarrassed him. So what if Reggie had said he could play so well the gods would come down from heaven to listen? Or, as Reggie told him in later years when he heard him playing his own compositions, that he could write music as if the ghost of Mozart was whispering in his ear?

None of what Reggie said mattered, though. Philip Ransford the Third's path in life would not be making music. He would follow in his father's and brother's illustrious footsteps. He would go to a top college and business school, buy out companies, break them apart, and resell them for fun and profit. Yes, that would be his future. Not some crazy instrument made of wood.

And yet...he never seemed able to leave the house without his music notebook. He ate his egg sandwich in the back of the limo while Reggie tried to engage him in conversation.

"Big day for you, eh?" Reggie asked.

Philip didn't answer. He didn't feel like talking.

"I mean, heck, you've been waiting, what, five, six years?"

"Seven," Philip muttered.

"Seven years!" Reggie whistled. "That's a long time to hold a grudge."

Philip finished off his piece of toast and carefully wiped his mouth with his handkerchief. Tucking it back in his pocket, he said, "I've told you a hundred times. I'm not holding a grudge. I just want to get back at that kid for what he did to me."

"Oh, I see. That's different, then."

Reggie was being sarcastic, but Philip didn't really care.

He didn't expect anyone else to understand what he'd gone through.

They were in downtown Spring Haven now, only a few blocks from the factory. Reggie turned down a side street and parked. Philip glanced out the window. They were sitting outside **Miss Paulina's Candy Palace**. "Why did you stop here?"

Reggie turned around in his seat, swinging his arm over the back of it. He pointed to the store window. "You see this candy store?"

"Of course I see it."

"You can go in there anytime you want, right? Well, anytime it's open, I mean."

Philip rolled his eyes. They both knew he could get in whether it was open or not. "And your point is?"

"My point is, you can get all the candy you want a hundred different ways. Why is it such a big deal that you were kicked out of the factory?"

Philip didn't answer right away. He had to decide what to say and what to leave out. He hated being put on the spot. Finally he just said, "Because it was...humiliating. And unfair. Logan had *asked* to see the little plastic truck. It wasn't *my* fault he didn't catch it and it landed in the vat of chocolate and broke their stupid machine. Then he just stood there, watching it slide deeper into the vat while Dad dragged me out of the room."

He hated how whiny his voice sounded. This whole thing just brought out the worst in him. He'd be relieved when it was behind him.

Reggie clearly wasn't going to let it go so easily, though. "You expected the boy, only five years old, to stand up to *your* father?" he asked.

Reggie didn't have to say the rest. Philip knew he was thinking, *when* you *can't even stand up to him.*

He glanced at his watch in exasperation. "It's not that Logan didn't stand up to my father, it's that he didn't stand up to *his*. He just let the Candymaker pull Dad aside and tell him I wasn't welcome to come back. Logan just stood there, watching that stupid truck fall into the stupid chocolate."

Reggie stared at him, shaking his head slowly. "A lot of things can change in seven years, remember that."

Philip scowled. He knew a lot of things could change. He'd changed a lot himself. He'd grown much taller, his hair had darkened, and his freckles had disappeared, coming back only when he was forced to spend time in the sun.

He bore no resemblance to the boy he'd been at five, the one whose favorite day of the year had been the candy factory's annual picnic. The one who thought he'd finally made a friend.

He stared out at the candy store as they drove past it. He'd never been inside, not even once since it opened five years earlier. He hadn't eaten a single piece of candy since the day they kicked him out of **Life Is Sweet**. He'd tried a jelly bean at Easter once, but it tasted like sand and he spit it out.

They drove the rest of the way in silence. When they reached the front entrance of the factory, Reggie opened the car door for him. Philip brushed past him without a word. Let Reggie think what he would, Philip had every intention of following through with his plan to win the contest and humiliate the Candymaker's son. And he would use any means necessary.

A boy and a girl were watching him with curiosity from the front steps. Philip figured the boy must be Logan. His mind raced with all the things he wanted to say to him, but he knew he couldn't, not until he'd won the contest. The fact that he had received the invitation to the factory in the first place meant that they no longer remembered him. He needed to keep it that way. It would make everything much easier.

As he got closer, Philip realized with disappointment that this boy was much too small, his hair much too dark, to be Logan. He turned his attention to the girl, who stuck out her hand and said her name, which he only half heard. As he met her eyes, four thoughts ran through his head:

THOUGHT NUMBER ONE: *she's very pretty*.

THOUGHT NUMBER TWO: *she hates me already*.

THOUGHT NUMBER THREE: *same as number one*.

THOUGHT NUMBER FOUR: *the more people dislike you, the more they stay away from you and the more you can get away with*.

He hadn't really considered how he would act around his fellow contestants, how he would get the privacy he needed, but this girl — he couldn't remember her name, some kind of tree or flower — had made the decision for him. He would be as unpleasant as possible.

Daisy started making a fuss about not bothering Logan with something, but Philip had no idea what she was talking about. For the past seven years he had tuned out any news about the factory or its inhabitants. In his mind, Logan was still five years old, still staring into that vat of chocolate as the toy truck sank, although of course Philip knew that wasn't the case.

It didn't take long to get the other boy, Miles, to dislike him as well. All he had to do was tell him the truth about the afterlife, which really, no one but little kids (and perhaps Reggie) believed in anymore.

The longer they stood out there, the more eager he was to get things moving. Unable to wait any longer, he tried and failed to get inside the factory. This only made him more anxious, although it seemed to entertain the girl (Fern? Rose?).

His hand twitched with the need to pull out his notebook and jot down a scale or two, but he didn't want the others to see it. Instead he started arguing with Miles until the door finally swung open. "It's about time," he said, ready to step inside.

Then he looked up.

A lot could change in seven years, Reggie had said. True

words, as it turned out. Logan, whose face Philip still recognized, had most definitely changed. He guessed this was what the others had been referring to earlier. Logan began to recite some poem, which gave Philip a few seconds to gather himself. Whatever had happened to Logan didn't change what he had come there to do. Not at all.

And if he didn't look at Logan, not directly anyway, he could almost believe that.

• • • • • • • • • • • • • • • • • •

CHAPTER TWO

• • • • • • • • • • • • • • • • •

Philip tried to ignore the others as they oohed and aahed about the factory and its wonders. He couldn't take his eyes away from the Cocoa Room. *Here's where it all went down.* The machines had clearly been upgraded since he had seen them last, but he still recognized them. One of the workers popped out from behind the bean grinder and waved at Philip. He quickly turned around and rejoined the group before the guy could get a good look at him.

Daisy was reading the awards on the wall. *Time to ramp up the obnoxiousness.* He took a deep breath. Without looking directly at Logan, he said, "Must be a lot of pressure on you, huh? I bet your parents expect to see your name right here. Too bad you have to be up against me. I don't lose."

That did it. The others jumped right in to stand up for this kid whom they'd only met five minutes before. Too bad they didn't know that Logan would never show them the same loyalty. He would turn his back on them just as he had on Philip seven years ago.

Philip's dad always said people didn't change, they

just got taller. He doubted that a few scars had changed Logan.

He knew he couldn't let his guard down, so he continued to argue with Daisy, who honestly got prettier as her cheeks got pinker. She got so mad when he asked if her father was a carpenter that she swung her ponytail at him. The smell of flowers and fruit instantly filled his nose. Not entirely unpleasant.

When Daisy said her father was a violinist, all he could think to do was make fun of it as his grip tightened on his briefcase. The mere mention of the instrument had caused music to explode in his brain. He turned on his heel and saw the fountain with its bubbling chocolate right in front of him. He did the only thing he could think of to keep from reaching into his briefcase and grabbing his notebook. He reached into the fountain instead.

So warm. So soft. But instead of distracting him, the chocolate had the opposite effect. The feel of it on his hand made the notes pop into his head all the more. A line of melody he'd been working on for the last few months suddenly burst into his mind, fully formed and perfect. It would be futile to fight against it.

He wiped off his hand, announced something about the fountain being unsanitary, and grabbed his notebook. He wrote down the sequence of notes so he wouldn't forget them and slammed the cover shut before the others could see. It was bad enough that he was cursed with this; he certainly didn't intend to let any of *them* know about it. He needed to keep the upper hand.

Logan introduced Max Pinkus, and Philip recognized him right away. He considered ducking his head, but how could he do that for two whole days? His brother's words about hiding in plain sight came back to him. Might as well try that. So he stuck out his hand, put on his most polite voice, and prayed the man wouldn't recognize him and kick him out.

When that didn't happen, Philip breathed easier. If Logan and Max hadn't recognized him, the only ones left to worry about were Logan's parents. Hopefully they'd be too busy running the factory to pay much attention to the other kids.

Max began to talk about touring the factory, and before Philip could stop himself, he had pulled out his notebook again. His hand drew F-sharps and B-flats and quarter notes and, his favorite, eighth notes. He knew the others were watching, but his hand refused to quit moving across the page.

He hated the feeling of not being in control. He'd been working on this piece ever since he'd discovered the violin under a box of his mother's old summer clothes. It wasn't as if anyone was going to hear it performed—why did his brain insist on putting it down on paper? At school he was sure the other kids thought he was just taking notes. He didn't know what the kids here were thinking, but he hoped it was the same thing.

"There won't be a test on this," Max said.

Philip wrote the last note and stuck the pencil back inside the notebook. Why hadn't he just left it at home?

A few minutes later, Daisy disappeared to go to the bathroom, and Philip felt both relieved (not to have her glaring at him) and annoyed (he wanted to get this show on the road). If he had to wait for the group all the time, it was going to drive him crazy.

He leaned his forehead on the cool glass windows of the Cocoa Room and closed his eyes. He could remember standing on the other side of that very wall, just inches away from the machines.

"In the afterlife," Miles said, "no one has to use the bathroom."

Philip wanted to bang his head against the wall. What *was* it with this kid and the afterlife? Why couldn't he understand that when you left the party, you left for good?

Daisy finally came back with some excuse about getting lost. He doubted her story. She was probably scoping out the place, getting in good with the workers so they'd help her in the contest.

He tried to pay attention to Max's explanation of the chocolate-making process, but how could he concentrate with the Candymaker's son standing a few feet away from him, just as he had seven years earlier? Philip glanced over at Logan, who seemed totally absorbed in watching the process unfold, as though he hadn't seen it every day of his life. You'd think it would have lost some of its appeal.

He turned away quickly, not willing to linger too long on the scars. Better to ignore them, as Logan apparently did. In a way, he almost flaunted them, wearing short sleeves instead of long, pushing his hair back instead of letting it fall over the sides of his face.

Then Max told Daisy, "Ah, my dear. You have stumbled upon one of the Candymaker's few trade secrets."

Philip's ears perked up. He watched the worker place the tin back into the cabinet. If he could get his hands on whatever was in that box, he'd win the contest for sure.

"What's a trade secret?" Daisy asked.

Philip explained it, but what he really wanted to say was, *"I knew it! My brother was right! Girls can be pretty or smart, but not both."* He managed to keep that inside, though. Antagonizing her was one thing, but letting her know he thought she was pretty was another thing altogether. For a few seconds he allowed himself to plot how he'd sneak away from the group, slip into the room, and take some of the secret ingredient before anyone even knew he was missing.

He quickly realized that that would be totally unnecessary. The secret ingredient was already mixed into the chocolate he'd be using. That meant, of course, that the other three contestants from Spring Haven would all have the same advantage, which was annoying. But he wasn't too concerned. No way would their contest entry be better than his.

As Max led them to the Taffy Room, Philip had to work hard to keep from smiling. He'd done it! He was back at the factory on his own terms, walking the halls like he owned the place. If the others hadn't been there, he would have patted himself on the back.

Of course *Daisy* volunteered to stretch the taffy. She clearly wanted to get on everyone's good side and didn't care how obvious she was about it. As he watched her, something strange began to happen. A memory floated into his head that he hadn't seen before. He and his mother were sitting on a bench by a pond. She handed him a piece of warm taffy and said, "Try it. But make sure you chew really well before you swallow it."

"But it's purple," he had replied. He hadn't eaten anything purple up to that point.

She'd laughed and said, "Sometimes the best things look the strangest."

So he popped it into his mouth and chewed, as she'd said to do.

That was it. There wasn't any more to the memory.

When Max tossed him a piece of freshly made purple taffy, he quickly tossed it back. If he tried to eat it, he'd throw up.

Daisy practically launched herself at him. "Why would you want to create the world's best new candy if you don't even eat candy?"

He couldn't very well tell her the truth about why he was there. Or why he didn't want to eat that taffy. It was much easier to lie.

As fun as it was to upset Logan, Philip knew he needed to

get out of that room. The sickly sweet smell and the hostile glares and the ghost of long-ago taffy were just too much.

The hallway was better. He could breathe there. No one followed him, not that he'd expected anyone to. He was angry at himself for allowing himself to get so upset. He had to pull himself together. He faced the wall, using the shiny surface of the Taffy Room sign as a mirror to straighten his tie and smooth his hair.

"Are you all right, young man?" a woman asked.

Philip turned around, startled. He'd thought he was alone. The woman wore the same outfit as the rest of the employees, had the same dusting of sugar in her hair and splattering of chocolate on her apron, but he'd know her anywhere. Logan's mom. The Candymaker's wife.

He squared his shoulders. "I'm fine, Mrs. Sweet," he replied, then immediately wanted to bite his tongue for adding her name. He forced a smile. "Just getting some air."

"Are you one of the contestants?"

He nodded. "Philip."

Her cheery expression didn't change at the mention of his name. His pulse slowed back down again.

"You enjoying yourself so far, Philip?"

He nodded again.

She pulled a tissue out of her apron pocket. Quick as a whip, she leaned toward him and wiped the wetness from under his eye. He stepped back, horrified that he'd let his emotions get the better of him.

"Nice to meet you, Philip," she said, tucking the tissue

away. "I've got to go find out why the bags of Snorting Wingbats are coming off the line with fifteen wingbats instead of sixteen." She laughed. "Rough job, eh?"

He watched her dash down the hallway. If he saw her again, he would tell her he was allergic to something in the factory. What she'd seen was nothing more than his eye watering.

He could hear the others saying their goodbyes to the taffy workers. He took a deep breath and arranged his face into a mask of disinterest.

Daisy glared at him as the group filed out of the room. No one said anything, so he just fell into step. The rest of the tour was uneventful. In each room, the candymakers couldn't wait to show them their particular candy. *Smell how the peppermint and spearmint oils combine to make the Icy Mint Blobs so icy! See how the Some More S'mores have exactly the correct ratio of marshmallow to chocolate to cracker! Feel how the Oozing Crunchoramas ooze onto your tongue from tiny holes in the wafer-thin crust!*

He would smell and he would look, but he would not taste. Every ten minutes or so, he'd have to write down a few bars of his concerto. He knew what he needed to make his candy, and all this felt like a waste of time.

As they trudged to yet another candy room, Miles asked Max why they didn't hold tours anymore.

Philip, who had begun to tune out whenever Miles began to speak, almost missed Max's reply. The words *toy truck* reached his ears, and he stopped to listen. His eyes grew wide as Max explained that the truck had jammed up the machines and it had been really hard to fix.

"After that, we had to stop giving tours."

Daisy and Miles started to speak, but all Philip could hear was the voice in his head yelling, **IT WAS ME. I'M STANDING RIGHT NEXT TO YOU! IT WAS MY FAULT THEY STOPPED GIVING TOURS.** He forgot to breathe. He must have made some sort of gasping or choking sound, because everyone suddenly turned toward him.

Then the hiccups began. He couldn't get enough air into his lungs. Max brought him water, and he gulped it down. Finally, they stopped, leaving him spent. He'd sabotaged the factory, and he hadn't even realized it. It should have made him feel great. Why didn't it, then?

"Serves you right," Daisy whispered.

If she only knew! But she didn't know. None of them did. They didn't even ask why he had reacted that way. He started to feel hotter and hotter as they walked, although he did his best to ignore it. Had his choking fit given him a fever or something? Then he realized that everyone was sweating. Max pushed a button, sliding doors swished open, and he saw why.

A jungle inside a room! Tall, smooth trees with bright green and yellow leaves. Short trees with huge pods hanging from low branches. Bushes and grass and nuts and vines. The *outdoors* wasn't supposed to be *indoors*. It violated the whole natural order of things.

The room seemed to make his competitors do strange things. First Logan hugged a sticky, gooey gum tree, then Daisy hugged and sniffed a cinnamon tree, and later Miles looked like he was about to faint just because Max pulled a lever and the ceiling started to move. Honestly, the three of them were just no competition at all.

At this point, all he wanted to do was get to work, but no, some sort of crisis had arisen in the Bee Room that only Logan, apparently, could fix. This he had to see.

Not surprisingly, Miles was scared of the bees and didn't want to go in. That kid really had to get some backbone or he wasn't going to survive in this world, let alone the contest.

Philip was slightly annoyed to see that Daisy didn't look any less pretty wearing the silly goggles. If anything, it made her green eyes even brighter.

He kept to himself in the Bee Room, glad not to have anyone looking at him for a change. Miles had some sort of crisis over a butterfly, of all things. The boy was so easily distracted. He often had this faraway look on his face that made him seem like he was half here and half somewhere else entirely. Philip hoped he didn't look like that. It didn't inspire confidence.

Paulo, the bee guy, was yet another person who greeted Logan as if he were some kind of god, making him out to be this helpful, caring person, when anyone could tell he was a few cards short of a full deck. First Max, then all the workers in the candy rooms, Avery in the Tropical Room, and now

Paulo. They must all feel sorry for him because of the scars, and Logan milked it for all it was worth.

As he watched Logan pretend to care about helping the bees, a thought occurred to him. *Maybe the scars aren't even real.*

That idea was still churning in Philip's head when the group (minus Logan) entered the Marshmallow Room. He actually planned to pay attention here, because he intended to use marshmallows as part of his project. Max introduced them to Henry, the marshmallow maker.

Henry shook Daisy's hand first, then Miles's. Philip stuck his hand out, but Henry didn't take it at first. Instead he stared directly into Philip's eyes. It felt like hours, but was probably only a few seconds, before Henry finally shook his hand. No one else seemed to notice, but Philip knew exactly what had just happened.

Henry had recognized him.

CHAPTER THREE

P hilip inched away from Henry. The only place to go was toward a large steel kettle full of some bubbling yellow liquid. He could feel the heat rising from it.

"Wonderful to meet you all," Henry said, glancing back at Philip, who stopped inching. "Are you here to see how we make marshmallows? It's a fascinating process. I never tire of it."

"Not right now, Henry, ol' boy," Max said, checking the huge glass thermometer sticking out of the kettle. He gave a satisfied nod, then continued. "We just stopped by on our way to lunch to tell you to expect a fresh batch of honey. The bee problem has been dealt with."

"Excellent," Henry said, rubbing his hands together in excitement like a little kid who was told he could have another cookie for dessert.

"Would you like to join us for lunch?" Daisy asked. "Logan told us it's chocolate pizza day!"

Would the girl never stop? Why did she care if the marsh-mallow man liked her? Why'd she have to go and do that?

Philip shrank back even farther, until he was practically on top of the kettle.

"Careful there, son," Henry said, switching off the flame.

Philip scurried out of the way.

"Lunch sounds lovely," Henry said, placing the sticky thermometer in a bucket of water. "I never pass up chocolate pizza!"

Henry didn't even glance back at him as they all walked to lunch. Perhaps he was being paranoid. Maybe Henry just thought he looked like someone he knew. A grandson or something.

But that theory went out the window when Henry volunteered to stay behind with him in the cafeteria while he waited for some real pizza. The firmness of the hand clamped on his shoulder told Philip all he needed to know. Why couldn't he have just taken the chocolate pizza? He could have thrown it out and avoided this situation.

Henry guided him toward a small round table to wait. "Would you like a taste?" he asked, holding up a slice.

Philip glanced at the mixture of dark and light chocolate sauce, the melted marshmallow cheese, the flaky crust. He had to admit it looked delicious. But he knew it would taste like cardboard. He shook his head.

"Suit yourself," Henry said, taking a big bite.

Philip watched the others leave through the back door. He had thought he'd be happy to see them go, but now he'd give anything to be with them.

Among the many things Andrew's notebook had taught

him was that when you're cornered, you always make the first move. So he pushed his chair back, wincing at the scraping sound it made. "I should check on the pizza. I'll just wait up there if it's not ready."

Henry waved him back down.

Philip hesitated, then sighed and sat down again. This guy wasn't going to make it easy.

"Mary will bring it," Henry said. "Let's you and I get to know each other."

"What do you want to know?" Philip asked, hoping his voice wasn't shaking but fearing that it was.

Henry folded his napkin and laid it neatly beside him. "Well, for starters, I'd like to know why you came back after all this time."

"Um, I don't know what you mean." *Where was that pizza!*

"I never forget a face," Henry said.

Seriously. How long did it take to throw some tomato sauce and cheese on a slab of dough? Philip tried to recall what the notebook said to do if the first move failed. All he could remember was something about giving your opponent the silent treatment.

So he crossed his arms over his chest.

Henry waited for a minute and then began to eat his second slice. About halfway through, Mary showed up. She placed two paper plates on the center of Philip's empty tray with a steaming piece of pizza on each.

"Just one is fine," Philip told her, handing her back one of the slices.

She raised an eyebrow but took the plate.

"Looks good," Henry said.

Philip stood up. "I should go now. Er, thanks for waiting with me." He picked up his tray with one hand, his briefcase with the other, and turned to go.

Henry put down what was left of his last piece. "You don't want to talk?"

Philip shook his head. Nothing got past *this* guy.

Henry stood up as well. The unmistakable smell of marshmallows rose from him. Did the man bathe in them?

"If you don't want to talk, perhaps you'll agree to just listen."

Philip glanced at the door. "They're probably waiting for me."

"I always prefer to talk while working anyway," Henry said, picking up his own tray. "How about you come by early tomorrow morning before you meet the others. We'll go down to the pond. Pick us some mallow roots."

Going down to the pond to pick mallow roots with Henry ranked as the last thing Philip would ever want to do at any point, ever, even once. "Thanks for the offer," he said, "but I really don't think I —"

"Do come," Henry insisted. "It'll be fun. Wear tall rubber boots."

"I don't have tall rubber boots." Philip began walking toward the door the others had gone through.

Henry followed. "Logan keeps a spare pair in the Marshmallow Room. You can wear his. He wouldn't mind."

"Of course he wouldn't," Philip muttered.

"What's that?" Henry asked.

"Nothing," Philip said, pushing the door open with his hip only far enough to let him squeeze through.

"Okay, then," Henry called after him. "I'll meet you out front at seven o'clock."

The door swung shut. Philip groaned. Looked like he'd be picking mallow roots, whatever *they* were. He debated going back inside and telling Henry he couldn't possibly meet him that early, but he had a strong feeling the invitation wasn't optional.

He had no idea what Henry could want to talk to him about, but he was afraid that if he didn't go, Henry might decide to tell Logan what he knew. Philip had always intended for Logan to find out, but on *his* terms.

He looked around the huge lawn covered with red-and-white-checked picnic blankets. With the pond and rowboats in the background, the corn and wheat fields to the left, the perfect rows of blueberries and raspberries alongside the red barn, he felt like he'd walked into a postcard. The air smelled so...fresh. And clean.

He had only the vaguest memory of being out here before. He remembered that there was only one rubber duck left for the race and he let some other little kid have it. His mom had been proud of him then.

Max's bald head made him easy to spot. Philip just wanted to eat in peace, and he refused to get drawn into a stupid game of Name That Cloud. Unfortunately, when he saw the cloud out of the corner of his eye, four more measures of his concerto popped into his head. He put down his pizza. Nothing he could do except get it out of his head and onto paper.

He barely noticed when Logan and Miles left. He was still getting down the last few notes when Max said, "If you don't mind me asking, what is it you're always so intent on writing in that notebook of yours? Are you a budding young author, perhaps? Daisy loves to read, maybe the two of you could work on a story together one day."

"I do," Philip replied, not looking up.

"Sorry?" said Max.

"I do," Philip repeated, "mind you asking."

"Oh." Max chuckled. "I see. Well, I'll let you keep at it then."

But he had finished for now. "Can we go make some candy? The contest is in two days."

Max swallowed his last bite. "Go get Daisy, and we'll find the other boys."

He let Max take his tray for him, and headed over to Daisy. He hoped the grass wouldn't leave stains on the bottoms of his pant legs.

She was leaning against the tree trunk, her eyes closed. He watched her for a few seconds, wondering what she was thinking about. Probably girl stuff, like hair and makeup and boys. He'd heard girls in school whisper about which boys they thought were cute. Once or twice he'd heard his name mentioned, and he had to admit, it was a lot better than most things people whispered about him.

He wanted to tell her she looked pretty, with those wisps of blond hair flying free from her ponytail. Instead, he said, "Thinking about how you're going to lose on Saturday?"

She snapped at him, then stomped off with Max to find Logan and Miles.

Philip trailed behind. As much as he didn't enjoy being out in nature, he enjoyed being around Logan even less. He arrived at the row of low bushes to find everyone peering at something white dangling from a leaf. He bent for a closer look and then pulled back. It looked like something from a horror movie, like a mummy. Like something trapped. It gave him the creeps. He wanted to be far away from it.

The lab was a welcome change, with its temperature-controlled environment and stations for each of them to work at. It was a relief to have some breathing room from the others.

Since he already knew what candy he was going to make, Philip paid attention only when Max discussed things that could actually be of use to him. While the others were entertaining themselves by making things fizz and smoke (or, in Logan's case, boiling things till they overflowed), he was laying out the ingredients he'd need and experimenting with adding just the right amount of mint oil to just the right amount of cocoa powder. He knew they weren't supposed to be working on their projects until the next day, but he didn't win all the time by following other people's schedules.

At the exact moment that the container of powdered sugar flew up in his face, he was thinking about how easy it was going to be to win this competition. As the sugar floated down on his head and shoulders, a piece or two landed on his lips. He quickly licked them clean, surprised by the brief sweetness.

He knew the others were laughing at him, but he figured he'd let them have their fun. After all, their fun would end on Saturday in total humiliation. He threatened to send Max the dry-cleaning bill and stormed out.

The halls were quiet for a change. That morning they had been filled with a steady stream of workers pushing carts loaded with trays of candy in various stages. He supposed the machines were up and running full force at this time of day. He brushed the powdered sugar from his arms, but succeeded only in smearing it more.

A young guy carrying a bucket of strawberries turned the corner. He took one look at Philip and burst out laughing. "Guess you're looking for a bathroom?"

Philip nodded grimly.

The man shifted his bucket under one arm and pointed to a door down the hall. "There's a sink right in that storage room. If it's locked, the regular bathroom is back that way, next to the Taffy Room."

Philip shuddered. He didn't plan to go near the Taffy Room again. "Thanks," he muttered.

The guy chuckled and headed off, whistling.

Philip hurried over to the storage room, hoping to find it unlocked. He hadn't noticed the room before, and he knew they'd been in this corridor before. All the other doors at the factory were the kind that swung open. This one had a regular knob and blended into the white walls.

He put his hand on the knob and was relieved when it turned easily. He opened the door and felt around for a light switch. All he could feel was rough, unpainted wood. His fingertips were so toughened from years of pressing on violin strings, though, that he didn't fear any splinters. He had to open the door wider to let in more light from the hall, and that's when he saw the string hanging from the ceiling. As he stepped toward it, something squeaked under his foot. He bent down and retrieved a small yellow duck wearing a sailor's hat. He stashed it in his jacket pocket. The factory had finally given him his duck.

It took two tries, but finally a dim lightbulb crackled on. He shut the door and looked around. All the stuff he remembered from the factory's annual picnics waited in the small room, piled high in boxes and barrels or just bound together with twine. His eyes landed on a stack of instrument cases in one corner, and he made his way over to them.

The black violin case on top of the pile had a good half inch of dust on it. He almost blew it off but realized the dust would just fly up in his face. He reached around the side for the latch, and the case popped right open. For a minute, all Philip could do was stare down at the most beautiful violin he had ever seen. Then, with shaking fingers, he gently lifted it out.

The shimmering pine of the belly. The deep, dark ebony of the chin rest and tuning pegs. The golden scroll at the top carved into the shape of a lion's head. The craftsmanship was far superior not only to anything he'd ever played but to anything he'd seen outside a museum.

He held it up to the dim bulb to read the inscription on the back. *Antonius Stradivarius Cremonensis Faciebat Anno 1727.* He almost dropped it. His heart rate doubled. He was holding a Stradivarius. One of only four hundred thought to exist in the world. The D string was missing entirely, and the others were loose and a little frayed, but it wouldn't take much effort to fix that.

The pegs turned smoothly, and he quickly tightened the three remaining strings. A tuning fork would have helped him make sure that they were perfectly adjusted, but he usually relied on his ears for that anyway.

He checked the case and found a cloth, an empty tin of rosin, and a pair of earplugs. But no bow. He quickly wiped down the strings, then plucked the E string with his fingers and held his breath for the fraction of a second it took the instrument to respond.

Like a single raindrop falling on a tin roof. A perfect note. He plucked G. And then A. Both flawless. Every ounce of him wished he could stay there and experiment with what the violin could do. And, of course, he hated that he wanted to.

Hearing a voice outside the door made the decision for him. The violin went back into its case, and the case back on the pile. He had one hand on the lightbulb string when he realized he hadn't done what he came to do. The workers on this hallway must use this sink pretty regularly, he thought, because the paper-towel roll and soap dispenser looked quite new. He dampened a few pieces of paper towel and ran them over his arms, chest, shoulders, even his hair. A quick look in the mirror assured him he'd gotten everything.

He pulled the string and was halfway out the door when he realized that the voice he'd heard had been Daisy's. He hoped she hadn't heard him tuning the violin. She was standing a few yards away from the lab, leaning her right hip against the wall. He couldn't catch her words, but she was definitely still talking. He wondered who was on the other end of the phone. One of her parents? Her friend Magpie that she always talked about?

A boyfriend?

But when he got closer, he realized she had no phone. She was talking to herself. He thought he'd seen her doing that before, but each time he listened more closely, she had stopped. This time it wasn't his imagination.

He snuck up behind her so close that he could smell her flowery shampoo again. "Talking to yourself can be a sign of a serious problem. This isn't the first time I've seen you do it."

She whirled around in surprise. Before she could answer,

Philip walked around her and into the lab. He loved getting the last word.

"Dad?" Philip said, slipping into the backseat of the limo. "What are you doing here?"

"Can't a father come pick up his own son?"

You never have before, he almost said. Instead, he just nodded. Reggie closed the door behind him, and he stashed his briefcase on the seat.

"So?" his father asked as the car pulled away from the factory. "How was it? Have you gotten this whole crazy idea out of your system?"

Philip felt his palms begin to sweat. Only his dad could make him feel like a little kid who didn't know what he was doing. "Why is it so crazy to think that I could win the contest?" he asked. "I win all the time."

"Come on, son. This is different. It's a *baking* contest. I'm not certain you'd know how to find the oven in our own house. And how many other contestants did you say there are?"

Philip wanted to yell that it wasn't a baking contest, like at a state fair. He wasn't trying to make the world's best apple pie. But he had learned that it was futile to argue with his father. He tried to keep his voice level. "Four from each region. Eight regions, so thirty-two kids."

"And the Candymaker's son? He's in the contest, too?"

Philip nodded.

His father shook his head. "Sorry, kiddo. If you win I'll eat my hat."

"Thanks for the vote of confidence, Dad." He caught Reggie's eye in the rearview mirror. Reggie winked at him.

"You know I have confidence in you," his father said, folding up his newspaper. "I simply don't believe in wasting time on a contest you can't win. I don't start a business deal if I'm not nearly a hundred percent certain I'll be able to make it happen. Just makes good sense."

Philip didn't respond.

"Now tell me about the factory itself. Tell me everything."

So Philip did. He told him about the different rooms, the grounds, the people. He left out mention of the Taffy Room and the Cocoa Room, not wanting to jog his father's memory about the whole banning episode. His father must have completely forgotten about the incident, because when Philip had originally been accepted and told him **Life Is Sweet** was going to host the local contestants, he'd just nodded and said nothing.

"How about the chocolate?" his father asked now. "Did you see any being made?"

Philip paused, then nodded. So much for leaving things out.

"You saw the whole process? From beginning to end? You saw them add something from a small tin box?"

"Uh-huh," Philip said, raising his brows. "Why do you ask?"

His father didn't answer. "So in your opinion the company is thriving?"

"I guess so, but why are you asking me this stuff?"

His father just smiled and flipped open his cell phone. When someone answered, he said, "Got confirmation. As soon as our inside man gets the secret ingredient you'll be able to put 'em out of business. Yes, I knew you'd be pleased." He shut the phone, leaned over, and ruffled Philip's hair. "Good job, son."

Philip was only vaguely aware that his father had actually complimented him for something. That alone would normally have been a shocker. But if that conversation meant what it seemed to mean, then Logan and his factory were about to be dealt a much greater blow than the one he had planned to deliver.

Forget about losing a contest. They were going to lose everything. He should feel happy about that. Shouldn't he? Oddly, the thing that popped into his mind was the Stradivarius. The perfect heft of it. The softness of the polished wood. The purity of the tone. He wondered what would happen to it when the factory was sold off.

The limo pulled into their driveway. "How long have you been planning this, Dad?"

His father chuckled and picked up his own briefcase from between his feet. "About seven years, give or take."

"Seven *years?*"

"Some projects take longer than others."

Reggie opened the car door, and his father swung his

long legs out of the car. "But as I said, I only do the deals I'm confident will succeed." He got out the rest of the way, and Reggie shut the door behind him.

The conversation, apparently, had ended. Philip waited for Reggie to come around to his side of the car, but instead he returned to the front seat and began to back out of the driveway.

"Um, I'm still in here," Philip called out.

"We need to go for a little drive," Reggie replied.

Philip lowered his window to tell his father he'd be back shortly, but his father had already disappeared inside the house. He hadn't even looked back to see if Philip was with him. By now he was used to his father's short attention span. After all, he was a busy man.

"Where are we going?"

"Just lean back and enjoy the ride."

Philip groaned. "We're not going back to the candy store, are we? Because I can have all the candy I want now and I still don't want any."

Reggie shook his head as they headed away from the center of town.

Philip leaned back and closed his eyes. He hoped the ride wouldn't be long. He had a lot to do in the twelve hours before he had to return to the factory. To his surprise, the car stopped only a few minutes later. Philip looked around. They were in the old section of town in front of a four-story apartment building that had seen better days.

"Why are we here?"

Reggie shut off the car and got out.

Philip waited for him to get in the back, as he had that morning. But Reggie opened the door and gestured for him to get out. Philip hesitated. He had a strange feeling this wasn't the first time he'd been at this building, but more than that he couldn't recall.

"Come on," Reggie said. "It will only take a minute."

Philip sighed and stepped out onto the sidewalk. "This better be good."

Reggie said only, "Do you remember this place?"

Philip shook his head. "Should I?"

"Probably not," Reggie admitted. "You were very young the last time you were here."

Philip turned to look at the building more closely. Gray brick. Nondescript iron railing. A cracked window on the third floor. He certainly didn't remember ever being inside. "Is this one of the buildings Dad owns or something?"

Reggie shook his head. "This is where your mother grew up. She used to bring you and your brother here to visit."

Philip felt an icy chill, as if someone had just splashed cold water on his back. He whipped his head around to face the building again. He had no memory of it at all other than that initial fleeting familiarity. Not meeting Reggie's gaze, he asked, "Why did you bring me here?"

"Because your mother wanted more for you than what she'd had. But not at a price. She never quite felt comfortable with your father's way of doing business. When she got sick she made him promise to teach you boys about art and music and about being grateful for what you have, not just how to compete and make money."

Philip still wouldn't turn around.

Reggie continued. "Well, as you know, your father didn't do too good a job with that. Can't really blame him. Winning in business is all he knows."

Philip slowly turned to face Reggie. "What's your point?"

"I think you know."

They stared at each other for a few seconds. "I'm getting back in the car," Philip said, breaking away. "I'd like to go home now."

He climbed in, lay down on the backseat, and pulled his knees up tight. In only one day, he'd gone back to the candy factory where he'd been banned, spent eight hours with his archenemy, found a Stradivarius (arguably one of the most valuable instruments on the planet), learned that his father was trying to destroy **Life Is Sweet?** for his own financial gain, and visited the house his mother grew up in.

He didn't expect to get much sleep that night.

CHAPTER FOUR

By the time Philip awoke the following morning, his father had already left for work. He had been out at a dinner meeting until very late the night before, and although Philip heard him come in around midnight, he didn't go down to greet him. He had no idea what he would say or where even to start. Better to take some time to figure it out first.

He slipped on his suit, which the maid had already cleaned and pressed. He knotted his tie, then stepped back to admire his reflection. Hopefully no one would look close enough to see the dark circles under his eyes.

Reggie was already waiting in the limo by the time Philip got outside. "Wearing the suit again, eh?"

"Nothing's changed," Philip said, climbing in. Once he had set a plan in motion, he saw it through, that's all there was to it. He had come to this conclusion after tossing and turning half the night. It was the only thing that made sense. He would make an excellent candy (or cheat, if need be), and he would win. That's all he had to concern himself with.

Reggie slid into the driver's seat and turned around. "What about your father?"

Philip unwrapped his egg sandwich. "Nothing to do with me."

"What about your mother, then?" Reggie asked.

"What about her?"

"I thought perhaps you gave some thought to what I told you. Maybe you'd want to rethink your plan."

"Why would I want to do that?"

Reggie sighed loudly and turned back around.

Philip pushed the button to close the window between them. He didn't expect Reggie to understand.

"Here you go," Henry said, barely waiting until Philip got out of the car to thrust a pair of tall yellow rubber boots at him. Henry was already wearing boots that went all the way up to his knees. He looked like a deep-sea fisherman.

Philip reluctantly took the boots, clutching them in one hand and his briefcase in the other.

"Marshmallow?" Henry asked, holding one out to him.

Philip hadn't even seen him reach for it. He shook his head.

"C'mon then, we're headed this way." Henry popped the marshmallow into his mouth and led them around the side of the factory to the huge lawn in back. Philip trudged behind. He slipped a few times on the dew-covered grass but managed not to fall. A toddler played catch on the lawn with her mother, and some workers waved as they walked to the fields. Other than that, only birds and the occasional bullfrog made any noise. Philip felt very out of place.

"You can leave your briefcase here." Henry pointed to a bench beside the pond. "We're going to walk around to the left side of the pond, but it gets a little marshy. I recommend putting your boots on now."

Philip sat down on the bench but didn't make a move to slip on the boots. "I can just watch from here, if it's all the same to you."

Henry lifted a boot from where Philip had set them down and silently handed it to him.

Philip couldn't believe he was doing this, but Henry had the power to get him kicked out of the contest. He didn't have a choice. On went the boots.

He trudged behind Henry once again, this time making sure his feet didn't slip out of the boots with every step. The ground beneath his feet gradually got mushier, until he couldn't tell where the ground ended and the pond began.

Henry pointed a few yards ahead to where a large canvas tarp was lying spread out on the ground. "That's where we're heading."

By the time they reached the tarp, the water was up past Philip's ankles. Instead of grass, the vegetation here was denser — large green plants with long, flat leaves, smaller plants with spindly brown stalks. Frankly, to Philip they all looked like weeds.

Henry walked right into the pond, and after a brief

hesitation, Philip followed. The cold water encircled his legs but didn't seep in.

When they came to a section filled with the weedlike plants, Henry reached out, grabbed one of the largest stalks, and yanked. It seemed to come up pretty easily. He tossed it onto the tarp. "Give it a go," he said, gesturing to the stalk next to the one he had pulled.

Philip doubted he'd ever touched a plant in his life, let alone a wet, slimy one. But he did as Henry instructed. Water splattered up at him as the plant flew out of the ground. When he tossed it, it fell a foot or so short of the tarp. Henry waded over and flung it onto the shore.

"Well done," he said, grinning at Philip. "That's all there is to it."

So they kept pulling and flinging. Philip learned to adjust how hard he pulled, and by the fifth or sixth time, he didn't even cause a splash. He had to admit there was something relaxing about the process. It became almost rhythmic.

He had just tossed his eighth mallow root onto the tarp when Henry, not looking at him, said, "Do you know how Logan got his scars?"

Surprised, Philip let go of the stalk he'd been about to pull up. "It's none of my business," he said. He figured the less he knew about Logan, the easier it was to go on hating him.

But Henry continued talking as he pulled up another root. Philip had no choice but to listen. "One day about seven years ago, the Candymaker was giving a tour of the factory to a local businessman and his two sons. At that time they were still offering tours to the public, you see. Anyway, one of the boys was Logan's age, and growing up in the factory as he was, well, Logan didn't have much chance to be around kids his own age."

Philip felt a shiver run though him that had nothing to do with the cold water.

"So this other boy, he was real nice to Logan and seemed interested in being his friend. They ran around the factory together, sampling all the candy until the Candymaker's wife warned them they'd get a bellyache. Then in the Cocoa Room, this other little boy tossed a toy truck to Logan, but he missed and it landed square in a vat of chocolate."

"I've heard this story," Philip said, interrupting him. "Max already told us. They stopped giving tours because the truck messed everything up."

Henry shook his head. "Not exactly. So anyway, the truck went in, the little boy's father yelled at him, and the boy started to cry. The Candymaker assured the businessman that it was no big deal, not to worry the boy over it."

Philip felt himself sway and grabbed onto a tall stalk for support. The Candymaker had said it was *no big deal?* But that made no sense.

"You all right?" Henry asked.

Philip gave a tiny nod.

Henry continued, "In fact, the Candymaker asked the businessman if his son could come back to play, since Logan enjoyed his company so much."

A numbness began to spread up Philip's fingertips into

his palms. He squeezed his hands hard, but it didn't help. He wanted to tell Henry he'd heard enough, but the man just kept on.

Henry pulled up another stalk, tossed it on the pile, and continued. "Then the family left, and the Candymaker went to get his tools. He hoped to get the toy out before it entered the pipes. Alone in the room, Logan was fascinated by the patterns the truck made as it descended into the thick chocolate. He decided that as interesting as it was to watch, he wanted to get the truck out to give it back to his new friend. By the time he realized how hot the liquid was, his arms were all the way submerged, and half of his face."

Philip felt as if all of the air around them had turned to brick. It was *his* fault Logan had those burns? Guilt was not an emotion he had ever entertained. He had no experience with it at all. But now he felt it in his gut like a punch in the stomach. The blue sky above seemed to swirl and swoop downward. He swayed and nearly toppled into the marsh. Henry reached out and steadied him.

"All that trouble," Henry said, continuing the story as though Philip weren't about to pass out, "and the little boy never even came back to play with him. Broke Logan's heart, although he never complained. Bless him, that boy never stopped being the great kid he always was. Kind and generous, and happy, too, even after what had happened."

"But...but," Philip stammered, struggling to get enough air to speak. "The boy was banned from the factory. He couldn't come back."

"Banned?" Henry repeated, seeming genuinely surprised. "Why would he have been banned? No. The Candymaker even called the boy's father afterward, but the boy never came back. Wasn't interested, I suppose."

Philip literally pinched his arm to make sure he wasn't dreaming. "Are you making all this up?"

Henry shook his head. "Just thought you might find the story interesting, is all."

"Just so I'm clear," Philip said, his voice shaking. "The boy was never banned at all?"

Henry shook his head again. "To my knowledge, the Candymaker has never kept anyone out of the factory. That'd be against his very nature."

The shock Philip felt at Henry's words was nothing compared with the fury that now entered his veins. It overpowered even the guilt. "If you'll excuse me," he said, his voice like ice, "I have to go make a call."

Without waiting for Henry's permission, Philip stormed out of the pond. Water splashed up at him, but he barely noticed. When he reached the bench, he flung off his wet, slimy boots and dug the cell phone out of his briefcase. He pressed speed dial and began to pace up and down the path. Reggie answered on the third ring.

"Have fun in the water?" he joked. "Those boots looked real —"

"Reggie!" he shouted. "I wasn't banned from the factory at all!"

At first all he got was silence from the other end. He

thought for a second that he'd lost the connection. Then Reggie said, "I wondered about that."

"What do you mean? You knew this and you didn't tell me?" As far as he knew, Reggie had always been honest with him.

"I didn't know for sure," Reggie insisted. "I was out in the car the whole time. I only knew what I was told."

"But why would my father say something like that? Why would he want to keep me from the factory?" He wanted to tell Reggie about Logan's burns but couldn't make himself say the words.

"Who knows your father's motives for anything?" Reggie said. "From what he said in the car yesterday, it sounds like he was interested in taking over the factory even back then. Maybe he thought a friendship between you and the Candymaker's son would complicate things in the future. He could have been looking out for your best interests."

"Do you really believe that?"

Reggie paused. "Anything's possible."

"Where is my father now?"

"Still at his breakfast meeting in town."

Philip thought for only a minute. He knew what he needed to do. He'd known it since the car had pulled away from his mother's old apartment. He said a quick goodbye and dialed his father's cell.

After seven long rings, his father finally picked up. "I'm in a meeting, Philip. Can this wait?"

A jumble of words tried to make their way out of Philip's

mouth. *Why lie about the banning? Why not follow Mom's wishes about how to raise him?* But all that would have to wait. He couldn't risk getting into a fight. Instead he said, "If I win the candy contest—"

"Philip, we've been through this. You're not going to win. So what? You'll win the next contest."

Philip would not be distracted. "But if I *do* win," he insisted, "if I can pull it off, will you agree to drop your plans to take over the factory?"

He heard silverware clinking against a plate. He heard his father chewing, then swallowing. It took all his self-control not to scream.

Finally, his father said, "Philip, why would I do that? I've been working on this deal for a long time. I'm a business-man, it's what I do. It's nothing personal against the candy factory."

Philip began to pace again. He knew Henry was watch-ing, but he didn't care. "If you're so sure I won't win, you've got nothing to lose. And if I do win, I could give you all the prize money and whatever money I'd earn on the candy once they start making it. That way you'd still make money on the deal. Come on, Dad. I don't ask you for much."

His father laughed. "You're serious about this?"

"Yes."

His father held his hand over the phone for a few seconds, and Philip could tell by the muffled laughter that he was sharing the offer with the people at the meeting. Philip clutched his phone tighter.

"All right," his father said, returning to the line. "You've got a deal. But don't worry, if you do win, you can keep the prize money. That's how sure I am that you won't. Again, no offense or anything."

"Fine." Philip hung up before he could say anything he'd regret. He looked up to see Henry standing on the other side of the bench, the tarp rolled up under his arm. Clearly he'd heard the whole thing. "I have to get to the lab," Philip told him, grabbing his briefcase. "I've got a contest to win."

"I can help you."

Philip hesitated. The only time people had ever helped him win something was when they didn't know they were helping. Andrew's notebook said that if someone else knew more than you did and wasn't actually competing against you, it could be valuable to enlist his help. Henry fell into that category. Plus he was the only person who knew what was going on. Or at least knew enough. Philip gave a single nod.

"Good," Henry said, reaching into his pocket and pulling out a surprisingly dry marshmallow. He held it out to Philip.

"No thanks."

"Too soon?" Henry asked.

"Yes."

They walked across the lawn toward the back door. Laughter reached them from all sides as groups of workers took the last sips of their coffee and the last bites of their chocolate chip bagels before starting their shift. Philip watched them wearily. Could saving a hundred people's jobs really be on *his* shoulders? Would he be doing it for them or only for Logan? Or for himself?

They passed the bush with the chrysalis hanging from the leaf. Philip glanced over at it. It was still there, maybe a little more translucent now. He thought the outline of the butterfly was easier to see. He felt as trapped as it must feel.

"What are you planning on making for the contest?" Henry asked, pushing the back door open.

Philip hesitated again. He hadn't planned on telling anyone his idea. Once you do that, you lose the element of surprise and, therefore, the upper hand. But things had changed. He'd have to adapt.

He waited for two workers to pass by on their way to the Pepsicle Room before whispering, "It's a square of chocolate with mint in the center."

Henry stared. "That's it?"

This reaction unnerved Philip. "Actually," he said, crossing his arms, "if you must know, there are crushed-up pieces of cashew nuts and a little marshmallow in the mint."

Henry crossed his arms, too. "Again I must ask, *that's it?*"

"It tastes very good!" Philip insisted.

"Have you actually *tasted* it?"

"As a matter of fact, I have." He didn't mention that it had been nearly ten years since he'd eaten his mother's World-Famous Chocolate Mint Squares. But he had no doubt they'd taste as good now as they did then. People used to come from the other side of town when they heard she'd cooked up a fresh batch.

"Listen," Henry said, putting his hand on Philip's shoulder. "I'm not trying to put down your idea. It's just that the candy industry moves really fast, with new products competing for shelf space in every candy store. The candy that wins this contest has to be so new, so special, that no one has ever even conceived of it before. Do you understand?"

Philip opened his mouth to argue, but he had to admit that what Henry said made sense. He should have known his mom's candy wouldn't stand out enough to win. "Well, what should I make, then?"

Henry shook his head. "That's up to you."

Philip threw up his arms. "But I don't know anything about candy. How am I supposed to come up with something in one day that's good enough to win?"

"I honestly don't know," Henry said. "Are you smart?"

"Yes," Philip replied without hesitation.

"Enterprising?"

"Definitely."

"Then I'm sure you'll come up with something. Think of things that interest you and start there."

The workers had begun to stream in, and Philip knew he had to get to the lab. "You're not gonna tell anyone, I mean, that I, um —"

"I'm not going to tell anyone anything," Henry assured him.

"Thanks," Philip said, then turned and ran in the direction of the lab.

"Your tie is wet!" Henry called from down the hall.

Philip undid his tie as he ran, the wet ooze of the marsh seeping into his fingers. He balled it up and looked around for a trash can. He didn't see one. He was about to shove it down deep into his suit-jacket pocket when he came to the storeroom where he'd washed off the sugar the day before. For the briefest of seconds he pictured himself cradling the Stradivarius in his arms instead of facing what was ahead of him. Without coming to a full stop, he opened the door, threw in the tie, and kept running.

He stopped short right before he got to the lab. How was he supposed to act now? Did he go to the others for help? Maybe they'd agree to drop out of the contest so he'd have a greater chance of winning. But what would he tell them? Everything? Or just the stuff about his father trying to buy the factory? He knew he'd never be able to tell Logan the whole truth. He wouldn't be able to handle the look on his face when he heard.

If he told them about the deal he'd made with his father, they'd probably think he was making up the whole thing just so he'd win. No, he had only two options. One was to come up with an idea amazing enough to win; failing that, he had to get the others to *believe* that his idea was so amazing they shouldn't even bother to compete.

Only Max was in the lab, fully absorbed in taste-testing something from a tray in front of him. Philip was surprised that none of the other contestants had arrived yet. According to his watch, they all should have been here by now. He was relieved that he wouldn't have to face Logan just yet. It was hard enough yesterday, but now, knowing he had been the cause of his scars, it would be a million times harder.

Philip watched as Max picked up what looked like a pink-and-yellow blob the size of a quarter, took the tiniest nibble, jotted something on his clipboard, took a bigger bite, made another notation, then popped the whole thing in his mouth.

Philip cleared his throat.

Max swallowed and smiled. "Good morning, Philip, didn't hear you come in. Would you like to try something we've been working on?" He picked up the tray and held it out. "It's the inside of—"

"No," Philip snapped.

"Oh, right," Max said, plunking the tray back down on the table. "I keep forgetting. Candy is bad."

"That's not exactly what I said," Philip began, then stopped himself. He couldn't apologize for anything. If he did, he might actually find himself being *nice,* and that wouldn't do at all. Not now. He quickly turned away and got busy organizing the ingredients at his station as they'd been instructed the day before.

Miles and Logan arrived, and Philip did his best to ignore them. It helped that they didn't expect him to do anything else. Daisy came in a little later, looking a bit rumpled. As she passed by him on the way to her own station, he got a distinct whiff of peppermint and something else. *Horse?*

He didn't have time to think about Daisy or anyone else.

Max jumped right into demonstrating the candy machines that had been set up in the center of the room. Philip hadn't really noticed them before — he couldn't focus on anything but what kind of candy he should make. Hard? Soft? Chocolate? Gum? What other categories were there? Perhaps he should have paid a little more attention yesterday. Henry had said to think of his interests. His interests were winning trophies, ribbons, plaques, and, on the rare occasion, cash. He didn't think a chocolate trophy was what the judges were looking for.

Max handed him a measuring cup filled with some kind of red goo and apparently expected him to do something with it. So he tossed it in the direction of the nearest machine. It didn't occur to him to hold on to the cup as he did it. He watched with a mix of horror and fascination as the cup bounced off the machine, hit the ground, and sent the red liquid flying. Not his finest moment.

"Don't worry," Max said, "that's why they call them accidents."

"Accidents?" Philip repeated. Was that what everyone thought had happened to Logan? That he'd had an accident? But that wasn't really the truth of it.

The others were looking at him. He had to snap out of it and focus. Fortunately, being obnoxious came easily to him, and in no time he had everyone convinced that he knew exactly what kind of candy he was going to make and that it was a secret. Telling everyone that he didn't trust them not to steal his idea was just icing on the cake.

"I prefer to win the contest first," he said when they argued with him. "And then I can control what happens next." As he expected, they didn't like that answer. But that was the point. He might have kept the argument going, but for the first time that day, his notebook called to him. He darted over to his station and grabbed his pencil. Musical notes flew across the page so fast he could barely keep up.

The door swung open a minute later, and Philip didn't need to look up to know it was the Candymaker and his wife. His cheeks burned as he remembered his short exchange with Logan's mother in the hallway outside the Taffy Room. Had she told Logan he was crying? He sure hoped not.

Henry had recognized him as soon as he'd seen him. What if the Candymaker did, too? He kept his head down and hoped they'd leave before he had to talk to them. But then the Candymaker's wife said, "Nice to see you again, Philip," and his heart sank.

He looked up to see the Candymaker striding straight toward him. He held his breath as he waited for recognition to cross the man's face. Yesterday he'd been worried about being known as *the kid who broke our machine and got banned,* and now he'd be *the kid who caused the Candymaker's son to get burned and then never came back to play with him.* Much, much worse.

But all the Candymaker said was something about Henry being impressed with his ambition. Philip breathed a sigh of relief. The Candymaker's wife didn't embarrass him; Henry wasn't going to tell anyone what he knew; the Candymaker himself didn't recognize him. He was free to continue with his new plan, which, now that he thought about it, wasn't any different from the old plan. His goal had always been to win the contest. The only thing that had changed was the reason why.

He couldn't believe his luck when Logan admitted he hadn't asked anyone at the factory for help with his project. That meant the odds of Logan coming up with anything good enough to win weren't as high as Philip had previously feared. But time was running out, and the others would soon see that he didn't have anything.

So while everyone was already annoyed at him, he figured he'd annoy them even more by demanding that Max put a barrier around his station. That would keep prying eyes away.

Max sent them off to do research, and when Philip saw that no one was moving, he realized that Miles and Daisy hadn't the slightest clue about what to make either. He could only hope the other twenty-eight contestants were similarly unprepared. He doubted he'd get that lucky, though.

He'd had every intention of heading directly to the Marshmallow Room, but somehow he found himself turning the knob on the storeroom door instead. With a backward glance to make sure he was alone in the hall, he slipped in and pulled on the light. No way would the Candymaker leave the door unlocked if he knew the riches it contained. How could anyone be in possession of a Stradivarius and not know it?

Ten seconds later he was cradling the violin in his hands, mentally playing his concerto on it. He was sure the notes would be so pure, so perfect, they'd set the stars on fire. "What am I talking about?" he asked out loud, shaking his head. He'd been hanging around Reggie too long. The only thing he needed to set on fire was some chocolate.

But while half his brain was yelling at him for being in here instead of doing research for his candy project, the other half had the brilliant idea of checking the cello case for a bow. He sighed, wishing, as he did every day, that he wasn't a slave to this instrument. Holding the violin aloft in one hand, he awkwardly brought the cello case to the ground.

The three rusty latches were a little tricky to open with one hand, but he did it. The cello itself was in even worse shape than the violin. All but one of the strings was missing, and a crack extended halfway across the neck. But beside it lay a bow!

The hairs were frayed and bone-dry, but it might still work. Unable to help himself, he brought the bow up to the violin. Right as he was about to draw it across the three strings, his eyes landed on a small shiny envelope stuck against the side of the cello case. Could it be? It was! Two extra violin strings! He quickly got to work replacing and tuning the D string. He stuck the extra one back in the violin case for safe keeping. Unable to keep the smile from his face, he raised the bow again just as Miles's and Logan's voices drifted past the room. Philip froze and prayed they wouldn't have any reason to come in.

Afraid to move, his eyes darted around the room for a place to hide if they did come in. Nothing. He did notice a plastic bin under the sink that he hadn't seen before, though. It held small plastic harmonicas, brightly colored Super Balls, and wooden yo-yos. The outside of the box said PRIZES.

The voices passed, and once he could breathe again, he crept toward the box.

CHAPTER FIVE

A candy harmonica?" Henry repeated.

"Yes! But not just candy in the *shape* of a harmonica — my harmonica would really play!"

Henry didn't answer right away. He stirred his marshmallow mixture one more time, then his face lit up. "I love it!"

"Really?" Philip asked. Then he scowled at himself. He sounded like a little boy. "I mean, you think it's good enough to win?"

"It could be," Henry said. "It depends on how well you make it. What ingredients you use, how you create the mold, how you get it to play the right notes...hey, are you okay?"

Philip was rubbing his temples. "Sure. I'm just great. The fate of the whole factory is in my hands, and I have no idea what I'm doing."

Henry turned off the flame and took a notepad and pencil from his desk. "Okay, let's go through it together. What do you see the harmonica being made of? Hard candy? Gummy candy? Chocolate?"

Philip thought for a minute. "How about hard candy? Then it won't melt when you play it."

Henry nodded thoughtfully. "That would be the obvious choice, but..."

"But?"

"Well, for the contest, the judges are looking for something truly different and inventive. You may have to dig deeper."

Philip stared into the pot of gooey marshmallow, willing the ideas to come. A few minutes later, one actually did. He looked up, excited. "What if I made the outside a mix of different kinds of chocolate, with something thicker inside, like a cookie maybe, so it won't get too mushy after the person starts playing it? And it could come with a tin of something gummy that you could stick into the little openings on the side of the harmonica to create different notes?"

Henry scrawled down Philip's suggestions. When he was done, he tucked the pencil behind his ear and said, "Sounds great."

Philip grinned.

"You look good when you smile," Henry said. "You should do it more often."

Philip rolled his eyes. "I'll get right on that. Now, what's my first step?"

Henry held the notepad up again. Before he could answer, Philip's cell phone rang.

"Sorry, be right back." He pulled his phone out of the

briefcase and stepped into the hall. He knew by the ring that it was Reggie.

"What is it?" Philip said. "I'm creating a work of confectionary art here."

"Well, it better be really tasty, because your father didn't call off the guy he has on the inside. He's still trying to get that formula."

Philip gripped the phone tighter. "Are you sure?"

"I heard him confirming on the phone that the guy was still in place. You didn't hear it from me," Reggie said before hanging up.

Philip stayed in the hall until his head stopped feeling like it was about to explode. He supposed he couldn't blame his father. After all, if he *didn't* win the contest, his father would still continue with his plans for the factory. Business was business. Nothing he could do about it.

Or was there?

He pushed open the door to the Marshmallow Room and said, "Can you write down the ingredients for me? I've gotta go do something."

"Should I ask what?"

Philip shook his head. "Better that you don't know."

Henry nodded. "Be careful. The walls have eyes around here."

"I will," he promised. Then he turned back. "Not, like, real eyes, right? Like cameras?"

Henry shook his head. "Only outside. But still, word spreads fast here."

"Got it."

His first stop would be the lab, to retrieve a tool kit he'd spied in the closet. His stomach growled as he strode past the cafeteria, but he had no time to eat. Although if he got caught doing what he was about to do, he might be eating bread and water for a good long while.

The laboratory hallway was empty. Everyone must be at lunch, which meant no one would hear him. This time he didn't even fight it. He ducked into the storeroom, picked up the violin, put the bow in position, and pulled it across the strings.

The violin sang.

Even with the strings in such bad condition, it outshone any he'd ever played. Philip closed his eyes. His fingers and the bow moved without him even thinking. He lost himself completely to the music. When he finished playing the new section he'd written the day before, he put down the bow. He always felt exhilarated after playing, but this, this was a whole different thing. He felt as if he could fly.

It took a few minutes before he could make himself put the violin back in its case. He opened the storeroom door a crack to make sure the coast was clear, then hurried to the lab. He stopped short when he saw Miles with that ever-present backpack over his shoulder. What was *he* doing here? What if he'd heard him playing?

Philip stared at him, daring him to say anything about the music. Instead, Miles wound up telling him all about Logan's project. He could tell Miles regretted it as soon as he'd said it, but hey, that should teach him to be more on his toes. He was too much of a pushover.

Miles left the lab in a huff, and Philip pulled out the toolbox and opened it. He chose a few screwdrivers and a pair of pliers. Usually he had these sorts of tools in his briefcase, since he never knew when breaking and entering would be necessary in the course of a contest, but with so much else to think about, he'd forgotten to pack them.

He wrapped the tools in a rag that he found in a drawer and stuck them in his jacket pocket. Being sure to stay on the opposite side of the hall from the storeroom so he wouldn't be tempted again, he ran without stopping to the place where everything began.

He had hoped to find the Cocoa Room empty. Instead, the Candymaker himself was in there, along with the two workers from the day before and two men in suits Philip did not know. They were all talking and laughing and having a grand old time. The Candymaker was leaning over one of the machines. His voice was loud enough to carry through the glass. "And this, my friends, is how we get our signature swirl on the top of all our chocolate."

"Bravo!" the older of the two men shouted and clapped. Then they all laughed again.

They didn't look as if they were leaving any time soon. Well, if *he* couldn't get to the secret ingredient, then neither could his father's guy. He had turned to go when he heard knocking on the window behind him.

He turned back to see the Candymaker waving him in.

He'd rather be anywhere than in that room with the Candymaker, but he figured he couldn't exactly run away now. He squared his shoulders and tried to look as tall and old as possible in case the Candymaker's memory kicked in.

He swung the door open, noting as he passed through that it had no lock after all. "Hello," he said uncertainly.

"Hello, Philip," the Candymaker boomed, striding forward and putting his arm around his shoulders. Turning to the group, he said, "This is another one of our contestants."

Lenny and Steve nodded to him and then retreated to the other side of the room to crack open some more pods with those long axelike things. In between loud *thwacks,* the two men in suits introduced themselves as fellow candymakers here for a visit before the convention.

"Whipping up something really special to wow the judges?" the younger of the two asked.

Thwack!

Philip jumped a little. "I hope so." And then, since he figured it would be a good idea to get on the Candymaker's good side, he added, "I'm sure it's not as good as whatever Logan's doing, though."

"Couldn't tell you that," the Candymaker said. "He hasn't confided in me."

Thwack!

"Really?" the older visitor said. "I assumed he'd have gotten help from his famous papa."

They all laughed again, and the Candymaker shook his head. "Logan wanted to do this on his own. I think he believes he has something to prove to us, which of course he doesn't."

The older man said, "Do you think he'll follow in the Sweet family's shoes and be the next Candymaker?"

"Hey, I'm not gone yet!" the Candymaker joked. "Don't rush me into retirement!" This got a big laugh. Philip smiled, too. He wasn't used to adults talking so freely around him, as if he were one of them.

Then the Candymaker's expression turned serious. "I'm not sure, to be honest. He might prefer to be more, ah, behind the scenes, as it were. Because of his … situation."

"Ah yes," the older man said, nodding. "That makes sense."

"He's a brave boy, he is," added the younger.

Thwack!

Philip looked from one to the other. Were they talking about Logan's appearance? They must be. He didn't know Logan very well, but from what he'd seen these past two days, Logan didn't seem bothered at all by his scars. Maybe he just hid it really well.

He had to get out of that room before the guilt threatened to swallow him whole.

"I should get back," he said, inching toward the door. "Gotta, you know, make that candy and all."

"Good luck," they called out.

As the door swung shut behind him, he heard Steve (or was it Lenny?) say, "He'll need it!" Followed by *thwack!*

Why would someone say that? Did he know something?

Was the contest rigged? He sure hoped not, or all his efforts would be wasted. Annoyed at not being able to do what he'd set out to do, he had no choice but to head back to the Marshmallow Room.

As he approached the cafeteria, the toe of his shoe sent a folded piece of paper sliding across the floor. The room was full of people eating, but no one seemed to be missing anything. He picked the paper up and unfolded it.

Hi guys, have lunch without me,
went to go check on ~~Magpie~~ the horse.
Hugs, Daisy.

Aha! He *knew* he smelled horse!

He held the note up to one of the lights in the ceiling. Underneath the crossed-out section he could see the word *Magpie.* He lowered the note. She confused her best friend with a horse? What a strange girl.

So that meant Miles and Logan were off eating lunch instead of working on their projects. Good. He ran the rest of the way and burst into the room.

"Okay, Henry. What have you got for me?"

Henry, carrying a huge tray of cooling marshmallows, gestured with his chin to the notepad on the desk.

Philip read the list: *dark chocolate, milk chocolate, cookie wafer, beeswax, marshmallow, mold tray.*

"Pretty straightforward, really," Henry said after placing the tray on a high cooling rack in the back of the room. "And it's not because I'm biased, but I think marshmallow goes better with chocolate than gummy does, so I went with that."

"What's beeswax for?"

"I think if you use it to coat the cookie, it will keep its shape better. Also form a barrier between the chocolate and the cookie. But I've never tried to make anything other than marshmallows, so Max will have to help you from here on."

Philip tore off the page and put it in his jacket. "Thanks, Henry." He extended his hand to shake Henry's, but the man had already begun stirring a pot of marshmallow mix, humming as he stirred.

Philip pulled his hand back and smiled.

When he arrived back at the lab, he nearly dropped his briefcase in surprise. Max had erected temporary walls around each of their stations. Excellent!

"So what do you think?" Max asked, coming out from behind one of the walls.

Philip wiped the smile from his face. "It'll do." Then he remembered he needed Max's help. "Can you, um, help me a little?"

Max's eyes widened, but he recovered quickly. They walked around to Philip's station, where he handed Max the list.

"So you've been to visit Henry?"

Philip felt the blood drain from his face. Had Henry told Max everything? Who else knew? "Um, how did you know?"

Max held up the paper. "I recognize the handwriting."

"Oh," Philip said with relief. "Yes, he helped me put this list together but said that you would take it from here."

"Okay, but you'll need to tell me what you're planning — how else could I help?"

In response, Philip took out the plastic harmonica and laid it on the table. "I want to make this. But out of candy. And I want it to play real notes."

Max held up the harmonica. "Interesting. You didn't happen to make a mold already, did you?"

Philip shook his head. He didn't want to admit that this was a new idea.

"No? Well, that's okay, you'll figure something out without one."

"But how will I keep it in the right shape?"

"You're going to have to form them by hand," Max said. "It would take too long to make a mold now."

Philip heard noises in the station next to him and caught a glimpse of a blond ponytail. "Can we talk about this later?" Philip asked, anxious that Daisy not overhear anything.

Max nodded. In a low voice he said, "But you should know, candymaking is a very collaborative process. If you win the contest and enter the candy business, you'll have to learn to get along with others."

Without waiting for a response, Max headed toward the back of the room.

Philip hadn't actually considered what would happen after he won. In the beginning it was just about making

Logan lose, and now it was about saving the factory. But he hadn't thought about the rest of it, and there wasn't any time to think about it now.

For the rest of the afternoon, Philip barely paused to breathe. Every hour on the hour, he excused himself and ran to the Cocoa Room, hoping to find it empty. He'd learned from years of watching his father's different businesses that the workers' break time usually fell at the top of the hour. But every time he went, either Lenny or Steve or both or random assorted others were in there. He lingered in the hall, pretending to read the plaques or admire the statue, but they refused to leave. Once or twice he saw Daisy walk by on her way somewhere, and he wondered briefly what her project was. For a split second, he thought of confiding in her. He couldn't talk to Logan, of course, and Miles was too much of an unknown quantity and too close to Logan anyway. But as a girl, Daisy was sort of an outsider, too. Maybe she'd help him.

But as soon as she caught his eye he chickened out and turned away.

The most annoying part of the afternoon was getting candy all over himself, his workspace, the pages of his notebook. Once he was forced to lick a dot of chocolate off one of the pages. It had fallen right in the middle of a staff, and he didn't want to come across it later and think it was a whole note and play it! If the taste of the paper hadn't come with it, he might have actually enjoyed it.

He abandoned his suit jacket and rolled up his shirt-sleeves, but he was still covered with sticky, gooey candy ingredients. Every time he tried to shape the chocolate into an even slightly recognizable shape, it just collapsed. Everywhere.

Working with the marshmallow was proving hopeless. Way too sticky to take in and out of the little pipes. Caramel was even worse. Paulo's beeswax helped, but he struggled with getting the cookie wafers to bend in the right way. Maybe if he had a week, he could do this.

At one point, when he knew the noise of one of the machines would drown out everything else, he put his sorry excuse for a candy harmonica to his lips and blew. Air whooshed through it, but it made no musical note. He'd taken the plastic harmonica apart earlier, and now he picked up one of the halves and examined it more closely. Somehow he'd have to make the tiny flaps that allowed the instrument to make the different notes. How was he going to make tiny flaps out of candy?

He rested his head in his hands. This served only to get caramel all over his face, but it gave him a reason to go back to the storeroom. The violin was just where he had left it. He washed up thoroughly, but as he lifted the bow, his sleeve slipped down and revealed the time on his watch: 4:45. Fifteen minutes till closing. His candy harmonica was nowhere near ready. He hadn't foiled his father's plans to steal the secret ingredient. How would he accomplish both these things in the next fifteen minutes?

The answer came swiftly. He *couldn't* accomplish them,

plain and simple. He dug his phone out of the pocket where he'd stashed it earlier and hoped he'd get reception inside the tiny room.

Reggie picked up right away. "I'm almost there."

"Don't bother," Philip said hurriedly. "I'm going to have to hang out here until I can get into the room with the secret ingredient. I don't think my father's guy has been able to get in there either. It's been busy all day."

"Won't they kick you out?"

"Not if they don't see me."

Reggie groaned. "Can't you just forget about this one, come home and polish your trophies?"

Philip had to laugh. "You know I can't stop something once I've started it."

"Be careful," Reggie warned. "Call me when you're ready."

"Okay," Philip promised, hanging up.

Back in the lab, Philip placed all his prototypes in a small plastic container, separating each layer with wax paper. He secured the lid, then put the container in his briefcase. He made up other small containers with various ingredients and added them to the briefcase, too. He'd stay up all night in the kitchen if he had to.

After Max gave them their instructions for the next day, Philip raced from the room. He made it to the storeroom before anyone else left the lab. He turned the lock on the inside of the door and sat against the far wall, between a wicker basket of beach balls and a pile of potato sacks. He didn't dare turn on the light.

He heard footsteps only a moment later, and the sounds of the other three talking. When the voices passed, he finally allowed himself to relax and close his eyes.

The next thing he knew, he awoke curled up on the potato sacks. He bolted upright. He'd fallen asleep! What time was it? He pulled the light switch and was relieved to see that only an hour had passed.

The thought occurred to him that he could easily slip into the lab and ruin the projects the others were working on. He could "misplace" their lists of ingredients. The candies could have an unfortunate accident with a Bunsen burner or the drain in the sink. It wouldn't be the first time he'd sabotaged a competitor's project. The end would justify the means, right? Andrew had underlined that concept in the notebook he'd passed along.

But he knew he couldn't do it. Even if he would be destroying them for the greater good.

This time when his stomach growled, it wasn't a friendly reminder to eat something. It was a command. He hadn't eaten since his egg sandwich at breakfast, the dot of chocolate in his notebook notwithstanding. The hunger began to gnaw at him.

He put his ear to the door, and when he didn't hear anything, he unlocked it and slipped out. The halls were empty, with only the hum of a candy machine here and there to interrupt the silence. He crept toward the Cocoa Room and hid behind the chocolate fountain.

Unbelievable! Steve was still in there, dragging a pile of

cocoa beans across the room. Didn't these people ever stop making chocolate?

Then an idea hit him like a bolt of lightning, and he stumbled, bonking his head on the top rim of the fountain. He ducked low again, rubbing his head. What if Steve or Lenny was the inside guy? They had the easiest access to the place. Andrew's notebook had stressed that when trying to achieve something, you always take the simplest route first. Surely his father would have done the same.

But if it WAS one of them, then they already had the ingredient, and it didn't matter if Philip got it or not.

Or did it? Philip stood up fast, whacking his head again in the same place. He thought he heard something go *plop* this time, but he didn't see anything. He ducked again and rubbed his head.

It DID matter if he got it. If both he and his father were in possession of the secret ingredient, then he'd have a bargaining chip. It wouldn't do his father any good to have it if everyone else did, too. And Philip would threaten to make sure that everyone did.

He watched for another few minutes, and then his empty stomach prevailed. Creeping low, he went around the corner and headed to the cafeteria. All the smells from the day still lingered in the halls, which only made him hungrier.

The cafeteria was dark. He tried the door. Locked! With a deadbolt, too! If he'd had his tools, he could probably jimmy the bottom lock open, but the deadbolt was another story. He could see through the cafeteria to the lawn outside. As distasteful as it was, maybe he could find something to gnaw on out there to keep his hunger at bay. A piece of fruit or something.

He remembered seeing a back door past the Pepsicle Room, so he headed there. He was about to reach for the door handle when it turned.

All he could think to do was flatten himself against the wall behind the door. He held his breath, not even daring to blink. A second later, Logan and Miles burst through the door, sparing his head by about three inches. Logan must have invited Miles to stay for dinner. He wondered if he would have gotten an invitation if he hadn't left the lab so quickly. Probably not.

The two of them weren't laughing and joking the way they usually were, but Philip could hardly worry about that. He continued holding his breath and began to pray. *Please don't look back, please don't look back.*

As soon as they were twenty feet away, he ducked around the door and slipped outside. A few workers were still in the fields, and two of the rowboats were out on the pond. He didn't see any way to wander around without being seen. He certainly stood out in the suit. He sighed and sat down next to one of the bushes, wondering briefly if the flowers were edible. It had come to that.

He noticed something white and puffy on the ground, like a sticky cotton ball. A closer look revealed it to be the caterpillar's cocoon or whatever Logan had called it. He glanced over at the next bush and there it was. A black, yellow, and red butterfly with wings so thin he could see right through them.

Usually he had no interest in insects. But this butterfly held his attention. He watched as it rubbed its antennae together, cleaning itself, without a care in the world. Philip figured it was simply happy at no longer being held prisoner in that white cage.

The butterfly fluttered a bit and turned so its head was pointed right at Philip. It waved its antennae around in a circle. And then, quite deliberately, it flew right at him, landed on his nose, and fixed its eyes on his.

Philip toppled over backward in surprise. By the time he scrambled to his feet, the butterfly had flown away.

Did that just happen? Had a butterfly just stared him down?

The open cocoon lay by his toe. It didn't seem quite as gross as it had when he first saw it yesterday, still hanging from its thread. It seemed wrong to leave it there on the ground, so he used his handkerchief to pick it up. When he went to stick the handkerchief into his suit pocket, it felt like something was missing. A duck-shaped something. He didn't remember taking the duck out of his jacket pocket at home the night before, but he guessed he must have. At least if he failed to win the contest and save the factory, he'd have something to remember his failure by.

He hurried back inside. Steve was *still* in the Cocoa Room! The man honestly must *sleep* there. Philip crept back to the storeroom, where at least he felt safe. He stared longingly at the violin but couldn't risk it, especially when Miles and Logan might be roaming around.

His empty stomach continued to growl at him. For a second he actually debated eating his attempts at a candy harmonica, but reason won out. He waited another few minutes before venturing out again.

When he entered the hallway, he was surprised to see how dark it had gotten. The main lights were off, and the dim bulbs along the ceiling barely shed enough light to see three feet ahead. Now that all of the machines were quiet, he noticed how loudly his dress shoes echoed in the hallway.

He doubled back to the storeroom and pulled out the first-aid kit in the hopes of finding a flashlight. He found not one but two. Neither worked when he switched them on. He began pulling apart boxes. Inside the third box lay three mechanical monkeys with cymbals for hands. He emptied out all their batteries, and by mixing and matching he was able to get one of the flashlights to work. He had to keep banging it against his hip to keep it on, but that was a small price to pay.

But what to do about his noisy shoes? He searched the room, including what looked like a bag of gardener's clothes, and wasn't surprised when no shoes turned up. He'd just have to take off his shoes and go in his socks.

So that's what he did. Flashlight at his side, he crept back into the hall and toward the front entryway. Whatever they used to shine these floors really worked — he had to be really careful not to slip with every other step. When he reached the corridor that led to the Marshmallow Room, an idea occurred to him. The boots!

He managed to make it there with only one near wipeout. He found both pairs of boots in a metal closet that creaked when he opened it. When he pulled out the ones he'd worn that morning, a pair of blue-and-white sneakers tumbled forward.

Sneakers would be even better! The streaks of yellowed marshmallow confirmed that they were Henry's, and a few sizes too big, but he tied the laces really tight and they worked fine.

As he passed the bathroom by the Lightning Chews Room, he thought he heard water running. He listened for a minute, and when it didn't shut off he decided it was likely just the pipes.

The Cocoa Room was finally dark! He breezed through the door and promptly fell right over a pile of bean pods, sending them skittering everywhere. He lay there, panting, waiting for someone to switch on the light and yell, "We got you!"

When no lights came on, he pushed himself up and began to restack the pods. Why would Steve have left them right in front of the door? When that was finally done, he hurried to the end of the room, where the cabinet awaited. He'd seen the workers go into the cabinet a dozen times today, and he knew it wasn't locked. He was about to reach for the handle when he thought he heard a sound in the hallway outside.

He swung the flashlight toward the window, only to find

himself staring at his own reflection inside a circle of light. A memory formed in his head. He turned back to the cabinet and for a moment let himself remember a game he and Andrew used to play when they were little. They'd turn off the lights and use flashlights to make shapes in the mirrors. Sometimes they'd spell out words for the other person to guess. Maybe not the coolest of games, but it was the last time he could remember playing anything at all with Andrew.

He shook the memory from his head and reached for the knob. It didn't budge. He tried again. Nothing. Impossible! He'd never seen them lock it!

He moved the flashlight up and down until he found the small keyhole. Reaching into his jacket, he pulled out the screwdrivers, chose the right one, and got to work. A minute later, the lock popped open.

He reached up and grabbed the tin. It weighed practically nothing. His spirits soared. He'd done it! He'd gotten it before they did.

Then he heard it. A distinct sliding sound. He counted to ten, then whirled around. A figure was crouched on the ground. He'd seen enough movies to know what to do next.

He shined the flashlight directly in the person's eyes. "Looking for this?" he asked, holding up the tin.

Then he saw who was on the receiving end of his flashlight beam. For a long moment, neither of them spoke. Then, without warning, Daisy leapt forward. Philip had only a split second to raise the tin above his head before she was in front of him, grabbing for it. He lost his balance, and the two of them went toppling to the ground.

When they landed, they both scooted backward, Daisy hitting the leg of a table, Philip nearly knocking over a huge container marked BUTTERFAT. The flashlight flew out of his hand and rolled under the huge bean grinder.

They stared at each other in the shadows.

"What are you doing here?" she hissed.

"Me? What am *I* doing here? What are *you* doing here?"

"*You're* the one holding the secret ingredient."

"It's not what it looks like," Philip insisted.

"It looks like you're trying to steal the secret ingredient so you can win the contest."

"No! Well, sort of. But not for the reason you think. I'm only taking it to keep someone else from getting it."

Daisy's eyes narrowed. "Really? Who?"

"My father, if you must know. He hired someone to steal it. He's planning to buy out the company."

Daisy gasped. "*Your father* is my client? Your father is *Big Billy?*"

"Who? No! His name isn't Billy. Wait, what do you mean your *client?*"

They didn't take their eyes from each other's face. In that instant Philip felt reality unravel in front of him like a spool of thread. Was *Daisy* his father's inside man? *Daisy?*

Her face, the floor, the huge bean grinder above them, it all began to blur.

Then someone sneezed.

Daisy looked at Philip. Philip looked at Daisy. Daisy put her finger over her mouth. Philip nodded.

They stood up.

PART FIVE

LOGAN
AGAIN

CHAPTER ONE

Maybe they didn't hear," Logan whispered to Miles in a choked voice. Miles was holding his hand over his nose, squeezing it tight so he wouldn't sneeze again. They both instinctively pressed themselves farther into the corner. There really wasn't anywhere else to go without revealing their hiding spot under the table.

Logan was having trouble sorting through what they'd just overheard. It sounded as if Philip was trying to steal the Candymaker's secret ingredient. Or was it Daisy? Nice, sweet Daisy? How did they even get inside? The factory doors were all locked at night.

Why were they talking about Big Billy? Everyone who knew Big Billy (and everyone in the candy business did) knew that the owner of **Mmm Mmm Good** was one of the nicest guys anywhere. Sure, maybe he liked to place bets on which candies would be successful that year and which would go the way of the Salami-Flavored Chocolate Nubs, but he'd never do anything to *hurt* another candymaker.

And, most important, how could Philip's father buy the company when it wasn't for sale?

Logan's eyes widened as two pairs of feet appeared in front of their table. Miles held up his paper-towel roll like a sword, ready to do battle. Logan would have laughed if the situation weren't so dire. They both pressed themselves against the wall, as though they'd be able to melt into it.

No such luck.

It was Daisy's face they saw first. Even in the near darkness, her yellow hair glowed. "Rats," she said softly when she recognized them. She kneeled beside the table and put her hands over her face.

"Rats?" Philip echoed. "There are rats in the factory? I didn't know a rat could sneeze."

"Cover blown, awaiting instructions," she said. Or at least that's what it sounded like to Logan.

"Huh?" asked Philip.

"I wasn't talking to you," she replied.

"Who were you talking to, then?" he asked. "And you still haven't told me what you're doing here."

Logan had heard enough. "C'mon," he said to Miles, who was still frozen in place, paper-towel roll at the ready. He took Miles by the arm and pulled him forward until they had cleared the table. Above the roaster was a heat lamp, and as Logan stood up he reached over and switched it on. It shed enough light to see everyone clearly now.

Philip gasped and jumped backward, knocking over an entire container of cocoa-bean shells. Some fell onto Daisy's head and slid down her ponytail, but she didn't even seem to notice. The rest scattered all around them, bouncing a few inches as they struck the hard floor.

Logan was reminded of when the powdered sugar spilled all over Philip the day before. That was back when things made sense. Now nothing did.

He turned from Daisy to Philip and back again. Daisy looked miserable, her eyes red, her usual smile nowhere to be found. As usual, Philip wouldn't even meet his eyes.

His voice shaking, Logan asked, "Would someone mind telling me what's going on?"

"Yeah," Miles added, still holding the paper-towel roll in front of him defensively. "Tsuj s'tahw gniog no ereh?" Then he quickly said, "I ... I mean, just what's going on here?"

Logan watched as Daisy did something that, even years later, he'd have trouble believing. She reached into her ear, dug around, and pulled out a shiny plastic object about the size of a pencil eraser. She placed it on the floor beside her. Then she stood up. "I think we all need to talk."

"Daisy?" a male voice called out from somewhere. *"Daisy? What did you just do?"*

Unbelievably, the voice seemed to be coming from the tiny object on the floor. Logan and Miles and Philip all crouched down around it. The world's tiniest cell phone, maybe?

"Daisy!" the voice barked. *"Come back here!"*

The boys looked at one another with identical wide-eyed expressions. Logan realized that this was the first time Philip had actually held his gaze for more than a second. Philip must have realized it, too, because in that instant his eyes softened and Logan saw something he'd never expected to see — regret.

"Come on," Daisy said. "We need to talk *somewhere else*." Bean shells crunched underfoot as she hurried from the room. No one else moved. Finally Miles shrugged and headed after her.

Logan and Philip continued to stare at each other. Logan broke the silence. "Why were you trying to steal my father's secret ingredient?"

Philip opened his mouth, then closed it again. He retreated a few steps and picked up the metal tin, which had been forgotten in all the excitement. Wordlessly, he handed it to Logan.

Logan looked down at the dented old tin clutched tight in his hand. He'd wanted to see inside it as long as he could remember. The corner was scratched and dented, and he wondered if that had happened just now or if it had been that way for years. He knew he could easily pop off the lid, but instead he handed it back to Philip.

"Here. If you need it so badly, you should have it."

Clearly surprised, Philip didn't do anything at first. Then he shoved the tin into his jacket pocket. "Daisy's right. We need to talk." He said this in a voice much different from the one he'd used with Logan before. Gone was the sarcasm. In its place was something like … respect?

Logan stumbled after him, hardly able to believe all this

was happening. How quickly his life had gone from a nice, easy routine to ... to ... whatever it was now. As the door to the Cocoa Room swung shut behind him and he joined the other three in the hall, he thought back to the words he'd greeted them with only a few yards from this spot. *Be not forgetful to entertain strangers, for thereby some have entertained angels unawares.* He looked at the faces of his fellow contestants and wondered just who he had been entertaining.

The four of them trudged, not speaking, toward the Tropical Room. Logan had decided that would be the best place to go. It was where his parents expected him to be, plus he always felt safe there and protected by the trees.

As they approached the cafeteria, Philip stopped. "Um, I know this might not be the best time, but I'm really, really hungry. Is there any way..."

"Now you suddenly care about food?" Daisy asked.

"Hey, I haven't eaten in twelve hours," Philip said.

Logan sighed and pointed to the ledge above the door. "The key's up there if you can reach it."

Philip stood on his toes and reached up. He tried jumping, but his fingers only grazed the bottom of the ledge.

"Oh, I'll do it," Daisy snapped.

Philip barely had time to step aside before she leapt into the air, swiped the top of the ledge, and landed with the key in her open palm.

"Wow," Miles said. "Are you, like, a superhero or something?"

"Something like that," Daisy replied with a wink.

Logan took the key and opened the door. The lingering odor of food and cleaning supplies greeted him as they entered. Never a great mix.

He'd been in the cafeteria at night many times fetching last-minute ingredients for dinner or attending the occasional after-hours meeting. But he'd never been there without his parents' knowledge, and never before with friends.

If these *were* his friends.

He led the group behind the counter and over to one of the huge refrigerators that lined the back wall. "You can make a sandwich from here if you like."

Philip pulled open the doors of the nearest one and began filling his arms with bread, sliced turkey, a block of cheddar cheese, a jar of pickles, a container of mustard, and, at the last second, a tomato. He plopped it all down on the counter.

"You weren't kidding when you said you were hungry," Miles commented as he ran his eyeglasses under the sink faucet. Logan wondered how the glasses had gotten chocolate on them, but there were more pressing things on his mind.

Philip stared at the food spread out before him. His face turned pink.

"Do you have a problem with the food selection?" Daisy asked, her hands on her hips. "Because I think I speak for all of us in saying that you're lucky you're getting anything to eat at all."

Philip shook his head quickly. "No, it's not that. I just ... I've ... I've never actually, er, made a sandwich before."

Logan expected Daisy to have something to say about that, but she didn't say a word.

"Let me get this straight," Miles said. "You've never made a sandwich before? Like when you put a bunch of stuff between two pieces of bread?"

Philip shook his head.

Miles sighed and picked up the knife. "I'll help you."

Logan went into the pantry to collect some snacks. Crackers and juice and gumdrops. He had a feeling they'd all be hungry by the time they were done talking.

Ten minutes later, they were settled on the ground under the sapodilla tree, where Logan had left the sleeping bags and duffels. Philip, although clearly not happy sitting on the dirt in his suit, didn't complain for once. He had inhaled his sandwich on the walk from the cafeteria and had even grudgingly thanked Miles for making it. It was the nicest thing Logan remembered hearing Philip say to Miles since they'd met.

"I'd like to know—" Daisy began, but Logan held up his hand to stop her.

"I'm sorry, but I should get to go first." He felt a little awkward saying it, since usually he was happy to listen. But this time was different. They had broken into his family's factory. He had questions.

Daisy nodded. "Sorry, you're right."

Of all the answers he wanted to hear, one was most pressing. "What I want to know," he said, forcing himself to look Daisy straight in the eyes, "is whether you were just pretending to be my friend in order to steal the secret ingredient."

"No!" she said hurriedly. "Not at all! And I *didn't* steal it — Philip did!"

"Hey," Philip said, jumping up, his head just barely missing a low branch. "That's not fair. You *would've* stolen it if I hadn't gotten there first."

"Actually," Daisy said, crossing her arms, "I wasn't trying to steal it at all."

Logan frowned. "But Miles and I heard you trying to take it from Philip."

"Yes, but I wasn't trying to steal it." She began pulling on her ponytail the way she did when she got nervous. "I mean, okay, in the beginning I was. But once I knew someone was going to use it to ruin the factory, I was trying to sabotage their plan instead."

Logan tried hard to follow what she was saying, but it didn't make any sense. "I don't understand."

She began pulling up blades of grass around the base of the tree. "I was, um, how should I put this... planning on mixing in some soap shavings so the chocolate would taste really bad."

The three boys' mouths fell open.

"Soap?" Logan repeated. "You were going to put soap in our chocolate? But why?"

Daisy pointed a finger up at Philip, who was pacing back and forth. "So *his father* wouldn't be able to sell it to a competitor, or whatever underhanded plan he had in mind!"

Philip stopped pacing. "You don't know that. You told me someone named Big Billy hired you!"

"Big Billy would never try to steal anything from us," Logan insisted. "I've known him my whole life. And what does he mean by 'hired' you?"

"So maybe I'm wrong about Big Billy," Daisy conceded, ignoring Logan's question. "But I'm not wrong about someone hiring me to steal it. Someone who calls himself Second Enterprises."

Philip reddened and plopped down onto a rolled-up sleeping bag. "Yeah, that would be my dad. Philip Ransford the Second. Second Enterprises. He uses that name when he's doing research on a company and doesn't want people to know yet who he is."

Logan turned to Philip now. "So you didn't know who he'd hired, but you knew your father hired *someone* to steal the tin? Then why were *you* trying to get it?"

"I didn't know about his plan until last night. I figured I had to take it to keep *him* from getting it."

"Ha!" Daisy said. "And we're supposed to believe that? Why?"

Philip hesitated for a second, then said, "The same reason you were trying to make it taste bad. You didn't want anyone buying the factory, right?"

"Right. So?"

"Well, why is it so hard to believe that I had the same reason?"

"Because you hate this place," Daisy pointed out. "All you care about is winning the contest."

Philip hung his head. "I don't hate this place."

No one said anything for a full minute. Then Miles spoke for the first time since they'd sat down. "Siht si yzarc! I thguoht ew erew sdneirf! Tub uoy erew tsuj ereh esuaceb enoemos diap uoy!"

"Huh?" Philip asked.

Logan felt a pang of concern. This wasn't the first time he'd heard Miles blurt out nonsense. What if something was seriously wrong with him?

"I know it seems crazy," Daisy said, laying her hand on Miles's arm. "And we *are* friends, I promise. At least, I hope we are."

Miles's eyes widened. "You understood me?"

Daisy nodded. "I know a lot of languages. Including how to speak backward. I can also sign, do Morse code, and decipher Egyptian hieroglyphics. "

Logan turned to Miles. "You were speaking backward?"

Miles nodded, reddening.

"That's a relief!" Logan said. Then, turning to Daisy, he said, "I still don't understand. Why would anyone have hired you to steal anything?"

Daisy covered her face with her hands. For a second Logan thought she might be crying. Then she lifted her chin and met their eyes straight on. "Because, as you've probably already figured out, I'm a spy."

Her words hung in the air for a minute. Logan thought back to the tiny device she'd taken out of her ear. That had seemed so strange he hadn't known what to make of it. But a spy? *Daisy?*

"Let me get this straight," he said. "You're a spy, like on TV? Where you sneak into places and have gadgets and wear fake mustaches?" It all seemed impossible to believe.

Daisy smiled for the first time since the events in the Cocoa Room. A kind of calm seemed to have settled on her, too. "Well, I don't usually wear a fake mustache, but the rest sounds about right."

"But how can you be a spy when you're still a kid?" he asked.

"I was born into it," she explained. "My whole family are spies."

Logan and Miles looked at each other in amazement.

"I've never told anyone that before," she added.

"What about Magpie?" Miles asked. "You must have told her. She's your best friend. Unless . . . she's also a spy?"

Daisy pulled at the grass again. "Um, not exactly. She's gone on some missions with me, but she's . . . my horse."

Philip tried to stifle a laugh but wasn't very successful. "Your best friend is a horse?"

"Hey, Magpie isn't afraid to hang out with me because I'm the boss's granddaughter. And she's not always trying to get the best missions or be the first to try the newest gadget from Research and Development. She's always there for me."

Philip rolled his eyes but let it go.

"So we're really the only people who know?" Miles asked. "Why did you tell us? You could have made up some story for being in the Cocoa Room. You could have said you were there to stop Philip."

She pulled at her ponytail again. "I told you because I've never had friends like you guys before. Friends who liked me for me, or at least as much of me as I could show you. I figured when everything went sour in the Cocoa Room, I might as well come clean. It's a relief, actually. I hated lying to you."

"So you're not really in the contest?" Logan asked, thinking of all the people who had wanted to get in but didn't.

"I *am*," she replied. "I didn't really care about winning, though. Not until I saw *him*." She gestured with her thumb at Philip.

Philip's eyes widened in surprise. "Me? Why would meeting *me* make you want to win?"

"If you must know, it's because you blew my cover. Twice now!"

"What are you talking about? I never even met you before."

"Harrison Elementary, three years ago," Daisy said, her eyes suddenly cold. "Regional spelling bee. You caught me trying to investigate cheating judges. I got reassigned to a dairy farm. I had to milk cows all day to bust up an illegal milking ring. My hands swelled up and I had to keep them in buckets of ice for hours."

Philip paled. "That was you? But that girl had red hair. And glasses."

"I was undercover. We need to look different for every job."

"So you wouldn't normally wear bright yellow dresses and two different socks?" Logan asked.

Daisy shook her head.

He felt a little disappointed at that, and also a little relieved.

"Well," Miles said, shaking his head in amazement. "This explains why you two hated each other so quickly."

"I never hated her," Philip muttered.

"A real live spy!" Logan said, finally accepting it. "Is that why you're so strong? And can jump so high? And know all those languages?"

She nodded, leaning against the tree. "I can do a lot of things. Run really fast, carry heavy things, hold my breath a long time, do advanced calculus. The training is really rigorous."

"What kind of training?" Logan asked.

Daisy shrugged. "Like I've had to run twenty miles in a hailstorm, climb trees with a thirty-pound weight on my back. Things to prepare us for any situation. A few years ago I had to swim across an entire lake underwater. I was supposed to be practicing for a job in Italy where I'd have to swim out to an island without being seen. The gig went to someone else, though." Daisy grimaced at the memory.

Miles made some sort of gagging sound and went as white as a cloud. "When...when did you swim under the lake?"

Daisy looked surprised at the question. "I'm not sure, maybe a year ago? Why?"

Miles inched closer to her. "Was this at Verona Park, a few miles outside Spring Haven?"

She nodded. "Why do you ask?"

He started to shake all over, like the epicenter of his own personal earthquake.

Logan rushed over to him. "Are you all right?" Miles didn't seem to hear him. All his attention was focused on Daisy.

"Did you have brown hair then?" he asked.

"Probably," she said, squirming a little. "That's my real color. Why are you asking me all these questions?"

Miles continued to shake. Logan worried he was having some sort of fit. Maybe he should use the intercom and get his parents.

"And you ran straight into the water?" Miles asked.

Daisy looked at Logan for support, but he was clueless, too.

"And the bees?" Miles asked, his voice quivering. "What about the bees?"

"I don't remember any bees," she said, frowning. "My dad pressed a stopwatch and told me to go, so I got up from the beach and ran in. I held my breath and swam as close to the bottom as I could. I remember swimming under a boat or two, and then I came up on the other side, where my parents and grandmother were waiting. That's all I remember. Pretty basic training exercise. Why are you ask—"

But she didn't get to finish because Miles launched himself through the air and wrapped his arms around her.

"You're alive!" he cried, tears suddenly streaming down his face. "You're alive!"

Logan stumbled backward in surprise. Even Philip jumped up, sending the sleeping bag he'd been sitting on rolling down the path toward the vanilla vines.

"What are you talking about?" Daisy asked as Miles clung to her, weeping, then laughing, then weeping again. He couldn't answer, due to the weeping and the laughing.

When it became clear he wasn't letting her go anytime soon, Daisy put her arms around him and hugged him back. This just made him hold on tighter.

"Do you think we should do something?" Philip asked Logan as the minutes passed.

"What should we do?"

"Maybe we should pry him off her."

Logan nodded. That seemed like a sensible idea.

Miles tried to hold on as Logan and Philip each took one of his arms, but he eventually allowed himself to be separated from Daisy.

"You okay, buddy?" Logan asked.

Miles wiped his eyes with the back of his hands, laughed again, and then said, "I was in that boat. The one Daisy swam under. Only I didn't see her. All this time I thought the girl—I mean Daisy—had drowned and I hadn't been able to save her."

Daisy's hand flew up to her mouth. "Oh no! I'm so sorry!"

"Is that why you talk about the afterlife all the time?" Philip asked.

Miles nodded. "The girl lives there." Then he laughed. "No, she doesn't! No wonder I felt the girl was here at the factory. She WAS here!" Then, before Logan or Philip could stop him, he threw his arms around Daisy again.

This time she hugged him back right away. "I'm really sorry. I didn't think anyone saw me run in. It must have been awful for you."

Still clutching tight, Miles said, "At least you didn't get stung by those bees. Being allergic and all."

"Honestly, I didn't even see them."

For some reason, that started Miles laughing and crying all over again.

Philip rolled his eyes. Then he said, "Um, speaking of bees, are there supposed to be bees in here?"

"Paulo brings a few in sometimes to pollinate the vanilla flowers," Logan replied. "One or two might cling to the vines every once in a while. Why?"

Philip pointed about a foot above Daisy's head, where a black-and-yellow bee was circling.

"Daisy!" Logan said, pulling on her sleeve. "There's a bee near you."

"So?" she said, still comforting Miles. The bee was now about two inches away from her left ear.

"Aren't you allergic?"

"Oh, right," Daisy said, untangling herself from Miles. "I keep forgetting. Hazard of the trade when you're always pretending to be someone else. I sometimes forget my real story." She stepped forward a few feet, but the bee followed her.

"Can't you charm it or something?" Philip asked Logan.

Logan shot him a look and tried shooing the bee away. It refused to go. "It must be attracted to your hair," he told Daisy.

As if to prove Logan's point, the bee flew right at Daisy's head at top speed. She shrieked and shuffled backward, her foot catching on a tree root. The others all gasped, but it happened too quickly for them to do anything. She flailed her arms, but it was of no use — she'd lost her balance and was on a collision course with the ground.

So fast that Logan could only half believe he'd seen it happen, Miles ducked, grabbed his backpack, and pushed it right to the spot where, a split second later, Daisy's head landed.

She lay there panting. The bee was nowhere in sight, perhaps scared off by all the drama.

Miles grinned and said, "Huh. I guess this thing did save your life after all."

"What's in there?" Daisy asked, still lying on her back.

"A life jacket. I sort of carry it with me everywhere. It's crazy, I know."

But Daisy shook her head. "It shows how much you can care about saving someone you've never even met. And now you saved me! I think *you're* the superhero here."

Miles pushed his glasses back up his nose and coughed.

"Better watch out," Philip teased. "I think she likes you."

Daisy groaned. "Philip Ransford the Third, do you have *any* redeeming qualities?"

"Hey," Logan said, "he *did* just save the factory. Even if he had to steal to do it."

"That's true," Miles said.

"Yeah, about that . . . ," Philip began.

"Let me guess," said Daisy, pushing herself up to a sitting position. "You made up that whole story and were just trying to steal the secret ingredient so you would win the contest."

"Not exactly."

"I knew it!" Daisy shouted.

Philip sighed. "Will you let me finish?"

Daisy grumbled something unintelligible.

"I was going to say that taking the secret ingredient might slow my father down, but there's only one way to make sure he won't buy the factory." He paused, pulling nervously at a leaf dangling above his head. Logan tried not to cringe. No one was supposed to pull the leaves.

"Well?" Daisy asked. "What is it?"

"I have to, um, win the contest."

Daisy hooted. "You're kidding, right?"

"It's true," Philip insisted, looking them each in the eye. "My father promised that if I win, he won't try to buy the factory."

No one spoke for a minute. Logan really wanted to believe him. But believing Philip meant that he'd have to give up his own dream of winning. That was a lot to give up based on the word of someone who hadn't said one nice thing to him until that night.

"But why would your father agree to that?" Miles asked.

"He doesn't think I could possibly win, so he's not too worried about losing the bet."

"Well, then," Miles said matter-of-factly. "We'll just have to make sure you win."

Logan's eyes widened in surprise. Philip had been the meanest to Miles. Why would Miles believe him so easily?

"Are you serious?" Daisy asked. "You actually believe that story?"

Miles nodded.

"What about your mother?" Daisy demanded of Philip. "What does she think about all this?"

"You'd have to ask Miles about that," Philip replied. "He's the expert on the afterlife."

It took Logan a few seconds to figure out what Philip meant. He'd never met anyone who didn't have a mother. Well, not that he knew of.

"Oh," said Daisy, lowering her head. "I didn't know."

Philip shrugged. "Why would you?"

"When did it ... I mean, when did she ..." Daisy trailed off. It was the first time Logan had seen her at a loss for words.

"When I was three," Philip said. "She got sick. I don't remember her too well, but I know she liked chocolate a lot. I think she'd be happy I'm here."

Logan had no clue what to say or do. He considered offering gumdrops but knew that wasn't right.

Miles must have known just what to do, though, because he walked straight over to Philip and put his arms around him.

Philip stood as stiff as the sapodilla tree next to him, but Miles didn't let go.

"You might as well hug him back," Daisy recommended. "He won't stop until you do."

So Philip raised his arms and awkwardly placed them on Miles's shoulders. They stood like that for another minute until Philip broke away. "Uh, thanks," he said awkwardly. "I think I'm good now."

Miles gave him one last pat on the arm and then retreated.

Daisy cleared her throat. "So, um, is your candy good enough to win?"

Philip shook his head. "Not yet. Maybe if I had another week."

Logan knew what he had to do. It was a choice that two days ago he couldn't have imagined making.

"Well, what are we standing around here for?" he asked. "We've got to get to the lab. You don't have a week, but you have us. Between the four of us, I'm sure we can come up with something great." He looked at Daisy and Miles. "If you guys agree, that is."

"I'm in," Miles said. "I don't need to win anymore. You know, due to the whole Daisy-not-being-dead thing."

Daisy grinned and hit him playfully on the arm.

"Ouch," Miles said.

"Sorry."

"What about you, Daisy?" Logan asked.

She nodded. "Just because I failed to plant the soap in the tin doesn't change anything. I still want to help save the company. It's a shame, though," she said wistfully. "My contest entry is really good."

The three boys looked at one another and starting laughing.

"It's a green glob of goop!" Miles shouted.

"True," Daisy admitted. "But it tastes like a summer's day."

"Doubt that," Philip said, sounding for a second like his old self.

"I know you guys like to argue over anything and everything," Logan said, "but we don't have much time left."

"What about you?" Daisy said. "Your grandfather and your father...winning the contest is a family tradition. This is your only chance. Can you really pass it up?"

"I have to," Logan said, feeling both sad and determined. "I want to be a candymaker, right? Well, it's time to go make some candy."

Miles came toward him, arms outstretched, ready to hug. Logan held up one hand. "Seriously, dude, I'm good."

Everyone laughed. They started down the path toward the door when Miles pointed in the direction of the cinnamon tree. "Um, I think we have company."

At first Logan thought the young man who stepped out from behind the narrow tree was Avery. Mostly because he hadn't heard anyone come in, and he couldn't imagine anyone else being there. But he was wrong. *How did everyone get into the factory after closing?* He'd have to talk to his dad about beefing up security.

"What are you doing here?" Daisy asked.

Before the guy could answer, Miles turned to Philip. "This is Daisy's cousin, Bo. He can pull motorcycles with his teeth." He lowered his voice to a whisper. "Can't talk, though. Lost all his teeth from the pulling."

"I didn't really lose my teeth," Bo said, pointing to a mouthful of pearly whites. "See? All there."

Logan and Miles both jumped back at the sound of his voice.

Bo glared at Daisy. "And my name's AJ, not Bo. Not a cousin. Just a really annoyed handler." He thrust Daisy's pocketbook at her.

"Boy, Daisy!" Miles said, shaking his head. "It's a good thing I'm still happy you didn't drown, or I'd be really ticked off at you for all the lies."

Daisy hung her head sheepishly. "I'll make it up to you. To all of you, I promise."

AJ still glared at Daisy, apparently unmoved by her remorse. "From what I've overheard, you have compromised not only your mission but our entire organization. We need to leave the premises. Now."

Daisy reddened. "I didn't tell them *everything*."

AJ scowled. "You were pretty detailed."

She shook her head. "Not true. Like, I left out the part about me being thirteen."

AJ groaned and slapped his hand against his forehead.

"What?" Logan, Miles, and Philip shouted in unison.

"You're *thirteen?*" Logan looked at Daisy in a whole new light. Thirteen! That was a teenager!

Daisy held up her hands. "Hey, don't blame me. I just found out myself."

"You didn't know your own age?" Miles asked, clearly skeptical.

Daisy shook her head. "Long story."

"You know you can't be in the contest now," Philip said. He didn't gloat about it, though.

Daisy's eyebrows shot up. "Oh! I guess you're right. Well, it doesn't matter anyway, since we're all helping *you* win now."

Logan put his hand on her arm. "Maybe AJ's right. This doesn't have to be your fight. I don't want you to get in trouble."

Daisy stood up straight. "Daisy Dinkleman never walks away until the job is finished."

"Dinkleman?" Miles repeated. "I thought your last name was Carpenter."

"Daisy," AJ said, gritting his very real teeth. "Please think about this. What am I going to tell your grandmother? She's at the mansion waiting for our report."

"Just tell her the truth."

AJ shook his head. "That's for you to do, not me. I'll stall her until after the contest tomorrow, but that's it. You're on your own."

Daisy nodded gratefully. "Thanks, AJ. You've been a good handler." Then she winked. "And a good cousin."

AJ just grunted.

Philip cleared his throat. "This has been a lovely family moment, but I think we'd better get moving. It's late already."

Logan turned to say goodbye to AJ, but there was no sign of him. Just a faint rustling of leaves on the other side of the room.

"Wow," Miles said, looking around. "He moves fast!"

Daisy nodded. "He always gets the jobs where you have to disappear really fast. Speaking of moving fast, we really do need to get going."

As they hurried from the Tropical Room, Miles said to Philip, "You know, you kinda look like AJ."

"You mean because we're both so incredibly good-looking?"asked Philip, tilting his head and grinning.

Logan groaned.

"Good-looking?" Daisy repeated, pretending to look Philip up and down. "Nah, I don't see it."

Philip rolled his eyes.

"You really should get that checked," Logan said.

Wait here while I get my candy," Philip instructed them when they reached the lab. He switched on the lights and ushered them in.

"Isn't it in the refrigerator with ours?" Miles asked.

"Just wait here," he repeated. "I'll be right back."

As soon as Philip had left the room, Daisy turned to Logan. "I know all this must be a big shock. I'd feel terrible if I thought I'd hurt your feelings in any way. I really just want to help."

Logan nodded. "I know, I believe you. I mean, you're still the same Daisy ... unless, um, Daisy isn't your real name?"

"It is," she promised.

"And your last name's Dinkleman?" asked Miles.

Daisy laughed. "No, not really. That's sort of a joke." Then her smile disappeared. "Actually, I don't know my last name."

Logan and Miles shared a look.

"What do you mean?" Miles asked.

Daisy sighed. "The spy world is really secretive. Sometimes the less we know about ourselves, the safer we'll be."

"But couldn't you just ask your parents?" Miles asked.

She shook her head. "I don't see them very often. It's complicated."

Logan felt sorry for her then. No matter how cool the gadgets or how fun the adventures, he couldn't imagine not knowing his own last name or seeing his parents every day.

The three of them were quiet when Philip burst in, his briefcase clutched in one hand, a big plastic container in the other.

"Ready to lay your eyes on the world's best new candy?" Philip asked, his hands poised over the container.

"We've been ready for ten minutes," Miles replied, drumming his fingers on the one lab table not hidden by the temporary walls.

"If you don't open it soon," Daisy said, "I'm going to push for submitting my green glob of goop instead."

"Anything but that," Philip said with a shudder. He lifted the lid and held the box out to them.

"Um, what is it?" Logan asked, seeing only a rectangular lump of chocolate lying on a sheet of wax paper.

Miles peered closer. "Is it a chocolate cell phone?"

Philip rolled his eyes. "No, it's not a chocolate cell phone! It's so obvious!"

Daisy bounced with excitement. "I know what it is!"

"See?" Philip said. "I told you it was obvious!"

"It's a brown glob of goop!" she shouted.

Logan and Miles laughed. Philip frowned. He placed the container on the lab table and lifted out the layers one by one. Logan could see milk chocolate, pieces of cookie, marshmallow, and what looked like strips of dried-out honeycomb. He'd seen a lot of candies before — hundreds, if not thousands, of candies in all different stages. The world's greatest new candy invention this most definitely was not.

"We don't mean to laugh," he said to Philip. "But seriously, what is it?"

Philip surveyed the table before him. "Well, I admit it doesn't look like much."

"Forget what it looks like," Daisy said. "How does it taste?" Without waiting for an answer, she grabbed a large piece and shoved it in her mouth.

"That's not how you're supposed to eat it," Philip cried, reaching for it. But it was too late. Daisy was already chomping away.

Logan watched as her expression went from skeptical to surprised and landed on *very* surprised. She swallowed and grinned. "I've gotta admit I wasn't expecting much. But this is really good! You have a gift! Who'd have thought it?"

Philip glowed under Daisy's praise. "Really? It's good?"

She nodded. "It's great. You really haven't tried it?"

He shook his head.

In the glare of the bright fluorescent lights, Logan thought he spotted some freckles on Philip's cheeks that he'd never noticed before. They reminded him of something, but he couldn't think what.

Miles reached for a chunk of chocolate, but Philip stepped in the way. "Wait, that's not how it works."

Miles pulled his hand back. "What do you mean, 'how it works'?"

Philip pointed to one of the blobs, which looked vaguely rectangular. "It's a candy harmonica. Or at least it's supposed to be. It doesn't quite work yet."

They all leaned in closer. Daisy shook her head. "Sorry, don't see it. It tasted good, but I'm pretty sure it didn't play music."

Logan knew what to do. He'd seen Max do it a hundred times. "Okay, everyone," he announced, stepping away from the table. He waited before continuing until they were all facing him. "This is the plan. We lay out all the ingredients Philip used. We try each one separately, we try them together. We add new ones, we take some away. We write down how it tastes, how it feels on our tongues, how long it takes to chew. We rebuild it until it plays like a real harmonica." Turning to Philip, he asked, "You'll be in charge of that last part. Do you know anything about music?"

Philip hesitated. "I know enough."

"That'll have to do. Miles, you'll work on the molds." He pointed to a shelf lined with candymaking books. "Those will help you. Daisy, you'll make up batches of chocolate. Sound good?"

"Ready, boss!" Miles said with a wide grin.

Logan felt his cheeks grow warm. "I'm not the boss, I just—"

"You're the Candymaker's son," Philip said. "If anyone can make this work, you can."

Logan looked down, both surprised at the compliment and afraid to admit it might not be true. "I'm not so sure," he said. "I'll try my best."

"You can do it," Philip said confidently. "This is what you were born to do."

At those words, Logan felt a new determination rise up inside him. So what if he hadn't always been the best at following through with things? So what if he sometimes got distracted and his attention wandered? *Now* was what mattered, and now he would give it all he had.

"Well, well, Philip Ransford the Third," Daisy said, nodding appreciatively. "You really are full of surprises."

Philip winked. "You ain't seen nothin' yet."

Before anyone could ask what he meant by that, the door to the lab swung open, and they froze.

"You all look like you've seen a ghost!" the Candymaker boomed.

Logan glanced at the others. They wore identical expressions of shock and fear. He was sure he did, too.

The Candymaker held up a plastic bag with something square inside. "I thought you might need a snack."

No one spoke. The others were still frozen in place. Logan snapped out of it first, his heart rate slowly lowering. "How did you, uh, know we were here?"

The Candymaker laughed. "I went to the Tropical Room to see if you needed anything. You weren't there, so I knew I'd find you here. This is exactly where I was the night before the contest thirty years ago!"

Logan could sense the others relaxing a bit, but still no one moved.

"I didn't expect to find all four of you, but hey, the more the merrier. I'll go rustle up some extra blankets." To Philip and Daisy he asked, "You're planning on staying the night, I presume?"

When they didn't answer, Logan said, "Yes, is that okay?"

His dad handed him the big plastic bag and said, "Of course it's okay. Just remember the contest rules. All contestants deserve privacy while they're working on their entries."

Logan nodded, not daring to even glance at the others.

The Candymaker turned to Philip and Daisy, who still hadn't moved. "Hey, either of you want to share how you got in without showing up on the video monitor?"

Philip began to stutter some sort of answer, then gave up. Daisy tugged on her ponytail so hard she let out a little yelp.

The Candymaker laughed. "I figured as much. I'll leave the blankets in the Tropical Room." He turned to go, then glanced back at Philip, his head tilted as though trying to remember something. Then he shook it off and was gone.

"Wow," Miles said. "That was . . . unexpected."

Logan turned to Daisy. "You're the expert at sneaking around. Wouldn't it just be easier to tell my parents what's going on?"

She shook her head. "We can't tell anyone else at the

factory, because the only way to stop Philip's dad is for the harmonica to win fair and square. That way no one can claim someone here influenced the judges."

"But they'd never do that," Logan said.

"Sometimes in business people are ruthless. They could make things up. We can't take any chances."

Logan nodded. He knew she was right. But he didn't have much practice lying to his parents. The one time he'd lied—about doing his homework when he hadn't—his mom threatened to send him to a *real* school, with *standardized tests!* Logan didn't know what standardized tests were, but he didn't like the sound of them. He couldn't even bring himself to think about how awful it would be to tell them he wasn't submitting the Bubbletastic Choco-Rocket after all.

"Are you going to get in trouble for bringing us here?" Philip asked.

Logan shook his head and lifted up the bag. "If I was in trouble, he wouldn't have brought us chocolate pizza!"

Miles lunged for it, but Logan held the bag over his head. Miles jumped for it but still couldn't reach. "Sorry," Logan said, "but we can't eat it yet."

"Why not?" Miles cried.

Logan stepped away from Miles and slid the bag under the lab table. "Because we can't clutter up our taste buds."

"M'i gnilliw ot ekat eht ksir," Miles grumbled.

"I'm going to ignore that," Logan said, using his foot to push the pizza even farther under the table.

"C'mon, let's get to work," Philip said, heading toward the cabinets. "I'll show you what I used."

The next hour flew by in a flurry of activity. Logan tasted different portions of the harmonica, focusing on the delicate balance of ingredients. He suggested adding a little dash of vanilla to the chocolate for a kick of sweetness, spreading a thin layer of caramel on top of the cookie for bulk and stability, and laying down the honeycomb in a crisscross pattern. This would strengthen the inside of the harmonica in case the person playing it gripped it too hard. He also thought they shouldn't use the marshmallow chunks to block off sound in the ends of the tubes, because history (in the form of **Life Is Sweet**'s great Chick-in-the-Egg debacle) had taught them that packaging two different confections together was inevitably disastrous. One always melted or cracked before the other, or they got separated in shipping and the customer wound up with only half of what he'd been promised.

Meanwhile, Daisy tempered the chocolate by hand, her considerable strength speeding the process along. She tapped her foot impatiently whenever the chocolate entered the cooling phase and she was left with nothing to stir.

Philip spent a good ten minutes trying to explain that the different chambers of the harmonica had these things called reeds and that the air blowing through them was what made the different notes. Then there were reed plates and combs, which supported the whole structure. Logan wondered where Philip had learned so much about music. Even though he couldn't follow half of what Philip was saying — stuff about how the reeds had to be open at one end and closed at the other, and some holes were for drawing in and others for exhaling, and the seventh hole was sometimes reversed — he was still impressed by Philip's understanding of the instrument.

Eventually Philip, growing weary of the others' attention clearly drifting off, went to the back of the lab to prepare the honeycomb as Logan had shown him.

Inside his cubicle, Miles pored over a book from Max's shelf on how to make a mold. Logan had just finished adding a cup of flour to the cookie recipe when Miles reappeared, the book clutched in his hand. "I'm afraid what Max told Philip is right," he announced. "There's no way to make the molds in time. We're going to have to do each one by hand."

Daisy lifted the glass thermometer out of her pot of chocolate, checked it, and slid it back in. "Not necessarily," she said. "We could make the mold out of wax."

Miles shook his head. "Metal is the best, or plastic. Wax would melt when we poured the chocolate in."

Daisy grinned. "Not *my* wax."

CHAPTER FOUR

Pssst, Miles," Logan whispered. "Are you awake?"

"No," Miles replied, his head almost completely hidden by the top of his sleeping bag.

Logan smiled in the near darkness. "If you weren't awake you wouldn't have answered me."

"Maybe I'm talking in my sleep," he mumbled.

He lay only a few feet away, but Logan couldn't tell if Miles's eyes were open or closed. The moon cast only a pale light through the glass ceiling, and the trees threw shadows everywhere. There was nothing like the Tropical Room at night. Except, Logan assumed, the real tropics. Which had snakes.

"I'm pretty sure you're not," Logan replied. He had tried to fall asleep himself, but after going through his gratitude list (which had grown considerably after recent events), he found himself more awake than ever. Some pretty big things hadn't gotten settled, and the questions nagged at him.

Logan pushed himself up on his elbows. "It's just that we haven't really talked about tomorrow," he explained. "We're supposed to show up with four new kinds of candy, not one."

Miles rolled over, pushing the sleeping bag away from his face. "You're right. We have to come up with a really good reason why we're dropping out. Let's go ask Daisy."

They wiggled out of their sleeping bags. Miles leaned around the tree and called out for Philip.

"He's not here," Logan said.

"Not here? Where is he?"

Logan shrugged. "He was writing in his notebook, and then the next time I looked, he was gone. Maybe he needed more light or something."

As they headed across the room to the cinnamon tree, Miles asked, "What do you think he writes in there?"

Logan shook his head. "Whatever it is, he's really secretive about it."

"Maybe he's a spy, too!"

Logan laughed. "I sure hope not. It's hard enough with one!"

Even from across the room Logan could see the glow of Daisy's flashlight. As they got closer, he saw that she was holding her book, a red blanket draped over her shoulders. She was reading out loud again, but not loud enough for him to hear the words.

She heard them approach and quickly closed the book.

"Did the farmer's daughter marry the rancher yet?" Miles joked.

"The story's turning out different from what I expected," she said, rubbing her eyes. "Nice pajamas, by the way."

Logan looked down at his familiar blue plaid pants and

top. Miles was wearing an identical pair, except in green. His were a little big, though. He'd almost tripped twice.

"What are you guys still doing up?" Daisy said. "It's the middle of the night."

Logan squinted to read the clock on the wall above Avery's office, but it was too dark to see. When they left the lab it was well past midnight. They'd worked for hours, trying to get the recipe exactly right. Miles had figured out a way to use Daisy's seemingly magical wax to shape molds that looked exactly like real harmonicas. Well, like halves of real harmonicas. They'd have to freeze the molds overnight and then stick the halves together and enrobe the whole thing in chocolate. And they'd have to refreeze them on the way to the contest. But the final test would be blowing into it. A candy harmonica that didn't actually *play* might as well be a lump of chocolate.

"Can I use your flashlight to see what time it is?" Logan asked Daisy.

"I don't have one," she said.

"But weren't you just using it? I saw it glowing."

She sighed and reached for her romance novel. "That would be this."

Miles reached for it first. "Your book has its own light? How cool!"

"It's not exactly like that," she said at the same moment Miles opened the book.

"No," he agreed. "Not exactly like that."

Logan leaned over to see what Miles was seeing. At first

he thought his eyes must be playing tricks on him in the dark. A screen? A bunch of keys with letters and numbers on them? Her romance novel was really...a computer? He looked quizzically at Daisy.

"We call it a comm device. Short for communication device. I plug in someone's exact coordinates, the person shows up on my screen, and we can talk or pass data back and forth. Pretty standard spy stuff."

Miles narrowed his eyes at her.

"I know, I know, the book was another lie. Just remember how happy you are I'm not at the bottom of that lake."

Miles sighed. "I'll try!"

"So what do you guys want?" she asked, pulling the blanket tighter around her. "Not a bedtime story, I hope."

Logan laughed, although to be honest, he wouldn't have minded one. "We just wondered what you thought we should say tomorrow. About why only Philip is going to be in the contest."

Her expression turned serious. "I was thinking about that. The best thing to do would be to each come up with a different, believable reason for dropping out. We don't want anyone to link us together, if possible. Mine's easy. I'll just tell them my real age and they'll have to disqualify me."

"That's a good one," Logan said with a nod. "What about for Miles?"

"I know!" said Miles. "I can submit something against the rules, like a pie!"

"Perfect!" Daisy said.

Logan nodded. "We'd have to hide it from Max, though. If he saw it he'd know something was up."

Miles suddenly frowned. "Where will we get a pie by tomorrow morning?"

Daisy patted her comm device. "Let me take care of that."

"What about you?" Miles asked Logan. "Yours is going to be the hardest to come up with."

"I don't know what to do," Logan admitted, a feeling of dread washing over him. "With my grandfather and my dad both winning, people are going to be talking about me."

"Hmm," Daisy said. "Maybe you should still be in the competition."

"But what if he wound up winning," Miles asked, "and then his family's factory got sold anyway?"

"I still don't understand that part," Logan said. "How can someone buy something that isn't for sale?"

"It's complicated," Philip's voice came from behind, making both Logan and Miles jump. He was still wearing his suit, but the shirt was untucked and the jacket discarded. "There are many ways to force someone out of business," he said without apologizing for sneaking up on them. "If the candy stores could be convinced to stop selling your candy, you'd last maybe a year or two, tops, before having to sell everything off."

"But why would the candy stores do that?"

Daisy answered that one. "We suspect Philip's dad is working with the owner of a rival candy factory. That owner could threaten to withdraw all his candy from the stores unless they agree to only sell *his* brand. And they could offer their candy at such a huge discount that the candy store couldn't refuse."

"Oh," Logan said. "That stinks."

"And that's just one possible tactic," she said.

"To keep up your reputation as the Candymaker's son, you'll still have to submit something really good," Philip said. "Only not as good as our harmonica."

"You mean *your* harmonica," Logan said.

Philip shook his head. "It's all of ours. It would still be a brown glob of goop without you guys."

"True," Daisy said happily.

"We'll all help you, too, Logan," Miles said.

But Logan shook his head. "If I'm really going to submit the Bubbletastic ChocoRocket, it has to be mine alone."

"Are you sure?" Daisy asked.

"I think he's right," Philip said. "He needs to follow the rules completely. That way, if anyone questions him, he won't have to lie. Something tells me he hasn't had much practice doing that."

"We better go to sleep now," Logan said, still feeling queasy. "It's gonna be a big day tomorrow."

"Before you guys go," Daisy said, "we still need a name for the harmonica."

"Can't we just call it the Chocolate Harmonica?" Philip asked.

Logan shook his head. "It has to be really creative. The judges like to see that."

But no one could think of anything, so Daisy suggested they sleep on it and figure it out in the morning. She spread out her blanket and rested her head on the life preserver as a pillow.

The boys said good night and headed back to their own tree. Not even ten minutes had passed before Miles sat bolt upright and shouted, "Harmonicandy!"

Logan smiled in the dark. *Perfect*.

Miles dug into his chocolate-chip pancakes as if hadn't seen one in years. Which, Logan recalled, he actually hadn't.

"These are really great, Mrs. Sweet," Daisy said, spearing a second one from the platter. "Thank you for having all of us for breakfast."

"It's my pleasure," Logan's mom replied, refilling their milk glasses. "It's wonderful to see you all getting along so well. Competition sometimes brings out the worst in people."

"Or the best," Daisy whispered when Mrs. Sweet stepped away. Philip shoveled the pancake in faster without looking up, but everyone knew Daisy was referring to him.

After breakfast, Logan hurried off to shower. A quick glance in the mirror reminded him that he really should comb his hair for a day as important as this one. He gripped the comb tightly and ran it through his wet hair. Maybe a haircut wouldn't be such a bad thing.

After that, he rubbed an aloe leaf up and down each arm and along the side of his face and neck. It always felt good to do that right after a hot shower. It helped the sap to penetrate deeper.

He hurried back to his room and dressed quickly in his usual outfit, only instead of a white short-sleeved shirt, he put on a long-sleeved one, struggling to button each button. Usually his mother helped him when he wore shirts with a lot of buttons, but he didn't want to bother her, since they had guests.

He stood back and faced the long mirror built into the inside of his closet. The shirt was definitely dressier than his usual outfit, more appropriate for a big event. Even with the aloe, though, his arms itched where the shirt rubbed against them.

He took one last look, then ripped the shirt off and put on his nicest short-sleeved one instead.

Logan held his breath as he watched Philip flip over the Harmonicandy molds, which they had coated with cocoa powder to keep from sticking. They all cheered when the harmonica halves slid right out.

Now all they needed to do was paint the insides with melted caramel (carefully, so it wouldn't clog up the tubes), then stick the two halves together and enrobe it. Miles and Philip took care of the caramel part, and once Logan showed Daisy how to set up the enrober, she refused to allow anyone else near it. They'd just placed the final product in the freezer when Max walked in.

"Good morning, young candymakers!" He slipped his lab coat on over his suit. "When can I see everyone's creations?"

"Mine still has to harden," Philip said. "We'll need to keep it cold in the van, too."

"Not a problem," Max promised. "The van's set up for that. How about the rest of you? Is everyone else's ready to go?"

"I still need to work on mine a little," Miles said.

"What did you decide to call it?" Max asked.

Miles hesitated. Logan knew he didn't feel any better about lying to Max than *he* did. Miles had shown them all his bee candy. It was a shame no one else would be seeing it today.

"I'm going to call it...Bee Happy," Miles said finally. "Like *bee,* with two *e*'s?"

"Wonderful!" Max clapped. "And you, Logan?"

"Mine needs some work, too," Logan said truthfully. "I can get it to turn from chocolate into gum, but not so much on the back-again part."

Max nodded. "We knew that would be a challenge."

"I'm going to try adding more carrageen."

"Good idea."

"Mine's all finished," Daisy said proudly, as though it were still going to be in the contest. "It's called the 3G's! Short for the Green Glob of Goop."

"Interesting," Max said uncertainly. "May we taste it?"

"Sure!" Daisy ran over to the fridge and returned with a small tray. She peeled a glob for each of them off the wax paper. The cooling process hadn't done anything for the candy's appearance.

They all took a bite at the same time.

And precisely two seconds later, they all spit it out into their hands. Only Daisy kept chewing hers.

"What?" she said when she saw everyone staring at her. "It's good!"

"No," Philip said, "it's not good. It's the opposite of good. No offense."

"Did you mash and boil the flowers before mixing them in?" Max asked.

Daisy shook her head. "Was I supposed to?"

"Did you cut away the base of the flowers first, or did you use the whole thing?"

"Um, the whole thing, I think."

Logan could tell Max didn't relish the news he was about to give. "I think perhaps you should consider starting—"

"I'm thirteen!" Daisy blurted out.

The other kids gasped.

"What do you mean?" Max asked.

This time it was Philip's turn to kick Daisy on one shin, while Miles did it on the other. Logan just sent her a pleading look. If Max knew her real age, he'd have to follow the rules and alert the Confectionary Association. Telling Max now would mean she'd have to stay behind. Logan needed her to be there. They all did.

"Daisy?" Max prompted.

"Um, I mean, I tried to make it thirteen times already, so, you know, I don't know how much better I can do."

"Well," Max said, "perhaps fourteen is the magic number, then."

Logan breathed a sigh of relief.

"Now let's all get to work," Max continued. "Philip, you may want to take an iron to your suit...it's quite rumpled. Almost looks like you slept in it!"

"Our driver is bringing me a fresh one," Philip explained, trying in vain to smooth down his creased pant legs.

"Excellent," Max said. "You want the judges to take you seriously, and looking professional helps." Max glanced at Daisy and cleared his throat. "Will someone be bringing you a change of clothes, too?"

Daisy's jeans were streaked with dirt and chocolate. Her T-shirt hadn't fared much better. "My cousin will be here soon. No worries."

"Good." Max checked the clock over the large sink. "I have to go sort out the directions and make sure we have all the paperwork we'll need. Meet out front at ten sharp, with your candy securely packed up. And don't forget to write out the recipes. Make sure you list every ingredient you used, even if it's just a pinch." He beamed at them. "I'm so proud of all of you! This is going to be a day none of us will ever forget!"

"That's for sure," Philip said under his breath.

As soon as the lab door swung shut, Daisy held up her

hand. "Before everyone yells at me for telling Max my age, or trying to anyway, let me just say it wasn't my idea. AJ told me to do it when Max started questioning me."

At their confused looks she pointed to her ear. "He's back. He says he's my handler till the end." She paused for a second, turning slightly away. "Of course I had to tell them! We're all in this together."

Turning back to them, she said, "Sorry. AJ says hi."

"No, he doesn't," Philip said.

"Well, okay, he doesn't. But don't take it personally. Pretty much the first rule of spying is not to get attached to the people around you. He'd really like you guys if he knew you." She gestured toward Philip with her head. "Well, maybe not you."

"Ha ha," Philip said.

Logan found he was actually glad that AJ would be nearby in case anything went wrong. "But why did he want you to disqualify yourself before we even got to the contest?"

"Don't be mad, he's just trying to protect me. The whole *get in, do the job, get out* thing. In fact, he's outside now with my clothes. I'll be right back." But instead of heading toward the front door of the lab, she ducked inside Max's small office and closed the door.

The boys exchanged puzzled glances. A minute later Daisy emerged wearing the same yellow dress she'd worn the first day they met her, except someone had sewn on pockets! She pulled at the collar and scowled. "AJ's warped idea of a joke. Here's your pie." She thrust a white bakery box at Miles. "It's peach cobbler."

Miles took the box. "But...how?"

She gestured with her thumb toward the office. "Window."

Logan was pretty sure he didn't want to know how AJ and Daisy knew that Max's office had a window. Wait! That window didn't actually open! When he pointed this out, she held up what looked like an ordinary silver pen.

"Cuts through anything," she explained, slipping it back into her dress pocket.

"But..." He was about to explain about how the lab needed to be kept at exactly 71 degrees with 40 percent humidity, when Daisy said, "Don't worry, the other end of the pen reseals it."

Logan must have looked doubtful, because Daisy said, "Not to change the subject or anything, but this is for you." She held out a note.

"What is it?" he asked.

"I don't know. Your mom gave it to me this morning while you were showering."

Once he heard it was from his mom, Logan knew it must be his daily special message. He felt a little strange opening it in front of them, but he knew they were curious. He cleared his throat and read: *"'List your blessings and you will walk through the gates of thanksgiving and into the fields of joy.'"*

He folded it back up and stuck it in his pocket. He didn't need a note to remind him to be grateful, but maybe he needed a nudge to tell the others how he felt. "I just want you guys to know…whatever happens this afternoon, I'll never forget what you're doing for me. And for my family."

"Oh, it's not for you," Daisy assured him. "It's for the candy!"

They all laughed.

"But seriously," he said, "you're all risking so much. When I counted my blessings last night, you guys were at the top."

"Me, too," Miles said. "You know, if I'd actually counted them."

"Ditto," Daisy said. "About you guys."

Philip just stared down at his shoes.

"You okay?" Miles asked him, nudging him with his elbow. "This is where you make fun of us for talking about things like blessings and counting them."

Philip shook his head. "I don't deserve blessings."

"What kind of thing is that to say?" Miles asked. "Of course you do. Look at all you've done in the last few days. Before you were all about winning, about being the best."

"I still am," Philip said. "Nothing's changed."

Logan shook his head. "Before you wanted to win for you. Now you want to win for me. That's very different."

"Trust me," Philip snapped. "If you had a better memory, you'd know I don't deserve any thanks."

"What do you…" Logan stopped midsentence. He watched as Philip grabbed his briefcase from the floor and stormed out of the lab.

"Where's he going?" he asked the others.

Daisy rested her hand on Logan's arm. "Don't worry about him," she said. "He's just nervous about today. I'm sure he didn't mean anything by it."

"Yeah," Miles said. "And I don't mean to point out the obvious, but you've got like a half hour to make your Bubbletastic ChocoRocket turn from chocolate into gum and back again."

Logan groaned. "You're right."

"Sure we can't help?" Daisy asked. Then, with a sidelong glance at her 3G's, she added, "Well, maybe just Miles could help."

He agreed to let them watch while he tweaked the recipe, but they weren't allowed to speak. Once it was as ready as it was going to be, he rolled it into the shapes of small rockets.

"Here goes nothing," he said, biting into one end. It tasted pretty good. It even blew bubbles. But it stubbornly remained a gum.

"Maybe it's for the best." Logan sighed, taking out the piece of gum and tossing it in the trash beneath his lab table. "We don't want it to win anyway."

"You'll make it work one day," Miles promised.

"It's time," Philip said. He'd exchanged his briefcase for a duffel bag, which probably held his old clothes. He was now dressed in a crisp black suit, a blue button-down shirt, and shiny black shoes. He'd combed his hair and no longer looked like he'd slept on the floor. Not much could be done about the purple shadows under his eyes. Logan figured they all had those.

Philip peered down at Logan's tray. "Those are pretty good rockets."

"They don't work."

Philip shrugged. "They will."

Logan wanted to ask what Philip had meant about his memory being bad, but he didn't want Philip to storm off again. So he hurried to pack up his candy and joined the others at the door.

With a last glance behind him, he forced himself to swallow the familiar doubt that threatened to rise up inside him. He had to trust they'd done everything they could. He followed the others out of the lab and into what would surely be the biggest day of his life.

The thing about leaving something behind for the very last time is that you rarely realize you're doing it.

CHAPTER SIX

T he two-hour drive was quiet. After some small talk along the lines of how pretty the country-side was at this time of year, they fell into staring out the windows, lost in their own thoughts. Max tried to liven things up by suggesting they play car games, but when no one jumped at the chance, he let them be.

Logan knew the others were nervous, too, but he bet he had them all beat. He couldn't stop thinking about how upside-down everything had become. Was he seriously entering the contest — the one he'd dreamt about his whole life — with the hope of *losing?* Back at the factory, Philip's plan had made sense. But now, only hours away from the moment he'd thought would make his parents see that he was worthy of carrying on the family business, everything was getting fuzzy. Maybe if he *did* win, they'd find some other way to save the factory?

The rolling hills gave way to a small town, then a bigger one, and finally the city lay spread out before them. The convention was in the city center. The closer they got, the more Logan thought his nerves would get the best of him.

Maybe he shouldn't have eaten that last chocolate-chip pancake.

A large truck ahead of them moved out of the way to reveal a two-story-high banner strung across the entrance of the huge convention center:

WELCOME CANDY LOVERS TO THE CONFECTIONARY ASSOCIATION'S ANNUAL CONVENTION!!! WE'RE NUTS ABOUT SWEETS!!

Max drove the van up to the front door, and they all piled out. Logan's parents pulled up behind them. His mom climbed out first, followed by Henry, who had come to the convention every year Logan could remember. Henry gave a big stretch and then waved, his white hair even wilder than usual from the Candymaker's habit of driving with all the windows down. Just seeing Henry made Logan instantly feel better. He'd missed him.

One by one, Max pulled their boxes of candy out of the van's refrigerated section. When he handed Miles the box labeled BEE HAPPY, he said, "My, those bees are heavy! How many are in there?"

"Um, just one?" Miles said, somewhat truthfully. "A really big one!"

Max laughed, having no idea that the box held one large peach cobbler.

While Max and Logan's father went to park, the rest of them gathered in front of the building. A steady stream of people flowed by them. Occasionally someone's eyes would linger on Logan for a few seconds longer than was polite, but he only half-registered it. It felt good to be out under the sky, and he was enjoying the feel of the air blowing on his face. Even though it was city air, and the clouds were too scattered to form recognizable shapes, being outside was always better than being inside. Except at the factory. Then it was a tie.

"Let's go in, future candymakers of the world!" the Candymaker shouted.

Logan shook off the dark thoughts of losing the contest and disappointing his parents. The Candymaker made it impossible not to be happy around him. They all laughed as they tried to trap each other in the revolving door.

"How cool is this?" Daisy asked as they tumbled inside, nearly landing on top of one another. They quickly straightened up and looked around the huge, cavernous lobby. In the center of the room sat an enormous chocolate fountain. It must have been at least ten times the size of the one at **Life Is Sweet**. Big enough to dance in, if one were so inclined.

"Try not to stick your hand in," Logan told Philip.

"Wouldn't think of it," Philip replied.

Logan pointed at Miles. "You either."

"Who, me? Never."

The registration desk filled the back half of the room. A long line of candymakers and candy distributors and candy-store owners joked and chatted while they waited to receive their badges. Logan recognized many of them, some of whom he only saw at this annual event.

Next to the long desk an archway opened into the enormous exhibit hall. Hundreds of people crisscrossed the room, bags of free samples dangling from their wrists. The salespeople from **Life Is Sweet?** had likely been there since dawn setting up their booth.

The exhibit hall had always been his favorite part of the convention. He loved seeing the new innovations in the candy world, not to mention all the samples. He hoped they'd get a chance to wander through there. He'd love to show it to his friends.

"That's us!" Miles shouted. He pointed to a large sign that read:

CONTESTANTS FOR THE CONFECTIONARY ASSOCIATION'S ANNUAL NEW CANDY CONTEST, THIS WAY

A huge black arrow pointed up an escalator. So many multicolored helium balloons surrounded the sign that Logan wouldn't have been surprised if it suddenly lifted off the ground.

Max and Henry went off to get the badges for everyone, while Logan's parents led them up to the contest floor. The walls of the upstairs room were covered with huge photographs of the previous winners, posing alongside their creations. Logan quickly found his dad and the Neon Yellow Lightning Chew, and then Grandpa and the Pepsicle. Seeing that picture of his grandfather, so young and full of hope, made Logan miss him. But it also felt as if his grandfather were here in the room, cheering him on, reminding him that the factory Samuel Sweet had built practically with his own hands was worth fighting for. The factory was bigger than any one person's dreams of glory. Hoping that Philip's candy beat his was the right choice, he knew that now for sure.

He tore himself away from the posters and looked around the room. Twelve-year-olds were everywhere — huddled in groups, sitting in pairs on the folding chairs that were set out in long rows, or just walking around on their own, their faces full of anticipation. A few of the kids waved, and Logan waved back. He was not the only Candymaker's son (or daughter) to turn twelve that year. He bet they all felt they had something to prove.

It occurred to him for the first time how many kids would have to lose in order for the Harmonicandy to win. He felt a pang of sadness about that. He didn't like having to root against anyone.

They hadn't gone too far into the room when the greetings began.

"Richard Sweet, you old dog!"

"Big Billy!" the Candymaker exclaimed, clasping the short, thin man's hand. "Have you grown taller?"

Billy patted his practically nonexistent belly. "Only out, my boy, only out!"

The men guffawed as if that were the funniest thing they'd ever heard.

"How much you got on the contest this year?" Logan's dad asked.

"Got a ten-spot on your boy," Big Billy said with a wink.

"A whole ten bucks! Wow, **Mmm Mmm Good** must be having an excellent year!" They guffawed again until Big Billy began to wheeze and had to take a puff from his inhaler.

Daisy nudged Logan. "That's him? *That's* Big Billy? He's, um, not very big. And he's *old*."

Logan nodded. "Eighty-two, to be exact."

"Eighty-two! Why didn't you tell me that before?"

He shrugged. "I told you he wasn't involved."

Daisy mumbled something, probably to AJ, and then motioned for the three boys to come closer. Logan kept one eye on his parents, who continued to greet old friends.

"AJ thinks whoever Philip's dad is partnered with will likely be hanging around the judging table, checking out the competition. So we need to keep an eye on anyone asking a lot of questions, especially about the secret ingredient."

The others nodded.

"I just got a text from Reggie," Philip said. "My father's sending someone over to the factory today to get the secret ingredient. Apparently the person originally assigned to the job failed in his mission."

Daisy rolled her eyes. "Everyone always assumes it's a guy. Almost all the spies at the mansion are girls!"

"That's not really the point of the story, is it?" Philip asked.

Daisy grumbled.

Logan grew concerned. He didn't like the idea of someone trying to get into the factory when no one was around. "What should we do?" he asked. "We can't let them get it."

"They won't," Philip said, pointing to his briefcase. "Remember? You gave it to me when we left the Cocoa Room last night."

Logan's eyes widened. "You still have it?"

"What else was I supposed to do with it?"

"You were supposed to put it back!" Daisy said.

"Good thing I didn't, though, isn't it?"

She grumbled again.

Logan had to ask. "Did you, um, look inside?"

Philip shook his head.

"Why not?" Miles asked. "No one could blame you, after all you're doing to help save the factory."

"It just wouldn't be right," Philip said. "You heard what Max said that first day. It's only for candymakers. When Logan turns eighteen and officially becomes one, he'll be able to look inside. I shouldn't know before he does."

Logan swallowed hard. "Thanks."

Philip just shrugged.

Miles held up his pie box. "So, should we get this over with?"

They all turned to look at the long table, where kids were still pulling candy out of boxes and lifting it off trays. "Guess we have no choice," Daisy said.

Still, no one made a move to head over there. Through the thickening crowd, Logan caught a glimpse of Max and Henry stepping off the escalator, a pile of badges in their hands. "Hey," he whispered. "Let's go do it now, before anyone sees us."

So they ducked low and hurried over to a table that ran the length of the far wall. A spot had been set aside for each contestant, with a large name card and a white ceramic plate. Seeing his name in big letters made it all feel so real to Logan. The others must have felt the same, because they were all hanging back. Daisy looked particularly bleak. Logan didn't envy her the task of having to tell the judges she lied about her age in order to get into the contest. Even though she hadn't lied, they'd agreed that confessing the lie was more believable than saying she didn't *know* her age.

"You know . . . ," Philip told her. "If you don't want to tell them about being thirteen, you could just submit the 3G's. It's not like you have to worry about winning and messing up the plan."

Miles chuckled. "Even when he's trying to be nice, he insults her."

"Actually, he's got a good point," Daisy said. "But it doesn't matter. I didn't bring the 3G's with me."

"I know." Philip reached into his jacket pocket and pulled out a plastic bag. "But I did."

"My 3G's!" Daisy said, snatching the bag. If possible, they glowed an even brighter green than in the lab.

Daisy whirled around and plopped the bag on the plate

395

in front of the card that read DAISY CARPENTER. Her face instantly brightened.

Up and down the table lay candies of all shapes (a starfish! a miniature globe!), sizes (the smallest looked like a cluster of snowflakes, the largest a life-sized boot!), and colors (every one in the rainbow and a few that weren't, like Daisy's). Hard candy, soft candy, things made out of milk chocolate and dark and white chocolate and every mixture in between. Some were impaled on sticks. One looked like a lollypop wrapped in bacon! Upon closer inspection, it turned out to be just that.

The one that Logan kept coming back to was a bowl with different flavors of ice cream, except that the scoops weren't ice cream, they were candy. It was a great idea, although he couldn't imagine how they'd package it for sale or how the kid who made it got it to look so real.

"You may want to arrange your candy on the plate, dear," Logan's mom said, startling all of them.

"Okay." Daisy hurried back to her spot and tipped the 3G's out of the bag. They bounced and slid around as she tried to spread them out on the plate. Truly, there was no way to arrange them, nicely or not.

Mrs. Sweet put her arm around Daisy's shoulders. "I bet they taste better than they look."

"You'd lose that bet," Philip said under his breath.

Logan tried not to laugh.

"And what about yours, dear?" Mrs. Sweet asked Miles, pointing to his name card, next to Daisy's. "Where are they?"

Miles looked pleadingly at Logan.

Logan made himself a quick promise to clean his room every day, then pointed across the room. "Hey, Mom, isn't that Miss Paulina from **Miss Paulina's Candy Palace** over there?"

"Paulina?" his mom repeated. "She told me she couldn't make it this year."

"I'm pretty sure I just saw her turn that corner," Logan insisted. "By the restrooms."

"I better go see if I can find her," his mother said, hurrying off.

Logan felt queasy.

"Nice one," Philip said. "I'm impressed."

"You're impressed that I just lied to my mother?"

Philip shook his head. "No. I'm impressed that you did it so well!"

Daisy went to kick Philip in the shin, but he darted out of the way before her sneaker made contact. "Come on," she said, "let's get the other candy out, and then we still have to submit our recipe forms. AJ wants me to scout out anything — or *anyone* — suspicious-looking before the contest starts."

Logan stared at his spot on the table. How he'd longed for the day when he'd have his own LOGAN SWEET name card at this contest, and now there it was. A black card with his name in big fancy gold letters. He lined up the Bubbletastic ChocoRockets on the plate as nicely as he could, then didn't want to look at them anymore. "Okay, your turn," he told Philip.

Philip lifted the lid of his plastic container and placed the Harmonicandys gently on his plate. "Don't you think we should test them first?" he asked.

They all looked down to check them out. The beeswax Logan had suggested brushing on top gave them a nice gloss, and the bright lights hanging over the table really made them shine.

Daisy let out a low whistle. "They look sooo great." After a quick pause, she said, "Oh, sorry, AJ. Won't do it again. He has a headache," she explained. "He said my whistling went through his skull." She rolled her eyes. "Teenage boys are so very dramatic."

"I don't think we have time to test them," Logan whispered as a woman wearing a light blue dress began walking down the length of the table. She was stopping in front of each contest entry, marking something down on a clipboard. Logan had seen this woman at previous conventions. She owned a chain of candy stores, he seemed to recall. The judges were always kept secret until the actual event. One year Logan's dad had been a judge, and he hadn't even told the family until the morning of the contest!

"Who's that woman?" Daisy asked, narrowing her eyes suspiciously. "She seems awfully interested in what each person made."

Logan laughed. "She's one of the three judges. I promise you, she isn't trying to steal my father's secret ingredient."

Daisy placed her hands on her hips. "Hey, more often

than you'd think, the last person you suspect is often the person who did it."

"Who did what?" Miles asked.

"You know, *it*."

"Ah, that clears that up."

"I hate to interrupt this fascinating conversation about the meaning of the word *it*," Philip said, glancing nervously at the rapidly approaching woman. "But she's checking to make sure everyone's candy is in place." He looked pointedly at Miles, whose candy was the only one missing out of all thirty-two entries.

Miles looked pained, as if he'd just eaten way too much chocolate pizza.

"I'm really sorry you have to do this, Miles," Logan said. "Look at it this way. If your Bee Happy candy wasn't so great, you'd be able to risk entering it. You know, like Daisy can."

"You're right," Miles said, brightening.

Daisy pursed her lips. "I think I was just insulted again."

Miles slid the pie out of the box and balanced it in his hand.

The woman was only a few spots away now, and Logan knew his mother would soon realize that Miss Paulina hadn't come after all. He glanced behind them to see that Henry and Max had gotten stopped by admirers, but they wouldn't be held up for long. "Now would be good," he urged.

Miles stepped up to the spot marked MILES O'LEARY and placed the pie in the middle of the plate.

"Now let's get out of here," Daisy said.

They hurried away from the table, not looking back. Logan knew he wasn't the only one who had no interest in being there when the judges (and Max! and his parents!) saw that pie.

Once they had filled out their information forms with the name of their candy (or pie), a description, and the ingredients, there was nothing to do but wait and try to avoid Max, Henry, and Logan's parents. Daisy had gone scouting, and she told the boys to keep out of sight. She directed them to wait inside a back stairwell that led down to an emergency exit. From there they could peer around the corner and see what was happening in the room, but no one could see them.

After she'd gone, Philip said, "I'm going to talk to Henry. I'll make sure he keeps the others away from the table as long as possible. Once they see the pie, they'll start asking us all sorts of questions."

"*You're* going to talk to Henry?" Logan asked, surprised. "What will you say?"

"Trust me, I know what I'm doing." Philip strode off into the crowd before Logan could ask anything else.

Miles and Logan watched the woman with the clipboard stop in front of the card with Miles's name on it, stare, turn the pie around on the plate, stare some more, then pick it up along with Miles's card. Miles whimpered a bit as the woman strode purposefully through a door marked JUDGES' ROOM.

"She's probably in there trying to figure out if the pie is real or made out of candy to *look* like a pie," Logan explained. "Like the ice cream up there."

"That's not real ice cream?"

Logan shook his head.

The woman came out a minute later and returned both the pie and Miles's name card to his spot on the table. Except now the word DISQUALIFIED was stamped in red across his name.

Miles sighed and took a step back, out of sight again. He leaned against the wall. "That is not a nice word. Usually I like words with the letter q in them, but not that one."

Logan, leaning on the wall next to him, nodded solemnly. He figured this was as good a time as any to ask a question that had been nagging at him since the night before. "Does it bother you that you went through all that, you know, *grief* when you thought Daisy drowned?"

"I thought about that a lot on the drive this morning," Miles replied. "And I decided that it wasn't for nothing. I mean, if it hadn't happened, I wouldn't have learned how to make up my own languages — and I'm really good at it. I've also learned lots of really interesting things in the library, not only about the afterlife but about all sorts of things. Looking for signs, even when I don't find them, kind of helps me pay more attention to what's going on around me. My parents think the whole thing made me withdraw from the world, but in a weird way, it made me more a part of it."

"Wow," Logan said. "You really *did* think a lot about it!"

Miles nodded. "The whole thing taught me a lot about life and losing things. I can kind of see things in people now, like I know when someone else has lost something, and that makes me understand them better."

Logan wasn't sure how to interpret that. "Like Philip losing his mom?"

Miles nodded. "Or like if someone's been through something big." He met Logan's eyes when he said the last part. And he kept them there.

At first Logan waited for Miles to explain what he meant. And then, all at once, in a rush of understanding, Logan knew what Miles was referring to. How could he not have realized it? Just because he never thought about his burns didn't mean others hadn't. It had been so long since he'd been around people he didn't know that it hadn't occurred to him to think about it. But it wasn't really normal not to have even given it a second thought. Why hadn't he?

That question set off a whole explosion of others. Had his parents kept him hidden from new people because of how he looked? Had they...had they canceled the tours because of him? The annual factory picnic?

He felt queasy. How could he have been so blind?

Miles put his hand on Logan's arm. "Hey, you look like you need to sit down. I'm really sorry. I didn't mean anything by it. Forget I said anything, I'm just rambling. Ignore me."

Logan shook his head. "No, it's my fault. I should have said something right at the beginning, the first day."

"You don't have to tell me anything," Miles said. "I'm sure it's really hard to talk about."

"No," Logan said, a little more forcefully than he intended. "It isn't, that's the thing. It's not hard to talk about. I barely remember a time before the accident. So when I look in the mirror all I see is me."

Logan reached back to that day, seven years before. He hadn't thought about it in so long. "I remember leaning into a big vat of chocolate. I was trying to get a toy that a friend of mine threw in by mistake. I don't know why I did it. I knew how hot it was. I was sort of mesmerized by that little truck making this really interesting path as it slipped down deeper. But I really wanted to get the truck back. So I just didn't think."

After a pause, Miles asked, "Did it hurt a lot?"

"I'm sure it must have, but I don't remember. When I get older, I can get skin grafts that will hide most of it."

"Well, that's good, right?"

"I guess so. It's just...I don't know, it's stupid—but what if I don't feel like me afterward?"

Before Miles could answer, a pair of arms grabbed Logan from behind and hugged him tight. So tight that it could only be one person.

"Daisy?"

The grasp tightened even more. "You'll always be you," she said. "It doesn't matter what you look like on the outside. You'll always be Logan, the Candymaker's son who's kind and funny and sweeter than all the candy in his candy factory."

"I think you're squeezing the air out of his lungs," Philip said.

Logan couldn't see Philip from his current position in Daisy's choke hold, but clearly he and Daisy must have arrived sometime during the conversation. How much had they heard? Enough, apparently.

Daisy slowly released her grip, and Logan took a few deep breaths.

"Any ribs broken?" Philip asked.

Logan felt around. "All present and accounted for."

"Good," Daisy said. "Because the judges are about to start tasting!"

Logan's heart began to pound hard as the four of them left the stairwell.

Philip walked next to Miles and whispered, "I only had a minute to make up a story for Henry to tell the others about why you handed in the pie instead of your Bee Happys, so I admit I wasn't in top form. Just go with whatever you hear."

Before they got any farther, Max came running through the crowd that had gathered by the candy table. "Oh, Miles, we heard about what happened! Losing all the Bee Happys at once! What were you thinking, bringing them into the bathroom with you? Couldn't you have handed them to someone while you went into the stall?"

Miles's mouth fell open slightly, but he recovered quickly. "I know, it was pretty stupid."

Henry put his arm around Miles's shoulders. "How could you have guessed they'd fall down the toilet like that?"

"Yeah," Miles said, glaring at Philip. "Who'd have seen *that* coming?"

Logan knew that laughing wouldn't be an appropriate reaction, but it was hard to hold it in. He turned away so Max and Henry wouldn't see his efforts and watched as his parents broke free from a crowd of fellow candymakers and headed his way.

As soon as he saw his mother's face, the way her eyes lit up when she saw him, then clouded over for a split second with worry as she scanned the faces around him, he knew, just KNEW he'd been right about his parents protecting him all those years. Or thinking that they were. He thought maybe he should feel angry, or at the very least, resentful. But all he felt was grateful that he finally knew the truth. Now he could set them straight.

A podium had been set up at the head of the contest table. A hush fell across the room as soon as the three judges stepped up to it. The woman they had seen before was now wearing a sticker on her jacket with the words JUDGE CAROL printed in thick black marker. Alongside her were two men, the taller of whom Logan recognized as Old

Sammy, the owner of the world's largest cocoa-bean processing plant (not everyone grew their own trees!). He didn't know the shorter man with the white chef's hat perched on his head, but his name tag declared him JUDGE EDGAR.

Logan's parents reached the group just as Judge Edgar stepped up to the microphone. With a twinkle in his eye, he called out in a deep, velvety voice, "So what are we gonna do today?"

The crowd cheered. Philip groaned, and although Logan couldn't see, he'd bet an eye roll accompanied the groan. Then the whole crowd shouted, "Make some candy!"

Judge Edgar beamed and sang, "And why are we gonna do it?"

"To make the whole world smile," the crowd belted out.

Judge Edgar joined the crowd for the last line. "Make the whole world smile!"

Everyone cheered and pounded one another on the back.

Logan's mom wiped a tear from her cheek, and Logan realized he was choked up, too. Every year the contest kicked off the same way, and it never failed to move the crowd.

Old Sammy took the mike now. "It's wonderful to see so many familiar faces and so many new ones, too!"

The crowd clapped. Logan recognized the Golds, the father and son candymakers who had been visiting the factory the day before. He waved and they waved back.

Old Sammy continued. "I'd like to extend the warmest welcome to our thirty-two young contestants here today!"

Judge Carol tugged on Old Sammy's sleeve and whispered something in his ear.

"Oh, yes, quite," Old Sammy said. "I meant to say, thirty-*one* contestants."

Miles slunk behind Logan.

"Now please keep in mind, children, even though there can be only one winner, that doesn't mean that many—if not most—of these submissions will someday be found on the shelves at your favorite candy stores. You just have to keep working hard, keep thinking sweet thoughts, and you'll get there."

The crowd cheered again. This time it was mostly the grown-ups, though. Logan would bet the kids were thinking of winning, not of someday getting their candy made if they tried hard enough. He knew the Bubbletastic Choco-Rocket had a long way to go before it would ever be ready to hit the candy-store shelves.

Judge Carol leaned into the mike. "Let the tasting begin!"

A white rope had been set up about four feet away from the table. It extended the length of the table, and only the judges were allowed inside. Logan saw that the information forms they'd filled out earlier were now alongside their entries.

A hush fell over the crowd as everyone pressed up toward the roped-off section to watch. The judges spread out. Old

Sammy approached the table from the right side, Edgar took the middle, and Carol started at the left end. Clipboards in hand, they began to taste. One girl squealed, "That one's mine! He's tasting my Bacon Pops!" But mostly everyone remained quiet, not wanting to distract the judges from their task.

The first judge to get to the **Life Is Sweet** section was Sammy, although Edgar was fast approaching, too, from the other side. Logan couldn't help holding his breath as Sammy picked up the Bubbletastic ChocoRocket. Beside him, he heard Miles inhale, too. Daisy slipped between them and grabbed both their hands. Together, they watched as Sammy read the information form, which explained what the candy was supposed to do. Then he took a big bite.

He chewed contentedly for a few seconds. At that point, Logan knew it should be turning into gum, and indeed, just then Old Sammy blew a bubble. It popped loudly, and the crowd chuckled. Logan and Miles let out their breath. The Candymaker clasped him on the shoulder and from behind whispered, "I'm so proud of you, son!"

"Thanks, Dad," Logan whispered, embarrassed that everyone must have heard the Candymaker's whisper, which was as loud as most other people's regular voices. "But it's supposed to turn back to chocolate now."

They watched as Sammy continued chewing for another few seconds, then dropped the gum inside a small bucket where it landed with an audible *plonk*.

He sighed. Well, that was that.

"I'll tell you a secret," his father said. This time he actually spoke quietly enough that only Logan and his friends could hear. "I couldn't even have made it turn into *gum!*"

Logan turned around, surprised. "Of course you could have."

His dad shook his head. "Not without help. That's why I surround myself with such smart people. Making candy is a team effort." Then he winked and gestured to the candy table. "But you knew that, didn't you?"

Miles, Daisy, Philip, and Logan exchanged wide-eyed looks. What exactly did the Candymaker know about their team effort?

Old Sammy had moved on to Daisy's plate, which gave Logan an excuse to turn back around without responding to his dad. They watched as Old Sammy popped a 3G into his mouth and almost instantly spit it into the bucket and reached for a cup of water. Miles giggled. Daisy kicked him, but her heart clearly wasn't in it, because Miles didn't even yelp.

A boy's voice in the crowd said, "Wow, that one must have been *really* bad."

Daisy's shoulders slumped. Before anyone else could comment, Philip reached out and patted her awkwardly on the back. Then he stiffened. Logan saw why: Judge Edgar had picked up the information form for the Harmonicandy.

Daisy reached out and took Philip's hand now. He flinched slightly but didn't pull away. Logan didn't dare even breathe. *Please play. Please play at least one note.*

Edgar cupped the ends of the Harmonicandy with the palms of his hands. Closing his eyes, he exhaled so gently his lips didn't even move.

A crisp, clear note filled the room. Logan and Philip and Daisy and Miles gasped and clutched each other tight. Any whispering from the crowd stopped. The two other judges turned at the sound, midchew.

Edgar held it out and examined it from all angles, an amused expression on his face. He brought it back to his mouth and blew a quick succession of notes. It sounded exactly like a real harmonica. They'd done it! Max and the Candymaker were thumping Philip on the back. Henry wiped a tear from his eye.

Judge Edgar finally stopped playing and took a bite. He turned back to the table, so Logan couldn't see his expression as he marked something down on his clipboard.

Logan could hardly contain himself. Inside he was soaring. Miles was bouncing up and down on the balls of his feet. Daisy and Philip hadn't moved, but they were both wearing broad grins. Logan's mom reached over and ruffled Philip's hair. At that moment, for the first time since Logan had known him, Philip looked like he was about to cry. He recovered quickly, though, blinking away any tears.

Daisy tugged on Logan's arm and whispered, "We may have a problem. Follow me."

"We'll be right back," he told his parents as the three of them hurried after Daisy. She led them back into the hidden stairwell.

"The judge loved it!" Miles cried once they were all safely inside. "Did you see his face?"

"That's all well and good," Daisy said. "But AJ told me that while we were watching Judge Edgar eat the Bubble-tastic ChocoRocket, the woman judge was tasting the ice cream one. Apparently she couldn't stop eating it. She gave it the highest score!"

"How does AJ know what score she wrote down?" Logan asked, feeling his joyous mood deflating.

"Trust me, he knows."

"Does it really matter?" Philip said. "I bet we'll get the top mark, too. At least from Edgar."

"You're probably right," Daisy said. "But AJ thinks we've got some serious competition with that ice cream. He said people have been talking about it all day. Apparently, before we got here, the kid who made it gave out a bunch of free samples, and everyone kept asking him for more."

"Are you even allowed to do that?" Miles asked Logan.

"I've never seen anyone do it before, but I don't think it's against the rules or anything."

"Then maybe they broke the rules in some other way," Daisy said. "Like using an ingredient that they didn't list or something."

"But how would we know *that?*" Miles asked.

"We need to get a sample," Philip said. "Are there any left?"

Daisy shook her head. "AJ already tried to find some. Our only hope is that the judges leave some on the table."

"But what good would it be to taste it?" Miles asked.

"Logan would know if anything was left off the list," Philip said. "Right, Logan?"

Logan nodded. He *would* know. But how did Philip know that? "Even if we tried to get some once the judging ended, we'd never get near the table without being spotted."

No one answered. Then Philip announced, "I'll distract them."

"How?" Daisy asked. "By climbing up on the couch and shouting about how candy rots your teeth? That would sure get everyone's attention. They'd throw boxes of toothpaste at you!"

"No, I'm not going to climb on the couch."

"You could stand on your head," Miles suggested. "Or wait, you could do a song and dance. Can you sing?"

Philip shook his head. "I won't need to shout on a couch or sing. Trust me. When the judging's over, I'll get everyone's attention. You just get a piece of that ice cream thing." To Daisy he said, "What do they call it, anyway?"

She paused while AJ talked in her ear. "What? That's not very creative. Oh. Okay, I get it. AJ said they call it 'I Scream.' Sounds like ice cream, but it's spelled like the letter *I,* then the word *scream,* as in, 'I'd scream really loud if it won, and not in a good way.'"

"That's pretty good," Logan admitted.

Philip scoffed. "Just find some way to disqualify it."

"I doubt I'll find anything," Logan said. "Why would someone risk not listing all the ingredients?"

"I know it's a long shot," Daisy said. "But it's all we've got. Too much is riding on this contest to risk anything."

Logan knew exactly how much was riding on it. He nodded. "I'll do my best."

They ducked back out in time to hear the crowd clap as the judges finished. Judge Edgar took the mike and said, "That was delightful!" He patted his belly. "I might not eat again for a week!"

The crowd laughed politely.

"It will take us about a half hour to tabulate the scores. Relax, go visit the exhibit hall, and you should all congratulate yourselves. An outstanding group!" He joined the other two judges, and they filed into the small room where Judge Carol had taken Miles's pie before.

"We're going to run down and check on the booth," Logan's mom told them. "Will you guys be okay up here? Max or Henry could stay if you like."

"We'll be fine," Logan assured her. "Have fun."

"All right," Philip said when the grown-ups left. "It's now or never."

"Tell us what you're going to do!" Daisy demanded.

Logan could tell she didn't like being left out of things. Especially things like this.

"I'll do *my* job," he replied, picking up his duffel from the floor. "You just worry about doing yours." With that he made his way through the crowd.

"Maybe he's going to recite passages from *Love's Last Dance*," Miles suggested. "No, wait, that's not a real book!"

He scooted out of the way just in time to avoid Daisy's foot heading for his shin.

At first the music was muffled by the din of the crowd, and Logan wasn't sure what he was hearing. He glanced at the candy table to see if someone had picked up the Harmonicandy and was playing it. But everyone was still standing on the other side of the rope.

As the music got louder, the sound of talking grew quieter as people looked around the room for its source.

Miles saw him first. He pointed to a cluster of chairs right beneath the poster of Logan's grandfather. "There! It's Philip! And he's...he's...*playing a violin?* Where did he get a violin at a candy convention?"

Logan's and Daisy's jaws fell open. Philip was indeed playing the violin, and not just playing it — he was making notes come out of the instrument that Logan had never *heard* before. The whole room was silent now. Everyone had begun to move closer to the boy playing like a world-famous violinist.

Philip had his eyes closed, an expression of calm concentration on his face. Logan couldn't tear his eyes away. This was Philip? *Their* Philip? The music was the most beautiful thing he'd ever heard. All around the room people were beginning to whisper. Others shushed them.

"I've heard this piece before!" Miles said in amazement. "I thought it was the radio!"

Daisy gasped. "I've heard it, too! Years ago! He was playing it back at that school where he blew my cover. I thought the music teacher was playing a record. But it was him!"

"Well," Logan said, "he did say he had a few more surprises up his sleeve."

"AJ is yelling in my ear," Daisy said. "We have to move now. You guys stand guard. If anyone's watching me, just cough loudly."

Logan and Miles nodded. Daisy darted behind them and was back before Logan remembered he was supposed to be guarding her. He'd gotten so caught up in the music that a life-sized Gummysaurus could have walked into the room and he wouldn't have noticed.

"Did anyone see me take it?" she asked.

Logan and Miles shared a guilty look. "Um, nope?" Miles said.

"Good. Let's go." She ran off to the hallway, and Logan and Miles hurried after her. She pulled a chunk of mint chocolate chip I Scream out of her dress pocket and handed it to Logan. "This is all that was left. The judges ate more of this one than of any of the others."

"This should be enough," Logan said.

"And here's the list of ingredients." She pulled the information form out of her other pocket.

"You took that, too?" Logan asked. "What if someone notices it's gone?"

"As long as Philip keeps playing, I doubt anyone's going to notice anything." She looked down at the paper in her hand. "Come on, Alex Gruber from Clover City. Show us what ya got."

Logan turned the candy over in his hand to see what he could tell from the feel of it. It had a smooth consistency, a little slick, but with a solid heft. It wouldn't crumble too easily. It was thicker than taffy and not at all sticky. So far he was impressed. "Okay. I'll name the ingredients, and you check them off as I go along."

She nodded. "Good luck."

Logan broke the small piece in half and put it in his mouth. He swirled it around on his tongue to make sure he picked up all the different flavors. Philip's music in the background actually helped him focus. It took only a few seconds before he was able to start distinguishing ingredients. "Sugar," he said first. "A lot of sugar."

Daisy nodded. "Check."

"Milk, butter, cream."

"Check, check, and check."

"Salt."

"Check."

"Soybean oil."

"Check."

Logan swallowed and put the rest of the piece in his mouth. "Cocoa powder."

"Check."

"Coconut oil."

"Check."

"Cornstarch."

"Check."

"Mint. Green food coloring and corn syrup."

"Check and check." She sighed. "That's everything. I guess we'll just have to hope for the bes—"

"Wait," Logan said, reaching out his hand. "There's something else."

"Really?" Miles and Daisy asked.

"It's barely noticeable. I'm not sure what it is." He closed his eyes and tried desperately to identify it. It wasn't so much a *taste,* exactly, as a *feeling*. But what was it? "You're sure there's no more on the table?"

Daisy shook her head.

Logan's heart sank. Whatever the other ingredient in the I Scream was, he couldn't figure it out. "I'm sorry. Maybe it's just my imagination."

"It's okay," Daisy said. "It was a long shot anyway. It's probably all legit."

"I guess you're right," he said uncertainly.

"Maybe the other judges won't like it as much as Judge Carol did," Miles said.

"Maybe," Logan said, but he doubted it. The I Scream had been really, really good. Almost better than real ice cream, if he had to be honest. All his taste buds had come alive while he ate it. It had sort of an *energy* to it. No wonder the judges wanted to keep eating it. He did, too.

Daisy left to return the information form to the table.

"What you just did was really cool," Miles said to Logan as they followed her out of the stairwell.

"But I didn't find anything that wasn't on the list." Or nothing he could determine, at any rate.

"Maybe not," Miles said, "but you did find everything *on* the list."

"I guess, but I'd trade that skill to be able to figure out how many ounces are in two thirds of a cup."

"But lots of people can do that," Miles argued. "Almost nobody can do what you just did."

Logan stopped. "I never thought of it that way."

Philip must have seen them emerge from the hall, because the music abruptly ended. And when it did, a huge burst of applause echoed through the room. Some people even yelled out, "Bravo! Bravo!" Others blew their noses loudly. Then, just as suddenly, the music started again, but a much different tune rang out this time. "Is that what I think it is?" Logan asked.

Sure enough, Philip had launched into "The Candyman" song and had the whole crowd singing along. Logan wouldn't have thought it possible that the old song could even be *played* on a violin, let alone that Philip would know how to play it.

When the song ended, Philip took a bow and the applause erupted again. The room now held about twice as many people as had been there before. People must have come up from downstairs when they heard the music.

Daisy returned from the table. Raising her voice over the sound of the applause, she said, "We better go rescue him before he's mobbed by admirers."

They zigzagged their way through the crowd until they reached Philip. He had just secured the violin in its case when Daisy grabbed him by the arm in one of her death grips and yanked him away. Logan and Miles hurried along on either side of them like bodyguards. People were calling out, asking for an encore, asking for his autograph even!

"Did you find out anything to disqualify the ice cream candy?" Philip asked as they ran. They all shook their heads. They couldn't go back into their stairwell, because the crowd would just follow them. But Daisy seemed to know exactly where she was going.

Which turned out to be the men's room! She opened the door a few inches and called out, "Anyone in here?" When no one answered, she opened the door the rest of the way and pushed Philip inside. Logan and Miles slipped in after them, and Logan locked the door.

"I'm pretty sure there's a strict no-girls-allowed policy in here," Philip said, leaning against the wall. His cheeks were flushed, but the rest of his face was unnaturally pale. His usually hidden freckles had popped out again.

For a split second, Logan had a strange feeling, almost like déjà vu. But it quickly passed. "Are you all right?" he asked.

Philip closed his eyes. "I'm just a little freaked out. I've never ... played in front of anyone before."

Daisy stuck her hands on her hips. "Philip Ransford the Third! Here's what *I* would like to know. How could you make fun of my father for being a violinist when you are obviously one yourself?"

"But your dad isn't actually a violinist, is he?"

"Well, no," Daisy sputtered. "But that's not really the point, is it? You didn't know that at the time."

Philip rolled his eyes. "I refuse to feel guilty about lying when you were lying, too. And first, I might add."

Daisy opened her mouth to argue, then closed it again with a sigh. "Fine."

Philip stepped over to the sink and began splashing water on his face. It splashed onto his suit, too, but he didn't seem to care. Not like the time he'd spilled powdered sugar all over himself. He had really changed.

Someone knocked hard on the bathroom door, but Daisy yelled, "Use the one downstairs!" and whoever it was went away.

When Philip was done drying his face, he turned to Logan and Miles. "Why are you guys looking at me like that?"

"Like what?" Miles asked.

"Like you've just seen a ghost."

Logan glanced at Miles and then said, "You were just really, really good. Like seriously good. Like monster good. It was just a little, um, *unexpected*."

"Right," Miles agreed. "What he said."

"How did you learn to play like that?"

Philip shrugged. "It's like Bach said: it's easy to play any musical instrument. All you have to do is touch the right key at the right time and the instrument will play itself."

"Trust me, it's not that easy," Logan said. "Your dad must be really proud of you."

Philip shook his head. "He doesn't know that I play. And trust me, if he did, he wouldn't be proud. He'd think it was a waste of time."

After a pause, Logan said, "Maybe he'd surprise you."

"Doubt it."

"We've got a situation," Daisy said, springing into action and unlocking the door. AJ squeezed in, looking like a real grown-up in a suit and tie. He locked the door behind him.

An official-looking badge hung around his neck, and they all leaned closer to read it:

BO DINKLEMAN

CONFECTIONARY ASSOCIATION

NEW CANDY CONTEST COORDINATOR

They all laughed at the name he'd chosen for himself. "I won't ask how you got the badge," Logan said.

"It's best you don't."

"So what's the problem now?" Daisy asked.

"Old Sammy wants to ask Logan if he'll change his product description."

"Huh?" Logan asked. "What do you mean?"

AJ turned to him. "He told the other judges that if you're willing to take out the part about the ChocoRocket turning back into chocolate, he'll declare you the winner. They sent me to find you."

Logan stared. "But that's not fair to everyone else. Why would they do that? I mean, Old Sammy is a friend of my family's..." He trailed off as another thought occurred to him. "It's not because they...they feel sorry for me, is it?"

AJ pulled at the collar of his shirt. It was enough of an answer.

Logan's head swam. He reached out for the wall and barely registered its coolness against his palm.

"I'm really sorry," AJ said earnestly. "I didn't want to have to tell you."

"Are you all right, Logan?" Daisy asked, taking his other hand in hers.

After the initial shock faded, Logan found that he wasn't really that surprised. "I'm okay. It's just...so strange. I mean, I've wanted to win this contest my entire life. But not like this. Not with a candy that isn't ready yet. I don't understand why anyone would feel sorry for me. Some people have scars on the inside, and other people's are on the outside. It shouldn't matter."

"I don't think everyone realizes that," Miles said. "I think they just care about you."

AJ nodded. "Old Sammy thinks you deserve to win for being so brave."

"Brave?" Logan repeated, confused. "How am I brave?"

"You're brave," Daisy said, "because you never stopped being *you*. And a lot of people would have."

Logan's eyes stung. "Really?"

She nodded. Philip and Miles did, too.

"So what should I tell them?" AJ asked.

Logan took a deep, shaky breath. "Tell them I appreciate the thought, but one day the Bubbletastic ChocoRocket will do what it's supposed to do. Turn from chocolate to gum...and back again!"

"You got it," AJ said, slipping back out.

Now it was Logan's turn to splash water on his face. He felt the scars as his hands brushed over them. Why was everyone else more bothered by them than he was? The faucet wouldn't turn all the way off, and the water dribbled into the metal sink.

"Time to go," Daisy announced. "AJ said the judges are coming out."

"Does he know who won?" Philip asked.

She shook her head. "It's in a sealed envelope."

"If I lose," Philip said, "I promise I'll do my best to keep my father away from **Life Is Sweet?**."

"You could say they've got rats!" Miles suggested.

"Whatever it takes," Philip promised.

They reached the main room to find it even more crowded than when Philip had been playing his violin. Word of the judges' arrival had spread fast. Rows of folding chairs had been set up, and they were all filled. People leaned against walls and sat in the aisle. Logan spotted AJ in a chair near the podium. Someday he'd have to explain how he'd gotten the judges to believe he was part of the Confectionary Association. He really was an excellent spy.

"There you are!" Mrs. Sweet said, appearing before them. "We heard the strangest rumor downstairs."

"Really?" Logan glanced uneasily at the others. He hoped they hadn't heard about the judges' offer...and that he'd turned it down.

She put her arm around Philip's shoulders as they walked toward the rows of seats. "We heard that one of the contestants—a young man—just played the most beautiful violin concerto. Would you happen to know anything about that?"

"I never listen to rumors," Philip replied.

They joined the Candymaker and Max and Henry, who had saved seats for them in a row near the back. Logan sat down next to his father, and the others filed in after him. The Candymaker dug through a canvas bag full of candies and pulled out a grape Blast-o-Bit. He offered it to Logan. Never one to turn down candy, Logan accepted. The familiar flavor was comforting. He felt a pang of homesickness for the factory, as he always did when away from it even for a few hours.

"We had thirty-one outstanding entries," Judge Edgar said from the podium. The buzzing of the crowd instantly stopped. Logan knew the people in his row weren't the only ones holding their breath right now. He wondered where Alex Gruber was sitting. If only he could have figured out what that final ingredient was in the I Scream. If there even *was* one.

"But in the end," Edgar continued, "we were able to narrow it down to two candies that fulfilled everything we were looking for. Something truly innovative, something never seen before."

Logan would bet everything that those two were the Harmonicandy and the I Scream.

Judge Edgar handed the mike over to Judge Carol. "How did we choose between them?" she said. "Well, one of them had a special something that we couldn't put our finger on."

Logan's heart sank. He knew they were about to announce that I Scream had won. He knew it as well as he knew his own nose. On the other side of the Candymaker, he noticed Henry's leg jiggling up and down. The only time he'd ever seen the usually unruffled Marshmallow Man do that was after he'd had too many cups of coffee at the factory's holiday party. Logan glanced away and then nearly sprang straight up out of his chair.

He knew what was in the I Scream!

He grabbed Daisy and whispered straight into her ear, "AJ! It's caffeine! Alex Gruber put caffeine in the I Scream!"

Things began happening quickly. Judge Carol handed the mike over to Old Sammy, who held the envelope in front of him. AJ jumped up and reached for Old Sammy's arm. Surprised, Sammy almost toppled sideways. AJ steadied him, then whispered into his ear.

"Are you certain?" Old Sammy said after hearing him out. AJ nodded.

Turning back to the audience, Old Sammy said, "I'm

sorry for the delay. But the judges will need to see all the contestants who trained this week at **Mmm Mmm Good**."

A murmur ran through the crowd. Four kids stood up, two boys and two girls. Logan didn't know which of the boys was Alex. If he had to guess, he'd say it was the one who had gone as pale as a sheet of paper.

Judge Carol picked up the mike. "Big Billy, we'd like you to come, too."

The murmurs intensified as Big Billy pushed up from his chair and followed the kids into the Judges' Room. The door shut behind them. Logan's dad and the other candy-makers gathered in the aisle to try to figure out what was going on.

"Now what?" Logan whispered.

"Now we wait," Daisy said. "And hope he admits it."

Philip leaned over. "Do you think Big Billy is the guy working with my dad after all? Maybe that was the backup plan — have someone from his group win and become more powerful that way."

"It's possible," Daisy said, "but I don't get that sense from him."

Logan was relieved to hear her say that. He hoped that Big Billy didn't have a part in the I Scream plot. Slipping caffeine or any other substance like that into candy was a very serious offense. Logan wondered why Alex Gruber would have taken such a huge chance, especially when the I Scream would still have been great without it. He must have *really* wanted to win.

It seemed like forever, but it was probably only ten minutes until the group came back out. Everyone except Alex and Big Billy. Logan watched the door for a minute until Judge Edgar cleared his throat into the microphone.

"Pardon the interruption, everyone," he said. "Some unexpected excitement. I won't keep you waiting any longer. The winner of the Confectionary Association's Annual New Candy Contest is ..."

"... Kimberly Bowker and her Bacon Pop!"

CHAPTER EIGHT

Logan's heart stopped as a single thought sped at top speed into his brain. *The factory is gone! We've lost it!* Then, in almost the same instant, he realized it was Miles who had fed that last line into his ear while Judge Edgar had paused.

"Very funny!" Logan whispered, elbowing him.

"Philip Ransford the Third, with the Harmonicandy!" Judge Edgar shouted.

Logan jumped out of his chair, along with everyone else from **Life Is Sweet?**, whooping and shouting. The rest of the audience applauded loudly. Logan knew a lot of kids were disappointed that their entries didn't win, but that's what he loved about the candy business. Everyone supported everyone else.

The **Life Is Sweet?** group took turns hugging one another. The Candymaker leaned close to Logan and whispered, "I'm sorry, son. I know how much winning this contest meant to you."

"But I *did* win, Dad. Trust me, we all won as soon as the Harmonicandy played its first note."

His father clapped him on the back. "Spoken like a true candymaker!"

And as his dad spoke the words, Logan believed them for the first time. He truly *was* a candymaker. They all were. He knew that the next time he stepped into the lab it would feel different. He wouldn't doubt himself anymore. He couldn't wait.

"You've got to go up there," Logan's mom told Philip.

"Will you come with me?" he asked, sounding younger than Logan had ever heard him. In his suit, it was sometimes hard to remember he was only twelve.

She hesitated for a second and glanced at Logan, who nodded. The crowd kept clapping as the two of them made their way to the front.

"Hey, that's the kid who was playing the violin!" a girl in the middle called out. Everyone started buzzing about that, then clapped even louder.

By the time Philip reached the podium, his face was as red as when he had his hiccupping fit the first day.

Judge Carol had the mike now. "Our newest staff member, Mr. Bo Dinkleman, will now present the winner with his prize."

Daisy, Miles, and Logan collapsed in giggles as AJ stepped up to the podium. "As a newcomer to your wonderful organization, I am thrilled to present this plaque to Philip Ransford the Third, for his invention of the Harmonicandy! The first chocolate harmonica that really plays!"

The crowd rose to its feet.

"And here is a check for one thousand dollars," AJ/Bo said, handing Philip an envelope. "I was told that **Mmm Mmm Good** had been selected to produce the winning candy this year, but Big Billy has an announcement he'd like to make."

The audience instantly started whispering. Clutching his envelope awkwardly, Philip stepped aside as Big Billy slowly made his way up to the podium. He took the mike, and the room quieted.

"Hello, my old friends. Well, not as old as *me,* but still plenty old!"

Everyone laughed.

"I had planned to announce this next month, but something happened today that made me realize the time is right. A few things occurred under my roof that didn't make me proud, and I realize that **Mmm Mmm Good** has grown too large, and I have grown too old. **Mmm Mmm Good** will be closing its doors, and I will be splitting up my candy production among the other factories represented here today. If they'll accept them, that is."

A shocked hush fell across the room.

"We can discuss the details at the Factory Owners' Dinner later today. Being a member of the candymaking community has brought me decades of joy, and I know that my old friends will take as good care of our candy as I would. I'd like to congratulate our newest winner here, even though I lost my bet!"

The audience laughed. Logan swallowed hard against the knot in his throat. One of the world's greatest candy factories would soon be gone. To think how close **Life Is Sweet?** had come to sharing the same fate. He had to remind himself that this was Big Billy's choice and that he'd found a way to keep his candies alive.

Billy handed the mike back to AJ and made his way to his seat. AJ said, "Well, you heard it here first, folks. Big changes are afoot!"

"Someone better get that mike away from him," Daisy whispered to Logan and Miles. "I think he might actually believe he works here!"

"Everyone enjoy the rest of the convention, and remember our motto, 'We're nuts about sweets!'"

By this time the crowd had begun to move, the grownups toward Big Billy, the kids toward the candy table. The contest entries were now fair game for anyone to try.

The organizers of the contest whisked Philip away to get his picture taken alongside a Harmonicandy, which they had put aside before anyone finished them all off.

"Let's go make fun of him so he messes up the picture," Daisy said.

They made their way through the crowd to find Philip posing in front of the plate. He stood so stiffly he almost looked like a cardboard cutout of himself.

When he saw the other three, he visibly relaxed, and the photographer snapped his picture.

"Got it!" the man said, lowering the camera.

"Bummer," Daisy said. "I missed my chance to make you mess up!"

"I'm sure it won't be your last chance," Philip said dryly. Just then his phone rang.

"The fame begins already!" Miles said. "Probably Hollywood calling to make a movie about your life story."

"Hello?" Philip said loudly, pressing the phone tight against his ear. "What?" He looked around the room, panic clear in his voice. "He's *here?* Like in the building? All right. Thanks for letting me know."

He closed the phone and said, "My father's here. Well, he'll be here in ten minutes."

"Do you think…" Logan began. "Do you think he might still go ahead with his plan?"

Philip didn't hesitate. "No. I'm sure he only came to verify the win."

Logan could see from Miles's and Daisy's faces that they weren't so sure. After all, the man had put a lot of planning into this takeover. Maybe he wouldn't be put off as easily as he'd promised. Fortunately, Philip was too worked up to notice their worried expressions. He turned to Logan. "I need to speak to your dad, okay?"

So once again they had to act as Philip's bodyguards. He graciously accepted everyone's praise as they crossed the room, but it was obvious he wasn't comfortable with the attention.

Logan pulled his dad away from the group surrounding Big Billy. "We need to talk to you for a minute. Out in the stairwell."

Once they were sure no one had followed them there, Philip reached into his jacket pocket and took out the secret ingredient. He handed the tin to the Candymaker, whose eyes grew large.

He looked down at it. "Why do you have this?"

The four contestants exchanged looks. They knew one another so well by then that words weren't even necessary.

"It's a very long story," Philip said. "But I wanted to give it back to you and apologize for taking it."

"I'm sure you had a good reason," the Candymaker said. He always, ALWAYS, gave people the benefit of the doubt.

"He did, Dad, I promise."

His father tapped the lid with his finger. "So I suppose you've all seen inside?"

They shook their heads.

"Really? Well, no time like the present." He began to lift off the lid.

Logan put out his hand to stop him. "Wait! I thought you didn't show people the secret ingredient until they were officially assistant candymakers."

"That's correct," he replied, pulling the lid the rest of the way off. He held out the tin. "Have a look."

"Really?" Logan asked, unable to believe it.

His father nodded.

Daisy squeezed Logan's hand as the four of them clustered around the tin.

Logan didn't know what he'd been expecting to see — maybe some ground-up powder or specially aged cocoa beans from an exotic island. Instead, he saw their four faces, full of anticipation, shining back up at him.

$\bullet\,\bullet\,\bullet\,\bullet\,\bullet\,\bullet\,\bullet\,\bullet\,\bullet\,\bullet\,\bullet\,\bullet\,\bullet\,\bullet$

CHAPTER NINE

$\bullet\,\bullet\,\bullet\,\bullet\,\bullet\,\bullet\,\bullet\,\bullet\,\bullet\,\bullet\,\bullet\,\bullet\,\bullet\,\bullet$

I t's empty?" Logan asked. "Did it spill out?"

The others looked just as confused as he did. Philip felt around in his jacket pocket. "I don't feel anything."

The Candymaker smiled. "What did you see when you looked in?"

"Our faces?" Logan replied uncertainly. "The bottom was mirrored."

"And what do you think Steve and Lenny see when they look in?" his father asked. "Or me, or Max?"

"I guess everyone would see his own face?" Logan said, his brow furrowing.

His father nodded. "That's right. And that's our secret ingredient. We put a little of ourselves into our chocolate."

Daisy beamed and reached out for the tin. "I know exactly what you mean," she said. "I felt like that when I was in the lab. Like I was a part of what I was making."

"Exactly!" the Candymaker said. "To tell you the truth, every candy factory has the same tin. It's a tradition, passed down from candymaker to candymaker. It's what makes each factory's candy taste distinctly their own."

Philip's jaw fell open. "You mean to say, there's no secret ingredient at all? At any of the candy factories?"

The Candymaker shook his head. "We all select our own ingredients, of course, and prepare them in a certain way. And where the cocoa beans are harvested makes a huge difference in taste. But that's about it."

Philip burst out laughing, followed by Daisy, Miles, and Logan.

"Someday you can tell me what you all find so funny," the Candymaker said, sticking the tin into his own pocket. "But I've got to get back out there."

He put his hand on Philip's still-convulsing shoulder. "Congratulations. I hope **Life Is Sweet** is chosen to produce your Harmonicandy. Great name, by the way."

Barely able to catch his breath, Philip gasped, "Miles thought of it."

"Did he?" the Candymaker asked. "We always have room at the factory for someone good with words."

Miles beamed, his eyes glassy with tears from laughing.

The Candymaker chuckled as he left them. "You four are gonna be trouble, I can tell."

That made them laugh even harder. For a moment Logan forgot that Philip's dad would be on his way up any minute.

When he arrived, everything would turn upside down. Again. But it wouldn't be about taking over the factory. It would be a lot more personal than that.

DAISY leaned against the maple tree and opened her comm device. Her mother's face quickly came into view. Gone were the snowy mountaintops of a few days ago; in their place were palm trees and a small hut. Her parents must be on a new mission already.

"Hi, honey!" her mom said, adjusting her straw hat to block out the bright sun.

"Don't '*hi, honey*' me!" Daisy scolded. "I'm thirteen? Seriously?"

Her mom's smile wavered a bit. "Oh. Found out about that, eh?"

"I guess that means it's true," Daisy said, even though she'd known it was the moment AJ had told her.

"We were going to tell you before your next birthday."

"Well, now you don't have to."

Her mother sighed. "AJ warned me this might not be a pleasant call."

Daisy narrowed her eyes at the screen. "When did you talk to AJ?"

"Last night. When you guys got home from your mission."

"But I tried to reach you all night, and your coordinates just flashed WE'RE AWAY at me."

Her mom adjusted her hat again. "Well, I may have been avoiding your call a bit."

"Mom!"

"Sorry, hon. But I wanted to give you some time to cool off. AJ told me you were a bit emotional. You're usually so level-headed."

Daisy sighed. "I know. And I'm not really too mad at you. The last couple days have been very...strange."

"How did the job at the candy factory go?"

Daisy hesitated. How could she possibly explain everything in a few minutes? It was going to be hard enough to tell her grandmother later. She'd feigned exhaustion when she and AJ had returned from the convention last night, and she'd left the house this morning before her grandmother could catch up with her. "Can you just wait to read it in my report?"

"Sure, if you'd like." Her mother came closer to the lens. "Is everything all right?"

"Well, I was wondering...is it all right if I take a little break from the whole spy biz? Just a few months. Go to a real school, that sort of thing? Just to kind of...think about everything?"

Her mother raised one eyebrow but didn't seem as surprised as Daisy thought she'd be. "Of course. Just because you're good at something doesn't mean you have to do it. Maybe you have another path in life."

"I do love being a spy," Daisy insisted. "Mostly. But I'm hoping things can change a little. Like I want to pick my own cases."

"We can talk about it when your father and I get home next week."

Daisy brightened. "You're coming home?"

Her mother nodded. "For at least a week. We'll have plenty of time to catch up on everything. I have a feeling you have quite a story for me." Her mother leaned in close again and looked around. "Hey, where are you? All I see is the bark of a tree."

Daisy turned her book so her mother could see the lake, the boats moored on the sandy beach, the merry-go-round off to the side. When she turned it back around, her mother asked, "Is that Verona Park?"

Daisy nodded.

"What takes you back there?"

Daisy smiled. "I'm waiting for some friends."

Her mother raised her eyebrow again. "Wow, that's new. Anyone I know?"

Daisy shook her head. Movement along the path on the far side of the lake caught her eye. "I've got to go, Mom. I think they're here. Say hi to Dad for me."

"Have fun, honey. We'll see you in a week. We're just

making a quick pit stop to see your brother, then we'll be home."

Daisy drew a sharp breath. "My WHAT?"

Her mom waved as the screen darkened. "Bye, honey! See you soon!"

"Wait! My what?" Daisy frantically pressed buttons but only got her mother's WE'RE AWAY message.

Daisy groaned in frustration, shut the book, and laid it down in the grass. She and her parents were SERIOUSLY going to have to talk about the importance of honesty in the parent-child relationship.

MILES saw the girl leaning against the tree, so much like the girl from his memory. But this time he knew what was going to happen next, and it wouldn't involve her running into the water and not coming back up.

He waved. She waved back.

His father untethered the rowboat from the post sticking out of the water. "You're sure you're ready to do this?"

Miles nodded. "It'll be good."

"Is that her?" his father asked, following Miles's gaze up the beach.

"Yup." Last night he'd told his parents about Daisy,

leaving out the fact that the reason she'd swum under the lake was that it was part of her spy training. At first they'd been really upset and even angry at Daisy and her parents for doing a stunt like that. But he tried to convince them that all the distress he'd gone through had not been for nothing. He had figured out a lot about life in the past year that he never would have otherwise. He knew they were still upset, but he also knew they'd slept better last night than they had all year. In fact, his mom was still asleep!

"Well, I'll leave you, then," his father said, checking that the boat was secure on the sand. "You have everything you need?"

Miles smiled. "And more."

And if the universe and everything in it might not actually exist (as one of the books from the factory's library had told him), then at least he'd made three friends. Three!

Dna yeht t'ndid neve erac taht eh semitemos ekops drawkcab!

"*That's* the boat?" **PHILIP** asked, joining Daisy on the walk down to the lake.

"You were expecting a yacht? And what *are* you wearing?"

Philip looked down at his Hawaiian shirt, long shorts, and tube socks that nearly reached his knees. "What, this? Isn't this what people wear outdoors?"

"Not normal people! I can barely see your face under that hat!"

He pushed the visor up a little. "That's the point. No sunburn." Reggie had given him the outfit, and the hat. And the sunblock, bug spray, and canteen filled with water, which were in his duffel bag. Reggie had tried to tell him he didn't need all the supplies for one hour on the lake, but Philip had insisted on bringing everything. If he had to be outdoors, he needed to protect himself from the elements as completely as possible.

They had almost reached the beach when Daisy stopped and put her hand on his arm. He didn't even flinch this time. "Have you spoken to Logan?" she asked.

Philip shook his head. "Not since my dad showed up at the convention yesterday. Logan's father kind of dragged him away."

Daisy nodded. "I know, that was kind of weird. I didn't see him after that either. I hope he's okay."

Philip nodded. He was eager to talk to Logan, too. He had something to give him. He also wanted to tell him that when his father found out about his violin playing (thanks to the Candymaker's wife), he hadn't freaked out. All he'd asked was "Are you any good?" Philip had nodded, and his father said, "Okay, then." That might not sound like a lot to most people, but for them it had been a real bonding moment.

"Let's ask Miles if he's spoken to Logan," he suggested as they started walking again.

Daisy agreed. But by the time they reached Miles, they saw Logan approaching from the other direction. Philip was relieved to see that he looked perfectly normal, his usual happy self.

"I have something to give you," Philip said to Logan when they all met by the water's edge.

"And I have something for *you!*" he replied.

"I have something for Logan, too!" Daisy said.

"I don't have anything for anyone!" Miles shouted.

They all laughed.

Philip opened his duffel bag and pulled out a violin case. "This is yours. I meant to give it to you yesterday, but I couldn't find you."

"Max took me home," Logan said hurriedly.

Philip waited for him to explain why, but he didn't. He just took the violin case, balancing it awkwardly.

"Did you just say this is mine?" Logan asked.

Philip nodded. "I took it from the storeroom down the hall from the lab."

Logan held it back out to him. "You should keep it."

"Trust me," Philip said, "you want this violin. If anyone tries to buy the factory again, this could buy you two *new* factories!"

"Really?" Logan and Daisy and Miles all asked at the same time.

Philip nodded. "It's very old and very rare."

"Hey," Daisy asked. "You never told us why you brought it with you to the contest in the first place."

"I'm not really sure," Philip admitted. "I think I just wanted it near me." Taking it had been a last-minute decision. He'd hidden it in the duffel bag Reggie brought to the factory. Philip was supposed to put his dirty clothes in there. Instead, the clothes went into the backseat of the limo along with his briefcase, and the violin went into the duffel. "It's kind of hard to explain."

"Ah, the special relationship between a boy and his violin," Miles said. "Who are we to question such a pairing?"

Philip stepped forward and kicked Miles in the shin.

"You ain't got nothing on Daisy," Miles said, pointing to a big purple bruise under his left knee.

"I did that?" Daisy squealed. "I'm really sorry!"

Logan laid the violin case down next to himself and reached into his pocket. "This is for you."

Philip reached out his hand and Logan gave him a small box, about the size of two decks of cards. He couldn't imagine what was in it. Unless it actually *was* two decks of cards, which seemed unlikely.

"This goes with it," Logan said, handing him a folded piece of paper.

"Should I open them now?" Philip asked, suddenly apprehensive.

"In a few minutes, okay?" Logan asked.

Daisy reached into her pocketbook and pulled out a large brown envelope. She handed it to Logan. "I thought you might want this."

Logan turned the envelope around in his hands. He held it up to the sun but couldn't see through it. "Well, at least I know it's not a violin!" he said with a grin.

"Well, I don't have any mysterious envelopes or packages, but I've got a boat rented for the next hour!" Miles said, tapping the side of the rowboat with his foot. "Make that the next fifty minutes now."

"We're all supposed to fit in that thing?" Philip asked, casting a doubtful look at the boat. "Is it even seaworthy?"

"Actually," Logan said, "I'm going to wait on the beach."

"Why?" Miles asked with concern. "You love rowboats."

"I know, but I'd kind of like to be somewhere else when Philip opens that box."

Philip almost dropped it. "Nothing will jump out at me, will it? Or smell really bad?"

Logan smiled. "I guess you're going to have to take your chances."

"Hey," Daisy said, "we'll be on that boat, too!"

"Don't worry, you'll all make it back to shore unharmed. Unless Philip is rowing — then you better be wearing your life vests."

"Got that covered," Miles said, pointing at the four life jackets piled in the front of the boat.

Philip rolled his eyes. He couldn't help it. "Let's get this over with," he said, nudging the boat closer to the water with his foot. He was eager to open the box, which was wrapped in blue paper, like a present. He didn't often get presents.

"Do you want me to stay here with you?" Daisy asked Logan.

Logan shook his head. "I'll be fine." He reached into the boat and grabbed one of the life jackets. "I hear this makes a good pillow."

"That it does," Daisy said.

Miles pushed the boat the rest of the way into the water. "All right. Climb in, guys."

Philip couldn't help noticing the two feet of water between the shoreline and the boat. "Um, how are we supposed to get in?"

"Like this," Miles said, pulling off his sneakers and socks and stepping in.

"It looks cold," Philip said, taking a step backward.

"Oy!" Daisy exclaimed. She tossed her bag into the boat on top of the life jackets, then marched over to Philip. Without a word of warning, she reached out, grabbed him around the waist, and hoisted him over her shoulder.

Philip was so surprised, he couldn't even shout out. His hat fell off onto the beach, but he only half noticed. Daisy carried him out to the boat, which had now drifted a few feet farther into the lake. By the time he recovered from the shock, she'd plopped him on the middle bench between the two oars.

"There," she said, with a satisfied nod. "You didn't even get splashed."

Philip could see Miles and Logan doubled over laughing on the shore. "Hey!" he shouted, his cheeks hot with embarrassment. "At least I'm dry!"

"Do you want me to come back for you, Miles?" Daisy called out.

Miles bounded into the water. "No thanks!" he said, reaching the side of the boat. "You should have seen your face," he told Philip. "Priceless. I'll never forget it."

"I'm so glad," Philip said, wishing he could think of a better comeback.

The boat rocked as Miles climbed in, and Philip clutched both sides to steady it. Why people wanted to be in boats he couldn't imagine.

Daisy jumped in last. She picked up the oars and gestured for Philip to move to the back bench. He didn't need to be asked twice — he had no interest in rowing. Miles tossed each of them a life jacket as the boat began to move.

Philip looked down at the box and the folded paper still clutched in his hand. He was surprised he hadn't dropped them in the lake when Daisy picked him up. He doubted he'd ever live that down. But truth be told, he was kind of pleased that he didn't have to get wet.

"Are you going to open it?" Miles asked.

"I guess," Philip said. He placed the box on his lap and unfolded the paper. "It's a letter."

"Is it to all of us or just you?" Daisy asked, twisting her head around to see.

"Hey, eyes forward," Philip commanded.

Daisy groaned, but turned back around. "Remind me never to drive you anywhere when I get my license. Which, as you know, will be a year before you guys get yours!"

"No problem there, if this is how you drive on water," Philip replied. He looked back down at the letter. "It's addressed just to me."

"You should read it to yourself, then," Miles said.

Philip nodded. "It's probably just about the contest."

But it wasn't.

Dear Philip,

Yesterday, when your father walked into the convention, I knew I'd seen him before. As soon as my dad saw him, he recognized him, too, and yanked me away with some excuse that Max needed my help back at the factory. Max and Henry kept trying to entertain me on the ride home with stories of the olden days in the factory (which I usually love), but something about your dad and the way he looked at me before my dad yanked me away kept nagging at me. Right before we got back to Spring Haven,

I realized where I'd seen him. And then I knew who you were. I blurted it all out in the car. Then Henry filled me in on your side of the story. I didn't think you and Henry had spoken more than two words to each other.

I just wanted to tell you, I never blamed you for what happened to me. I was just a kid, and I thought that if I could get your truck back for you, we could be friends. I just wasn't thinking when I reached into that vat.

Last night when my parents came home, I told them I wanted them to start the tours up again, and the annual picnic, and when it looked like they didn't want to, I told them that I don't mind so much when people look at me for, like, a minute too long. It's not their fault, they're not trying to be hurtful. And the burns will get better—they already are.

I know you were just trying to protect your-self by being kind of awful when you first came back to the factory. It was probably hard for you not to tell me who you were, and I'm kind of glad you didn't, what with everything else going on. These last few days with you and Miles and Daisy have been the greatest days of my life. And I've had a lot of great days. You guys all treated me like I wasn't any differ-ent at all, and that's all I want. I've never worked so hard on anything before the Harmoni-candy project, and now I know I can. Anyway, this is the longest letter I've ever written. I hope you'll come back to the factory to hang out. I promise if you throw me something and I miss it, that I won't climb into another vat of chocolate. ☺

Your friend, Logan
PS No more secrets, ok?

Philip blinked a few times as the note rustled in the breeze. He realized they'd reached the center of the lake. Daisy had crossed the oars over her lap and was watching him.

"So?" she asked. "What did it say?"

He hesitated for a minute, not sure if he really wanted to show them. But Logan was right. No more secrets. He handed Daisy the note and hoped they wouldn't hate him when they read it.

With shaking hands, he unwrapped the box. Inside sat a small plastic truck on a bed of cotton. *His* truck.

Clutching it in his hand, he turned around and looked back at the beach. He could barely make out Logan lying on the sand, the bright orange life vest beneath his head, no doubt trying to decide what the cloud above him resembled. Philip looked up. *A Bubbletastic ChocoRocket,* he decided. *Definitely.*

A Harmonicandy, **LOGAN** decided. *Definitely.* Then he turned away from the cloud and sat up. He tried to slide his finger under the flap of Daisy's envelope. When that didn't work, he ripped off the top, hoping he wasn't harming anything inside. He reached in and pulled out a photograph with a small note attached in Daisy's handwriting.

> If nothing ever changed, there'd be
> no such things as butterflies.
> xo, Daisy

He smiled. She was right. He lifted off the note to see the photo underneath. It took a few seconds to register what he was looking at. Was that...him? He brought the picture closer. It had been taken a long time ago, before the accident. The little kid in the picture had no scars on his face and neck, only a wide grin. The butterfly on the tip of his nose was hard to miss. Yellow and black and red, just like the one in the chrysalis. Like the ones in the chrysalises every year. So a butterfly really *had* visited him before, even if he didn't remember it. This picture was proof. Maybe no one ever got to witness the exact moment of transformation. Maybe some things were just meant to be private.

It finally occurred to him to wonder who had taken the

picture and how Daisy had wound up with it. He'd ask when they returned. Or maybe he wouldn't.

He lay back down, the photo resting on his chest. By now Philip would have read the note. The others probably had, too, which meant there were no more secrets between them anymore. Well, except maybe for one...

Someday he'd tell Philip that the Stradivarius was actually made by Samuel Sweet—grandfather, candy factory founder, and woodcarving enthusiast.

But not yet.

After all, they'd be busy for a while. They were candymakers now, and they had a whole lotta candy to make.

READER'S GUIDE

1. The four main characters in *The Candymakers* have very different lives. Whose life would you most like to have? Why?

2. If you could make up a new candy for the candymaking contest, what would it be? How would it taste? What would it be called?

3. Out of all the candies described in the book, which one would you most like to try?

4. What would be your favorite room to work in at the candy factory?

5. Did you guess who was trying to steal the secret ingredient? If not, who did you think it was?

6. Why do you think Logan's parents worked so hard to protect him after his accident? Do you think he needed their protection? Why or why not?

7. Miles likes to make up codes and other languages. Do you know any other languages? Would you like to learn one?

8. Daisy's spying takes her all over the world. Is there an undercover assignment you'd like to have?

9. In the end, Daisy decides to spend less time as a spy. Why do you think she takes this step back? What did the candymaking contest teach her?

10. Why isn't Philip proud of his musical talent? Why does he feel the need to hide the talent from his father?

11. Henry and Philip spend a lot of time together during the contest. How does Henry help Philip? Why do you think he does this?

12. Philip finds out his father lied to him about being banned from the Life Is Sweet candy factory. Have you ever been lied to by an adult? Do you think he or she had a good reason for doing so? How did it make you feel?

13. Both Logan and Philip think they have something to prove by winning the candymaking contest. Have you ever felt that way?

14. In the end, the four children unexpectedly become friends. Have you ever become friends with someone you didn't expect to? Did that experience teach you anything?

15. Who do you think took the photograph of Logan as a child that was in Daisy's file?

THE
CANDYMAKERS

and the
Great Chocolate Chase

Available spring 2016!

Note: The following excerpt has not been edited
and may change for the finished book.

"You will travel in a land of marvels."

—Jules Verne

From the desk of Mr. H—

You! With the dirty knees and the leaf in your hair. You with the sticky fingers and the smudge of chocolate on your chin. And you with the flashlight under your covers after Mom said lights out. And, yes, *you* with this book in your hand trying to decide whether you're going to read it. You don't know me very well—not yet, anyway. But a lot of people went out of their way for me, so I figured I'd pay it forward and look out for *you*. I'm not gonna lie—this is a long book, and there are things you should know if you're going to spend your precious time turning the pages. After all, what is more valuable than your time? As a man much wiser than I once said, "Time is the coin of your life. Don't let anyone else spend it for you."

If you do read this book, here's what's in store for you: Hidden treasures. Secret worlds. The open road. Rivers of light. Maps of awe. A sky of many colors. Gadgets and gizmos. New friends and old enemies. Old friends and new enemies. Love. Fear. Bravery. Hope. One very small and very loud cat who thinks he's a dog.

And candy. Lots and lots of candy. *Boatloads* of it, in fact. Soft and chewy, hard and crunchy, sour and sweet.

If any of that stuff doesn't interest you, feel free to close the book now. No hard feelings. I won't take it personally. I should mention, though, that if you don't stick around, you'll miss seeing one of the world's most famous magicians attempt the most dangerous trick of his career. And did I mention the chocolate waterfall? No? Well, there's one of those, too.

I'd better go now. I need to sleep. Got a big day tomorrow. So do Logan, Miles, Philip, and Daisy. Only to them it's just an ordinary Tuesday. Life is like that, ya know? It's never the things you worry about that get you.

After spending exactly twelve years and five months living inside a candy factory, Logan Sweet knew all the best places to hide. That's not to say he hid often. In fact, all the folks responsible for creating, packaging, selling, and shipping the dozen different types of candy produced at the **Life Is Sweet?** candy factory considered Logan to be a visible, helpful (some would say *indispensable*), and always cheerful presence on the factory floor. But from time to time, Logan found the need to be alone. Usually, these times coincided with the due date of a homework assignment. Since all his teachers worked at the factory (and in the case of his parents, lived in the same apartment), he had to be creative if he wanted to ditch them.

Logan had found his first favorite hiding spot when, at age seven and a half, he saw no reason to go to all the effort of building a diorama of the Amazon rain forest when, really, the factory's Tropical Room was as close to a real rain forest as one could get without visiting the equator. Most of the candy rooms didn't have any boy-shaped hiding spots, but then he discovered the perfect place in the Icy Mint Blob Room, which offered the additional benefit of being all the way down at the end of a long hallway.

He couldn't simply walk in and hide, though. Preparations had to be made. Logan had carefully gathered his supplies and then parked himself in one of the oversize chairs in the factory's library and pretended to read up on the rain forest. He waited as patiently as possible (which is to say, not patiently at all) while, one by one, the workers shut down the factory's candy machines for the night. This process was a lot more complicated than merely turning off a switch. The oil that made the machines run smoothly had to be drained and disposed of properly. All the pipes, tubes, trays, bins, compressors, oscillators, tumblers, conveyor belts, ovens, stovetops, kettles, vats, pots, pans, funnels, and barrels had to be scrubbed and stored. He nearly fell asleep in the chair!

When the coast was finally clear, Logan had run down the quiet hall, wedged a pile of pillows behind the stack of old peppermint-oil barrels, and stocked his new space with comic books, drawing pads, and snacks. He'd made it back up to the apartment just in time for his mom's famous Veggie Loaf Surprise dinner. (It should be noted that his mom's substitution of chocolate chips for peas hadn't been a surprise for many years.)

Logan wound up spending many lazy midday hours tucked away in that hiding spot, lulled into an almost dreamlike state by the thumping of the nearby panning machine. The panner—which looked to him like a space-age washing machine—spun the Icy Mint Blobs and coated them with blueberry syrup until they shone. It also muffled the sound of Logan crunching/slurping/chomping on the latest candies that had been deemed NQP (not quite perfect) by Randall, the head of the quality-control team. As much as Logan loved all the candy **Life Is Sweet** produced, he particularly loved the pieces that came out too oddly shaped to fit in the packaging, or that were stuck together, or that came off the conveyor belt too sticky or too hard or the wrong shade of brown/red/orange/yellow/neon green. He possessed an uncanny ability to show up exactly when a new NQP batch appeared on the counter of the employee lounge.

By the time Logan was nine, his legs had grown so long that his feet stuck out from behind the peppermint barrels. Rather than risk being discovered, he'd found a new hiding spot in the barn hayloft. This one worked out even better because the open windows let in a lot of fresh air (which also helped offset the smell of the cows below) and allowed him to play Name That Cloud without lying outside in the open. In one direction, he could gaze at the wheat fields and the corn, the fruit trees and sugarcane grove, the great lawn with its small pond. A glance in the other revealed the gleaming windows, tall chimneys, and deep red brick of the back of the factory.

When not drawing dinosaurs in his sketchpad, he would play one of his grandfather's old hand-carved wooden puzzle games. He wasn't very good at solving them, but he enjoyed the challenge. He could hum as he worked, and the noises of the busy barn drowned out the sound. The farmers below him milked the cows for fresh milk and collected eggs from the chickens, and if they knew he was there, they never let on.

As he got older, though, Logan began to enjoy learning more and more and hid less and less. Eventually, he forgot about hiding at all. But tomorrow candy history would be made when the first Harmonicandy glided down the conveyor belt. All eyes were on Logan.

So, obviously, he needed to hide. He needed to hide *fast.*

Unfortunately, the options were slim. A frenzied energy buzzed through the air. Along with it, visitors from all parts of the candy community filled the factory halls, the candymaking rooms, the library, the cafeteria, the Tropical Room, the Bee Room, the great lawn, and even his family's apartment upstairs. This made it very hard to hide in shadowy corners or even to slip into closets or back rooms unnoticed.

He wished his friends from the candymaking contest were there. They were the only people who knew him well enough to understand how he felt. Miles O'Leary, Daisy Carpenter, and Philip Ransford the Third were so different—not only from one another but also from anyone else he'd ever met (not that he'd met many kids, since his whole life had mostly been spent in the factory). But each of them made his small world bigger, and every night when he recited what he was grateful for, they were at the top of his list. Even Philip. Not that Logan would ever tell him that.

Logan had hoped Miles would have been there by now, but his grandfather was visiting, so he was off doing family stuff. Miles wasn't the best at hiding, anyway. He'd most likely sneeze or forget they were supposed to be hiding and then start to tell a story and blow their cover. Poor hiding skills aside, Miles was the best friend Logan had ever had. It helped that Miles hadn't had a best friend before, either. They were learning together how to be one.

If anyone could figure out a way to help Logan now, it would be Daisy. Hiding was basically her full-time job! But she was away on a spy mission, and even though she had given him one of her secret communication devices before she left, she'd made it clear the gadget was for emergencies only. No one knew when her mission would be over, but she promised she'd be back for the factory's annual picnic, at the end of the summer. As momentous as the next day's event was expected to be, the factory's first picnic in seven years would be an even bigger deal, but one he was looking forward to. He and the Harmonicandy wouldn't be the center of attention.

That left Philip. But even though the first Harmonicandy was about to roll off the line and Philip should have been dancing in the halls with joy and anticipation, he hadn't been around much. And when he *was* there, he never hung around for long before he had to go write a paper for school or something.

Plus he wasn't the best listener.

Logan pressed himself against the wall outside the Oozing Crunchorama Room to plot his next move. Maybe he could claim that his skin felt clammy and hide out in the nurse's office. It was always empty, so he'd have lots of privacy. The worst thing the nurse usually saw during the course of the day was a beesting. The Candymaker made safety his number one priority, which made it all the worse that the only serious workplace accident had occurred when his own five-year-old son tried to reach into a vat of chocolate fudge and sustained third-degree burns.

Logan quickly dismissed the idea of the nurse's office. He'd spent enough time at the doctor's after the accident. Plus he would feel terrible lying to anyone.

He glanced behind him. Last month the Oozing Crunchorama had fallen to third on the candy best-sellers list, after being at the top for nearly a decade. Max and the other candy scientists responded to this disappointing turn of events by tweaking the recipe. All they did was chop the hazelnuts into smaller pieces and add a touch more cream to up the "ooze factor," and the candy community went wild. A week later the Crunchorama was back on top. Now the room bustled with activity as they tried to keep up with the demand. Logan sized up the corner behind the hazelnut-warming table. It would provide good cover from the workers mixing the hazelnut-praline mixture into the huge vats of milk chocolate. First he'd have to figure out a way to distract them, though.

"I don't think I've ever seen you stand so still," a familiar voice said with a chuckle. "Usually you have only two speeds—fast and faster."

Logan jumped. Then he turned to face Henry, the man who had single-handedly run the Marshmallow Room since the factory opened fifty years earlier. Henry had always been like a grandfather to him, even when Logan's own grandfather—the original Candymaker and founder of **Life Is Sweet**—was still alive. Logan had been so busy these past few months that his usual morning visits with Henry had become less frequent. With his mess of white hair and easy smile, Henry was the only grown-up Logan didn't mind seeing right now.

"Can we go back to the Marshmallow Room?" Logan asked, tugging Henry on the sleeve to follow him. Logan knew they'd be alone there. Henry guarded the marshmallows the way a mama bird guarded her eggs, and he was extremely choosy about who he let get too close.

Henry nodded, and Logan took off in a run. He darted through crowds of smiling guests, their arms laden with bags of free treats. He did his best not to meet anyone's eyes. He knew this behavior was uncharacteristic of him, but he couldn't stand having one more person grip him on the shoulder and follow with some words that were supposed to make him feel better but that had the opposite effect. Comments like "We're still rooting for you, kiddo!" or "This must be tough, but hang in there!" Or, if the person was a particularly nosy or thoughtless journalist, "Your grandfather won. Then your dad won. What's it like watching your father's company produce the contest-winning candy when you're the first member of your family for three generations to lose?"

Ugh, it was exhausting.

By the time Henry showed up in the Marshmallow Room, Logan already had the large Bunsen burner up and running and two marshmallows speared on the tips of their favorite toasting sticks. The smell of freshly roasted vanilla beans had calmed him down a little bit, but not much.

"Let's hear it," Henry said, sitting down on the wooden stool next to Logan's. The stool groaned under Henry's weight.

"No one believes me when I say I'm okay," Logan complained as their marshmallows toasted over the low flame. He didn't like the way his voice sounded. Until recent events, he'd never had reason to complain about anything. But he couldn't help it. "They pat me on the arm," he explained to Henry, "and tilt their heads at me with their eyes as gooey as a fresh batch of chocolate." It wasn't until the candymaking contest a few months earlier that he'd begun to realize that people always looked at him with sympathy—or at least ever since he'd gotten the scars that ran across the side of his face and along his arms and hands. Other than having to massage aloe into them, Logan never gave his scars much thought. It hadn't occurred to him that others would think about them. Looking back, he was embarrassed that he hadn't been smart enough, or aware enough, to realize that of course others noticed.

"You can't really blame them for thinking you might be disappointed," Henry replied. "You have to watch the Harmonicandy get all the glory. Under your own roof, no less! And after you worked so hard on your Bubbletastic ChocoRocket."

"I might not have worked *that* hard," Logan said.

"Perhaps it wasn't your best effort," Henry agreed. "But most people don't know that. All they know is that the kid who was rude to everyone won the contest, and you didn't get what you wanted."

"But losing the contest *is* what I wanted," Logan insisted. "I mean, not before it started, but once I got to know the others, everything changed. The Harmonicandy was really a team effort, even though only Philip can take the credit. You know he isn't really as obnoxious as he acted while he was here, and then when we were able to save the factory, I really *did* win!" Logan shoved his marshmallow into his mouth to keep himself from rambling even more.

"*I* know all that," Henry said gently. "And I understand your frustration. But you have to see it from the other side."

Logan let his shoulders slump and crossed his arms.

Henry chewed his marshmallow and laid the stick next to Logan's on the counter. He turned off the burner. "Perhaps you're being oversensitive and a bit overdramatic."

Logan would have argued that perhaps he wasn't being dramatic *enough*, but then Randall rapped on the glass door and Logan straightened up. He didn't want Randall to see him sulking. He jumped up to open the door.

Randall balanced a large brown box under one arm while he chomped on a green apple held in his free hand. He grimaced with every bite. He'd once confided to Logan that he didn't like apples but had to eat them when he was taste-testing different candies. Sour apples neutralize chocolate. Bread neutralizes hot, spicy foods, and fortunately, Randall liked bread. He'd gone through two whole loaves in one day before giving the final approval to begin production on the Fireball Supernova. He could also always be counted on to have packets of crackers stuffed in his coat pockets, because they neutralized almost any taste—spicy, sour, bitter, or sweet. Logan found this all very interesting, but he didn't need to eat any of those tricks. His taste buds were always on full alert.

Randall tossed the apple over into the trash can by the door. "I'm sorry to interrupt," he said, laying the box on the counter beside the marshmallow sticks. "This package arrived a few minutes ago, so I offered to deliver it on my way to the Harmonicandy Room. Only a few more tests to go before the first one comes down the conveyor belt. Exciting!" Then he glanced at Logan, and his grin wobbled a bit.

Logan looked pointedly at Henry. This was just the kind of thing he'd been talking about.

Henry leaned over to look at the shipping label. He squinted. "It's all blurry," he said. "Is this the new vanilla-bean grinder I ordered?"

Halfway out the door already, Randall called back, "Nope. It's for Logan."

Logan and Henry looked at each other in surprise. "Me?" Logan asked. He pulled the box closer. Henry must need glasses, because the return label was printed in neat, even letters. The handwriting wasn't familiar, and the address didn't mean anything to him. Whom did he know who lived two states away? No one. "Maybe it's from Daisy," he suggested to Henry. "It doesn't look like her handwriting, but maybe that's on purpose to cover her tracks." Henry was the only grownup at the factory who knew Daisy's true identity. He'd promised to keep her secret, and there was no reason to doubt him.

Logan pulled at the tape on the side of the box but couldn't get a good grip. He would need scissors or a knife to cut through it. Logan and sharp instruments didn't mix well. "Will you open it for me?" he asked.

Henry nodded. "Certainly."

As Henry crossed the room to his metal supply cabinet, Logan thought how much he appreciated that Henry hadn't jumped up to help before Logan even asked for assistance. He'd become very sensitive to people doing that for him.

Henry returned and got to work cutting through the thick tape. When the flaps were loose enough, he stepped back to let Logan pull the box open.

Logan thought it might contain a game or a puzzle or something funny that Daisy had come across on her travels. She knew he didn't leave the factory very often, so she liked surprising him with random things from the outside world. A few weeks earlier she'd sent him a painting she had bought at a rest stop on the highway. It showed a cat waving a magic wand while wearing polka-dot pajamas. The painting now hung over his bed.

"So what's in there?" Henry asked.

Logan carefully lifted out a thick stack of crumbly, yellowed newspapers and dusty spiral notebooks tied together with brown twine. "I don't think it's from Daisy," he said, plopping the contents on the counter. His new friends knew he didn't have much patience when it came to reading. He'd once told Miles that he usually read the last page of a book first, and Miles was so horrified he didn't speak to Logan for the rest of the day. Talk about being overdramatic.

"I bet this will tell us," Henry said, pulling a long, thin envelope from underneath the twine. He handed it to Logan, who turned it over in his hands. The envelope was new, while the rest of the stack looked as if it had been rescued from someone's attic or basement. Logan tore open the envelope and unfolded a typewritten letter. He held it up so that Henry could read it alongside him.

Dear Logan,

We have never met, but your grandfather—the one and only Samuel Sweet—and I spent our boyhoods together. We lived two houses away from each other, and I believe I spent more time at his home than at my own! His had the best smells! (And I don't mean your great-grandmother's cabbage, which did not smell good AT ALL!)

I recently found this box of Sam's old journals and candymaking research, and I know he would want you to have these things. Even though my life took a different path, I do keep up with candy news because it reminds me of my dear friend and the world he treasured. I heard of your defeat at the annual contest and that your family's factory was given the honor of producing the winning Harmonicandy. I hope you will be comforted by seeing all the notebooks your grandfather filled with ideas for candies that never worked out. Don't give up! I am old and coming to the end of my days, but there is greatness ahead for you—I am certain.

Very sincerely yours,
Frank Razinsky

Logan stared down at the letter. "Even strangers feel sorry for me. Still think I'm being oversensitive?"

When he got no answer, Logan looked up. He saw something he would never forget—tears streaming down Henry's cheeks.